PROTOTYPE

ALSO BY M.D. WATERS

Archetype

PROTOTYPE

A NOVEL

M.D. WATERS

DUTTON
— est. 1852 —

DUTTON
—• est. 1852 •—

Published by the Penguin Group
Penguin Group (USA) LLC
375 Hudson Street
New York, New York 10014

USA | Canada | UK | Ireland | Australia | New Zealand | India | South Africa | China
penguin.com
A Penguin Random House Company

LIBRARY OF CONGRESS CATALOGING-IN-PUBLICATION DATA
Waters, M.D., 1976–
Prototype : a novel / M.D. Waters.
pages cm
Sequel to: Archetype.
ISBN 978-0-525-95424-8
I. Title.
PS3623.A86889P76 2014
813'.6—dc23
2013032392

Printed in the United States of America
1   3   5   7   9   10   8   6   4   2

Designed by Nancy Resnick

For Jackson and Jameson.

I would collapse entire nations to protect you.

All changes, even the most longed for, have their melancholy; for what we leave behind us is a part of ourselves; we must die to one life before we can enter another.

—Anatole France

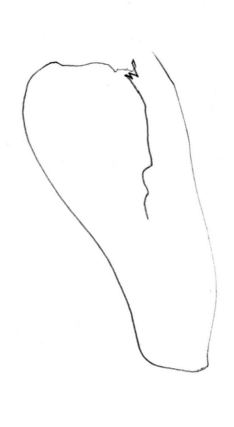

CHAPTER 1

I float in nothing.

The tether binding my incorporeal form keeps me from floating into the abyss that is arctic and as black as pitch. The restraint is also fragile. One wrong move and I will have nothing to hold me.

Wake up, Emma. It is only a dream.

Not a dream, though. My worst nightmare.

The abyss I float in threatens death.

I shoulder through the thick crowd of men, clinging to the straps of my backpack. Sweat streams down my spine. Gusts of wind have pulled strands of hair free from my knotted bun and they stick to my neck. Dust clouds the area, kicked up by children playing to the side of the uneven cobbled road and by the marching of heavy military boots. Militia patrol Zirahuén's street market to thwart any trouble in the otherwise friendly haggling system.

I keep my head down and sunglasses on to avoid eye contact. Any sign of interest on my part makes men too aggressive, too hands-on. It did not take me long to learn this in the year and four months that I have been free. Not every country's government is regimented to the slavery of women like the eastern half of America is, but that does not mean women are not wanted.

Needed, actually.

I keep my wedding ring—the ring Declan Burke gave me in the weeks before he died—on a chain around my neck. Sliding the set of diamonds on my finger has saved me multiple times. If men believe I am married, most tend to back off out of respect for my "husband."

The ring is the last of the jewelry I took from my old home, and I hate to part with it, but it is time. I am nearly out of money and have nothing to show for it. In the year I have searched for my parents, I have come up with only one promising lead: the name of a man who lives in Mexico, of all places. Zirahuén, Michoacán, to be exact. A village beside Lake Zirahuén in the central highlands of Mexico.

The man I seek is ex-resistance like my parents, who seem to be nothing more than ghosts. After escaping a prison in America's eastern territory more than twenty years ago, they disappeared without a trace. For all I know, they could have died. Either way, I have to know what happened to them. Maybe if I find them alive—I refuse to believe they are dead—I can finally figure out where I fit in this world.

Knowing I am Emma Wade—ex–resistance major, wife of Noah Tucker, mother to Adrienne—does not change the fact that I am still a clone carrying Her soul. That those I left behind could not bring themselves to accept me for who I am. I am forced to make a new life for myself, and this is all I hope to do once I find my parents.

I politely decline the hagglers stepping in my path on my way to the area selling produce. I am told the man I seek sells fruit, but this is all I know. Three blocks into the market, I find a row of five carts selling various types.

Stopping, I ignore the shoulders brushing past. Rubbing the tight muscles in the back of my neck, I blow out a gust of air. Five carts. Five men. And I do not speak Spanish.

I pass the first three because the men are too young to be the man I seek. The fourth is a man who cannot be younger than eighty, speaks no English, and cannot stop staring at my breasts . . . or the ring lying between them. I know he could be the right man, but my instincts say *definitely not.*

One glance at the last cart reveals another young man, late teens, and my stomach falls. Peter swore I would find him here, and though I spent only two weeks on his ranch in Montana, I trust him more than I have trusted anyone in a very long time.

The ex–resistance general took me in at my lowest point. A time when I was beginning to believe I would never find my parents. When thoughts of the family I left behind clawed at my guilt. But also a time when my abyss dreams had progressed into a true nightmare.

The peace I found with Peter could not have come at a better time. More than that, he gave me hope again with a single name: Cesar Ruiz.

An older man exchanges places with the young man behind the last cart and my heart leaps. I approach the cart, which houses red apples. Flies swarm the bruised skin, removing any appeal. The man behind the rotting wood wears a wide-brimmed hat and has a shock of salt-and-pepper hair flaring around his deeply wrinkled face. He rubs wide, stubby fingers over his mustache while studying me with dark eyes.

I remove my sunglasses and hang them from the front of my tank top. "Cesar Ruiz?"

Please speak English.

The man shakes his head and speaks rapidly in Spanish. He also avoids looking me in the eye.

I hold up my hands to stop him and try to regulate the air that has just become trapped in my lungs. This *has* to be him. "I do not understand. Do you speak English?"

The young man from before sidles up beside me. His black hair is pulled taut in a low-hanging ponytail. "What is it you need, American?"

"I am looking for someone. Cesar Ruiz?"

"Not today, lady. Tomorrow."

The boy's eyes shift quickly to the old man, and I know intuitively I have found the right place. This would not be the first time ex-resistance has lied to me about their true identity. Even in a whole other country than the Americas, they would not want to be found by the wrong person. I have to be careful not to scare him off.

"My name is Emma Wade," I tell him. "He knew my parents, Lily and Stephen. I am only trying to find them."

I finish with a pointed look at the old man. His head is tilted in a way that says he listens, but he swats at the hovering flies in an effort to deflect suspicion. I know this tactic and am not fooled.

Instead of nodding or giving me the brush-off, the young boy picks up an apple from the cart. "Not today," he repeats, squinting into the sun. He tosses the fruit in the air and catches it in his other hand, then rolls it between his palms.

The next time the apple flies in the air, I snatch it away. "Tell him I have come a long way and will not leave without the answers I came for."

The boy opens his mouth to respond when the old man steps around the cart, hands raised. "It is okay, Miguel."

I let out a relieved sigh. That did not take as long as I expected. "You are Cesar?"

He casts a furtive glance around. "Not for a long time. How did you hear of me?"

"An old friend of yours named Peter. I ran into him in Montana. He made me groom a lot of horses before telling me where to find you."

Cesar nods toward the shade of an alley behind his cart, shouting orders in Spanish to Miguel. Once we stand between the buildings, he glances around to determine if we are alone.

He removes his hat and fans his face. "You are resistance?"

"No." Not exactly a lie. Originally, yes, but I am not Her anymore. He does not need to hear my complicated story. "I have friends working against Burke Enterprises."

His eyes widen. "This will not be easy. Not after—"

"—the cloning. I know."

I am curious if Noah was as surprised as I was when the government practically begged Burke Enterprises to begin a cloning program on a much grander scale. They even went as far as to erase the charges against Arthur Travista for the murder of the two hosts of their first successful clones. Ruby and Lydia refused to press charges, anyway. And why would they? They are alive and well with healthy babies. A miracle of science.

No one knew the truth about me, thank God. The few friends Declan trusted with this secret have thus far kept quiet, believing Declan and I were kidnapped by the resistance. At least that is the story they tell the media. With the security system—put in place by Noah himself—there is no way they did not see my fight with Declan. I am not sure how far out the view went, but they know I was the last to see him alive, at the very least.

I shiver, suddenly cold despite the humidity. Declan will forever stare at me from the cold depths of that lake.

"Did you know my parents?" I ask.

"Stephen and Lily Wade, you say?"

I nod.

A single round shoulder lifts as he looks down the alley and into the market, where so far no one pays us any attention. "I knew a lot of men who went by the name Stephen, but no one by the last name Wade. The only Lily I knew was a Lily Garrett. Young woman with no husband. No children. Our time in the southeast region was short. It is possible she could have gotten married after I left."

My heartbeat races in opposition to the plummeting feeling in my stomach. "Peter said—"

"Pete and I have been around a long time. Have known a lot of people." He taps his temple. "We have good, long memories. If I once knew a couple by this name, I would, and could, tell you."

I should feel numb to these dead ends by now, but I am not. I clench my jaw and turn to hide the tears brimming in my eyes. They are more a sign of my mounting frustration than anything else. This and I am exhausted from the long day of traveling to get here. Crossing Mexico's border cost me a lot of my remaining funds; then I had to travel by aerotrain for half a day before reaching a working teleporter. All for nothing.

My thoughts are interrupted by the sound of three pitched dings in the street. Cesar and I step out of the alley and look up at the holograph image of an emergency broadcast filling the sky.

The blond male newscaster is American, according to his accent. The Spanish translation runs along the bottom of the holo-sky stream. I stare past the reporter in the video feed to the building behind him, a flutter of nerves winging through my stomach. The main office building of Burke Enterprises towers above all of Richmond, Virginia, a grand structure of glass and steel.

"Must be about the clones," Cesar says with a scowl deepening the wrinkles on his face. "Burke Enterprises wants the world to know how important they are."

These same broadcasts air in America. I had not expected them to stretch to other countries, but I should not be surprised. Infertility is a worldwide issue, and no doubt other countries are salivating for Dr. Travista's "cure." The one he keeps to himself and that other scientists are unable to replicate.

No one has figured out how the elusive doctor managed to transfer an entire soul into a cloned body capable of carrying multiple pregnancies. According to Dr. Travista's reports, we clones can even accept donated organs now; we are no longer as fragile as our predecessors were.

In a newsroom, a dashing man with too-white teeth speaks into the camera. *". . . a while since we've heard from the creator himself, Dr. Arthur Travista, so do you think he's making a rare appearance today, Tim?"*

The camera switches back to the man in front of Burke Enterprises. A strong wind tunnels through and lifts his carefully placed hair. *"That's a good question, Isaac, and the consensus here is that, yes, we will indeed be hearing from Dr. Travista today. It's possible he wants to add to the recent statement released from the White House regarding the rising number of successful pregnancies since the birth of a daughter from the Original Clone herself, Ruby Godfrey, just this past winter."*

The man, Tim, pauses and tilts his head as if listening to someone speaking in an earpiece. He glances behind him and says, *"It appears the moment has come, and I am told, Isaac, that it is* not *Dr. Arthur Travista. Let's tune in now to where the surprise speaker approaches the podium."*

The massive crowd surrounding the dais goes deathly quiet. Camera flashes burst sporadically as finely dressed men spill through glass revolving doors. In the center of this protective cluster is a tall man with cropped dark hair, his head bowed just enough to hide from the camera. Despite his hidden face, I know this man too intimately to be fooled. Yet it is impossible.

Knees weak, I brace a hand on the corner of the tan and red building to my left. This cannot be real. But I do not imagine the broad set of shoulders or the sure gait of the man who demands respect from everyone around him.

Declan Burke reaches the podium and looks into the roaring audience. Flashbulbs erupt in a frenzy as the photographers race to capture every angle of the man long believed captive of the resistance.

Off-camera, Tim gives the audience a brief rundown of the past year in an exuberant tone: Declan's disappearance, how without his financial aid and support we would not have the promise of a thriving future. If Dr. Travista is the "father" of cloning, Declan is definitely the "godfather."

Declan raises his hands for silence, casting the throng his devastating smile. Even now my heart skips. Despite our last days together, I loved this man too much for my own good. While our world requires men to think of their women as possessions, Declan treated me with more kindness and love than I deserved. His patience in those first months of my clone life went above and beyond what any other man would have deemed necessary. It has taken me a long time to admit this, but I am the woman I am now because of him. My past, what little I remember, has not defined me.

He has.

Declan tugs down on the dark blue suit jacket he wears—my favorite color on him—while he waits for the crowd to calm. Meanwhile, I study the small changes in him. He wears the shadow of a goatee and tightly trimmed hair. His crowd-pleasing smile does not reach his eyes. He is also thinner than I remember.

"It has been a long year," he says in his deep voice. Every syllable raises goose bumps along my skin. *"A year of many successes for the human race. God willing, the success will only continue to grow."*

His expression sobers and he shifts his weight. *"I am only sorry it was a year I could not celebrate with you. For me, it was a year of fear at the hands of the resistance, followed by several months of recovery. A year I will never get back, but a year I intend to be repaid,"* he finishes with a fist on the podium.

Arms rise in the air and obscure the perfect shot of Declan, who waits in silence while the men cheer. A taut line stretches his full mouth. This matches the fire in his eyes perfectly.

"I came here today not to discuss my harrowing year with these so-called freedom fighters but to beg you, the people of every nation watching this broadcast, to help me."

Declan's gaze falls, and a look of sheer loss paints his expression. The strong hands that know every inch of my skin slide up and grip the edges of the podium. His chest rises and falls hard beneath his fine suit.

Then his gaze lifts, and there lies a heat that had not been there prior. Through the camera, past all the miles between us, the intensity of his stare sears into me. As if he sees me. As if there is no distance between us at all.

"The resistance took my wife, Emma. And I want her back."

CHAPTER 2

My breath catches on the heels of his announcement. Why would he do this? Revenge? Have I not paid enough?

Declan continues, though his voice is nearly drowned out by my heartbeat rushing in my ears. *"I'm offering a reward in the amount of a hundred thousand dollars for any information leading to the rescue of my wife, Emma. But,"* he says in a sharp tone that emphasizes the word, *"bring her to me alive, and you will be a millionaire ten times over."*

My picture flashes across the hologram along with a phone number. It is an old picture—my hair was chin length then—taken from the showing of my art in a gallery. My first and last show.

Cesar pushes me into the wall, where I hit with a *thunk*. Pieces of the weathered surface fall and pebble around our feet. He grips my throat in his hand. For an old man, he is strong and fast. "What is your real purpose for seeking me out, Emma Burke, wife of the richest man in the Americas?"

I gasp for what little air his hand allows. "He lies. I escaped. Thought he was dead. I swear."

The old man backhands me, and I stumble into the cobbled street with a ringing ear and throbbing cheek. Men face me from every direction. Thanks to my image poised over their heads like a beacon, I am all too recognizable to this poor village.

They glance between me and the picture, and the potential threat urges me to take an unsteady step back. Then the whispering begins. Pointing. I take another step, my heart crashing against my sternum like a caged animal.

Go, go, go.

The men converge on me like a swarm of buzzing insects. Spinning, I jump on a stack of produce crates resting against the side of a one-story building. I pull myself to a red-shingled rooftop and roll to my back. I take one heaving breath before getting to my feet and crossing to the other end of the angled roof.

I jump to another building, this one with a flat top, that sits slightly lower to the ground. I am to the middle when several men jump down behind me. One of the men is fast and snags me by the pack I wear. I drop to my backside and scrape my palms on the concrete surface.

He reaches for me again. I swing a leg at his ankles and sweep his feet out from under him. By the time I get back up, the others have reached me. I nail one with an elbow shot. Another with a head butt that brings tears to my eyes. White dots float in my vision. Unsure I will be able to aim accurately again, I slide out of the grabby hands and run for the side of the roof.

I jump to the ground and roll in a thick patch of grass. The edge of the village is not far, and beyond that, a collage of pine, oak, and ash trees. I can lose myself in the sprawling hills of Michoacán. What I should do after that is anyone's guess.

The majority of my followers quit their pursuit before the village limits. They do not run every day like I do. I run because I must outrun them all, a lesson I learned from one of my most useful memories of last year.

I do not look back but instead listen to the dropping off of footfalls and, according to their tones, frustrated curses. I run into the trees and lose several more. Well into the first mile, I reach the entrance to a cemetery. Stone steps lead up the steep hillside. Aging statues of angels, heads bowed in prayer, frame either side of the entrance. Ivy winds up their ethereal bodies. Loose green leaves carpet each step. The sun shines through dense foliage, casting heavenly fingers around the blessed area.

I duck behind large headstones, hoping to lose whoever still follows. When I think I have been out of sight for a while, I push through the door of a mausoleum and close myself inside. Dust particles float in shafts of sunlight from small windows near the top. Three stone coffins fill the space. Dried flowers rise stiffly from dust-coated ceramic vases.

Voices sound close outside and I scramble to the nearest coffin to test the lid. The stone is heavy but scrapes aside with little trouble. A putrid and dank-scented cloud encapsulates the air around me. My gag reflex hitches and I cannot bring myself to look down at first. The raised calls outside grow closer, though, and force me into action.

Whoever the woman was, she has completed the decomposition process, making things easier. She wears the remains of a full-length white dress, pearls at her throat, and a diamond ring to rival mine.

I could sell those.

I grip the coarse stone edge and shake my head. I cannot believe I just considered robbing a dead woman's grave. There are no circumstances that dire. Not even mine. Besides, I will owe her once I do what I am about to do.

Carefully, I push the remains aside and climb in. The interior smell is nowhere near as bad as the initial release, but it is still awful. I hold my breath and exert all my strength into shifting the heavy lid back into place. Soon, not even a slip of light passes through.

My next draw of breath drags in the foul air and pulls tears from my eyes. *Oh God, there is a dead woman next to me. Dead.* I want to cover my face but I dare not move. A sharp hip bone sinks into my back like a knife. The back of my head lies on a bed of ribs. I am living inside my nightmare. Trapped by the infinite dark with death at my back.

Outside, the unmistakable sound of the door opening makes me stiffen. Two men speaking in rapid Spanish are inside the mausoleum. The scuffling of shoes against concrete echoes in the space. I hear them travel between the coffins, taking their time. I hold my breath when one of them speaks directly over me, his voice muffled. Three taps, like palm slaps, sound on the lid. I flinch, then lie frozen, unable to do so much as blink. Soon, every muscle quivers beyond my control.

After what feels like an eternity, the sounds disappear, but I never hear the door close. Is the coffin lid on crooked? Was there dust on the floor to track my footprints? I do not remember. All I know is that someone could still be inside, waiting me out. Despite how badly I want to be free, I fear leaving the confines of this coffin more.

My heart drums, and sweat beads along my brow. Every muscle in my body aches from lying so absolutely still. I crane my neck to better listen for stragglers and jostle the rib cage under me. The skull loosens and rolls, then settles near the crown of my head.

A whimper escapes my throat and I slap a palm over my mouth. Humid breath travels across my knuckles in quick gusts. I try very hard not to think about the trauma that would have loosened the woman's skull from her spine, but in the dark, it is hard to think of *anything* else.

I listen hard past the rush of blood in my ears and still hear nothing but dead space. But I have to be patient. A few more minutes with a skeleton win out over even one second back in Declan's hands.

The time passes in slow, tense increments, and eventually I make the decision to check the room. I ease into position, careful of the loose bones lying behind me, and push. My adrenaline has slowed, and the strength I need to move the stone has waned dramatically. I cannot make the lid budge even a little.

My eyes widen and black dots fill my vision. I want to scream but can only mouth the word "no" into the space that now feels as if it closes in around me. I bite my lower lip and push again. The following scraping sound explodes in the silence and I startle back into the skeleton. A bone stabs my back. I lurch up and hit my head on the coffin lid. The dull throb manages to slow me down, but only for a moment.

I *need* out.

I heave my entire upper body against the lid and force it aside. Cool, fresh air accompanies a blinding light. I scramble up and topple over the side. I hit the ground with a *thud,* sending a jolt of pain into my hip and down my leg.

Leaning against the coffin's dais, I drag in every blessedly fresh breath. My eyes water in the sunlight, but after several blinks, I conclude that I am alone. I reach out and shut the door. They could still be out there, which is the only reason I have not run. If I stay where I am long enough, I will walk from here rather than run.

Except Declan's broadcast has ensured that I will always be running. He essentially put a price on my head that no one can or will refuse. In only a few minutes, and from an entirely different country, Declan Burke managed to snatch my freedom right out from under me. How can I continue my search now? Anyone who is or was resistance will assume I am a spy, and everyone else stands ready to turn me over for a pile of cash. I will face danger and difficulty no matter where I go.

Not everywhere.

I sigh and rub my temples. I cannot accept that running back to Noah is the only option I have. But if there is another, I do not know what it is. I would gladly go back to Montana, but putting Peter in Declan's line of sight is the last thing I want to do. No one else I have met has opened their home to me.

Damn it.

I stand and brush dust from my backside. "Just get out of Mexico, Emma. Worry about the rest later."

Getting out of Mexico is as simple as sneaking into the back of a cargo truck bound for Arizona. I avoid plenty of close calls by hiding my hair under a scarf. My sunglasses and lack of eye contact do the rest.

Twenty-four hours have not given me a better outcome to my issue. Even if it were a question of money, I could not simply sell my wedding ring to the first buyer. Not without being recognized. My luck got me across the border but will not hold out much longer.

Despite all that, I am still against asking Noah for help. After the way I left, the only help he may give is a hand back out. He probably despises me. He should. Even if I am wrong and he holds no resentment toward me, there is another truth holding me back. I am a coward and cannot face the guilt behind my own actions. Seeing him, seeing Adrienne, will be a glaring reminder of my mistakes.

I have one last option left, though it is not one I look forward to. But I am resolved to try. I waste no time and find the nearest public teleporter. The outside of the booth says ARIZONA PUBLIC TRANSPORT in black letters. Warnings below spell out the dangers of trying to port unlawfully out of the country. As the booth is an instrument that turns you into a billion tiny pieces, I would not risk unlawfully going *anywhere.*

Inside, the silver floor gives under my weight, and my stats—total mass, water, and body fat, as well as additional calculations based on the clothes I wear—appear in glowing red lights on the clear surface. Once the calculations are finished, a keypad appears. With shaking fingers, I type in the port number, breathe deep of the spearmint masking the rancid scent of the numbing agent, and watch the Arizona street melt away.

The second I step onto Las Vegas Boulevard, the desert sun envelopes me. The passersby on the main strip ignore me despite how I must look after my time in Mexico. This is exactly why I chose this destination. In Las Vegas, everyone is too concerned with their own bad luck to see mine. Even though the broadcast played everywhere, I have no reason to believe it has gone viral enough to make much of a difference yet. Even if it has, the gamblers are too focused on their game of choice, getting drunk, or sleeping. The crowd, too, is also so thick that to the video cameras I am merely one face among thousands. Even if Declan monitors the footage, the odds of finding me are slim.

I slide my large sunglasses on and duck my head as I weave through the men. Several slow their pace outside glass-encased booths where beautiful, scantily clad women showcase their goods. The women wink and smile seductively. They run their hands over their bodies to draw attention to their best assets. Dollar amounts flash on the glass when a man stops to look at the merchandise.

Marijuana merchants entice potential customers with promises of a good high from mobile stands they maneuver through the throng. Neon-colored tubes sprout from the top like flowers. Screens on the stands stream the names of the weed for sale. Blue Cheese. Amnesia Haze. Diesel. White Rhino. Despite the odd names, money changes hands at a consistent rate.

I turn into the nearest casino: the Crystal Palace. The structure is in the shape of a diamond and made entirely of glass. The lobby is white and gold marble. Bronze statues of ancient gods on pedestals adorn corners with tall sprouting plants. Fountains spray water high into the air.

I stand out amid such opulence. My hair is dirty, my skin and clothes covered in dust, and I am certain my exhaustion weighs heavy on my face. I crave a shower and a soft bed, so I use the last of my cash to pay for a room and hope the insanity of my plan is fueled by my lack of sleep. That when I wake, I will have a better plan.

Except this does not prove true. I wake knowing my latest idea is my only option next to running back to Noah, and I refuse to give in so easily. I dig clean clothes out of my bag: dark jeans, white tee, and black leather jacket. Under one pant leg, I strap on the only weapon I own—a knife, in case things go horribly wrong—then slick my hair into a low-hanging ponytail.

In the hotel's casino, amid the ringing of slots and clicking of chips, I patrol the tables until I find an unguarded cell phone beside a patron. His chips are stacked high to one side and his laugh soars above everyone else's. I lean on the table as if I have an interest in the game, smile at the man, who has crooked yellow teeth, and slide his cell off the edge.

"Good luck," I tell him as I walk away, hoping he does not notice the flush in my cheeks. One thing I never do is steal from others, but I have little choice. I cannot have my call traced to this location. With the cell phone, the best they can do is locate the nearest call receptor.

"Leaving so soon?" the man yells, but I never look back.

I find a shadowed corner near a large plant and slip behind, keeping my attention on everyone in the vicinity. With shaking fingers, I dial a number I wish I could forget as easily as my past.

A man answers the phone on the second ring. "Declan Burke's office."

CHAPTER 3

I recognize the voice on the other end of the line as Declan's assistant, Armand Tulley. "I need to speak with Declan Burke," I tell him.

"I'm sorry, miss, but—"

"This is Emma Burke." I press a knuckle into my temple, feeling the start of a headache coming on. "Put my husband on the phone."

The words feel foreign and wrong, but they do the job. The line goes quiet, leaving me to listen to the pleased laughter and groans of loss all around me. Sweat tickles my brow and I fan my shirt to cool my hot skin as I wait for Declan to answer. How will he act? Despite what he has told the world, he may want me dead. After all, I tried to kill him.

"Emma?" Declan's deep voice, filled with worry, causes me to jump.

I take a moment to wet my dry lips before responding. "Why are you doing this?"

"Doing what? Searching for my wife?" He sounds almost angry now. "I should be asking you the same question."

I grip the phone tighter. I have not been his wife since before Noah deleted all records of our union at Her behest. Something Noah explained to me a long time ago but apparently a fact Declan refuses to believe. "I am not your wife. Our marriage was erased years ago, remember?"

Silence envelopes both ends of the line. I imagine he searches for a new lie he hopes will lure me back. I lift the wedding band hanging heavy around my neck and slip it onto the end of my index finger. The diamonds catch and reflect the fluorescent lights and remind me how everything he represents is nothing more than a set of chains.

Finally, he says, "You were happy with me . . . before all this madness. I know you loved me just as I love you."

"After how things ended, I cannot believe you can so easily forgive. There is no reason why I should trust you to let me live."

"I've had a lot of time to consider what happened between us, and I understand why you felt compelled to act as you did. I understand why you were angry, and you had every right."

I lost my husband and daughter because of him. I lost my rightful place in this unforgivable world. What I feel goes beyond anger. "Tell me something, Declan. If I were to return, would we work through our issues like normal people?" I already know the answer, but I need to hear him say it.

"We aren't normal people. Would it be so bad to forget all that's happened? To get back to where we were?"

"You mean to the lies and deception?" Tears sting the backs of my eyes. Whether they are from anger or disappointment, I do not know. "I cannot live like that again, but I cannot live my life on the run either. Please rescind the offer for my return. I am no threat to you or your company. I am only trying to find some peace."

"With your other husband?" he clips out.

"No," I say too quickly, then take a deep breath to steady myself.

There is an audible sigh on the other end. "Emma, please come home. Let me take care of you."

A single, hard laugh bursts free from deep inside me. "By giving me limited access to the world? By forcing me into having your children, then giving my daughters to one of your camps?"

"Our children will never know that life. They don't have to, Emma.

There are benefits to being who I am. You only got a glimpse of what I'm capable of doing for you."

What he is capable of doing *to* me is the only thing concerning me, and that is why I will never return. "Will you call off the search or not?"

"What kind of man would I be if I gave up the woman I love more than life?"

"You do not know what love is. If you did, you would let me go." I hang up before hearing his response. The cell clatters to the marbled floor and I crush it under my shoe.

Why did I think that would work? I know Declan too well, and he always gets what he wants. *What he pays for,* as he so eloquently put it to me once. According to the laws in the east, I am his property. The Burke family purchased my host as a teenager, and because I am a clone his company created, he has every right to me. But I cannot accept that. Not with freedom still in my grip.

I step around the plant into the view of the casino. One glance into the teeming room reveals new trouble. White-and-gold-uniformed men stand near tables, their attention seemingly somewhere else, but I know this tactic. The red coats in Declan's labs used to trail me too. They are not as unassuming as they would like me to believe.

Two of the security men throw something that zips through the air so fast I am clueless about its purpose until my arms, elbows to shoulders, are strapped tight to my rib cage. My legs are restrained from knees to hips. They have used some sort of wire to snare me. I lose my balance and drop to my butt like a stone.

One man, the head of security according to the extra flair on his uniform, raises an arm. "We got her. Someone call the hotline."

They will *not* send me back to Declan. I twist my ankles around and pull up my pant leg. I finger my knife free, then run it up between my thighs, cutting the wire.

Patrons at tables scramble out of their seats, crowding the aisles. Others take to using the tabletops for their escape, toppling hundreds of chips on the way. Security fights to get through the mob while I work my way into a standing position.

I am unable to free my arms before someone barrels into me and we skid across the marble floor. My back hits a clay pot so hard the pot cracks open and potting soil spills all over me. I thrust the knife into my attacker's thigh. He yells and his weight disappears, taking my blade with him.

On my way back into a standing position, I shoulder another man in the stomach. After that, any route out I may have had closes like the lid of my recent coffin. I allow those buried fighting instincts to take over and ignore the alarmed warnings in my head, because *I will get out of this.* I have to.

Someone snatches my ponytail and yanks my head back. My back hits his chest and I slam my heel down on his instep. He cries out and pushes me right into another man, who catches me by the shoulders. The man looks nothing like Declan—none of them do—but he may as well be a perfect representation. The determined set of his jaw. The tight grip of his hands. Letting this man, or any other, take me so easily cannot happen. Not like this. I will die first.

I bring my knee up between his legs and he releases me with a grunt. I strike him in the chin with a solid kick, then immediately aim another to my right, connecting with a chest. I whirl around with a jumping roundhouse to the front again, then tilt forward to balance a kick back into the man coming in behind me.

Finally, the way is clear to run. Free of the main casino, I face a full hotel lobby. The men and few women disperse, willing to leave my capture to the multiple security guys behind me. The front doors have only begun to slide open on my approach when a heavy body slams into me. We crash through the window. I roll into the semicircular driveway with a scattering of glass shards. The fast-approaching *whir* of an electric car engine warns me to keep rolling across the drive. I am clear by only seconds when the squeal of tires rends the air, followed by a *thunk* as the vehicle hits the man.

My head spins and I feel as if I have been running for miles. I cannot remember which way to the nearest public teleporter, but I have to move. Shouts warn everyone to get out of the way. They are too close.

I roll to my knees and clamber to my feet, then take off down the street, refusing to look back. Something hot and wet oozes down the side of my face and tickles my cheek.

I duck into the first public teleporter I find. Through the glass, I can see the mass of white-and-gold-clad casino security continue to pursue me. I use my nose to type in an untraceable code followed by the port number I no longer have a choice but to use. The security draws too close, with guns raised. Spearmint floods the booth. My body numbs and the Las Vegas Strip disappears.

The resistance command center looks no different as I appear inside one of the ten teleporters lining the wall. Stations arranged in a semicircular pattern fill several rows of wide steps and face a cavernous room of monitors. Each station is in the shape of an elongated number three and manned by two resistance members. They stare at four video relay monitors apiece. The eight monitors per station are hooded by a shelf that gives off enough soft light to illuminate a single keyboard inlaid in a pale wooden desktop.

I find myself frozen inside the teleporter, unable to stop the port number to downtown Polson, Montana, from filtering into my thoughts. It is not yet too late to make the choice to return where I know I am welcome. Except Peter is too old to fight for me and I bring nothing but trouble. Especially now.

Swallowing my fear, I step out of the teleporter. People stand from their stations to face me, some speechless, others whispering to a close neighbor. Nobody welcomes me, the impostor who looks like Emma Wade.

I approach the nearest young man who does not look as hostile as a few of the others. "Can you tell me where I can find"—asking for Noah feels like too much. I am not ready—"Foster Birmingham?"

A man of average height steps forward and brushes the younger one aside. His hair is flaming red, cut short and spiky. His freckled face is rectangular and hard-edged. He is almost attractive, but not kind, according to the set of his jaw. Fierce green eyes take my measure, scanning me from scuffed boot to bound arms. I know I must look a sight—I can feel the tickle of hair sticking to the sides of my face and neck, not to mention the blood now dripping off my chin all over my leather jacket—but I wish he did not have to be so thorough in his assessment of my state.

"You made a mistake coming here," he says, squaring his shoulders and tucking his hands behind his back.

I balk for only a moment. "Who are you?"

"Major Clint Reid."

My thoughts trip on the word "major"—Emma's old position inside the ranks of this group. There is a pulse of indignation toward this man who takes Her place.

Still, I will try to be civil, though this man already sets my teeth on edge. "My name is—"

"I know exactly who you are, Mrs. Burke."

Heat blossoms in my cheeks. No one has called me this in well over a year, and I do not like it. "That is not my name."

He ignores me and uses two fingers to motion for someone to come over. "Lock her up."

CHAPTER 4

I expected several reactions when I arrived, but locking me up was not one of them. "What?"

Two men reach for me. I strike out with plenty of kicks, my only defense at this point, but am in the wrong place to fight back. These men are thoroughly trained to handle a threat, so one woman with her arms tied down is nothing. There will be no escaping this problem. They have me pinned to the ground in a matter of seconds, pressing my throbbing, bruised cheek to cold concrete.

"Get her out of here," Reid tells the men.

They haul me up so fast the room spins. My feet barely touch the ground as they lead me into the hallway. Sonya is there, and she stands as if made of stone, watching them drag me in the opposite direction. She has grown her hair out since I last saw her, and the tight black curls brush her narrow shoulders. A small child rests on her hip. A beautiful little girl with blond ringlets. The girl's pale skin is a sharp contrast to Sonya's darker brown. Despite the year and few months that have passed, I would know this child's face anywhere. I see it in my memory every day.

Adrienne.

I cannot take my eyes off her. That is, until Noah approaches Sonya with a soft smile that lights his eyes. His hair is cut short, his blond a shade darker than Adrienne's. He kisses Sonya's cheek and brushes a hand down Adrienne's back.

"Noah!" I do not know if I yell because I am in need of rescue or because I am witnessing a living nightmare. There is no mistaking the close relationship that has formed between Noah and Sonya. There is also no mistaking the fact that I hate it.

Noah spins in my direction. His complexion pales.

I drag my feet to slow the progress of my imprisonment, but the men tug me with little effort.

"Stop!" Noah darts around Sonya. "What do you think you're doing?"

"Major Reid ordered her locked up," a man tells him.

Our progression comes to a standstill, giving Noah a chance to catch up. "Let her go."

There are more than a few "buts" going around, and nobody moves to set me free.

Noah stares down the two holding me until they release my arms. "If Reid has an issue, he can take it up with me, his commanding officer, *and yours*," he finishes in a tone that makes me shrink back. I remember this dangerous tone of his all too well. He once used it to threaten my life.

The men retreat, leaving me alone with Noah. He runs a hand over his cropped hair and gives me a half smile. Laugh lines fan away from his eyes. There is color in his face, and his amber eyes are the brightest I have seen them outside a memory of my past. He looks a million times better since I last saw him. He looks happy.

"I did not know where else to go," I say. "After the broadcast—"

"I wondered if you'd come."

My heart trips over itself, and my feelings for him clamber to get free and act. I want to run my nails over his new tightly trimmed beard and along his sideburns. I want his arms around me so bad I ache. I want to bury my face in his warm, musk-scented neck and just *release.*

But I cannot let this need overtake me. I made my choice and, apparently, so has he. "I could use a place to stay for a couple of days. I need to—"

"Emma," he breathes, my name a sigh wrapping around me. His eyes close and he takes a deep breath. "Of course you can stay." His voice is firm again and he opens his eyes. "As long as you need."

I look away from the mask of indifference he gives me. The place where Sonya stood is empty now, Adrienne gone from my sight.

Rustling from him draws my attention back. He pulls a knife free from a pocket in his black uniform pants and nods at my bound arms. "I take it these aren't a fashion statement."

I force a chuckle as he swipes the knife through the tight wire. "No."

He looks at my bleeding forehead. "My guys didn't do this, did they?"

"A whole other group of men, actually." I massage my throbbing arms. "My luck has sort of run out since the broadcast."

"I saw the satellite feeds from Mexico. Close call, huh?"

"You saw what happened?"

He reaches into another pocket and frees a dark blue bandanna. "The entire world has by now. The networks are eating it up. Burke has successfully turned it into a botched attempt to escape your captors."

My stomach sinks as he carefully places the cloth over the wound on my forehead. The pressure sends a jolt of stinging pain down my face and I wince.

"You should let Sonya look at this," he whispers.

I replace his hand with mine and step away. The last thing I want is to set foot in their hospital wing. I plan to avoid doctors and their tests for the rest of my life. "I will heal."

"It looks ba—"

"She's beautiful," I say, cutting him off and motioning to the now empty corridor. I already regret coming here. He smells too good. Looks too good. And the mention of Sonya wrings my heart with fresh pain. "Adrienne," I clarify when he looks confused.

"Just like her mother."

The reverence in his tone snags my attention and I find his gaze seeping into me, though his expression gives nothing away. I cannot help but wonder if the adoration in his voice is for Adrienne or me. Maybe it is too much to hope for a little bit of both.

The way he looks at me is a trap I easily slide into. I shake myself free of his thrall and say, "You are with Sonya now?"

Noah's expression shifts to surprise, then embarrassment, and finally, determination. "Yes. She's been a good mother to Adrienne." His gaze lowers to the floor. "It just sort of happened."

I wonder why he feels the need to explain while conversely feeling I deserve an explanation. But a much stronger emotion clouds this: a sudden need to end Sonya's rights to my child. Not Emma-of-my-past's child. *Mine.* This is the first I have felt such a solid claim to her since living through her birth.

He opens his mouth to say something else, only to be interrupted by the bellow of a man who, in all of minutes, has made me despise him. We turn as one to face Clint Reid.

"You put us all at risk by harboring this fugitive," Reid says.

Noah sweeps an arm between us as if on instinct and glares at Reid. I stare at the appendage meant to stave me off, wondering why on earth he thinks the separation necessary. I may have a few choice words for this man, but I would never attack first.

"What the hell do you think you're doing?" Noah says. "She came here for help."

Reid glances calmly between us, a muscle ticking in his square jaw. "Or she came here to spy on us."

"I am no spy," I tell him.

The man's mouth twitches with amusement and derision all at once. He speaks to me now as if Noah no longer matters in this conversation. "Declan Burke returns from the dead with a story about his kidnapped wife, and you conveniently stroll into our headquarters a day later? I don't buy it. You've been planning this with your husband—"

"He is not my husband." The more this stranger goes there, the more I hate it. I want no further association with Declan than absolutely necessary.

"Funny. You sure played the wife role to"—his gaze slides over me in a salacious manner—"perfection."

I narrow my eyes, biting back the fighting words worming their way to the surface. I cannot let him bait me.

Noah shifts to stand in front of me. "You have no idea what you're talking about. Emma thought Burke was dead, same as us."

Reid's attention shifts slowly from me to Noah. "You can't prove she didn't meet him after she disappeared last year. They could have staged that little event in Mexico yesterday to throw us off."

"You're right," Noah says. "I can't prove it, but I know Emma better than anyone, and she would never turn on us."

"With all due respect, this clone is not Emma Wade. You'll be much better off once you accept the fact that your wife is dead. In fact, we'll all be much better off."

Noah strikes him in the jaw and Reid's head snaps to the side. Clearly Reid did not see that coming any more than I did. I doubt the major feels the same warm charge I do, though. It was a good hit, and well deserved.

Noah prepares to swing again and I come to my senses. One time is enough, so I take him by the arm. "Stop it, Noah. Let it go."

Reid wipes the blood coating his lip with the back of his hand, glancing askance between Noah and me. "That's the problem, Mrs. Burke. He can't let it go. Do us all a favor and open his eyes, will you? Remind him who and what you really are so we can finally move past the loss of a woman you will never be."

The fire zips through me so fast it burns out all rational thought. While proactive before, Noah is not quick enough to halt the stinging slap I lay across Reid's face.

Reid merely smiles and snorts a single laugh while rubbing the area. "Did I say something to offend?"

"I do not know you but am already sure every word out of your mouth is offensive."

Reid raises an eyebrow at Noah. "She doesn't know me. You hear that? How much more proof do you need?"

The words sink in and I realize Emma Wade knew this man. Because my memories are lost in some dark abyss, I have only proven his point. Noah cannot even look at me.

"This was a mistake," I tell them. "I will leave."

"You aren't going anywhere," Noah snaps, and gives me a look that dares me to argue. To Reid, he says, "There will be no further discussion on the matter." He then takes me by the elbow. "Come on. Let's get you settled."

CHAPTER 5

How do you feel today, Emma?

Any nightmares?

The internal voice comes in the curious resonance that can only belong to Dr. Travista. Why, I do not know. Maybe because I am living a new nightmare, trapped underground with Noah and Sonya, forced to wear Her clothes from a cardboard box marked EMMA'S in bold black letters. A box I refuse to look into too deeply. My past haunts me around every turn.

I stare in the full-length mirror at a version of Emma Wade that I, along with everyone else, would love to deny exists. She wears black pants with zippered pockets everywhere. Military issue. They are fitted but loose enough to move comfortably. The basic tee is white and fitted as well. With my dark hair hanging long and loose over my shoulders, I could easily be the version of Noah's wife who died more than a year ago. For half a second I am tempted to find scissors and cut it back to chin length.

I sigh at my reflection and run warm palms down the front of my thighs. "Pull it together."

A knock on the door startles me and I twist to face the steel surface. "Come in."

A whisper-soft *shiff* fills the space as the door slides into the wall.

Sonya peeks her head in and gives me a belated, tight smile. "May we come in?"

"We?"

Another head, male, bald, and shiny, ducks in nearly a foot below Sonya's. The man's smile beams from one unusually tiny ear to the other. He must be older by twenty years, but he looks far more youthful than I feel at the moment.

"Hello, Miss Emma," he says, and darts into the room with quick feet, stocky arm extended in greeting. He wears tan slacks and a rumpled button-down shirt striped in shades of brown. One of his shoes is untied. His palm, when I take it, is warm and moist but soft.

"Just Emma," I say.

"Phillip Malcolm. Call me Phillip." A nervous energy makes his hazel eyes dart, his smile twitchy. His head bobbles jerkily from side to side. "Or Phil. Or Dr. P."

It takes everything I have not to yank my hand free. "Doctor?"

Dr. Malcolm glances between me and Sonya, who leans cross-armed in the doorway. "Geneticist, actually. Or at least that's how I began my career. I like to dabble in all the sciences. You know, I once even tried my hand at ichthyology, which sounds boring except—"

"Phillip," Sonya cuts in. Her weary tone suggests she has to do this often.

The man flushes, but his smile never shows any hint of disappearing. "Anyway. My specialty is in genetics."

Sonya walks the rest of the way in, her hands sliding into the deep pockets of her white lab coat. Unlike Dr. Malcolm's, her attire is neatly pressed. "I told Phillip I wanted to take a look at that cut on your head and he insisted on coming along to meet you."

He raises both hands as if to stop me, though I stand perfectly still. "I am a huge fan."

What an odd little man. "Thank you. I think."

Sonya's hands reappear with a set of gloves. "May I?"

I step back. "I cleaned the wound myself, and it is not deep enough to warrant an examination."

Despite my words, she continues to snap on the latex. "Why don't I be the judge of that?"

Hold very still, Emma, Dr. Travista's voice says in my head.

My heart leaps. "The cut is not even bleeding," I tell her, retreating again, this time stepping on a wooden support leg jutting out from the standing mirror.

Dr. Malcolm tilts forward and back on the balls of his feet, waving a dismissive hand at me. "She's right, Sonya. You can't fix what ain't broke." He winks at me.

I blink.

Is this a trick? Why is he trying to help me?

I stare at the man so long I almost forget what I am doing—*escaping*—and Sonya nearly has her hands on me before I dart around her. "Okay, hold on a second. Please do not do that, Sonya. I did not ask for your help, and I do not need it."

Her espresso eyes meet mine, unblinking. "All right. Fine. But you've been doing a lot of traveling," she says, rummaging in her deep pocket. "I'm guessing you didn't have any immunizations."

"You want to know if I have had my shots?"

She eyes the wound on my forehead. "I wanted to look at that and then draw some blood. For the safety of the population, I need to make sure you aren't carrying anything contagious."

The last thing I want is to have a needle shoved through my skin. I do not believe I carry anything but would also hate to be the reason an entire underground population—

"Did you know there was once a virus," Dr. Malcolm begins, "that killed hundreds of millions a year? Up to eighty percent of all who contracted the virus died. It was unintentionally introduced in Veracruz back in the 1500s and killed millions of the native population." He wiggles his fingers over his forearm and squishes up his nose. "They'd get these tiny little pustules—"

"Phillip," Sonya says with a dark eyebrow raised at him.

He mimes locking his thinned lips and winks at me again. I cannot help but smile. He has also sold me on the needle, which I hope for his sake was not his master plan. "I guess if it could mean the life of hundreds of millions, you should check my blood for this deadly virus."

Dr. Malcolm chuckles and waves a hand in the air. "Oh, they eradicated smallpox in the 1900s. No worries."

Sonya motions for me to sit on the bed. She pulls a chair over to sit in front of me and focuses on preparing my arm for the blood draw. She is close enough that I cannot help but inhale her sweet scent. Like raw sugar and vanilla. The smell is too sweet for my tastes and I wonder if Noah likes it.

I am suddenly filled with images of the two of them together, making love, talking about marriage, raising Adrienne together. Maybe even having more children. Are they to this point in their relationship? Does he love her?

It is as if my rib cage constricts in reaction to this thought. More than anything, I do not want him to love her. Is this how he felt last year after seeing me with Declan? He had the means to watch every detail of my time with Declan, too. I can only imagine the torture he must have experienced.

The room grows eerily silent except for two sets of uneven breaths between me and Sonya and the measured set leaning around Sonya to watch. The air grows warmer by the second.

"Little pinch," Sonya warns, then slides the needle into a vein.

I wince and watch the vial fill with my blood.

"In the blood," Dr. Malcolm whispers unnecessarily, "are six *billion* letters making up a gene sequence." His gaze lifts from the vial to my eyes. "One single letter out of place in a single chromosome can lead to death." His smile lifts the corners of his eyes, causing lines to fan away from the outside edges. "Did you know that?"

I swallow hard, my suddenly dry throat clicking. "No. I did not."

His eyes twinkle. "But I am sure Dr. Travista has already checked you for these sorts of defects. I bet you're perfect."

Perfect. Yes, Dr. Travista used that term a lot. But I am far from.

Sonya looks up at me as if we are sharing in some wordless conversation. I do not know what that could be, nor do I care. All I care about is the order of my six billion letters in the hands of these two doctors. The last thing I want is to find out something is wrong with me, which will cause a domino effect of actions that can only lead to tests. Tests lead to a loss of freedom.

"I only give you permission to test for viruses," I tell her. "Not my gene sequence." I look pointedly at Dr. Malcolm. "All right?"

His beaming smile falters. "Of course. But if you ever change your mind, I'd love to spend some time—"

"I will not change my mind."

Sonya removes the needle and passes the full vials to Dr. Malcolm. While stuffing everything else back into her pockets, she squints up at my cut. "Looks superficial."

I lean away. "I told you it was not bad."

"Just doing my job, Emma. Keep it clean until the skin closes." She stands and places the chair back in front of the little desk. "Let me know if you need anything. You know where to find me."

"*Us,*" Dr. Malcolm amends. "I would love to chat with you while you're visiting, Miss Emma."

"Please. Just Emma."

"Are you staying long?" Sonya asks, then activates the door switch.

Dr. Malcolm darts into the hallway, stops, then spins to face the room with interest dancing in his bright eyes.

"No," I tell her.

"Too bad."

This is the last thing I expect from Sonya after how we left things. I will never forget the look on her face as she said the words that ultimately led me to leave in the first place: *You aren't his wife.*

She gives me a tight smile, then disappears into the concrete, box-like hallway. Dr. Malcolm waves enthusiastically before sprinting off after her.

Dumbfounded by what just happened, I start to close my door but stop when a very tall someone fills the space. Long, toned arms brace on either side of the steel doorframe. I beam up at the man whose skin is the color of milk chocolate and whose eyes have a grayish-blue hue.

Foster swoops in and scoops me off the ground in a swinging hug. I do not need all of my memories to feel bone deep that Foster Birmingham is my best friend in this entire world. He was the only one who accepted me without question after discovering my clone status last year.

Me.

Not Her.

He sets me down and holds me at arm's length, giving me a cursory once-over. His eyes shine with some private amusement. "All your limbs are still there. All ten fingers and toes?"

I wiggle my fingers in his face.

He smirks. "And look at how well they work."

I raise an eyebrow. "What am I missing?"

"Apparently nobody enough to warrant a simple phone call."

Over this last year, I have felt guilt for leaving Noah and, most especially, Adrienne, but never Foster. Until now. "I know. I am truly sorry for disappearing the way I did. I would have called eventually."

He straightens and folds his arms. His biceps strain against the dark-green T-shirt he wears. "I'm not a fan of eventually."

I need to divert this conversation away from me, so I turn and sit with folded legs in the middle of the mattress and hug a pillow to my chest. "What has been going on with you?"

He sits on the edge of my bed. "I was promoted to lieutenant a few months ago, which is really cool. I also had my leg cut off, which wasn't so cool."

I laugh, because he clearly has both legs. "Funny."

He does not laugh. Instead, he leans over and drags a black pant leg up. Dark-gray metal joints and curves of alloy muscle make up his left leg from the knee down. The metal ankle flexes in complete silence.

"Best cybernetic leg money could buy," he says, knocking knuckles on the artificial knee joint. He then points to his temple. "Complete with nanorobotics that communicate directly to my leg from my brain."

Belatedly, I realize I have not taken a breath since the reveal and fill my burning lungs. "But why?"

"Tucker was faced with discharging me from active duty because I never got full function back."

One of my memories pre-Declan is of Foster nearly losing his lower leg in the raid where I was shot. It was the same night Dr. Travista cloned me. Last I saw Foster, he limped all the time.

Foster focuses on lowering his pant leg and says, "Speaking of Tucker. You saw him? How'd that go?"

The idea of how it went creates a desert in my mouth. I stand and pour water from a pitcher, avoiding the look on his face. I do not want to see the pity or hope or whatever else could possibly lie there.

"That good?" he says.

I swallow half the glass before saying, "It was fine. He looks well."

"Well?" He laughs. "There's a time and place for political correctness, and that's never with me. Especially when it comes to you."

I set the glass on the table as if in slow motion, wasting time before turning to face him. I find him leaning on his knees, eyebrows raised and waiting.

"He looks happy," I say with a hitch in my voice, "and I am unhappy with the reason why. But"—I raise a finger to stop him from speaking—"I made the choice to leave him. I cannot blame him for moving on."

Frowning, he lowers his head, then nods. "You're right. You couldn't blame him." He looks up through lowered lashes. "If it were true."

I brace against the edge of the table. "I do not understand."

Foster stands, and each silent step he takes toward me is agonizing. He stops in front of me and folds his arms. "Nobody knows this, and I mean *nobody*—other than me, of course—but he's been looking for you since the day you left. You should have seen his face when you appeared in that feed from Mexico."

But Noah is with Sonya now. And I saw the way he greeted her in the hall. There is no mistaking the bond they have formed. "Why are you telling me this?"

"Oh, I don't know, Wade. Because I want to offer you incentive to stay put for once. Or because while I respect Sonya, Adrienne could use a little less I-learned-to-be-a-regimented-mother-from-a-handbook child rearing. Or maybe it's because I remember how happy you two were once upon a time. After all that, it's because you have a right to know. What you decide to do with that information is up to you."

CHAPTER 6

What do you have to say to those who claim you've managed to find a person's soul? That you can control the one part of us we've been unable to prove the existence of?"

Dr. Travista removes the wire-rimmed glasses from his bulbous nose and aims a thin smile at the interviewer, who speaks offscreen. *"Now, that would make me a god, wouldn't it? I'm merely a man of science."*

"A man of science who performs miracles."

The doctor responds with a satisfied smile and puffs out his chest. *"At least one a day."*

I lie blinking at the shadowed ceiling. The interview returns me to a time when I sat facing Dr. Travista, wearing white scrubs, and always curious. Curious about what I looked like. Curious about an accident it turned out I never had. Curious about why my husband was so reluctant to touch me. Curious about the man who grieved his lost wife in my nightmares.

He refused to let me go. Does he still?

How are you today? Dr. Travista's voice asks.

I finger the round piping edging the mattress. *Heartbroken.* That is how I am. Ashamed. Guilty. Curious.

Talk about that, Emma. What about this situation makes you curious?

Sighing, I rub the heels of my palms in my eyes until white spots appear. This has to stop. I am *not* curious about how Noah and Sonya started dating or why. Why he would look for me if he has moved on.

I am also not curious about why the resistance has a geneticist on staff.

Put the stirrups up. The ghost of Dr. Travista's past order is punctuated by the snap of a rubber glove. *May as well run a few extra tests while I'm at it.*

Shivering, I roll to my side and clutch the pillow under my head. This is not the same situation. I cannot let my imagination go there. Besides, I am no longer as naïve as I once was. And this place is big enough. I can avoid Dr. Malcolm, and maybe even Sonya if I have to. I definitely do not have to go near the hospital wing. And there is no one here with the means to order me to have tests run. I make my own decisions.

Exhaustion sucks me into a deep sleep. I dream of an office lit by sun reflected off snow, and walls lined with bookshelves. Furniture a deep shade of red. The quiet, watchful eyes of Dr. Travista as I trek along the path of one shelf. He motions for me to sit in my usual chair across from him. I do not want to. He will ask me how I am, and I will be forced into telling him more lies. I am tired of the lies.

I stand before my chair, and his smile is gentle, his gray eyes studying. He searches for the woman he tried to erase, but he will not find Her. I am too careful.

I sit, and—

—I float in nothing.

I lurch up to a sitting position and drag in a lungful of air. My skin is slicked with sweat, but my bones have brought back with them the frigid depths of the abyss. I jerk and flinch as I try to control the shiver that has taken over my body. The air tastes strange. Thin. Wrong. And the walls feel too close in the darkness. They tilt toward me and I scramble to free my legs of the tangled sheets.

I roll from the bed and my bare skin slaps against the floor. My already bruised hip flares, but I am more aware of the pain swathing my chest and throat. The tight nature of my lungs. I cannot breathe.

Exit. Where is the exit?

The shadowed steel beckons me from across the room. I race through the door hoping to breathe fresh air, only I face the underground corridor. It may as well be another tomb for all the good it does me now. Gasping in recycled air, I claw the sweat-dampened shirt away from my skin.

The slap of bare feet on concrete moves quickly toward me. "Emma? What's wrong?"

I face the voice and want to cry. Noah approaches in black sweatpants and a white tank top. I do not want him to see me this way. Weak. A child by comparison to the woman he remembers.

He reaches for me but I twist away, unwilling to let him touch me. His hands fist at his sides. "What is it? Talk to me."

Let's talk about your recent nightmare, Emma. Can you describe it for me?

I grit my teeth and rake my hands through my hair. I shake my head in an effort to rid myself of Dr. Travista's voice. He drifts away, but I feel him there. Waiting. Studying. The way Noah does now. There is no telling what he must think as I stand there shivering in my tank top and underwear, my usual mess following a nightmare.

"What are you doing out here?" I ask. The question comes out in a half moan.

"Never mind that," he whispers. "What's wrong?"

I need to see the stars. The old thought comes of its own free will for the first time since my time in the labs. "I need fresh air. That is all."

He enters my room and returns with a blanket that he wraps around my shoulders. Standing before me, he helps gather the front for the most coverage. I cannot help but focus on his handsome face and the caring, efficient way he handles the situation. I want to lean in and feel the solidity of his arms around me. I do not need anything else as long as he is there to hold me together.

But he does not. Cannot.

"Come on," he says, once finished.

He leads me through several corridors, and we end up in his office. He opens a door behind his desk and reveals a teleporter. "I had it put in after . . ." He pauses and seems to consider his next words carefully. "After you left."

The public port we arrive in is moonlit and free of people. I stare out at a large park surrounded by trees and benches that line a running path. In the distance rests a shimmering pond with a wide footbridge.

I draw the cool night air into starving lungs. The action is exactly what I need to ground me. So is the tickle of grass between my toes. The wind in my face. I am nearly lost in these sensations when I feel him. Noah's gaze touches me as if with fingers of its own. I look straight up rather than give in to the temptation of returning his attention. What I see is almost enough to distract me. The stars are incredibly clear here, except tree branches obscure a large section of the night sky.

Noah points at a grassy knoll near the bridge. "The best view is there."

We stroll in silence, with only the whisper of our feet brushing the grass. It takes a full minute to get to the spot despite how close it looked. I sit and tug the blanket tight around me before looking up and seeing how right he was. The sky spreads out nearly uninterrupted.

Noah sits and wraps his arms around upturned knees. "Ready to tell me what happened?"

I cannot look at him, nor am I ready to talk about what happened. I am too embarrassed. "What were you doing in the hall?"

He chuckles. "I feel like I live in that hall. Adrienne sleeps in my room. If I'm in there, she won't go down, so I wait in the hall. She woke up and caught me painting."

I am instantly jealous he has the means to do this. I have not touched a brush to canvas in too long. "Painting? At this hour?" Not that I know the hour, but it feels like it is very early in the morning.

"Couldn't sleep. Your turn."

I hesitate, wondering how best to explain, then decide on, "Bad dream."

"Now tell me something I didn't already know."

I look in his eyes before I realize what I have done. He looks tired behind his interest in my story. I do not want to tell him and break this content moment, but he will not give up until he hears the details. "I dream of death. I feel it pulling me, and every night, it gets closer and closer to taking me. I did not think I would wake up this time."

We turn away from each other at the same time. When he does not respond, I say, "Anyway, I was a little disoriented when I woke up, and I panicked."

"I'm glad I was there, then."

"Me too."

Silence envelopes us again. We lie back on the soft grass and stare into the sky. At the stories laid out in a series of constellations, most of which Noah knows somehow. I know only a handful of them and do not see the three he pointed out to me in one of my few memories.

"Will you tell me what you see?" I ask. "What story plays tonight?"

He is quiet for too long. I find him staring at me with unfiltered shock.

"You do not have to," I say, and look away. "If it—"

"Centaurus," he cuts in, then points straight up.

"I do not know which stars you are looking at."

Noah scoots closer and takes my hand, sending tingles racing over my arm. He opens my palm without pause, as if the fire I feel is mine alone. In it, he places dots in several places and then draws invisible lines to connect them.

When he is finished, I look up and find the grouping. "What is Centaurus?"

Our hands drift apart and lie between us. I feel the heat of his skin beside mine, so close, yet very far.

"Centaurus is about a centaur named Chiron," he says. "He was a wise half-human, half-horse who tutored Hercules and Jason. One day Hercules accidentally wounded him. Being immortal, he would live with the pain forever and begged the gods to put him out of his misery."

Noah pauses and drops his head to face me. I wonder if he has chosen this story on purpose. Am I supposed to be Hercules? He the wounded centaur unable to escape the pain I have inflicted?

"So did they?" I ask. "Put him out of his misery?"

"Yes. And gave him a place among the stars."

A protracted moment ends with us turning away at the same moment. The heat of his skin is suddenly too much and far too close. I sit up to end the intimacy of lying beside him.

"You always know the best stories," I say, thinking back to the memory of us on the beach.

He sits up and wraps his arms around his knees again. "Why don't you tell me one?"

The wind blowing through a nearby cluster of trees cloaks the release of my sigh. I am wary of where his question will lead. "What story would you like to hear?"

"The one where you tell me where you've been all this time."

"Nothing to tell."

One heartbeat.

Two.

I resist the urge to comb down his hair, which stands up in the wind.

"You never could lie to me," he says.

These words speak of a history together. The day I left, this was what I wanted from him more than anything. He could not give it to me then, and now that it seems he can, he is too far away to reach.

I stand and tighten the blanket. "I have been searching for my parents." I turn away once the words are out. I need to walk. Sitting with him feels dangerous.

Noah catches up to me at the end of the footbridge. "Did you find them?"

I do not answer until we reach the middle. I lean over the railing and watch the gentle ripples of water bathed in moonlight. "No."

My wedding ring falls and swings heavy from my neck, a reminder of the man who would rearrange entire continents to find me, thus halting my search. I lift and finger the band, staring absently at the water. "I thought I was finally getting somewhere in Mexico. The man I was meeting was ex-resistance. It turns out he only knew a woman named Lily Garrett. That was all I learned before Declan's announcement." I point to my bruised cheek. "That is when the man gave me this and I spent the following hour or so running from an entire village in the central highlands of Mexico."

Noah reaches out and takes the ring from where I roll the band around my fingertip. "Your wedding ring," he says, letting it drop.

I tuck the jewelry back under my shirt, mentally flogging myself.

I may as well have flaunted my marriage to Declan in his face. Careless. "I no longer have a luckenbooth to stave off any would-be husbands," I explain.

Noah rests his forearms on the railing. We look down at the branded luckenbooth on his right hand. I do not have a memory of him doing this, but I know he did it when we married. I loved him for it because he turned something tainted and ugly into a symbol of our love.

He pushes off the railing and backs away. "What will you do now?"

I turn and rest against the barrier. "The same thing I have done for more than a year. Look for my parents."

Noah stands with arms folded, his gaze cast far behind me. "The price Declan Burke has on you won't make that easy."

"All I need is shelter for a couple of days. Until I figure out a safe place to—"

"You're safe with me," he cuts in, his gaze fastening on me. A moment later, his arms fall, as do his eyes. His weight shifts. "Let me help you."

My head tilts to the side, drawn down with the cinching around my heart. "I cannot ask you to do that. If Declan finds me with you, it will wreck everything you have done using Tucker Securities."

It seems he can look at me again, and I am unable to tear my gaze away for even a moment. "He won't find you." He sounds so sure I almost believe him.

"Your men think I am a traitor, and if you protect me—"

"Let me worry about them." He takes a step closer. "Tell me you're staying, Emma."

He will thwart any excuse I throw his way, but in truth, I do not want to leave. Despite all warnings to the contrary, I want to be near him and Adrienne, and maybe with the access to his computers, I can make headway in my search.

"Okay."

He nods once and tries unsuccessfully to contain a smile. "Okay."

CHAPTER 7

Declan stands outside his building in Richmond, wind tunneling strong down the walkway. The erratic *whoosh* of air brushes the mic held by the reporter. The flash of bulbs adds light to the morning sun.

"Unfortunately," Declan says to the small gathering of reporters, *"what we hoped was a breakthrough in Emma's whereabouts ended shrouded in mystery. But at least I know she is still alive and trying to come home where she belongs."*

He looks directly into the camera, the sea in his eyes bordering on a storm. *"Emma, if you're hearing this, I will find you."*

Declan's warning races over my spine in the guise of an icy shiver. If his intent was to frighten me, it worked. I have no idea how I will get out of this situation short of ending up exactly where he wants me: on Dr. Travista's table.

I shut off the vid screen and toss the remote to the table next to my bed. Declan has managed an entire news conference before normal people have breakfast. He must be getting desperate. But why?

A knock sounds on the door, startling me. Who would want to see me this early? At least I am already dressed for the day. "Come in," I call out, deciding it must be Foster. He promised to take me to breakfast, but I assumed it would not be for another half hour.

The door slides aside for Noah, who has Adrienne propped on his hip. I jump off the side of the bed, unable to take my eyes off her. This close, I see the resemblance to my own face. She has my hazel eyes, my nose with its rounded tip, and my heart-shaped face. She also has Noah's full lips, as well as his naturally wavy hair. She is absolutely beautiful.

Noah closes the door, glances around the quiet room, and gives me a wary smile. "We aren't interrupting anything, are we?"

I wonder what he believes he would interrupt. It is not as if I have had time to plan a secret tryst. "No. I was just watching the news conference." I glance at Adrienne, who watches me from the corner of her eye, her head buried in Noah's shoulder. "Hi," I say to her, and the word is barely audible.

Noah bounces her when she does not respond. "Say hi, chicken."

"Chicken?"

A soft blush fills his cheeks. "Yeah. I've always called her that. Just sort of happened with no rhyme or reason."

I love this more than I can say, but I am also jealous of the obvious bond they share. It feels wrong that I am a stranger to my own daughter, but I did this. I put myself on the outside all on my own.

"Anyway," Noah says, casting his gaze around the room, "we were just getting ready to head to breakfast, and I thought you'd like to meet her."

I can only nod, not trusting my voice as I watch Adrienne watch me. Her little fists clutch tight to Noah's shirt, and she tries to be invisible, which is something she will never be. Not in a million years.

Noah kneels and sets Adrienne on the floor. She stands but does not release his shirt, forcing him to sit on the concrete floor with a sigh.

"She's shy," he tells me, and pulls her into his lap.

I kneel in front of them, itching to touch her but unable to move my arm to do so. "Me too," I admit.

He bounces her on his knee. "Let's see what we can do to change that."

Foster retrieves me for breakfast shortly after my visitors depart. The best Noah could do during their visit was to get Adrienne to walk freely around my room as she kept one eye on me at all times. She did not speak at all, but I learned she uses sign language to communicate with Noah. It was a good start.

Breakfast is a group affair, loud with the sound of laughter, conversation, and scraping of utensils. Foster leads me to one of the copious number of long stainless steel tables in the too-bright and cavernous cafeteria.

We are sitting no more than five seconds when I hear, "Hello, Miss Emma."

My tense shoulders slump and I force a smile up at Dr. Malcolm. "Good morning, Dr. Malcolm."

Foster waves a finger between us. "You two know each other?"

Dr. Malcolm beams almost as bright as the reflection of fluorescent lighting on his bald head. "I had the pleasure yesterday."

"He and Sonya left just before you arrived," I explain.

The doctor bounces and rocks on the balls of his feet, unusually quiet, as if in desperate need of something to say to prolong his visit. His fingers tap the underside of his tray.

I cannot take it and have no wish to be rude. "Would you like to sit?" I ask, and cross my fingers that he declines.

Dr. Malcolm slides across from me and is already sitting when he says, "Yes, thank you."

Foster's knee knocks against mine, but I am careful not to react.

"How was your first night?" Dr. Malcolm asks.

I stir my yogurt, watching the pink layers swirl. "Like every other night."

The doctor's eyes flick between Foster and me. "I'd be curious to know what you dreamed about, if you remember, of course. Did I tell you how I once spent some time studying oneirology? Fascinating what dreams can tell us about a person's—"

A silver tray clatters on the table beside Dr. Malcolm, startling the doctor into silence. A man begins to sit and Dr. Malcolm has to move before the man and his female companion sit on him. I do not know them but am already grateful for the interruption. The last thing I want to talk about is my dreams. Especially not with this doctor.

The woman is stunning. Layers of long brown hair roll down her back in large waves. Her eyes are simply unfair: bright green and in the shape of large almonds. Thinly trimmed brows arch to points over them. Her pink lips form a natural pout and her olive skin is flawless. She is tall, slim, and curvy. Unfair. Everything about her is unfair.

The guy with her is also attractive. Messy brown hair. One eyebrow permanently notched higher than the other. Full lips in a smirk. He is the guy who makes the kids laugh while making the adults exasperated.

The woman folds her arms over the table and leans forward, sharp eyes holding my gaze. "'Tis some visitor tapping at my chamber door,'" she says.

I recognize the line instantly. My Edgar Allan Poe fascination is fairly recent, and "The Raven" is one of my favorites. Peter gave me a new appreciation for classic literature that She never had. "'Only this and nothing more,'" I finish.

She angles me a single nod. "Hello, Clone."

"Hello, Human."

Her smile widens and she exchanges a look with the man beside her. She then reaches across the table for a handshake. "I'm Nicoleigh Bennett. You used to call me Leigh."

The guy next to her snorts. "That's not what she used to call you."

Dr. Malcolm turns to face the four of us, eyes alert, his entire body nearly vibrating with excitement. "This is a perfect display of establishing dominance in a social group. Typically, in this day and age, it would be between two males given the fact that there are so few females to fight over. You see, with her choice of mates, the female doesn't have to show her feathers, so to speak, when meeting another female. I find it interesting that the two of you—"

"Yes, Doc P. So interesting," Leigh says, smirking at me.

Her friend nods at me with a big smile. "I'm Miles Trumble. Best not get into what you used to call me, because you hated the fuck out of me."

I cannot imagine how I did not like either of them. I appreciate their honesty and willingness to socialize despite what the rest of the room must be feeling.

"Was the feeling mutual?" I ask Miles.

He leans forward and gives me a smoldering look that is no more serious in nature than Leigh's attempt at being mean. "Baby, I wanted nothing more than to get in those—"

"Finish that sentence and perish, my friend," Foster says. He aims a fork at Miles. "Try making a decent impression this time around."

Leigh's smile dims and, unfortunately, that does nothing to alleviate her stunning features. "Foster says you're having a hard time—"

"That's not what I said."

"—and I think you deserve a chance. Emma 1.0 would have given you one, and so, for her, I will too."

I am touched into speechlessness. This is the last thing I expected after they sat down.

Miles shrugs a single shoulder. "I just want another shot at the one that got away."

I chuckle. "Try holding your breath while you wait. We will see who caves first."

"Did you know," Dr. Malcolm says, "that it's physically impossible to hold your breath to the point of death?"

The four of us stare blankly at him. I do not know about anyone else, but I expect him to explain further. Instead, he simply dips a spoon into his oatmeal and eats as if nothing happened.

Leigh clears her throat and raises her eyebrows at me. "We're going to the range for target practice after this. Interested?"

I exchange a quick glance with Foster, wondering if he will signal this to be a bad idea, but he does not. So I say, "I am not fond of using any weapons. I do not even like fighting hand to hand."

Miles chokes on his orange juice.

Leigh blinks rapidly. "Excuse me?"

"If it is a last resort . . ." I trail off and shrug. The one and only time I held a gun was when Foster and I faced down an entire room of Declan's security. The guilt over taking lives has never lessened.

She holds both hands up as if to halt me in my tracks. "Let me get this straight. Declan Burke has the *entire world* looking for your ass, and you're going to . . . what? Sit on your hands?"

The plan was to hide and cross my fingers, but when the situation is put that way, my plan does not sound very smart. Not after what happened in Mexico and Vegas.

"I do not know if I am even allowed—"

"You're allowed." Foster pushes away his empty plate. "And Leigh's right. You need to be able to defend yourself."

"But Clint Reid—"

"—is Clint Reid," Leigh cuts in, and her tone suggests his name on her tongue has replaced a rather noxious expletive.

51

Foster adds, "A little training won't hurt you or anyone else."

Dr. Malcolm sits up straight. "Mind if I tag along? Certain traits, such as Miss Emma's ability to fight, for example, could be genetic—passed down from one or both parents—and will come naturally to her. It's clear to me from the news footage that you retained the physical responses to attack when cloned, so naturally I am curious if this will hold true—"

"Maybe next time," I say. When he frowns, I add, "I have not even agreed to go."

It is at this moment I hear a child's giggle and look to the other side of the room. Noah, Sonya, and Adrienne walk down the aisle to an empty table. Sonya tickles Adrienne, who is in her arms, and nods at something Noah says. He carries two trays of food and smiles down at Sonya.

Is that the same man who supposedly searched the world for me for more than a year? The same one who is all but begging me to stay? For what reason? To make me watch this show of their happy union?

Foster's hand covers mine and begins prying my fingers away from the butter knife I grip in my fist. In my ear, he whispers, "Ease down, Wade."

I let the knife clatter to the table. *What has gotten into me?*

Leigh peers over her shoulder and back. "Target practice must sound pretty good right about now, I'm guessing?"

"Yes," I tell her, and give the little family another look. They have not taken the same notice of me, and for that, I am glad. My reaction has shocked and embarrassed me. "Can we go now? I am suddenly very anxious to begin."

CHAPTER 8

Leigh slaps a small gun in my hand. "HK pistol with single plasma-pulse rounds. Don't let the small size fool you. She's a serious bitch."

I grip the weapon and slide my thumb over a tiny switch on the side. The handle hums almost imperceptibly as it powers up in preparation for use, which startles me. My muscles twitch from nerves, and I have to be careful not to inadvertently pull the trigger.

I look into the long concrete room behind protective glass. On either side, deep insets in the wall face each other hiding God knows what inside their shadowed spaces. "What do I do?"

Leigh scoops her hair off her neck into a low ponytail. "You'll see. Miles and I will go first."

She slides her HK into the back of her black pants and tucks her black tank top in deeper than necessary, which accentuates her large breasts. Miles does not take his eyes from them, nor does he seem to care if she catches him looking.

When she does, she rolls her eyes, then smacks him in the forehead with the heel of her palm. "Get a good, long look so you don't shoot them out there."

Miles grins. "Try not to let them get in the way. Oh, wait . . ."

Foster chuckles and knocks me with his elbow as if we are sharing in our own private joke, only I do not know what it is. Emma would have known, and this only makes me feel like more of an outsider.

Leigh and Miles enter the concrete room. Foster opens a wall panel and keys in a code. The overhead lights dim and sounds of gunfire blasts fill the space.

Foster leans down near my ear. "They're running through a program that simulates a warlike atmosphere. This is *not* for amateurs."

Then I am in the wrong room.

I look through the bulletproof glass at the simulation in progress. Leigh and Miles spin back-to-back in a slow circle, HKs raised. Every few seconds, one of them shoots into the dark insets.

"What are they looking at?" I ask.

"Simulations of the enemy."

Just then the simulation of a man appears beside Leigh. She ducks to avoid the butt of the man's rifle and, poised on one knee for balance, aims up to administer a kill shot to the head. He disappears, but two more of the same man reanimate in his stead.

"The program I've given them doubles each enemy killed," Foster says, folding his arms.

"But they cannot possibly win against those odds. They will be outnumbered."

"It isn't designed to beat. Just to see how far you get."

Both Miles and Leigh are "killed" less than a minute later, but they are panting and laughing and giving each other high fives. A fine coating of sweat covers both of them.

They are barely in our protected space when Miles asks, "What are the stats? I know I got more kills."

Foster presses a button near the panel, and the protective glass comes alive with statistics. To the left of the numbers, a video play-by-play runs through what we just watched live. In the stats list are numbers for each head, torso, and limb shot as well as the percentage of accuracy of each shot fired. Their total death count puts Leigh ahead by two.

Miles's jaw drops. "What the fuck? Program is jacked."

Leigh smacks him in the shoulder. "Stop crying." To me, she says, "Your turn, 2.0. Whatcha got?"

The HK feels hot in my palm, though the air is cool enough to raise goose bumps along my exposed arms.

"Nervous?" Foster asks.

I peer into the nearest set of concrete insets, where soon the simulations of my enemy will appear. They are not very deep and vary in width. "Little bit."

"It'll come back to you."

"I will never understand why you have such confidence in me."

He tugs my ponytail and grins. "Just breathe and follow your natural instincts, Wade."

My natural instincts tell me to hand over the weapon and run for the safety of anywhere else.

Miles's voice sounds over a speaker system. "Ready?"

Foster raises a hand and twirls his finger, signaling the start of my imminent "death." The effects of battle filter through the speakers and sound very real on this side of the protective glass. The lights dim and flash in tandem with various bomb-like reports.

I go into full alert mode, eyes open for my first enemy target. Foster and I circle the room as the previous occupants had. This feels very natural, and not because we stood this way a year ago in Dr. Travista's lab. But because it is what he and I do.

The men appear around corners with HKs or plasma rifles. In the beginning, they are easy to pick off. My aim, surprisingly, is good. A little rusty maybe from the lack of practice. But a focus takes over that is familiar, though unfamiliar all at once. I block out the sounds, and even Foster—but only to a point, because I do not want to accidentally shoot him. I pay no attention to the small audience or the score of the game.

My adrenaline pumps strong through my veins as the numbers of my enemy increase. My movements have to be quick. Foster is no longer at my back; the two of us separated a while ago. The simulated men begin to swarm, and I shoulder roll through them. They jump out of the way as if I could actually knock them over. When I sweep kicks at their ankles, they fall. They grunt and curse and spit . . . everything I might see in actual combat. Without the pain, of course. They strike me and I feel nothing more than a mild jolt of electricity.

When I finally "die," I am on the floor, breathless and laughing. Foster yanks me to my feet.

"That felt amazing," I say, gasping deep for breath.

He rocks me in a hug. "I'm so damn proud of you, Wade. I knew you could do it."

Raised voices from behind the glass draw our attention, and the second I look over, the lights go up, blinding me. I raise my free hand to hood my eyes just as three men dart into the large space, guns pointed directly at me.

"Put the weapon down," one yells.

Foster puts himself between me and them, but I do as I am told. My blood runs cold and freezes the layer of sweat coating my body. My vision darkens and the ground seems to tug at me, beckoning with icy fingers.

"What's the problem, guys?" Foster asks.

His voice forces me back to the bright room and I shake off the abrupt dizziness. Skipping breakfast was probably not the smartest idea.

Clint Reid enters behind the men, and I know he has something to do with this. He, too, has a gun trained on my head. "Mrs. Burke. Kick the gun over and put your hands up."

Behind Reid, Noah appears, and his nostrils flare with each breath. His face is red. "Put your guns away. You've made your goddamn point, Reid. That's enough."

The men do as they are asked. Reid is a little more hesitant but finally manages to follow orders.

Foster moves closer to me and I have to peer around him to see. Clearly he is not as trusting of them as I would be. "Someone want to explain?"

"Mrs. Burke is considered high risk and isn't authorized to carry firearms," Reid says. "She shouldn't even be in this area of the hub."

So that is what they call this place.

Reid continues with a pointed glance at Noah. "If I had my way, she'd be locked away until this matter is cleared up, but—"

"—but she isn't and won't," Noah snaps. He looks at Foster. "Take her out of here."

Leigh and Miles appear in the doorway and Reid shakes his head at them. "The three of you"—he eyes Foster to include him—"are on notice. One more fuckup like this and I'll have your asses."

Noah raises his hands. "Okay, okay. Foster, Wade, out. Bennett, Trumble, you too. Everyone's dismissed. Except you, Reid."

Foster leads me by the elbow, his eyes focused on the four men who previously had their guns trained on me. When I pass Noah, he does not look at me, and muscles feather along his jaw.

Reid, on the other hand . . . "Don't even think about teleporting from this facility, Mrs. Burke. You're here for the duration."

My footsteps falter. *What?*

Foster pinches my elbow. "Come on, Wade."

I want to laugh. Maybe Emma Burke would exit this room without a word, but I am not that woman anymore.

Pulling free of Foster's grip, I spin so fast Noah and Reid stop arguing to stare in bewildered silence.

"You will not keep me here, Major Reid," I tell him, but shift my focus between both men in case Noah decides to join Reid's crusade. "I dare you to try."

I turn my back and shoulder past my slack-jawed audience.

CHAPTER 9

A*nd the top story today,"* the male anchor says from behind a desk, *"is, of course, the question at the top of everyone's mind: Where is Emma Burke?"*

Behind him, still images from a Las Vegas casino float in a holo-vid for the entire world to see.

"The latest coming out of Las Vegas, Nevada. Footage was leaked to our sources of Mrs. Burke trying to escape security in a local casino. After close examination, authorities have ruled the video feed a fabrication by the resistance in an attempt to divert attention away from her actual whereabouts.

"The hunt continues for the beloved wife of Declan Burke, the God-father of Cloning."

I shoulder a backpack with several items of clothing from "Emma's" box and shut off the vid screen. These continued broadcasts are going to make things hard, but it has become very clear what I face if I stay. I will not live down here with Noah's false sense of freedom as I once had with Declan's.

I zip up my leather jacket and exit the room. I already know I can-not leave through the command center. Major Reid will have cut off that escape route first. But I doubt he knows that *I* know about Noah's private teleporter, which is why I head directly to his office. Noah could be there, of course, and fighting him to get out is not something I want to do, but I will do what I must.

The sound of a large group of children makes me slow outside an open room. Inside are bright colors and low tables with tiny chairs. Soft mats cover the concrete floor. Pictures of animals and the alphabet decorate the walls. Children sit at the tables or in groups on the floor. Several older girls—they can only be in their late teens by the looks of them—appear to be the only adults in sight.

Adrienne sits in the lap of one teen, pointing at pictures in a cardboard book. The two of them name animals and re-create their sounds on each page. I drift closer, unable to tear my gaze away. She repeats the animal names but makes the sounds without prompting. I do not know if this is normal, but to me, she may as well be a genius.

Guilt like nothing I have ever felt before wraps tight fingers around my throat. I should have been here to witness these advancements for myself. I blink rapidly to dry my wet eyes.

Someone approaches from behind and stops beside me, startling me. Dr. Malcolm smiles into the open room of children, arms clasped behind his back, rocking between his heels and the balls of his feet.

"Children are a miracle," he whispers in order to not alert anyone in the room to our watchful presence. "Wouldn't you agree, Miss Emma?"

I clear my throat. "Yes, of course."

He nods toward Adrienne. "And your little miracle . . . Adrienne is a beautiful child."

My little miracle. The daughter I never planned for. *Is* she mine? I mean, *really* mine? My feelings aside, because God knows from the moment I saw her I loved her, do I have the right to call myself her mother?

Looking at what I am about to do, I know the answer is a swift and resounding no. Because here I am, once again, about to desert my daughter as if I hold no responsibility in her upbringing. What kind of mother does that?

"I can only imagine the relief you must feel when seeing her," he says. "Knowing the struggle behind her gestation period and birth." He stops and smiles up at me. "But it worked out perfectly, didn't it? Your daughter is here and healthy."

"Dr. Malcolm." I turn to face him. "Is she my daughter? I know it is a strange question, but I have often doubted the possibility because of my situation."

He beams up at me as only he can. I do not know how he does it. "Genetics are genetics, Miss Emma. Biologically, she is unequivocally your daughter."

Unequivocally.

My eyes are wet again, and I avert my gaze back to where Adrienne and her caregiver have moved on to a book of shapes. That precious creature is my daughter. There is no question in my mind that if I leave now, I will be unable to live with the guilt of what I have done.

Even if it means giving up my freedom. It is time to make a choice, and it needs to be one I can live with.

Dr. Malcolm swivels to face me. "Do you mind if I ask you a question?"

I am almost afraid to give him permission, but he has given me something I have been short on of late. Hope. "Not at all."

"Are you leaving us?"

I find him glancing at my backpack. I adjust the bag's weight and look back at my daughter. Mine. Not Hers.

Freedom be damned. I will figure out another way. "No."

I stand outside Noah's open office and reshoulder my pack. He sits behind his desk, head bent over a computer tablet. Nerves flutter in my belly at the sight of him. There is no distinction between the anxiety over the conversation we need to have and my attraction to him. Unfortunately for me, it may be a little of both.

He looks up and seems unsurprised to find me standing there. "I went by your room. We need to talk about . . ." He trails off as his attention falls to my bag. His lips form a thin line and he leans back in his chair, making the springs *skritch*. "I'm surprised you even went out of your way to say good-bye this time."

I drop the offending bag and bury my trembling fingers in my back pockets. He must see confidence, rather than the fear I feel right now. "Can we talk?"

His expression is set to one of impassivity, and his eyes may as well be closed to me, but he nods and waves me inside. "Close the door."

I take a single step inside, tap the door switch, and cut off the view to the people beginning to rubberneck in the hall. "I have been giving our situations a lot of thought."

"Have you."

This is not a question, and his tone lashes. A moment later, his gaze darts to my bag and back. If I had a match I would set the thing on fire. I should have taken it back to my room.

"I do not want you to do me any favors, which is why I will not ask you to make Major Reid back off. With that said, I will not live here like a prisoner."

He scoffs. "You're hardly a prisoner."

"Not all jail cells have bars. I know that better than anyone, and I refuse to let that happen to me again."

Noah leans forward and rests his arms on his desktop, linking his fingers. "Last I checked, you came to me for help. And that's what I'm doing."

"By cutting off my access to the outside world?"

"Let's not pretend you have somewhere else to go."

"I met someone." I purposely imply there is a more than friendly relationship between me and this "someone," who happens to be Peter. Noah's expression falls and I know he believes it. "He offered me a permanent home if I want it. There is no reason to believe I cannot live there undetected for a very long time."

He looks down and away. "If that's the case, why did you even bother coming here?"

"You know why."

Noah stiffens. The rash words take us both by surprise, especially since their meaning is clear. I fought an internal battle against coming here for a full day, but the truth is that he was my first choice. He will always be my first choice. I could not stay away from him if I tried.

"No," he says. "I don't know why. Why don't you tell me?"

I cannot tell him the truth. Mine could quite possibly be the only heart at stake, and I will not torture myself by laying everything out for him to feast on.

I detach my gaze from his. We have to get back on track. "I know you cannot risk losing the respect of your men by handing me my freedom without something in return. So I have a solution I think we can both live with."

Pausing, I meet his eyes to gauge his reaction to my change of subject. If he really wants to, he can press rewind and force the truth from me. I hope he does not.

He eases back in his chair. "I'm listening."

"Major Reid does not trust me, but if I were to help you with Declan . . . Finish what we started more than a year ago . . . Nobody knows him as intimately as I do. You can use me."

The last thing I want is to go anywhere near Declan, even if it is from the safety of this resistance hub, but I do not see another option.

"And in return," he says, "I get Reid to back off."

"That, and I still want to look for my parents. Any help you can provide in the way of computer access would be appreciated."

Those bright amber eyes study me as he rubs a hand over his chin. Sweat begins to prickle my brow as I wait. Will he let me stay?

Let me stay, Noah.

Finally, he says, "I'll talk to Reid."

My tense shoulders collapse, forcing the pent-up air from my lungs. "That is all I ask."

Foster jogs up to me outside my room. "There you are." Like everyone else has, he eyes my pack with suspicion.

"I am not leaving," I say before he can ask.

Nodding, he follows me into my room, where I toss the bag to the floor at the end of my bed. He lifts the tablet he carries. "There's something you need to see."

His grim expression kicks my heartbeat into a steady jog. "Okay."

Foster faces the vid screen on my wall. After tapping a few commands on his tablet, the screen blinks and shows a room I know well. Declan's office. The direction the camera faces is what Declan called his meeting space, with a couch, chairs, and a wet bar.

On the wall to the right are a series of winter paintings I had painted and hidden away and that he at some point unearthed. Opposite the paintings is a floor-to-ceiling view of downtown Richmond, Virginia. Sunlight glints off skyscrapers, though I know this is only a real-time projection. There are no windows in his office.

"Why are we looking at an empty office?" I ask.

Foster stares at his tablet, where, unlike what shows on the vid screen, the office footage moves at high speed. "Because I'm searching for the right spot. Here we go."

The footage now faces a different direction and my gaze falls instantly on Declan. He slouches in his chair, his left hand resting across his desk. He absently spins a glass with a shot of amber liquid in the bottom. Bourbon, if I had to guess. His gray suit jacket hangs open, his tie pulled loose. He stares across the room, barely blinking, let alone showing any hint of emotion.

"Pause," Declan says into the empty room, breaking the silence. *"Go back five seconds and hold."*

My stomach drops. On the wall opposite him, his computer runs a video feed I recognize, though from a wholly different angle. The footage he has paused is of me resting on the flat of my back on a slanted roof in the central highlands of Mexico. My exposed skin is grimy with sweat and dust. My hair is pulled back tight except for the few strands sticking to the sides of my face. My expression is one of determination, not fear, though I know I had been frightened. I barely remember the short stop after I first climbed on that roof and rolled to my back. It could have been only two seconds. Three at most. Not that it matters.

"Play," Declan says, and rubs his chin. He swivels his chair to face his desk, then sits forward and leans on his forearms. He watches my escape unfold with such intensity. It is a small wonder he does not have the ability to snatch me right from the video itself.

"What were you doing there, Emma?" he whispers, watching every step I take. My fight, my jump off the final roof, my large lead into the densely wooded foothills. But that is where it ends. Because of the thick foliage, the satellite camera loses me the moment I disappear into the forest.

Declan mutters a curse and runs a hand over the tightly shaven goatee he wears. The phone rings and he lifts the receiver without so much as a breath of air to announce he has done so. Whoever is on the other end begins speaking, though; I hear the hum of a man's voice.

"Say again?" Declan says, retrieves a stylus, and begins writing on a tablet computer. *"That's all he said?"* After a single nod, he hangs up.

"What the hell are you up to, love?" he says to the screen.

Trepidation sweeps through me. "What did he write down?"

Foster sucks in a deep breath before adjusting the camera's angle to show the front of the tablet. What I read freezes my blood. Names.

Stephen and Lily Wade.

"He knows you're searching for your parents," Foster says.

It is as if the floor drops out from under me. "If he finds them, he will use them against me." I drag my trembling fingers through my hair. "I will have no choice but to go back."

CHAPTER 10

*T*hank you for coming," Declan says to the camera crews airing the conference all over the world. He stands in the lobby of Burke Enterprises facing the outer windows. "*I know the hour is late, but I feel there's no time to waste.*

"*Questions have been raised regarding my marriage, such as where Emma was for the first eight years. In an effort to shield her from embarrassment, I have been quiet on the subject. That said, it has come to my attention that continuing to do so would be a risk to her personal health and safety.*"

The gathering explodes with questions, to which Declan only raises his hands to quiet them.

"*It was discovered shortly after we were married that Emma would not live long without intervention. The disease she has is a rare genetic mutation and was missed in all her prescreen exams at the WTC. If not for the work of Arthur Travista, she would not be with us today.*"

More questions echo in the lobby's space, bouncing from marble floor to high ceiling. Declan waits patiently for them to quiet again.

"*Her condition is private and took all of those eight years to manage. I will not further humiliate my wife by giving you every detail. I tell you only because Arthur has expressed concern that her remission is only temporary. Without treatment, she* will *die.*"

Declan raises his hands when the voices rise into a jumble of questions.

"The second thing I will tell you," he says, *"is that Emma's own parents may be involved in her kidnapping."*

I pace by the door, arms folded tight across my chest. Noah, Reid, and the office are a blur. The reality of what Declan has done clings to me like a fog I cannot escape. This move was brilliantly calculated. "I cannot possibly find them in time."

Noah rocks back and forth in his desk chair at a slow, even pace, rubbing a hand along his chin. He stares into the same distance that has sway over me. "You can't think like that. They're ex-resistance, which makes them resourceful."

I rake my hands through my loose hair. "Which also makes it that much harder for me to find them."

Reid glances between Noah and me from his perch on the edge of Noah's desk. A grin slides across his face, showing a perfect row of white teeth. "Gotta give it to Burke. That was a stroke of genius."

Noah glowers at Reid. "Is that really necessary?"

"No, he is right," I say, though I loathe agreeing with anything Major Reid has to say. "The entire world is now looking for Stephen and Lily Wade, and all without having to offer a new reward."

Reid tips his coffee cup at me and grins. "Time to ante up, Mrs. Burke."

He laughs and I stop pacing. "This is not a joke, Major. Not to me."

Noah's gaze lifts from a spot on his desk to meet mine. "Any thoughts on the gene mutation thing?"

"No, why?"

"He could be telling the truth. Or his version, anyway."

The fog I am caught up in parts, and I am swept up in words left unsaid. Noah's expression holds no sign of his thoughts, but I recognize the uneasiness in his eyes. Declan's ploy to gain sympathy from the world has had a different effect on Noah. While I have had nothing but concern for my missing parents, Noah wonders if I am dying.

I tear my gaze away from his. He takes me back to the day I died in the hospital ward, and I have no want to relive that time. "I have been gone a long time, and I was perfectly healthy before. Even if there were something wrong, he could not possibly know."

"But what if—?"

I snare his gaze with mine in such a way that stops him from continuing. "I am fine, Noah."

Major Reid's voice cuts between us, and I startle, having forgotten he was there. "Look at her. She's *fine.*" He drags out the last word and punctuates it with a wave of his hand.

"She's completely healthy," Sonya says from the doorway. She waggles a computer tablet and looks only at Noah. "Other than some predispositions to preventable diseases, there's nothing in her genetic sequence to suggest—"

"Wait, what?" I say. Did she say what I think she just said?

Sonya's next intake of breath is slow, and her eyes never leave Noah. "From what I can tell, Burke's lying. Dr. Malcolm agrees."

She did it. "You ran it. Without my permission?"

She finally looks at me with steely resolve, confirming my suspicions.

I never should have let her leave with my blood, and would not have if not for Dr. Malcolm and his long-winded story distracting me. "Unbelievable."

Noah drops forward in his chair and the wheels click and rattle on the floor. "What's she talking about, Sonya? Ran *what* without permission?"

She looks at Noah with little to no concern in her eyes. "In all fairness, I wouldn't have dared if not for the fact that you asked me to—"

"He *asked you to*?" I feel momentarily out of breath as I swing a glare at Noah. "You asked her to?" How could he do this to me?

Noah stands with his eyes wide and hands raised defensively. "Hold on a second." To Sonya, he says, "What *exactly* did I ask you to do?"

Reid slides into the armchair in front of the desk, effectively removing himself from this conversation. But according to the glint in his eyes, it has nothing to do with being uncomfortable. He enjoys being a spectator to the unfolding drama.

Sonya says, "You asked me to learn every detail of Travista's cloning process. So that's what I'm doing. That's why you brought Phillip Malcolm here, isn't it? I'd love to say we're managing just fine, but I can't. We're at a dead end."

She looks at me. "I'm sorry, but you are my first and probably last shot at getting my hands on a clone. The more we know, the better—"

"So this is about getting your hands on a *clone*? I am still a human being, Sonya, and I never gave you permission to run those tests. In fact, I expressly forbade it. I am not a project."

Reid leans forward and braces his elbows against his knees. "Wait a second, Mrs. Burke. Let me get this straight. You claim to want to help the resistance take down your husband—"

"He is *not* my husband."

"—and here we have a real shot at him except you're suddenly afraid of needles? Sounds awfully suspicious to me."

I should not be surprised he went there. Any excuse to make me look like the bad guy. "When did learning how clones function result in 'a real shot' at Declan Burke?"

"Emma," Noah says, and his is the only calm voice in the room. "I understand you're upset, but no harm was done."

No harm done. Dr. Travista's exact words following his attempt to wipe my memory a second time. I almost laugh, but there is nothing funny about this. "There never is in the beginning, is there?" He straightens, steeling his spine in reaction to the look I give him. "How do you think it begins? With a few harmless tests. Routine checks on the reflexes, hearing, sight." I look pointedly at Sonya. "Blood tests." I look back at Noah. "Nothing big, right? Next thing you know, I'm strapped to a table, surrounded by nurses and covered in wires, with my legs up in stirrups."

Noah's eyebrows knit together. His response is slow in forming. "You don't honestly think—?"

"There is no excuse for what Sonya did, and you need to stop pretending there is."

Noah grips the edge of his desk and his jaw tightens. After a deep breath, he is the picture of calm and collected. "If we lose another woman to the cloning process, it would be helpful to know how we can save her memory from being permanently erased."

"I will tell you how." I look directly at Sonya. "Do not let another host die."

Sonya flinches, and I am immediately flooded with the memory of how she tried to save me. The tugging in the lower half of my body. Her sharp commands. She fought desperately to control the loss of blood that eventually ended my host's life. Regardless of what she has done, she did not deserve the unwarranted remark.

"I am sorry," I tell her. "That was unfair."

Tears rim her eyes. "I tried to save her," she says to me, then shifts her gaze to Noah, who leans heavily on his desktop and does not look up.

"You mean me," I say. Her words sting, and they soak up some of my guilt. That experience was mine. Not Hers. "You tried to save *me*. Is that not what you meant?"

The silence that follows makes even Major Reid shift and avoid eye contact. I cannot bear it and excuse myself from the room. I need a few minutes alone so I can get my head on straight. Thanks to my outburst—warranted or not—we strayed from the matter of finding my parents. For their sake, I need to get back on track.

But how can I focus on finding them when I have to watch my back every second of the day? I stop at the corner and lean against the wall, blinking blurry eyes as I stare blindly across the vast space of the hallway.

"Emma," Noah calls from just outside his office.

My heart gallops in response to his voice. Despite everything I said, he looks at me with a soft set to his eyes.

He reaches me and his eyes latch with mine, refusing to let them go. He lowers his voice to avoid being overheard. "Are you all right?"

"I am fine."

"You can talk to me, you know." As if to punctuate the statement, he runs a warm hand over my arm.

I hate that he looks genuinely concerned for me, because it does not make being near him any easier. I will have to make him believe there is nothing to be worried about. Pasting on a smile, I reach out and squeeze his arm. "I am fine."

He rolls his eyes and twists to lean into the wall beside me. "No, you aren't."

"All right, so I am not fine. How could I be after what just happened?"

He lowers his voice. "I feel responsible. But while I don't condone Sonya's methods, you understand why we need to know more, don't you?"

"I do not know." I sigh. "What are the odds that you will ever see this happen again?"

"Not every woman going through Travista's clone process is a volunteer. You know that. It's important we gain all the knowledge we can. Knowing gives us control where there was none."

Is this the same excuse Dr. Travista tells himself to help him sleep at night? I have been on the receiving end of this need to control. No matter the intent, nothing good will come of this.

"I only want to help," he says. "What if the memories aren't actually lost with the host? Wouldn't you want—?"

"No." I will not get my hopes up over something I know is impossible. Her voice is gone, and with it, what is left of my memories. "You have to let this go." Let *Her* go, I do not say, because is this not what he is really asking for? His wife to return to normal? "Not everything can be fixed."

His chin declines in a half nod. "I know."

I push off the wall. "I do not want to talk about this anymore."

He takes my wrist, stopping me from walking away. His fingers are warm and callused. "You need a distraction." When I meet his gaze, he gives me a pleasant smile and stands upright. "Come somewhere with me?"

"I do not have time for distractions, Noah. My parents—"

"Give me ten minutes; then we'll talk. Promise."

Sonya exits the office and stops when she sees us. "There you are."

Noah's grip on my wrist tightens as if he believes I will use this opportunity to slip away. He is right to do so, because the idea has crossed my mind. I want nothing to do with his distraction, and I cannot stomach being so near Sonya right now.

"I'm going to get Adrienne," Noah says to Sonya. "Can we meet up later?"

Her eyes narrow very slightly. "Sure."

He wastes no time turning us away from her. "Let's go."

Curiosity flares, especially now that I know we are getting Adrienne first. "Where are we going?"

He gives me a smile that brightens his eyes. "If I told you that, it would ruin the surprise."

CHAPTER 11

Noah leads me into a large room with white walls, a white floor, and a white ceiling, but they are not painted. The surfaces are screen-like. I have seen a room like this many times before, but this is much larger.

"A hologram room?" I ask. Declan once had a room built special for me. It was my private paint studio for months, and the only place I had any real privacy from his security cameras.

Adrienne struggles to get down, and Noah sets her on the floor. She bounces and points straight-armed at the floor with an impatient grunt.

"We come here a lot," he explains, and picks up a small computer tablet from a dock station. "Hold on, chicken," he tells her in a patient tone.

He taps the screen a few times until an image appears around us. The beach with its crashing waves, and, so help me, the Heermann's gull in its breeding plumage comes to life all around me. I cannot feel the sand or the breeze or smell the brine, but a missing piece of me clicks into place and somehow all is right in the world.

"Mexico," I whisper. I want to cry from the relief I feel from seeing this so alive around me.

Noah nods. "Playa de Oro. Beach of Gold. It's north of Manzanillo."

After all this time, I finally have a name for my beach, the object of so many wonderful memories.

Adrienne squeals in delight and chases after a seagull poking its beak in the sand. The holographic bird does not move or startle off. When she runs through the image, she giggles and repeats the process over and over until the gull flaps into the air with a *caw*.

"We were married on this exact beach," Noah says. "Do you remember?"

I cannot look at him as I shake my head, and a knot has formed in my throat. The details of this moment overwhelm me. Finding out the exact location of my beach. Standing here with Noah and our daughter. Those things alone are enough to upset my fragile balance, but then he has used the word "we," and it is all I can do not to shatter.

Noah sits near the edge of the simulated water, arms wrapped around upturned knees, and looks over the expanse of ocean that seems to go for miles. "We rented a house for a month after. The beach sat empty for miles thanks to the South American War ravaging the entire coastline back in the day. Just us and the little house." He pauses and a small smile lights his entire face. "We were different people there. Relaxed and free of responsibility for the first time in our lives."

Adrienne skips into the simulated waves and starts spinning. When she grows dizzy, she tumbles to the ground and giggles. I cannot help but laugh in response. I wish I could experience every moment of my day with the same carefree attitude.

"We never did get back there," Noah says after a long moment.

I ease to the floor near him but not close enough to touch. I must keep my distance, especially faced with this memory. "Why not?"

"What we do here is important. We both knew that, so we put our future on hold, believing that was the right choice." He meets my eyes and says, "I still believe that."

My muscles tense, because just like that, we are no longer speaking of our past. I can only hope he does not ask me to help Sonya in return for the freedom I have requested. I am not the same Emma who believes in giving up Her life for the sake of what is important to their cause. Fighting Her fight lost me my husband and daughter. My memories. My entire life.

Tearing my gaze away, I focus on Adrienne, who chases another gull.

"I spoke to Reid about your request," he says.

"And?"

"And he agreed. He'll be keeping a close eye on you, though. Nothing I can do about that. He's always been a suspicious person."

Adrienne kneels beside me to watch a gull strut past my knee. She points to the sand where little footprints mar the surface, then smiles up at me.

"Footprints," I tell her, and am reminded of my early conversations with Declan and, later, with Ruby Godfrey. How I taught her simple things her husband, Charles, should have, the way Declan did for me. Things like footprints.

"Where is *your* foot?" I ask her.

She stabs the top of her left shoe and looks up for approval.

"Very good." I reach out and run a hand over her soft curls, and she lets me, though to be fair, her full attention has returned to the gull's footprints.

To Noah, I say, "Major Reid can keep as close an eye as he likes. I have nothing to hide from him. Or you."

He sighs, drawing my focus away from Adrienne. He watches his hand wring the opposite wrist. "I know you don't."

Adrienne runs off, leaving my palm cold. "What do we do now? I need to look for my parents now more than ever. I cannot let Declan find them first." I hope Noah is right and that they are resourceful enough to stay hidden. "But I also made you a promise, and I intend to keep it."

Noah leans back into his palms and spreads his legs out in front, crossing them at the ankles. He stares almost absently into the waves crashing in front of us. "I'll ask Foster to help you search some of our old files. There has to be a record of your parents somewhere. As for Burke . . ." He trails off and shakes his head.

"What?"

"I don't know. Just a feeling I can't shake, I guess."

"About Declan?"

He glances at me. "What do you think happened to him after he fell through the ice?"

Noah's words put me back in the freezing water of the lake, staring down at my unblinking ex as we sink to the bottom. "I really believed he had died."

But I was wrong, because he has returned with some fanciful story for the entire world. It was not as if I was around to see him for long, though. That was the time I kept returning to my host body as She died. I almost drowned in that lake with Declan because of it.

I flick a fingernail over an imperfection of thread in the knee of my jeans. "Maybe he was hurt so badly that he has been recovering this entire time. No one saw who pulled him from the lake?"

"The cameras don't reach that far. We based all our evidence on what we heard and saw from the people working for him. Nobody knew a thing. Because of the resistance involvement that night, they assumed he was kidnapped. We had Foster's account and believed he was dead."

"Did you ever go there? Look for ways he may have gotten out undetected?"

Adrienne walks around Noah and climbs into his lap, facing me while leaning against his chest. He rubs her back and kisses the crown of her head.

"I didn't see a need," he says. "Feel like taking a trip tomorrow? I have the morning free."

My heart *thunks* against my ribs. "You want to go to the lake?"

"Why not? Could answer a lot of questions."

"Just you and me?" I ask before I can stop myself. My inflection rises with my abruptly elevating anxiety level. "Why not send someone else?"

He looks at me with laughter in his eyes. "Yes, you and me. And yes, I could send someone else, but aren't you curious?"

Yes. Always curious. About everything. But this is the lake where I nearly died with Declan. If not for Foster, I most certainly would have. Then there is the fact that I will spend an unknown amount of time with Noah. Alone.

What are you afraid of?

I shake off the irrational fear. "Okay. A trip to—" I do not even know where Declan's home actually is. Mountains. That is all I know. "Where is this lake exactly?"

He chuckles. "Tennessee."

"All right, then. A trip to Tennessee sounds fun."

Noah glances down at Adrienne. "It's somebody's bedtime."

Adrienne yawns as if on cue. Her eyes look glassy, telling me she is already halfway there. We stand and Noah holds Adrienne close. She rests her head on his shoulder and lets her eyelids close.

I reach out and tuck stray curls behind her little ear. "She really is beautiful."

"I already feel sorry for the trail of broken hearts she'll leave behind," he says with a soft chuckle. "It'll look like a war zone."

Adrienne takes a shuddering breath and her mouth droops. Already asleep. I envy her this ease. "You should take her to bed."

We head for the exit and pause only so Noah can shut down the hologram. "You can use my log-in to access the system if you want to start searching the records for your parents," he says, docking the tablet. "My password is 'Europa.'"

The hologram of the beach is gone, but the memory is clear in my mind. Noah sitting behind me, holding me after we made love on the beach. Telling me the story of Zeus turning into a white bull to attract a woman he loved.

"The princess," I say.

He is careful not to react, and his voice is almost too controlled as he says, "You remember the story?"

"Yes. Along with the others you told me that night. It is one of my favorite memories," I admit. I do not remember making love, but I know it was the night he painted the luckenbooth into my sunset painting. I have always believed it was the luckenbooth that led me back to him.

Noah stares at me in silence; then his cheeks begin to turn pink and he looks away. "I need to put her to bed."

I open the door and he lets me exit first. In the hallway, I turn to face him. "Thank you."

He looks distracted as he closes the room. "For what?"

"The beach. It means more than you know."

Just like that, his attention is solely with me. He takes and squeezes my hand. "I know exactly what it means."

Taking my hand back feels like sinking my fingers into an existing rip in my heart and tearing it open further. I tuck both hands in my rear pockets and back away. "See you in the morning."

CHAPTER 12

Miss Emma."

I glance over my shoulder. Dr. Malcolm runs up behind me, hands clutched to his chest to keep his white lab coat from flying about. By the time he reaches me, he is out of breath and can barely talk. He holds a finger up, asking me to give him a minute to collect himself.

I do not want to give him a single second. Not after what I found out last night. He has been trying to get close to me in an effort to trick me into tests. I knew I could not trust him, and it has since been confirmed.

"Dr. Malcolm, I really do not have time. I am meeting Noah in two minutes."

He swallows hard and shakes his head in an attempt to pull himself together. "Sorry. I often intend to start working out. I understand you like to run. Maybe"—he points to me and back to himself several times—"you would let me tag along sometime? Show me the proper way to"—he swings bent arms front to back in a jerky, stiff motion—"move my arms for the least resistance. My knee joints aren't what they used to—"

"One minute," I cut in, glancing toward the command center, where I am to meet Noah. I do not want to be late.

He looks up as if I came out of nowhere, rather than the other way around. His bushy brows pinch together. "Are you sleeping well, Miss Emma? You look tired."

The nightmares grow worse, and my only defense is to stay up as long as possible. Not that it matters. The moment I fall into a deep sleep, I end up drifting into the clutches of the abyss. "Just adjusting to sleeping in a new place."

He nods and gives me his trademark smile for the first time since approaching. "The trick is to get on a regimented schedule as soon as possible. Up at the same time. Down at the same time. Exercise. Don't eat a heavy dinner. Oh, and no napping." He winks. "I'd personally have a hard time with the last one." He leans in as if telling me a secret. "I love naps."

I take a slow, deep breath. "Dr. Malcolm, I appreciate the advice, but I am going to be late."

His mouth forms a perfect oval. "Oh, right. I stopped you."

"Yes, you did."

He rocks on the balls of his feet and buries his hands deep in his coat pockets. "I owe you an apology. You see, I had no idea Dr. Toro meant to run your gene sequence, and by the time I found out, it was too late to stop it."

"But you could have?"

"Well—"

"You could have stopped it, yes? Destroyed samples or whatever it is you need to do? Erase files. Throw my blood down a drain?"

"Well . . ." He trails off, sighs, then nods. "You're absolutely right. You have been wronged. It will never happen again."

I give him a tight-lipped smile. "You are a scientist, Dr. Malcolm. You will not be able to help yourself."

A straight finger flies up between us, making me flinch back in surprise. He lifts both eyebrows. "Challenge accepted."

"I really have to go," I tell him, fighting the urge to laugh. He makes it so hard to be mad at him.

"We'll talk later?" he calls when my back is turned.

I lift a hand to wave rather than answer. It seems I will not have a choice in the matter.

Noah and I appear in Declan's living room. The sun is still rising in the mountainous background through the wall of solid windows on the other side of the room.

I step into the familiar setting, my heart drumming. Despite the fact that the fire has not been lit since the winter before last—I assume—the room smells of the burned wood. The lighting feels foreign, too, as I never lived here any other season than winter. There is no snow to reflect sunlight.

The security cameras are set to show a prerecorded feed so that no one is alerted to our arrival. Even so, I am nervous. If Declan ever found out I was this close, not to mention standing here with a man he respects . . .

I am looking into the open bedroom, the bed unmade, when Noah sets soft fingers on the small of my back. I startle.

"You okay?" he asks, his gaze dipping to my lips and back up.

My heart trips; then I realize we stand in the same spot where we first kissed. Post-cloning, that is. Right after that, he told me I was not his wife and dragged me away to prove it. That kiss was the last good moment I had that day. Truthfully, I have not had many since.

"I would like to leave," I say.

He glances around, his jaw clenched, and nods. "Yeah. Let's get out of here."

I follow him across the hardwood, each slat varying in shades from light to dark. One of my favorite throw blankets lies in a heap on the couch in the sunken living room. The kitchen counter holds a couple of days' worth of dirty dishes. Declan was never this untidy before. Blankets should be folded and tucked inside the chest near the fireplace. Dishes rinsed and placed in the dishwasher. Bed made. Even when I forgot to do this, Declan came in behind me to do it himself.

Pausing in the nook by the dining room table, I take another look around. This table was always set with a floral centerpiece and a crisp linen tablecloth. Always. The only thing on it now is a dirty plate with a half-eaten breakfast and a stale cup of coffee.

"Who has been living here?" I ask, because I am positive it cannot be Declan.

Noah stills with his hand on the sliding glass door handle. His eyebrows pinch together. "Burke. Who else?"

"You are certain?"

"Of course I am. I've seen him here myself. Why?"

I cannot tell him how unlike Declan it is to live this way. Doing so would be like throwing my unwitting indiscretion in his face. "Never mind."

Outside, the ground is patched with grass. Our boots crunch on the needles strewn everywhere. The thick mass of trees shields us from the brunt of the sun, but it does not take us long to break a sweat.

As we near the ledge where Declan and I went over, Noah lets me lead the way. I avoid the exact area and seek the path down the mountainside instead. When we near the edge—a good distance away from the spot where I threw Declan and myself over—Noah stops and looks over the side. He glances at me, then back down.

"You're lucky to be alive," he says. "That's quite a drop."

"Declan's body shielded me from the ice's impact." I turn and step onto the dirt path. "We can go down here."

The way down is narrow and steep. The soles of my boots slide on loose rock and dirt.

Halfway down, Noah says, "I heard Foster's version of that night. Saw the video."

The following silence takes hold of my curiosity and swivels me around to face him. He slows to a stop two steps away.

Shielding my eyes from the sun, I squint up at him. "And?"

"Just curious about your take on what happened."

The truth is, I do not want to talk about that night. Reliving the day I found out I was a clone, how Declan stole me from my family, that I would never be accepted back into my old life . . . That day is not something I want to think about ever again.

"You already know what you need to know." I start down the slope again and slide, losing my balance. Noah catches me under the arms as I am about to fall.

"Careful," he whispers. Whiskers tickle my ear. His breath is hot on my cheek. His fingers dig a little too deep.

Goose bumps rise on my arms and I step out of his hands. "Thanks."

Near the bottom, he says, "Where did you fall from?"

I glance between the lake and the ledge above us, searching for the spot. I point at an area extending out farther than most. Large gray rocks jut out from the side. "We went over from there."

He looks up, then lifts an arm to wipe his sweaty forehead across the green sleeve of his T-shirt. "Jesus, Emma."

My sentiments exactly. The drop looks worse from here somehow. But I shrug a single shoulder and look up. "It was not so bad."

He laughs and I cannot help but join. It eases the tension at least.

"Okay," he says, and looks around. "Foster said he didn't pass anyone, and no one ever saw anyone from the house feed. They had to come and go from another direction."

I point left. "You walk down that way. I will go right. Yell if you find something."

We part and I am both grateful and sad for the separation. I never should have agreed to come here alone with him. When it is easy between us, it is too easy. And it cannot be easy. Not while he is in love with Sonya.

Is he in love, though?

I shake my head. I cannot ask things like that. That will only lead to talking myself out of believing it to be true, which will only lead to hope. I gave up on a future with him the second I walked out of his office more than a year ago.

Despite the arguments I tell myself, I glance across the lake and watch Noah looking for another way out of this area. The lake is surrounded by cliff walls and trees on all sides and, according to what Noah told me earlier, man-made. The lake's dark shadow reaches almost to the edges, revealing how deep the bottom is. Not that I need a shadow to tell me. I am well aware of the lake's depths.

I turn and look at my own wall of mountainside. Tree roots curve out of the side of the dirt like the tentacles of some sea creature. Some gnarled and pointed ends have sprung free of the dirt. It is then I notice how the trees stagger upward at an angle. Upon closer inspection, I find a shaded trail behind them.

"Found it!"

Instead of waiting, I enter the trail, which is nowhere near as steep as the other. Leaves and needles coat the loose dirt floor. I walk at a brisk pace, anxious to see what I will find. But the path only ends in more forest.

Noah finally reaches me, breathing hard. "Thanks for waiting."

Ignoring his sarcastic remark, I say, "Should we walk through the forest? Maybe there is another residence."

He scans the area. Wind blows through the trees and shapes his blond waves, alternating between flattening and lifting the strands. The rising sun casts the shadow of swaying tree branches on his skin. "Look for a well-worn path. If we don't find one, we'll have to come back with some equipment. The last thing we need is to disappear for several days because we got lost."

I look down, seeking footprints on the soft forest floor. There is nothing that obvious to my layman's eye. We take opposite directions again until I hear him call back to me almost thirty seconds later.

The path he discovered is wide and made of loosely packed dirt. "No footprints," I say.

"Could mean it hasn't been used in a while."

"Only one way to find out."

We take the trail in silence. At the first patch of grass Noah comes to, he takes a long, wide blade and positions it between his thumbs. Soon he is blowing through them and making a rough, high-pitched whistle sound.

I chuckle. "You are like a child."

He cups his palms around the sound to change the tone. Then he is smiling too much to continue. He passes the blade over. "Here. Give it a try."

I shake my head. "No, thank you."

His grin tilts. "Because you can't do it." When I raise an eyebrow at his challenge, he scratches his chin and adds, "I even have a scruff disadvantage and can *still* do it."

I stop walking and take the blade from him, determined to prove that I can. "As if beard growth matters."

He chuckles.

We face each other on the trail and he shows me how to make the blade taut between my thumbs. He stands close enough to share his body heat and the sweaty scent of his skin.

"You have to blow hard," he tells me once I have the grass placed.

He watches me intensely as I place my thumbs against my taut lips. My cheeks fill with air and sting slightly from the exertion. It takes me several tries to finally make one excruciating sound.

His smile widens. "See? That wasn't so hard."

My belly flutters. His smile leaves me with little air to breathe. How does he do that? I stand frozen between closing the space between us and widening it.

His smile falters and his eyes lower to my lips before darting away. He clears his throat.

I hand the blade back, my cheeks warm from more than just the act of blowing. "Now that I have played your silly game, can we find the end of this trail?"

"Lighten up, Wade. We'll get there."

I follow him and in seconds he has exchanged his grass for a long stick to swing around. I cannot take the silence with the occasional swatting sound, so I say, "You said last night you have a feeling about Declan you cannot shake? You did not say what it was."

Noah sighs and squints down the trail at nothing in particular. "A year or so ago, I might have never considered it, but now . . ."

"Now what?"

"You're right to think he could have spent the last year recovering. Maybe he had a broken back or neck or something. Arthur Travista has proved he is capable of fixing just about anything."

I glance askance at him. I can tell from his tone that he does not believe this theory. "You do not think so?"

He meets my gaze. "I think Travista cloned him."

CHAPTER 13

I can no longer walk. *Why... why... why would they do that?* I bend and brace myself on my knees. The world seems to have gone utterly silent save the sound of the wind through the trees and my heartbeat pounding through my ears.

Declan a clone? To what end? Cloning was supposed to be a means to end infertility, not make a man like Declan Burke immortal.

"How can you be sure?" I ask, watching loose dirt swirl in the wind at my feet.

Noah stabs the ground with his stick. "You said he was dead, and I've always trusted your instincts."

I straighten and meet his eyes. "You have to base this on more than my word."

He casts his gaze down the trail. "All right. Clones are really thin after they're brought to life, and Burke looks thin to me. To reach his current level of fitness, I assume it would take at least a year."

"Maybe he lost weight because of his recovery time from a serious injury."

"So explain why he's been in hiding this entire time. Why make the world believe he was kidnapped if he was only injured?"

"A matter of pride?"

"If it was that bad, why not use the opportunity to show off more of Travista's lifesaving skills? Imagine the press they'd get."

I have to walk and think. Everything he says makes sense, and I would not put it past Dr. Travista. Declan Burke is the only man who has given him enough funding *and freedom* to play God.

Noah strolls up beside me, closer than he was before. He has given up his stick. "There's more."

My stomach rolls. "Do I want to hear this?"

"Rumor has it Burke was sterile."

I trip to a stop and he grabs my arm to steady me. "I do not believe that."

He tilts his head. "Last I heard you are as fertile as they come, yet somehow, you managed to escape pregnancy."

"I avoided—" I cut off short from telling him how I planned our sex life around my fertile days to prevent pregnancy. I nearly had it down to a science. "You are wrong. I witnessed his disappointment every month. If he were sterile—"

"Then Travista would have been experimenting on ways to reverse it. Burke may have been forced into the last resort: cloning."

I turn and walk away from him, my heart thundering in my chest. If this is true, then no one is safe. Not even men.

"You think the idea of Burke being a clone is crazy?" he asks, catching up to me.

"Yes. Crazy because you have to be right. It is the only thing that makes sense."

Noah tucks his hands in his pockets and looks out into the forest. Wind flutters through his hair. "Only problem will be proving it at this point."

"Why does it matter? It is not as if the world will think less of him."

He stops. "Clones have no rights, Emma. He'd lose his company."

An icy chill winds up my core. "What do you mean 'clones have no rights'?"

"Think about it. The only clones being created are female. Why would the government rush to give basic human rights to the female population when they could have full control over them? They wouldn't. And there's no need to clone men."

"Well, clearly there is if cloning cures sterility."

"We live in a world where men outnumber women. I wouldn't call that a need."

"But if Dr. Travista were to offer this option to men, the government would go directly into talks about establishing their rights, yes?"

"Probably. Eventually, powerful men will see other benefits. If Burke can circumvent death, so can they. But for now, no one's even asking questions. It's so early in the game, all these men and government officials can focus on is getting their hands on their own cloning project."

"Including you." I had not meant to say it, but it is too late to take back.

Noah steps away. "You can't compare me to them."

"Maybe not. But as an outsider looking in, it seems pretty obvious to me. You brought on a scientist specifically to figure out how cloning works. Do you think he will stop at saving memories? Your girlfriend went as far as to run my gene sequence without my permission. But I guess I have no rights, so it does not matter anyway, does it? She can do what she likes with my blood."

I turn and walk the second he opens his mouth to respond. The last thing I want is to argue with him, and I could have avoided it altogether, but the topic has me on edge. I have no rights and I am stuck in another situation where people want to study me. Of all the places I could go, ending up with Noah was supposed to be the safest. I am no longer sure it is.

Another, smaller path appears, and we take it in silence. No more than a minute later, we come upon a small cabin with a wraparound porch, complete with a swing.

Noah produces a gun that was tucked in the back of his jeans. His posture stiffens and his gaze darts in all directions. He leads us up the porch and to the front door. He taps the gun against the surface and presses his ear to the exterior to listen.

"I don't hear anything," he whispers.

Dirt coats the porch swing as well as the front windows. My instincts tell me no one has been here in a very long time. "Is the door unlocked?"

He tries the handle and the door swings open with a loud, drawn-out creak. He enters the house gun first, taking it slow. "Stay behind me."

I stand in a shadowed living room with two deep red armchairs facing a cold fireplace. A small kitchen sits unused in a back corner and the entrance to a perpendicular hallway in the other. The air smells musty.

Noah exits the hallway a moment later and tucks his gun back in his jeans. "Just one bedroom and bathroom in the back. There are a few personal items, but not much. Nothing to tell me who lived here."

I glance around the living room. While Noah approaches the teleporter near the kitchen, I look at the bookshelves. Heavy tomes with gold embossed letters; every subject has to do with one science or another. I even recognize the bookends because I saw their doubles at least once a week for months.

I pick up a framed photograph of a young woman sitting in a swing. Jodi. The woman Dr. Travista loved and failed to clone once upon a time. "Dr. Travista lived here."

"How can you be so sure?"

I flash the photograph at Noah and say, "I just am."

He may not know much about Jodi, if anything, but he nods, trusting my judgment. "Teleporter's busted," he says. "We won't be able to pull any destination data from the hard drive."

The only reason to destroy the data would be to hide the trail. I did that when I sent Foster through a teleporter just before I was shot two years ago. I used codes I retrieved from the resistance before leaving last year to hide my trail, but you cannot always trust that to work.

I take a deep breath and look around again. A fine layer of dust coats everything. He has definitely not lived here in a long time. "Okay, so Dr. Travista left the labs the night Foster and I went in. He came home, saved Declan from the lake, and took him to some super-secret hideaway?"

"Where he either healed Burke from a serious injury or cloned him," Noah adds.

"You realize cloning implies he had a second facility all along."

He shrugs. "And why not? Especially if they planned to do this on a grander scale."

"Would you not have heard them talk about this?"

"Burke doesn't trust anyone or anything. Hell, neither he nor Travista even used the word 'clone' for months; that's how careful they are. To this day no one knows where the facility is, not even the government. If they do, they're being very tight-lipped about it."

I link my fingers around the back of my neck. "This is insane."

He glances around, then takes a deep breath. "Well, at least we know where he disappeared to. We should head back. I have back-to-back meetings all afternoon."

I follow him to the front door. "Do you still run Tucker Securities?"

"Of course I do."

We close up the house and head back down the trail. Our boots crunch in sync on the needle-strewn floor. Birds sing to one another in the trees above, each note a temptation to believe a fantasy in which everything is right and harmonious in the world.

I tuck my hands into my back pockets and focus on the end of the trail ahead. "I thought you would have had someone step in and run the business for you. Is it not a lot to handle? The company and a resistance faction?"

"It isn't so bad, and I do have help. I only handle the bigger clients who have trusted me for a long time. I've worked too hard on my image to just disappear."

I remember the public image. The man's man. Everyone is drawn to him, including Declan. Noah is a very good actor, which I have to admit scares the hell out of me.

Noah blocks my path at the entrance to the larger trail and faces me. His gaze is cast down, and it seems to take an eternity for him to say, "I want you to trust me, too, Emma."

My muscles lock. I am unsure how he expects me to respond.

"I have very good reasons for the clone study," he continues, shifting weight to his other foot. "I can't share them with you, but you have to trust me."

I could easily say, *Yes, Noah, of course I will trust you,* because how could I say anything to the contrary? A year ago I might have caved. That will not happen today.

I force my gaze down to our dirt-dusted boots. "I need you to tell me something. Did you agree to let me stay because of my offer to help with Declan? Or did you see potential for your project?"

"I'd be lying if I told you it didn't cross my mind, but no, it had no bearing on my decision." I glance up to find him squinting off to his right. "Sonya knows she overstepped. It won't happen again."

For her sake, I hope not. I walk past him and enter the main trail. "We should get back."

"Hold on, Emma."

I do not want to hold on, because I want to let this go. He wears on my all-too-thin defenses. But despite this, I face him, steeling myself for what he would add.

He stands with hands hooked on his hips. Fingers of sunlight highlight every sharp angle of his face and play in his hair. He takes a shallow breath, then closes the distance between us. My heart flutters when he stops in front of me, close enough that the toe of his boot taps mine. I want to back away—to *look* away—but I cannot. I swallow hard against a dry throat.

"It won't happen again," he repeats. This time, his gaze holds mine without so much as a single blink. He will force his truth on me if it kills him.

Noah's chest rises on a shaky breath. He closes his eyelids for the span of yet another breath, then stares into my eyes as if searching for my soul. I even believe he finds it, because I am utterly ensnared by his intensity.

His voice lowers to a rough whisper. "I told you that you're safe with me and I meant it."

I have to summon my voice from somewhere deep inside. "I believe you."

And I do believe him. I only wish I could trust the people around him to make his truth reality. He may not realize it yet, but they will turn him into a liar without having to utter a single word.

CHAPTER 14

Leigh leans against the doorframe outside my room, arms folded. Her smile is immediate and genuine, releasing the built-up tension in my shoulders. "Ready to go?"

I peer out the door both ways. Foster is supposed to help me search files today but is running late. "Go where? I am waiting on someone."

"I know. Foster sent me in his stead. Got tied up with Major Reid."

"You are helping me?"

She lets loose a single, hard laugh. "Uh, no. That would be Miles's department. I'm just along for the ride." Her right hand lifts to the HK belted at her side and thumbs the safety switch on and off. "I have the afternoon free, and what better way to spend it than with the resident clone?"

I laugh, but the sound comes out forced. I am too distracted and nervous over how the search will go. "I will enjoy the human interaction as well."

We take a wide stone stairwell down a level. Two more right turns in the brightly lit hallways and we reach a corridor lined with doors that say GESTURAL INTERFACE. We stop at one and Leigh presses a silver-plated button to the right of the entry that reads G14. The door slides away with an audible *shiff,* disappearing into the wall, giving us access to a space a quarter the size of the hologram room.

A young woman nearly collides with us on her way out. Petite, with a thick platinum braid hanging to her midback, she looks too innocent to wear the set of HK pistols on her hip. She gives Leigh a tight smile and cuts me with a shoulder on her way by.

Leigh raises an eyebrow and glances between me and the girl striding away. "Miles's partner, Farrah Styles. She's . . . wound a little tight."

Miles yells from inside, snatching our attention. " 'Bout damn time. Are women always late?" The room is dark save the bright blue glow from wall-size vid screens. A curved glass table sits in the middle of the room on an elevated circular platform. Miles stands beside it, arms crossed.

"We're not late," Leigh says. "You're just early for once."

Miles hops down and walks toward us with a tilted grin. "What's up, Wade? Ready to do this?"

"Are you?"

He freezes and scoffs. "Please. Have we met?"

I cock an eyebrow at him. "Barely."

Leigh slaps his shoulder. "She's got you there."

Miles pushes her up onto the platform and I follow. He positions us in the center, then faces the table. On the clear surface glows the image of a computer desktop in white and blue.

He rubs his palms together and grins at the tabletop. "Hey, baby, let's warm you up." He strokes a small, illuminated blue square in a tight circle. "Oh, yeah, there's your sweet spot."

Leigh snorts beside me. "Said every disillusioned man in history."

He grins and starts typing on an illuminated keyboard. "I'm no man, honey. I'm a beast."

"I thought that was hair I saw on your back."

He spins around, eyes wide. "Take that back. That's how rumors get started."

She flicks a hand at the table. "Don't you have something you need to be doing?"

He points at a box near the top of the table and looks at me. "Foster said you'd have a password. Ours"—he motions between himself and Leigh—"will access only local files. He said you'd need to do a broader search."

He slips on a pair of black gloves with a metal circle over the pad of each finger while I debate the pros and cons of his password request. I may like him, and I am anxious to get the search started, but I do not know him enough to trust him with Noah's password. What was Foster thinking?

"I do not have a password."

He smirks, sucks in a deep breath, and exchanges a quick glance with Leigh. "Okay. Let me put it to you this way: I can hack in to help you, but they can't pin it on me if I don't actually *hack in*."

Leigh folds her arms and chuckles. "You couldn't hack a woman's bra, let alone Tucker's network security."

Miles straightens, obviously prepared to rise to the occasion. "Oh, I can. And I will. Which would you like me to prove first? Your bra or the network? Both with one hand tied behind my back?"

"That will not be necessary." I step up to the glass and type "Europa" on the surface keyboard, unwilling to let Miles risk getting into trouble because I am being too careful. Foster trusts him, so I will too.

Miles settles back in at the keyboard. After more typing, he reaches toward the center of the glass with his right hand, and thin blue rays of light connect between the fingertip pads of his glove and the screen. He draws his hand up, pulling the images from the table. Five different computer windows hover in the air over the surface. The blue glow of the walls serving as a backdrop dims automatically.

With his gloved fingertips, Miles slides the hovering boxes around. One tap enlarges one box. Two taps makes more windows appear.

"God, I love these rooms," he says, and stands back to look at his handiwork.

Now the title "gestural interface" outside the room makes sense. "Why have all those computers in the command center when you have access to this?"

"Nice, huh?" Miles says. "Only problem is it's not meant for long-time use."

He swings an arm like he is throwing a lasso, and the windows barricade him in a circle. Leigh and I now stand on the outside of his holographic wall, where he spins and reads from the inside. Every word on the see-through screens appears backward to me. He pushes at the air with both arms, and the windows fly back and around the perimeter of the platform, putting Leigh and me on the inside.

"Fun as it is, though, too much time with your arms above the heart will wear you out. We only use it when we need to access a lot of data at once."

Leigh laughs from behind me. "Well, for Miles, any excuse will do: work, pen pal correspondence . . . *Porn from the twenty-first century.*"

"Hey. It really was the kinkiest era," he says, then links his fingers and cracks his knuckles. "I'm all in. Now you tell me what you're looking for."

I allow myself to feel hope for the first time in days. I could find my parents today. "I am looking for my birth parents, Lily and Stephen Wade. They were resistance and imprisoned when I was around four. They escaped not long after."

He nods and scans the open data windows hovering in the air. "Cool." He acts as if I did not just hand him next to no information.

"A man I met in Mexico said he knew a Lily Garrett in the southeast region. She is not necessarily my mother, but she is the only lead I have."

Miles fingers through windows. They spin in a tight circle until he taps one and they stop. "Okay, let's find Lily Garrett, then."

Leigh taps the toe of her boot on the metal-grated floor over and over and over. When I cannot take the sound any longer, I say, "I did not realize that the resistance was split by regions. I thought they were one big group."

Leigh stops tapping and glances sidelong at me. "The resistance is one large hive made up of multiple cells. Each cell has its own lieutenant colonel in command." She pauses to look at me from under the bridge of her perfectly sculpted eyebrows. "The hive has generals and colonels to oversee the lieutenant colonels and their regiments. Lieutenant Colonel Tucker commands our hub but reports to Colonel Nathan Updike, who commands the mid-Atlantic region."

"Here we go," Miles says, and pulls forward a window, then uses his fingertips to widen the frame. "Southeast region." On the hovering window, he scrolls through a list of names.

I cross over to stand beside him as the names fly up the screen. "There must be a thousand names there," I say, my stomach fluttering with nerves. *Please find her.*

"But only one Lily Garrett," he says. He sweeps his arms and shoves aside all the windows but one. He taps her name, which opens a new window.

A holographic folder appears, and Miles fingers the image open as if it were real. He throws aside a picture of a blond woman about my age. Beside it, he tosses up a legal document. A death certificate.

My throat tightens, and I have to blink away tears as I read the dates. Lily Garrett died before I was born, on a mission meant to bug the main office building of Caulder Consolidated in Savannah, Georgia. She was never my mother. I am at a dead end.

Miles sweeps the hologram windows into a pile, balls them up in his fist, and throws them to the side, where they disappear. "I'm gonna go out on a limb and say she isn't your mother."

Blood rushes into my head and throbs at my temples. I clasp my hands behind my neck and close my eyes. I can just make out the white glow of the computer windows from behind my dark lids. "I laid in a casket with a corpse to find out the name of a woman who is *no one* to me."

"Listen to me." Leigh's assured tone snatches my attention. "If anyone can find them, it's Miles. *Believe* that."

The door slides open before I can respond, and Foster leans inside. "Wade. Tucker asked me to grab you. Something big is going on at Burke Enterprises."

CHAPTER 15

Nobody says a word when I follow Foster into the command center. Leigh and Miles follow close behind. It seems as if the entire room is standing to watch the wall at the far end. Twenty smaller screens are set as one large frame to view the lobby in Burke Enterprises. Surrounding screens show different angles of the same scene, one I cannot believe I am witnessing.

Charles Godfrey.

A very angry Charles Godfrey. I have been on the receiving end of his anger, and it was not a pleasant place. From the moment I met him, the man frightened me. Always glaring, impatient, and distrustful of my methods when dealing with his wife, Ruby. He assumed I was coaching her into playing dumb, when in fact, she was still learning how to be human. I had been the same way, only Declan had far more patience. My ex sat with me every day, teaching me new things until I became the loving wife he wanted.

The memories of those early days brush over me like a frigid breeze. It is hard to believe there was ever a time the idea of Declan caring for me made me warm with love for him.

Noah appears around the side of a nearby desk and shoulders through a grouping of men in front of me. He wears a light gray suit with a striped tie hanging loose at the neck. "Godfrey stormed in a few minutes ago," he tells me, and glances up at the screen. "He's demanding to see Burke and trying to force his way past security. They've been holding him back and waiting for Burke to arrive."

"Where's Declan?" I ask.

"Off grid."

Which means he is in an area they cannot monitor. He is probably with Dr. Travista plotting their next move against me.

I look up at the screen. For the first time, I notice someone hanging limply in Charles's hand, but it has to be a lie. It is too unreal. He clings to the upper arm of a thin blond woman. He holds her so tight his knuckles are white. Her free arm drags on the marble floor under her as he shifts around looking for a weak spot in the security line. The chin length, curling strands of her hair hang over her face, but I know who she is.

"Ruby," I whisper, and move deeper into the room for a better look. Tears burn the backs of my eyes. "She is not moving." *Move, Ruby. Please move. Whimper. Something.*

With each passing second, an invisible constraint around my chest tightens. I knew Charles Godfrey could not be trusted to care for her. And she knew no better. Like me, her mind had been wiped, only she never regained her memories because Dr. Travista murdered her host after he realized the tie binding the host body to the clone. The survival of my original body is the only reason I have the few memories I do.

"Where's Burke!" Charles yells at the line of security. The stocky man's face is red. Thick veins snake across his temples and forehead.

A young man pushes through the line, his soft-edged features impassive, but with piercing eyes focused on Charles. His dark-brown hair is short and teased in a way that makes him look like he just rolled out of bed. His dark beard is trimmed close to the skin and cut tight around the edges.

Someone stops just behind and to the side of me. Noah's soft musk wafts forward, and I do not have to look back to know it is him.

"Who is he?" I ask.

"Daxton Thomas. He's an intern working with Burke. He's also the son of Evan Thomas, the CFO who ran the business in Burke's absence."

On-screen, Daxton snaps down the brown jacket of his three-piece suit, then holds up his hands to the man dragging his wife around the lobby. *"Mr. Godfrey, I'm going to have to ask you to calm down. Mr. Burke isn't in the building at the moment, but if I could get you to come wi—"*

"You tell that motherfucker he owes me a new wife! I paid a lot of money for her, and he gave me a faulty product!"

I had hoped it was not true, but now there can be no question. Ruby is dead. Tears coat my eyes and I blink rapidly to force them back. I glance at Noah. "Do you know what happened to her?"

He shakes his head, attention focused on the screen. Then he points and says, "There's Burke." He moves forward to the workstation in front of me and leans straight-armed on the desk between two analysts. "I want this recorded from all possible angles," he orders.

Declan's security line steps aside to let him pass. I fight to keep from shrinking away from his screen presence: tall, demanding attention, the intensity in the sea of his eyes daring any man to cross him. His perfectly fitted three-piece black suit accentuates the broad line of his shoulders and the V shape of his torso. He stops and straightens his spine, expanding his chest.

"You and Travista did this, didn't you?" Charles asks. *"Payback for my disagreement with your traitor wife."*

I take immediate offense. Disagreement? He tried to beat the hell out of me for something I knew nothing about at the time.

"Why don't we go somewhere private?" Declan suggests. *"That way*

you won't be tempted to break any part of the nondisclosure agreement you signed. Let one of my men take the body off your hands and we'll discuss your concerns—"

"My concerns? Admit you and Travista sabotaged my wife. Admit you limited her life span to get back at me."

Declan's nostrils flare. His fists clench and release. I watch with bated breath as he works to maintain control of his temper. Will he hit him? Throw him from the building? There is no telling how far he will go.

Finally, he steps close to Charles and towers over him. *"If I wanted to do something as childish as what you're implying, I would have had Ruby disposed of the second you laid a hand on my wife."*

His tone is cool and even. Underneath it, even I feel the warning that lies there. He is still angry over the attack. For a moment, I glow with pleasure. That is, until I remember that Declan is *not* my husband and what he is doing to me makes him certifiable.

Charles grits his teeth. *"You really are a stupid fuck. I know what was happening to her. You want to screw with me?"* He drops Ruby's limp body at Declan's feet. Declan barely lowers his chin to acknowledge her. *"You better hope you can salvage what's left, or I'm taking you for everything you've got. This company and all its assets will be mine."*

Noah starts shouting orders again. "Somebody find me Dr. Toro and Dr. Malcolm."

On-screen, Declan jostles Ruby up and off the floor. He hands her to Daxton, who sinks under the weight, grimaces, then rolls her into the arms of the nearest security officer.

"Mr. Thomas," Declan says to Daxton, keeping his gaze level on Charles. *"Why don't you show Mr. Godfrey to my office? I'm going to see Arthur. Let's see what we can do to rectify this tragedy."*

In other words, let us see if we can grow him a new wife by tomorrow. How very diplomatic.

The security officer leaves with Ruby's body. No one takes a second to look back, not even Charles Godfrey. I am alone in this grief.

Sonya's voice breaks through my thoughts. "What happened?"

Noah turns from the desk and walks over to where the two doctors have stopped beside me. I have already taken an unconscious step away from them. Dr. Malcolm smiles up at me and waves but returns his attention to Noah the second he starts speaking.

I do not listen to the recounting but instead look back at the screens. The interior of Burke Enterprises is slowly clearing out. Declan and Charles have already disappeared. The semicircular security desk is now visible, with its five officers manning the station.

Someone resets the larger screen back to multiple small screens, but every video is set to watch the same scene from multiple angles. In one, Daxton Thomas stands off to the side with a phone pressed to his ear. He was supposed to be escorting Charles Godfrey upstairs, but it appears he has forced that job on someone else.

"Emma?"

Noah's voice snaps me out of my trance. I blink and return my attention to the room, where he and the two doctors stare at me. "Yes?"

"I asked if you remember what Godfrey said about Ruby just before threatening to take the company."

I think back to that moment and replay the conversation in my mind, then repeat it aloud. "He said, 'You really are a stupid fuck. I know what was happening to her. You want to screw with me?' Then he made the threat. Does that mean something to you?"

Sonya does not let him respond. "If he knew something was going on, we could watch some of their home footage—"

"There is none," Noah says. "Godfrey declined the security months ago."

I feel the burn of a stare and find Dr. Malcolm gaping up at me. I flinch in surprise. "Is something the matter?"

My question draws the others' attention.

Dr. Malcolm says, "You have an eidetic memory, don't you?"

"A what?"

He busies himself with digging in a pocket, then the other, shifting quickly between them a few times before settling on one. "Total recall," he says. "I bet if we look back, those were Mr. Godfrey's exact words." He pulls out a palm tablet and begins thumbing the tiny keyboard across the bottom.

"Are you keeping notes about me?" I ask. After our talk this morning, I cannot believe he is so quick to take advantage. Maybe I should have been more specific. "Dr. Malcolm—"

"Emma," Sonya cuts in, hand raised to stop me, "he's keeping a record of details that may help us."

Noah takes the computer from Dr. Malcolm, shoves the device back in the doctor's coat pocket, and looks directly at Sonya. The muscles in his jaw flex. "We talked about this." He looks at Dr. Malcolm. "And Emma has always been able to recall details perfectly, so this won't help you in the slightest."

Dr. Malcolm's eyes brighten and he bounces a few times on the balls of his feet. "But, you see, it does. Nobody knows the full extent of transference from host to duplicate. Are certain traits learned or genetic? Emma's memories aren't there, but it's as if everything else about her works on automatic. Muscle memory where there shouldn't be because her new body is, well . . . *new*. She fights as if she's done it her entire life. She handles weapons with above-average proficiency." He grins at me and reaches out to pat my arm. "Nice job in that simulation, by the way." He turns back to Noah in the span of an eyeblink. "If I'm right, she has complete sensory recall, which—"

"I've heard enough," Noah says, and I could not be more grateful. It is as if every word Dr. Malcolm uses siphons the air from my lungs.

"I won't ask you to respect Emma's privacy again. Can you find out how Ruby Godfrey died or not?" he asks Sonya.

"Not without access to her remains, but based on what Charles Godfrey suggested, it could be a defect. Not that we'll get a chance to find out." Her dark eyes focus on me. "It's not like I have another clone to look at."

I stiffen and curl my fingers into fists. I cannot believe she is resorting to guilt tactics.

Noah snaps his fingers in Sonya's face to get her attention. "If Godfrey says he saw what was happening, you can watch Lydia Farris. The Farrises have security monitoring their property."

"I'd rather have Ruby's body," she says. Her clinical tone turns my stomach. Ruby was a human. A mother. My friend. "We have people with pull at the medical examiner's office. If we intercept the transport—"

"You will never see her," I say. When they look at me, I add, "We are Dr. Travista's children. He would never let Ruby end up in the hands of someone else. He brought her into this world, and he will control how she leaves it." For this, at least, I am glad. I do not want Sonya using Ruby as she would use me or anyone else she came into contact with.

Sonya looks skeptical. "There are procedures that have to be followed. Laws against—"

"Laws that protect humans. You forget who you are dealing with." My throat feels tight, and I cannot take how they look at me any longer. "Anyway. I should let you finish this discussion in private."

Noah releases a long sigh. "I'll walk you out."

Sonya's eyes narrow at him. "She knows the way."

There is no need for words as he lengthens his spine and rolls his shoulders back. The tide of his reaction is a silent, encompassing fog. Sonya folds her arms across her chest, completely unaffected. She cocks her head pointedly at him, then looks directly at me.

Dr. Malcolm clears his throat, his bright, friendly smile faltering. He bounces on his toes and lets loose a stiff chuckle. He leans toward the middle of our perimeter and singsongs, *"Awk-ward."*

I have to get out of here. Tentatively, I face Noah. "Will you let me know if you figure out what happened to Ruby?"

He starts to nod, but Sonya releases a derisive laugh and rolls her eyes. "As if you care," she mutters under her breath.

Heat swirls in my face and chest. Swiping the palm tablet from Dr. Malcolm's pocket, I place it in his startled hands. "Take this note down. Clones run on the same human emotion as everyone else." To Sonya, I add, "Ruby was my friend. Not even you can take that from me."

CHAPTER 16

T*oday's top story has shocked the world,"* the newsman says from be-hind his large desk. Behind him in the floating holo-vid is a picture of Ruby. She laughs at the camera, the gold flecks in her eyes sparkling. Her long curls are folded into a loose braid over one shoulder. *"Ruby Godfrey, the Original Clone, was declared dead this afternoon. No word yet on the cause of death, but Declan Burke is expected to make a state-ment later today."*

I lie on a holographic beach, eyes closed to a sun, desperate for the surrounding solitude to take me away from recent events. But my heart hurts for Ruby and her child. I wish it hurt for Charles, too, but I know better than to believe him a grieving husband. Even if I had not seen his reaction with my own eyes, I know he did not value his wife the way he should have.

I am also bothered by Charles's words. They meant nothing to me until Noah pointed them out. One sentence in particular: *I know what was happening to her.* What could have been happening to her that would make him automatically believe her death was caused by a defect in the cloning process?

Dr. Travista's image fills my mind. I can see his office, with heavy books and nice woods and warm red colors. How he faced me in his chair, saying, *You're perfect,* with a considerable amount of pride in his tone. Little did I know at the time what he truly meant by this: a perfect re-creation with endless possibilities. More than he bargained for.

A cold shiver forces me to a sitting position. I blink at the holographic waves that a high tide has brought closer. The water recedes from under my feet and leaves behind white foam bubbles that sizzle and burst. A gray pebble gleams wetly under the sunshine, half-buried in the compact sand. Not unlike me, both free and captive in a place seemingly peaceful. But even a tide can drag a person down and steal her last breath.

What sort of tide took Ruby? Charles? Or is he right about her body failing her? Will mine fail, too?

You're perfect, Dr. Travista's voice tells me.

Am I? Are any of us?

I do not know, but I feel the need to see Ruby again.

A seagull struts through the computer tablet beside me just as I reach for it. I wake the screen to the long list of holograms. I noticed earlier they are merely a single file in the larger network. I tap out of the screen and take a few wrong turns inside the network but eventually find myself staring at a list of names. At the top, Burke Enterprises. I tap into the file and then into the lobby feed.

Because the tablet is set to holographic mode, the entire room transforms into the same lobby I watched from the command center a few hours ago. I stand in my surprise and jump when a tall, lanky man walks right through me to get to the security desk. I know I am not really in the room and that no one can see me, but it feels as though this is real. I even catch myself watching doorways for Declan to arrive and catch me.

I let my heartbeat settle before turning the tablet to voice command. "Computer, play current footage from marker thirteen hundred hours, sixteen minutes."

The live feed pauses and, in only a second, resets the room to the time I requested. The lobby is brighter than it had been in real time due to the time difference. The abrupt cacophony of voices startles me. Charles is yelling at Declan again.

"Mute sound."

The abrupt silence leaves me with a ringing in my ears and the hollow sound of my breathing. I walk around the projected men, heart pounding, and pause in front of my ex. He glares over my head. I had forgotten how much taller he is. I lay my hands on his chest, then let them fall through his image with a silent curse. After all this time, and after all he has done, I cannot stop myself from falling into familiar patterns.

Ruby's body appears under my feet. Arm lying across her chest. One leg bent awkwardly under her. "Computer, pause footage."

I step back and kneel beside her. Wide eyes stare up at me. I once loved their light brown color with flecks of gold and green, but the life in them is gone now. She looks otherwise peaceful despite being dragged and tossed and talked about as if she were a dysfunctional product. She looks *human.*

I wish I could hold her the way someone should hold her. With care. With love. I wish I could give her a proper good-bye. I wish I could shield her from the ogling men in the room. But it is far too late.

"Computer, resume footage." I stand and watch the feed continue. There is nothing to discover about Ruby's death in this little bit of video. No clue as to what Charles Godfrey could have been referring to.

What did he know?

Declan lifts Ruby off the floor and passes her to Daxton. I am about to stop the video altogether, but Daxton passes Ruby to a security officer and I recall how he ignored Declan's directive and ended up in a corner of the lobby on the phone.

I find myself strangely drawn to this man, who cannot be much younger than I am. The unwavering compliant front he airs for Declan drops the second he turns his back. Before, Daxton was like the rest of them. The way he looked up to Declan, the eager-to-please employee. But now, with no one looking on but me, he releases the unadulterated abhorrence in his blue eyes and has my rapt attention.

"Unmute sound," I say, and a flood of clicking footsteps and the hum of conversation fill the room.

Daxton tucks one hand deep in his pocket and lifts a phone to his ear while strolling to an empty part of the lobby. *"Charles Godfrey just dropped his dead clone off in the lobby."*

Miles slides the gestural interface gloves on, his usual comical expression serious while he listens to me recount Daxton's phone conversation. He brought us back to room G14 once I explained I needed his help with another search.

"Can you find out who he was talking to?" I ask after my long explanation.

That perpetual smile finally breaks free, and he spreads his arms wide. "Of course, Wade. You came to the right place." He pulls a blue stream of light from the clear table and assembles a group of computer windows in the air before him. The surrounding walls darken to a midnight-blue glow. "That is, of course, if he was talking to someone in our network."

"At the very least, trace the call. I want to know who he was talking to."

He pushes the floating windows to the outside of the perimeter, encasing us on the circular dais. "So bossy," he says, but winks. "I dig it, though. It's hot."

I rub my eyes. I had not meant to sound bossy, but I am still in shock over what I heard from Daxton's side of the conversation.

I stand near the table and out of the way to watch Miles work. With his arms raised and moving, lines of muscle flex from biceps to wrist. Even his shoulders, hidden under a black T-shirt, contract with every move. It occurs to me that if not for the messed-up nature of my life lately, I might have pursued Miles. Or at least allowed him to pursue me. He is tall, thin but sinuously carved in muscle, and funny. He is also more than boyishly cute. He is handsome in a way I doubt any woman could help but admire.

"Did I really dislike you before?" I ask him.

He glances at me, and there is amusement rather than surprise on his face at my odd question. "Without a doubt." His hands resume their search through the windows. "We dated a really long time ago. We were barely nineteen and I had too much energy to settle into one relationship."

"By 'too much energy' I assume you mean you cheated."

A grin peels across his face as he jabs a finger at a window. "And like the bastard I was, didn't even regret it. For what it's worth, I do now." He looks at me and jerks his head at the screen in front of him. "Come take a look. I think I found something."

I move up and settle beside him. He smells nice. Spicy. He taps into a few more screens until the outer area of Declan's office appears in the window to my left. The walls are silver with thick and thin black lines weaving around one another, designed to look like a computer chip. A young, sandy-haired man sits behind a mahogany desk, feet kicked up and crossed.

I gasp. "He called Declan's assistant?"

With a brief nod and eyes narrowly focused, Miles pauses the feed.

He sets to work inputting instructions on a second window. A moment later, the lobby of Burke Enterprises appears. He lines up the times to match and hits play on both feeds.

The phone beeps in the office and Armand lifts it free of its cradle. *"Declan Burke's office,"* he says in a chipper, professional tone that belies his laid-back posture.

I look at Daxton, one hand tucked in a pocket as he repeats the side I already heard. *"Charles Godfrey just dropped his dead clone off in the lobby."*

Armand drops his feet to the floor. *"What happened to her?"*

"I don't know. Crazy bastard probably dosed her up. He's blaming Burke. Threatened to take the company in a lawsuit. Anyway, we can use this to our advantage. Get ahead of the story in the media."

"Agreed. I can make an anonymous call to the Times. *Imagine the press Burke will get if the world thinks his missing wife—"*

Daxton, glancing furtively around the lobby, cuts in. *"As much as I'd love to put this on her, Burke won't stop until he figures out it was you, then, by extension, me. No, we start by putting this on the resistance. Once that news settles, we'll find a way to leak a connection between Emma Burke and Ruby Godfrey. The press will eat that up.*

"Lastly, we'll reveal who the real Original Clone is. How Burke's been misleading not only the world but three-quarters of his board and tainting his father's legacy. When all is said and done, the world will know what Emma Burke really is, and who she was. Resistance."

Armand is nodding, a slow smile spreading across his face. *"Brilliant. I'll make the call to the* Times. *By morning, the world will think the resistance was behind the clone's death. Will I see you later?"*

"Computer, pause feed." I nod at the frozen men in the room. "What do we know about these guys? Anything useful?"

Miles drifts close to Armand's hologram window with his arms crossed. "Obviously, you already know this guy. Nothing much more to say about him other than he likes to be in the know of every single detail. Sneaky bastard. Gets in where he can, how he can, and nobody's the wiser."

He faces the lobby and Daxton. "This guy . . . nothing. His parents, on the other hand . . . are confidential."

I am impressed he even knows what the word means. "Confidential meaning you are suddenly opposed to abusing privileges, or confidential meaning you will tell me anyway?"

He snorts a laugh. "Lower the eyebrow, Wade. I'm getting to it." He swipes a third window closer to him and taps until two personnel files appear. With a sweep of his arms, all other screens slide out of the way. "Meet Evan and Charissa Thomas."

I briefly met the Thomases at my gallery show last year. They, along with other members of the board, made me feel as if I were under a microscope. Now I understand why. A few of them knew me to be ex-resistance, as well as being the first successful clone. They were waiting for Declan's pet project to turn traitor. Based on things I heard, I believe Evan Thomas is one of the few who knew everything about me.

While the pictures show younger versions of the couple I met, the names on their files actually say Victoria and Ryan Owens. In the photos, they wear military-issue black. She has a heart-shaped face, soft pink lips, and sleek, dark brown hair. His dark hair lies in soft waves, and gray fans around his temple. His eyes are a beautiful shade of blue.

"I do not understand," I say, facing Miles.

"Neither did anyone else." He shrugs. "Or so I hear. We were barely out of diapers when they turned on at least four resistance cells. They're why those of us low in rank never know the locations of the other hubs."

"They were double agents?"

He nods. "Lived as loyal members of the resistance for roughly five years. Then things got hot, so they turned over what they knew, and Mr. Thomas got himself a sizable handful of shares in Burke Enterprises. Later, he was appointed to the board and promoted to chief financial officer.

"Mrs. Thomas became the typical American wife. Handed their daughter, Olivia, over to a WTC without so much as a parting tear. She stayed at home to raise their son into the devious little snot you see today."

A sour tang fills my mouth. "They did that to their own daughter?" I cannot imagine doing this to Adrienne, and I have spent only a handful of hours with her.

"I'd love to say it was hard on them, but the Thomases sold out entire families for shares in a company bent on owning the world. The children who survived were either distributed out to WTCs or adoptive families."

The idea of someone living among us, planning this very same thing, makes me want to run down the hall, snatch up my daughter, and steal my husband away from his responsibilities. I would take my family to Mexico and live out the rest of my days. But my family looks to Sonya in my stead. She is the mother and, maybe someday, the wife. The only family I have is a mystery. Captured and imprisoned—

"Oh my God," I whisper. My lungs struggle to maintain a consistent airflow while my head wraps around a sudden realization. "The four cells. This happened around the time my parents were imprisoned for being resistance. Is it possible they were caught in these raids?"

Miles seems to look past me; then his eyes begin to widen. "Holy shit, Wade, you're right. You may have just figured out where to find your parents."

CHAPTER 17

From an open doorway, the old man nods at a reporter, who must stand to the side of the camera filming his impromptu interview. *"I saw it happen, you see. She was on her way out to tend the garden, same as every day. I'm minding my business on my back porch, reading the* Times, *same as every day. One minute she's humming and walking; next she's standing there, still as stone. Then she just collapses. Thought she passed out, you see. I called out to her, of course. She didn't answer, so I went to check, but she was dead, you see. Just like that. Dead."*

Leigh sets a bowl of yogurt on my breakfast tray, then retrieves her own and continues down the stainless row. "Latest out of BE is that we poisoned Ruby Godfrey," she says over her shoulder, just loud enough for me to hear over the hum of conversation and scrape of silverware filling the dining hall. "One day I'm going to stop being surprised when they blame us."

Poison. I cannot help but wonder if that part is true, and if not by us, then by whom? Charles?

I pick up a small bowl of granola. All down the row, person after person reaches under the buffet glass for one thing or another. The aromas of cooked meat and saccharine confections fill the air.

"Do you think she was really poisoned?" I ask, claiming a container of apple juice from amid a sea of beverages.

"No. It was probably the best they could come up with on short notice after the neighbor talked last night." Her long ponytail swings forward as she lifts a plate stacked with pancakes and a side of syrup from the stainless warming table. "If it wasn't poison, it would have been any number of things. Strangulation. Snapped neck. Lethal injection."

And even if this liability had not been the first stage of Daxton's plan, Declan would have made similar accusations. The only difference being he would have spun the lie in a fashion aimed at getting me back.

I slide my tray off the shelf. "Any word on what really happened?"

Leigh turns with me and we head toward a table where Foster and Miles sit with full plates. "No. Her body went straight to Dr. Travista, and no one's said a word about it since. Nothing of any use, anyway."

When we are settled beside the boys, Foster says, "Miles was just telling me about last night."

My appetite disappears in a deep pit as I exchange a look with Miles. We made it through two of the four cells before calling it a night. Needless to say, I went to bed with my hopes freshly trodden. "I am beginning to think this is a huge waste of time."

Miles shakes his head. "We have two more to look at, and if your parents don't turn up there, there's still plenty more to go through. No worries, Wade. If they're there, I'll find them."

I have no doubt about that, but the question is, will he find them in time? Declan will never give up the search for them as long as I am still in hiding.

Leigh kicks me under the table and beams. "Now, slap a smile on. You haven't had to get inside a single coffin yet."

I roll my eyes but laugh.

Miles grins. "Exactly. We'll head back over after breakfast. You only have me till noon, though."

I am beginning to nod when the light *tap-tap-tap* of running feet heads right for me, followed by a soft *slap-slap-slap* on my leg. Startled, I find Adrienne in the aisle beside me.

She stomps a foot and lifts her arms. Gives me a high-pitched whine.

I blink. She wants me to pick her up? *Me?*

Foster elbows me in the side. "Well, don't leave the girl standin' there, Wade. What's wrong with you?"

I snap out of it and lift her into my lap. Her loose curls tickle my chin and she smells like sweet strawberries. She grips a slate-colored palm tablet in her tiny hand that she slaps screen down on the table as soon as she is settled.

Adrienne fists my spoon and dips into my yogurt. Everyone but me laughs, as I am too busy looking for Noah or Sonya. I cannot believe they would just let her wander off.

Foster points two tables down to the left. Noah nods once at me with a finger raised, then returns to an obviously heated discussion he is having with Sonya. Her back is to me, and she jabs a finger into the tabletop as if making a point. His cheeks are flushed, his lips set in a thin line.

Leigh glances over her shoulder and back. "Still at it, I see."

I look at Foster, who shrugs and bites off the end of a piece of bacon. Adrienne reaches for the remains of the slice and he hands it over without question.

"What do you mean?" I ask Leigh. "Still at what?"

Adrienne bounces happily in my lap and swings her legs. The heels of her shoes hit my shins, and I have to readjust her position to save myself from the inevitable bruises.

Leigh smiles affectionately at Adrienne and says, "They had a pretty serious argument in the hospital wing last night. She isn't happy about his opinion of you."

"Which is?" Foster asks.

Leigh leans over her tray and lowers her voice. "The one where he believes 2.0 is his wife and Adrienne's mother. Sonya is of the opinion that a clone does not an Emma make."

I smooth Adrienne's hair down, nonchalantly covering her ears to whisper, "Adrienne should not hear any of this."

"Can't be any worse than what she'd be hearing if she were at their table right now," Miles points out.

Foster twists and leans an elbow on the table, giving his full attention to Adrienne. He pinches her round cheek and grins. "Have I told you about the bugs living in my head?"

"Oh, here we go," Leigh says with an eye roll.

Foster looks at her with wide eyes and says, "I'm telling you, I can feel them itching around my brain."

"You can't feel nanites," Miles says. "They're microscopic."

Leigh elbows him. "Shut up. None of this is appropriate conversation." She reaches over and picks up the palm tablet Adrienne set on the table by my tray. "Whatcha got here, bugface? Can you say bug?"

Adrienne scrunches her face and says, "Bug," though it sounds more like "Ug."

Everyone laughs as Leigh flips the computer over. Leigh's laugh comes to a halt, her smile frozen on her face. She shows Adrienne, and by extension me, the screen. On it, images slide by at a slow pace. Images of me.

The pictures fade in and out and pull at me with a steel grip. I cannot look away. There I am, lying in the greenest grass, laughing. Painting on the beach in Mexico. Talking to a group of men in military-issue black. More pictures flash by, all of them of me, none of them familiar.

Leigh points to the screen. "Who's this, bug?"

Adrienne twists around and looks up at me with shining hazel eyes. With palm upright and fingers partially splayed, she taps her thumb to her chin.

The laughter dies at the table, and everyone watches me for my reaction.

"That's right," Leigh says, and slides the device back across the table. Her bright green eyes smile at me.

"What just happened?" I ask.

Foster lays a hand on my back. "She signed the word for 'mother.'"

Tears build, closing off my throat and burning the backs of my eyes. Is this Noah's doing? Is this part of the reason Sonya has become so angry?

Sonya's voice startles me. "Come on, Adrienne. Time to go."

Her tone is harsh, a juxtaposition to how beautiful she looks today. Her usual black curls have been straightened into soft waves that lie past her shoulders. While she wears only a simple pair of dark-green slacks and a pressed white button-down blouse, they accentuate curves I will never know without surgery.

Sonya's reach is swift and targeted. I angle Adrienne away on instinct, fearing she will get hurt in the pass-off. She is too close to the table and could get caught between me and the lip. Sonya looks too upset to think that far ahead.

"Emma." Sonya's voice is firm, low. "Hand her over before—"

"You are causing a scene," I whisper, glancing furtively around. Hungry attention zeroes in on us from every angle in the room. Noah seems unable to get by Major Reid, who has him stopped in the middle of the aisle.

"Then don't fight me on this."

Adrienne, unaware of the tension building in the mere seconds Sonya has been standing there, spoons another lump of yogurt, ignoring us.

I bend to whisper in her ear. "Can you sit in Foster's lap for a second?"

Foster reaches for her without hesitation. "Come sit with Uncle Foster." She lets him lift her up, and he settles her into his lap.

Standing, I tilt my head away from the table, and Sonya follows me, though she looks ready to explode.

I stop past the row of tables and out of earshot, sensitive to the fact that the entire room is not as loud as it was two minutes ago. "Maybe Adrienne should not be around while you and Noah are arguing. I can—"

A hard laugh shoots free of her chest. "You're giving me parenting advice? That's rich coming from the woman who deserted her family." In my stunned silence, she closes in on me, arms folded. Her too-sweet vanilla scent tickles my nose. "I'm the one who picked up the pieces and held them together. I stayed up nights feeding her and caring for her when she was sick. I clothe her and bathe her. I plan and care about her future. *I* am, for all intents and purposes, her mother. So you don't get to do this."

Heat rushes up my neck to my face. This conversation has little to do with Adrienne and everything to do with manipulating my guilt. She wants to hurt me and knows exactly where to strike.

"And to be honest," she adds with a hint of condescension, "your own rights are still up in the air as far as I'm concerned. You look like Emma, but until I have solid proof of this so-called *transference,* you're just another body who, unfortunately, looks like someone we used to care about."

The final blow holds the sting of a slap. I add two steps between us, blinking back the tears sneaking into my eyes. "That was unnecessarily cruel. Even for you."

"Cruel is you showing up here and tantalizing Noah and Adrienne with a possible future, when you have every intention of leaving the second it's all clear."

"I would never— That is not—"

I stop scrambling for words when I realize the entire room has gone quiet. Everyone has stopped pretending to ignore us, and our private conversation just echoed throughout the hall's acoustics.

"Oh no?" she continues, undaunted. "Isn't that what you told me the day you showed up out of the blue?"

Noah appears and jerks Sonya around with a grip on her upper arm. His expression is set in hard lines. The amber in his eyes flares with simmering heat. "What the hell is wrong with you?"

"Excuse me," I say, and start for the table. I will not be a part of this argument any longer. Sonya's arrows are dipped in acid and expertly aimed.

"Emma," Noah says, and it is as if he literally has to tear his glare off Sonya to look at me. "Watch Adrienne for me. Sonya and I need to go have a talk."

What he asks of me gives Sonya ammunition, but he offers me more time with Adrienne. I cannot pass this up. I meet Sonya's heated gaze. She is wrong about me. I will not hurt my daughter. What I will do is tear down the world to stay with her.

"Take your time," I say to Noah.

They pass me just as I retake my seat and resettle Adrienne in my lap. I hug her small frame to me and kiss the top of her strawberry-scented head. I move my yogurt closer. "Still hungry, sweet girl?"

Foster takes my quivering hand from the bench seat between us and squeezes. "About those nanites . . ."

CHAPTER 18

Leigh invites me for an afternoon run in the hub's gym, and I do not decline. Running has been my therapy for so long, and after my argument with Sonya, I need to clear my head now more than ever.

What I really need is to forget about Noah for a while. I hate the way my thoughts keep returning to their argument over me, and the way it makes me feel.

I find black track shorts, a white fitted tank, and running shoes in "Emma's" box. It feels odd wearing her things, but another part of me is strangely connected to these superficial bits of my past.

We step onto the empty blue-and-gray-striped track, which encircles a small arena where people train in some sort of martial art. The atmosphere is thick with the scent of sweat and rubber matting. A seven-foot glass partition separates us from the grunts, the curses, and the occasional laugh. Mirrors make up the outside wall, giving the impression of a much larger space than we are actually in.

Leigh spends the first three laps talking about the men and few women training: how long they have been with the resistance, who sleeps with whom . . . She does not say so outright, but it is clear she has few friends in the group. Being that I find Leigh a good person, I doubt this has anything to do with personality. She just simply does not let a lot of people in. I understand this, though. I trusted face value once, and that did not work out so well for me in the end.

Halfway through our fourth lap, I catch a glimpse of Foster strolling up to the group in the center arena. His new leg stands out among the other flesh-covered limbs around him.

I slow to a stop and draw a deep breath into my burning lungs. I approach the glass, watching Foster settle into a sparring match with the current instructor. He is very good.

Leigh leans a shoulder against the partition glass and wipes her upper lip with the back of her hand. Sweat glistens on her exposed shoulders and heaving chest. Those green eyes scan me root to tip as her hand comes to rest on a jaunty hip. "So what's going on with you? You've barely grunted two words since we got here. Still bent up over what happened at breakfast?"

I am, but Sonya and her accusations are not the only things on my mind. The sparring match in progress across the room blurs as the last few hours play back in my mind. How the GI room was full of jokes and heart-pounding anxiety but ended in silence and blinked-back tears.

"Miles did not find my parents in the other two cells."

She lays a hand on my back. "Oh, I'm sorry. But hey, it's not over, right? Lots of places to look."

I nod but cannot loosen the hopeless feeling entwined around me, heart and soul. "I am beginning to wonder if I should keep trying. Noah is right; my parents can take care of themselves if Declan finds them. They do not need me for protection."

"But that's only one reason you're looking for them," she says sagely.

Closing my eyes, I nod. It is only that I am loath to admit, even to myself, that I am wasting my time.

I back away from the glass. "If I find my parents and they discover what I am . . ."

"What you are? You mean human? Don't let the things Sonya said earlier—"

"Sonya has nothing to do with this."

"—get to you. She's just pissed about this thing between you and Tucker. I can't blame her, but she had to know this would happen."

Of course she would bring up Noah when I am currently working hard to forget he exists. "Nothing is happening."

She laughs and pushes off the glass. "Whatever you say."

I do not want to argue, so I step back onto the track and put one foot in front of the other, moving into an easy jog. The soft tap of each step has lost its calming effect.

Leigh appears beside me, arms pumping and ponytail swinging. "I hope you don't think I'm prying—"

I bite back a groan. "If this is about Noah—"

"Uh, no. I can take a hint. Subject dropped." When I do not respond, she continues. "With my room being across the hall, and the fact that I'm an insomniac on a good day . . ." She trails off, seemingly unsure if she should continue.

I glance over to find her focused on the track ahead of us, her lips pursed in a thin line. "Where are you going with this?"

"You've been having nightmares."

My toe catches the rubber and I stumble to a stop. This is the last subject I expected her to broach.

Leigh slows and backtracks. She takes a couple of labored breaths and swallows hard. "It's nothing to be ashamed about," she says, and takes another wincing breath, pulling her hands up to her hips. "If any girl comes out of a WTC free of nightmares, she'd have to be soulless. I guess what I'm getting at is that if you need to talk, my door is open."

She has somehow managed to introduce two topics so uncomfortable I would rather turn myself over to Declan than discuss them. Correcting her on the true nature of my nightmares will only lead to questions I do not want to answer, so I say, "I will be okay, but thank you."

She wipes sweat from her upper lip and stares past me, seemingly a million miles away. She continues as if I had not said a word. "I guess you could go to the doc for all the recommended medications. All the best from the west, their quick mental-instability fix. Except the past is still there no matter how regulated the happy thoughts become. She doesn't get that."

Now I am lost. "She who?"

"Sonya."

And we are back to the other name I hoped to avoid, but my curiosity has been piqued, so I do not mind as much. "Why would Sonya not understand?"

"Because she was born and raised free. She's only here because the resistance needed doctors, and word is she stayed to be near Tucker. They joined the same year."

Her gaze travels to the center of the room and, more specifically, to Foster. He pays us no attention while trying to wrangle a wooden gun free from his opponent.

Leigh returns to our conversation, tightening her ponytail. "I'm not saying she doesn't know what she's doing. She's a great doctor. Just wish she understood she can't fix everyone and everything with a drug or procedure."

"From what I have seen, it is all about the science with doctors. Dr. Travista tried to cure his girlfriend of infertility and she ended up brain-dead." Like Emma.

Leigh huffs out an angry breath and glares toward the ceiling. "What is it with men thinking infertility is a problem? Why can't they just accept us the way we are? I mean, look at Sonya. All she can think about are the clones, and finding a way to cure herself. God help anyone who stands in her way."

"Sonya cannot have children?" I ask.

She shakes her head. Thanks to her small tirade, I now have answers to questions I did not realize I had. So many things make sense now. Not only am I the woman who can potentially take Sonya's family, but I represent a cure to her infertility.

Leigh looks into—past, really—the room again, and I suddenly see her in a whole new light. Her anger has nothing to do with Sonya, or doctors, or even men in general.

"You cannot have children either?" I guess.

She glances at me and away. "No, and I'm glad you brought it up." She shifts her weight. "I've been wanting to ask—"

The door to the hall slides opens and Major Reid steps through. He looks around until his gaze lands on me. "Burke. With me."

He has the worst timing; not to mention the use of Declan's name grates on my patience more and more with every use. He turns his back and disappears as if I will obediently follow behind.

I fold my arms and wait for him to reappear. Beside me, Leigh bites back a smile, mirroring my stance. I lean close and whisper, "What do you think this is about?"

"No idea."

When he finally reenters the space a moment later, he looks thoroughly perturbed. "Mrs. Burke. I need you to—"

"I heard you."

He swings an arm at the exit in a wide, sweeping arc. "Then let's go."

"First, you will have to give me a clue as to where you are taking me. Second, a 'please' would go a long way." I would add the request to discontinue the use of that name, but he is incorrigible.

Reid glances between me and Leigh. His cheeks turn a light shade of pink, which I gather is from anger rather from embarrassment. "Lieutenant Colonel Tucker would like to see you in his office. *Please,*" he finishes with a forced smile and gritted teeth.

My heart *thunk*s triple-time against my sternum. I do not want to see Noah. Not after what happened this morning. He will want to talk about Sonya. He may even apologize for her, which is not his place; nor will it erase the words she spoke.

Leigh tilts her head toward Reid. "You should go see what Tucker needs."

"I guess so. See you later."

I follow Reid out. He walks ahead, slapping the shoulders of and slinging funny remarks at the men we pass without sparing so much as a glance in my direction. At the end of our second hallway, I start to turn right, but he takes the left. Opposite the direction of Noah's office. Where is he really taking me, and why lie about it?

I hang back and ask, "Where are we going?"

Major Reid halts and lets his head fall back. After a sigh, he swivels around. "I already told you."

"You said we were going to Noah's office."

He points straight up. "Upstairs. In Tucker Securities."

This gives me a jolt of surprise. "We are below Tucker Securities? In Richmond?"

"Last I checked, you didn't need to know all the answers." He starts back down the hallway. "Let's go."

Reid leads me to the command center, and for once, nobody stops what they are doing to take notice of me. They continue to chat and laugh. Two men sitting in different stations toss an oblong brown ball back and forth. The wall monitors flash with different video streams.

Reid stops at a set of shiny copper doors that part in the center. He presses a round button that lights up on contact, then folds his hands in front of him. He stares at the doors, tapping two fingers against his arms as if to some unheard beat. Finally, the doors part to reveal a box with a bright white light inside.

Oh no. I have heard of these. "An elevator? Why not just teleport in?"

He steps inside. "No one teleports directly into the building from here. At least twenty-five percent of our people go in to work every day. That many men, that many hidden port signatures . . . Sort of gives up the fact that we're hiding something." He focuses on the wall to his right. "On or off, Mrs. Burke?"

I step aboard and try not to think about how the floor creaks. About the fact that my life hangs in the balance. Literally held by cables connected to this ancient piece of technology. "Is this thing safe?"

He laughs in a way that says my question is the most ridiculous thing he has ever heard, and punches a series of numbers on a keypad. He never answers me, but I do not care. I am too busy memorizing his eight-digit security code.

We arrive at our destination seconds later and he allows me to step out first. Dark tan Berber carpet leads under a solid glass wall into a spacious office surrounded by windows. The furniture—desk, chairs, and tables—is either cherrywood or covered in dark leather upholstery. The little bit of wall space is off-white.

Reid and I stand to the far left side of the office watching as a clean-shaven Noah stands behind his desk, buttoning his suit jacket—a grayish-blue pinstripe. The jacket forms around his tight frame with each button, causing warmth to swirl in my belly.

I immediately glance away, forcing my lungs to draw breath. I cannot keep doing this to myself. Will I ever be able to look at him without reacting this way? Do I want to? I am beginning to think some twisted part of me enjoys the torment of wanting a man I cannot have.

I return my attention to Noah, who watches the door leading out of his office expectantly. "Can he see us?"

"The glass is one-way and soundproof," Reid says. "No one will know we're here."

This is good to know, because had Noah's visitor seen me, my entire world would have turned upside down.

Declan enters the office and strolls across the space to meet Noah's waiting handshake, his gorgeous smile brightening the room.

CHAPTER 19

My muscles lock, torn between facing the inevitable and fleeing. I know Major Reid said that Declan cannot see me, but my thoughts stumble over one another, crushing all rational cognition. Nothing more than a piece of glass separates me from him. Them. Declan *and* Noah.

I fold my arms, tucking my quivering hands under them. "What is this about?" The words are as tight as my chest.

"You're supposed to look for any changes in your husband," Reid says. "Missing scars or something. Whatever will help prove he's been cloned."

I nod but do not tell him Declan would have no such distinguishing mark.

"Good to see you, Tucker." Declan's gaze shifts over Noah's shoulder to an area of wall flanked by two bookcases—an area hidden to me from where I stand. His smile falters for only a moment before blowing full force again.

"Mr. Burke. Very good to see you," Noah says, and motions toward a set of leather chairs. "Please sit."

I would like to sit too. Maybe put my head between my knees. But I cannot move to do so. I am both frozen by and sick from the scene taking place. The last time I witnessed Noah and Declan in the same room at one time, I had no idea who Noah was to me. Now is a different story.

Declan takes a seat seconds before Noah, and they both unbutton their suit jackets. Declan wears a dark shade of brown today. For the first time, I note the sharp contrasts between the two men I have loved. Where Noah is light and haloed in sunlight, Declan is dark and shadowed by his own lies. Where Noah's eyes glimmer with gold, Declan's are a raging, storm-chased sea.

"What is it I can do for you?" Noah asks. "I've taken the liberty of looking over recent reports, and it seems your system is up-to-date and running smoothly. Have you been experiencing issues?"

Declan rests an elbow on the arm of his chair and rubs his chin. "No, no. This visit is personal in nature."

Noah sinks further in his chair, crossing an ankle across his opposite knee. "I'm intrigued." He blasts Declan with his own devastating smile. I catch the aftershock and stumble over a breath.

Declan taps his fingers on the leather arm, watching them absently. "You know my wife is missing."

I gasp reflexively. My ex is coming to my ex about me?

"Yes," Noah says, his smile faltering and then disappearing completely. Declan misses the flash of anger in Noah's eyes, but I don't, and it only succeeds in feeding my dark, tormented side. "I'm sorry about that, but I don't see how I can help."

Declan leans forward, resting both elbows on his knees. He lowers his voice to just above a whisper and pins Noah with a solid gaze. "We're both businessmen. Taking risks and crossing lines is an everyday occurrence. Part of how we keep our businesses thriving."

The following pause is heavy and brimming with hidden meaning. It is as if Declan requires some sign from Noah that it is safe to continue.

Noah finally nods. "Go on."

"A business like yours with top-of-the-line security systems . . . you must be everywhere."

"Not everywhere, no."

"But you are connected to your clients. You have complete access to their systems and must see a great deal."

My God. He wants Noah to utilize the very system we use against him to *find me*. Who else has he approached with these outlandish favors?

Noah lets a long moment go by in silence. "What you're suggesting would be against the law, Mr. Burke."

Declan smiles and leans back. "Yes. It would. But who am I to judge?"

Noah sits forward and lowers his voice. "If you're under the impression I give myself the same access you have, you're mistaken." I step closer to the glass to hear better, hugging my middle. A tease of fog coats the surface. "The most I have is for testing purposes only. Quarterly upgrades. I wish—"

Declan raises his hands. "No need to go on, Mr. Tucker. I understand your position."

"Good." Noah leans back and hooks an elbow on the back of his chair. "Believe me. If it were in my power to help find your wife, I would."

Declan glances at the wall behind the desk again, frowns, then looks at Noah. I am curious now as to what he keeps looking at. "Off the record, Mr. Tucker, I would consider it a tremendous favor if you were to use your resources to keep an eye out for her. Or even just an ear to the ground. It's imperative I find her quickly."

Noah runs the length of his forefinger back and forth across his lips, eyes narrow while considering. Finally, he lowers his hand to his lap and nods once. "Off the record, consider it done."

His answer knots my stomach. I do not believe Noah will turn me over, but this conversation is steeped in the surreal. Witnessing the lengths Declan will go to find me . . .

"Maybe," Noah says, "you would be willing to do something for me in return."

Excuse me?

Declan tilts his head. "Name it." In two words I hear how he will kill, maim, or steal if Noah asks.

"I have a close relative who would like to see a particular woman jump to the head of the line."

What woman? What is Noah up to? First he wants to study clones; now he wants to *make* them? I hope this is not because I have refused to allow Sonya to study me. He would not do something as drastic as all that, would he?

"What's her current wait time?" Declan asks.

"A year."

"Send me her name. I'll see it gets done."

"Thank you. I'll be in touch on both counts."

Declan smiles and stands. "Then I won't waste any more of your time."

Noah stands and walks him to the door.

Declan begins to step out, then stops abruptly. "Oh, I almost forgot." He dips into an inside jacket pocket and hands Noah an envelope. "Invitation to our upcoming Fire and Ice Ball. You own a tux?"

Noah chuckles. "Of course."

Declan claps a hand over his shoulder. "I expect to see you there with a beautiful woman on your arm for once."

Noah ignores the comment and looks up from the invitation, a line creased between his eyes. "Masquerade?"

"Yes. In honor of my late mother. She loved the idea of masquerade balls. A night where everyone is given equal opportunity to hide who they really are. To become someone else."

Reid releases a single, hard laugh. "Now, there's irony for you."

"Why do you say that?"

"The man doesn't need a single night, or even a mask, to hide what he really is. He does it every day in plain sight."

I meet his gaze, biting back several retorts. While the statement is aimed at Declan, I am offended. If "what" Declan is is a clone, then I am just as low a creature in his mind.

"I cannot say I blame him for wanting to hide with people like you around to make being 'what' we are such a horrendous thing."

I direct my attention back into the room. Noah stands alone, tapping the invitation in his hand, deep in thought.

"Not horrendous," Reid says, and presses a button near the elevator. "Just unnatural."

The glass in front of me parts before I have a chance to respond, opening the width of a door.

Noah faces us. The brightness he had in his expression moments ago is gone. He looks exhausted and his eyes are bloodshot. "I wondered if you made it in time. What do you think?"

I step forward just enough to stand in the new opening. "There is nothing different from what I could make out." It is the truth. Other than a shorter haircut, and the already observed drop in muscle mass, Declan is no different to me. Proving him to be a clone will be impossible. "I think it is time to consider the possibility he is not a clone. Or at least move on to other avenues to use against him."

Reid laughs opposite me in the doorway. "No, Mrs. Burke, it is not time to do any such thing."

"There are plenty of ways to deal with Declan Burke that have nothing to do with cloning. Why not focus on those instead?"

He gives me a wide, toothy grin. "Because this is more fun. Besides, you aren't in some kind of hurry to end this, are you? Got places you need to be?"

I ignore the jibe, because going into how I want this over more than anyone in this room will fall on deaf ears. And not even for myself. Declan still wants my parents, but I have to believe they are hidden too well to fall victim. "Dr. Travista would have made Declan the prototype from which all men will be cloned. He is perfect. Short of Declan revealing the truth from his own lips, we will never find out."

"That's enough," Noah says, punctuating his order with a resigned sigh. "Maybe it's time we moved on to something else. We'll get him another way."

I am glad he agrees and that my time here in his office is at a quick end. I would like to shower and figure out what my next step should be regarding my parents. Leigh may be right in saying Sonya got to me earlier, but I would like some time alone to consider it.

I start for the elevator. "Sorry I could not be of any use."

"Emma, wait," Noah calls, then appears beside me as the down button lights up under my finger. His musk is an assault stoking a fire in my body. I would give anything for the strength to tamp it out. "Stay for a minute, will you?" He turns toward Reid. "You and I will talk later."

The elevator rumbles open and Noah maneuvers me aside to let Reid enter. I am torn between staying and getting inside the box with the man I would just as soon throw over a cliff than spend time with.

"Come back inside," Noah says when we are alone.

I follow him into the office and look around for the first time. Movement from Noah's side of the one-way glass catches my attention. The words "Tucker Securities" bounce around the wall in a no-nonsense font on a beige background. The wall must be the screen saver for his computer.

"Would you like something to drink?" he asks.

"No. Thank you." I pace down the wall and end up at one of two floor-to-ceiling bookshelves behind his desk.

He walks to the window and leans straight-armed on the ledge, squinting out at the sun-brightened city. I know he wants to talk about this morning but is unsure how to bring it up. Because I want to avoid the topic, he will get no help from me. Besides, I have a more important question for him.

"You are having someone cloned?"

His chin lowers to his chest. "We have to find the cloning facility. Whether or not the volunteer will end up needing to complete the process depends on how things go."

So he is not doing it for the purpose of studying us. That is a relief. "I hope for her sake she will not have to."

"Me too."

I trace my fingers along the spines of his books and read a few of the titles. Business economics. I am not sure if this is better or worse than the books in Dr. Travista's office.

Noah turns and leans a hip on the ledge. "What did you think of Burke? Other than the possible cloning, I mean. Any thoughts?"

"I thought a lot. Like, for instance, I wonder how you plan to give him information regarding my whereabouts."

He presses his fingers into his eyes and rubs. "Let me worry about that. I'll come up with something. Anything else?"

"He seems desperate."

"How so?"

"He came here and asked you to break the law for him. From his perspective, you are a powerful man who could potentially find out what is really going on here. That I am not a captive but a willing participant of the resistance. Why take the risk?"

Noah's head tilts ever so slightly. "Because he loves you."

A simple reason that speaks volumes. I understand more than he realizes because I would risk everything for him and Adrienne. But that is my weight to bear, not his. I shake my head and look away from the glow in his eyes.

I walk past the bookshelf to the section of bare wall where Declan kept looking minutes before. My attention lands immediately on the painting and I gasp in surprise. Tears sting my eyes.

I finger the paint strokes creating waves on a beach. The sunset. The luckenbooth cleverly hidden in the sand dunes and beach grass. The sign I once told Noah would be my way of expressing my love for him. The only question is if this is the original we painted in Playa de Oro together or the one he purchased at my show. I am almost afraid to ask.

Noah passes behind me, then leans a shoulder on the wall beside the canvas. He tucks his hands in his pockets, making his suit jacket flare back. His amber gaze is bright as it sweeps between me and the art that once meant the world to me.

"You seem surprised to see it," he says.

I swallow a lump in my throat. "No, not really. You helped paint it if I recall correctly." It is not a direct way of asking, but I have to know.

Noah releases a slow breath, stands upright, then positions himself at my shoulder. "I wish I could take the credit, but this is all yours." He looks down at me. "An original by Emma and Emma alone."

He reminds me of a time I have not thought of in months. The moment the original version was painted, how he changed the colors in my sunset and added the first luckenbooth to the sand dunes.

But while this is a perfect re-creation, a clone of the original, it is *not* the same. It is mine. All mine. And he kept it.

My stomach flutters and I step back until I am stopped by the edge of his desk. I grip the curved wooden sides with straight arms. Noah sits to my right and crosses his arms. The two of us stare at the painting, a reminder of the time we once shared and lost. Something I held on to even when its meaning made absolutely no sense to me.

After a full minute passes, he bumps his shoulder against mine. "I'm sorry."

I blink up at my painting, desperately working to check my emotions. "You seem to be doing a lot of apologizing lately."

"I know, but—"

I bump his shoulder to cut him off and meet his eyes. "It is okay. Really. And I am sorry too. Especially for what my return is doing to your relationship with Sonya. The last thing I want to do is cause a rift between you two."

He chuckles. The gleam in his eyes is startling and warm. Encompassing. "You aren't sorry, but thanks. It means a lot that you care enough to lie. Even if it is badly."

I roll my eyes and smile toward my painting. Looking at him makes me forget my place. "I hate how you see right through me."

"It took years to discover your tell."

I gape at him. "I do not have a tell." All those months of lying to Declan and Dr. Travista are proof enough for me.

"You do. Your right eyelid twitches like you want to wink. It's cute."

His smile turns into a laugh, which makes me laugh. And just like that, we slip into that place of ease, where nothing outside our bubble matters. The tension dissipates like water on a hot day.

Then the laughter fades and is replaced with the blinding realization of proximity. Body heat. His soft musk, which I have always been fond of, even when I thought I loved Declan.

Noah's gaze lowers to where I have bitten my lip in an effort to stifle the sudden longing to kiss him. He wets his lips and I hold my breath.

He is going to kiss me.

He is not free to kiss me. Get off this desk. Try a chair. One far, far away.

But I do not move. Not even when the space between us begins to close. Whether this is my doing or his is unknown, and I cannot bring myself to care.

He tears out of the thrall first, and I release a long, silent breath. Stand upright. He follows suit and we walk to opposite sides of the desk, where we face each other.

There is no sense in denying what just occurred. What *has been* occurring. "We cannot keep doing this," I say.

His intentions are confusing. If he wants to be with me, why stay with Sonya? Unless he expects to make me the other woman, which I refuse wholeheartedly. No matter his reasons, I need for him to make up his mind. Maybe then I can move past this.

He casts his gaze down and braces himself with straight arms on the desk. "You're right. We can't. This thing with Burke could end soon. You'll have your freedom."

He does not say . . . *and you'll leave again.* The words lie there in the way he looks at me. Already hurt by the act I have yet to perform. Except I do not believe for a second the doubt is born of his own mind, but rather Sonya's. And he believes her.

I have made a huge mistake. "Maybe it would be best for everyone if we stayed away from each other for a while." My voice sounds tight. Renegade tears brim my eyelids.

Noah meets my eyes and very slowly begins to nod. "Agreed."

The acknowledgment stings, proving that no matter what he or Sonya believes, I am the one who will end up hurt by all of this. In fact, I already am.

CHAPTER 20

A note from Miles on my door invites me back to the command center. I wanted to be alone, but maybe a distraction would be the healthier option. Too much has happened today, and I will only end up wallowing in self-pity if I stay in my room. I have to move past this as quickly as possible or I will drown.

Miles lounges behind a desk in the command center. He is also deep in the cooler-than-necessary room, so I have to wade through the bodies standing around, suffering their unwanted attention. A few men do not move, forcing me to push against them. By the time I reach Miles, I am irritated on top of everything else.

He sits with his booted feet up on the desk, a tablet computer resting against his lap. While he looks at ease, I am keenly aware of the hum of male voices and how they surround me on all sides. My nerves jump, prepared for any of them to attack, verbally or otherwise.

Miles does not look up when I stop beside him, so I swipe at his feet and they drop like rocks. The blond woman sitting on his other side turns toward us. His partner, Farrah Styles.

Startled, Miles rocks forward and reaches into his right ear, where he removes a wireless earbud. "Jesus, Wade."

"Is there a reason why we had to meet in here?" My tone snaps unnecessarily, drawing the attention of the analyst at a nearby desk, but I am too wound up to care.

He reaches around me and pulls forward a chair on wheels. "Have a seat."

"I do not want—"

"*Have*"—he hands me a spare set of earbuds—"a seat. Have you met Farrah?"

I palm the blue-and-silver buds and sit. Farrah gives me a tight-lipped smile and I mirror the action precisely. "Not exactly. Nice to meet you."

"Hey," she says, and starts winding her long braid up into a low-hanging bun.

I lean toward Miles. "What am I doing here?"

He sends a thumb over his shoulder at Farrah. "We saw something earlier I thought you'd like to see."

"Did Declan do something?" He has yet to speak to the press about Ruby's death, so it is still likely he will find a way to spin this in a way to aid in his search for me.

"No. This is something else. Some*one* else." He rolls up to the keyboard inlaid in the wood of his desk. All four of his monitors blink on to a bright-blue screen.

Farrah glances furtively between me and Miles. "Major Reid doesn't want her—"

"Do I need to put you in a corner?" Miles asks without looking up.

Farrah seethes in silence and I bite back a grin. This is exactly the sort of distraction I need.

"What happened?" I ask.

"Our friend Daxton made a rare visit to his father's office this morning."

The four screens flick on to a paused scene, shown from different angles. Daxton is frozen in midstep as he walks into an office nearly the size of Declan's. The room is visually cold. Minimalistic. A floor-to-ceiling window wraps around one side and behind the desk. Early morning light glares in and reflects off glossed wood furniture. An older man whom I recognize as Evan Thomas sits behind the desk staring at a flat computer monitor. His silver hair lies in combed-back, natural waves.

I have just inserted the earbuds when Miles starts the footage. Daxton stops two steps inside the office, and the automatic door slides shut behind him. Evan does not look up, and Daxton tucks his hands in his pockets. The cold wall between them is palpable from here.

"Good morning, son," Daxton mimics in a deep voice. *"You're looking well."*

Evan glances at his son from the corner of his eye. *"What is it, Daxton? I'm busy. Someone told the media the resistance killed Mrs. Godfrey. But* someone *didn't give any details. Now* someone *has to produce proof."*

A chill races over my spine, and only a small part is due to the derision in Evan's tone. This happened this morning, which means Evan is the one who spun the poison story.

A corner of Daxton's lips lifts. *"Someone had to do it."*

Evan pushes away from his desk and faces his son. His fingers fold over a crossed knee. The pointed arches of thick eyebrows, the set of his lips, the arctic freeze in his eyes . . . Everything about him speaks of dangerous calculation. This man is practiced in the art of not reacting, and of course he is. He never failed as a double agent for Andrew Burke, and he has the position and power to prove it.

"You never think," Evan finally says in a tone that could just as easily have said *I like your suit.*

Daxton raises a hand while strolling closer to the desk. *"Now, that's where you're wrong."*

Evan motions for Daxton to sit. *"Pray tell, son. Let's hear your master plan. We both know you have one."*

Daxton unbuttons his jacket before folding into a chair. *"Let's just say that by the time I'm done, the board will hold a vote of no confidence in Declan Burke. Burke Enterprises will be yours for the taking. Ours."*

Evan lets a smile slide across his face that fails to meet his eyes. He steeples his fingers against his lips. *"Is that so? You have it all planned out, do you?"*

Daxton leans forward, his expression alight and hungry. *"Once the board learns Burke's own wife, the woman he's been dumping millions of dollars to find, is the Original Clone—"*

"No." Evan cuts him off with this single, cold word. He has not moved, but the minute narrowing of his eyes speaks volumes. *"Drawing negative attention to the clone project could be fatal to everything we've done."*

"What are you talking about? Arthur Travista is murdering human beings to complete the clone process and nobody cares. In fact, the government is begging him to do it. Hell, they're funding part of it."

"Any further attention could lead to the WTC project, and none of us wants that."

I straighten in my chair and dig the earbuds out of my ears. "What WTC project?"

Miles pauses the video, sits up, and exchanges a look with Farrah. According to the tight look on her face, she is against answering any of my questions. An eternity seems to pass before he answers in a hushed voice. "They're talking about clones. Put two and two together."

Farrah groans and spins to face her own quad set of screens.

I am too shocked to care what she thinks. "Clone" is not a word that should *ever* be synonymous with WTC. Ever. Unless . . . "Are they cloning the girls? Are you certain?"

Miles shrugs. "This is the first I'm hearing of anything remotely close to it, but this is Burke we're talking about. The man has no ceiling."

Before I left Declan I had discovered he had organized the kidnapping of young girls in the west to fill his training centers. He truly believes he will single-handedly save our race by not allowing those women to go to waste in a world that needs them so badly. It would not surprise me in the least if he were to go this far with his cloning project.

Then again, he cares enough about the girls in his centers to change their harsh treatment—or so he led me to believe. Maybe I am jumping to conclusions. There has to be another explanation.

I tuck the earbuds back in, sure the rest of the conversation will reveal more. Miles takes the cue and resumes the video. He rolls his chair close. His shoulder rests against mine and I feel the rise and fall of each breath.

In the video, Daxton leans back and drapes an elbow over the back of his chair. *"Not if we're proactive. We control the flow of information."*

"Like you controlled the leaked information about Ruby Godfrey? You left too many questions unanswered. Now here I am, cleaning up your mess. You lack the control needed to follow this plan through to fruition."

"Then help me. You want this company. I know you do. Let's take it together."

Evan's hands ease back into his lap. *"Your entire plan hinges on proving Emma Burke is the Original Clone."* This is not a question.

"That's part of it, yes. I want to show her connection to Ruby Godfrey, which will eventually reveal she's a clone. For the coup de grâce, I'll reveal her connection to the resistance. Burke won't have a single rock to hide under."

"I can't support this action."

Daxton grunts a humorless chuckle. *"Which part, exactly?"*

Evan purses his lips. *"I have work to do."*

The two stare, unflinching, until Daxton finally rises from the chair and buttons his suit jacket. *"Give my best to Mother."*

When Daxton reaches to activate the door, Evan says, *"I suggest you reconsider. The moment you bring the girl into it, Declan Burke will come down on you before you even utter the words pertaining to the next stage of your plan."*

Daxton smiles. *"I'm not worried."*

I remove the earbuds, disappointed I did not learn more about the plan using the WTCs. But I have come to a huge realization. This is bigger than any of us imagined. Bigger than what is happening with Noah. Bigger than building a relationship with my daughter. Bigger than my search for Stephen and Lily Wade.

Declan has to be stopped. Especially if he and Dr. Travista are involving the girls living in the WTCs.

I stand. "We need to tell Noah about this." I start for the aisle and stop because I was actually headed back up to Noah's office. The exact place I need to avoid. I turn and face Miles. "I mean you. You need to tell him."

Farrah looks up from her screens. "Major Reid has already been informed. He will handle it from there." She shoots a narrow look at Miles. "And I want it stated for the record that I had nothing to do with involving a civilian."

Miles's typical easygoing personality changes to irate so fast it is as if someone flipped a switch. "What the fuck is your pr—"

"You were never here," I cut in. I cannot have any more problems arise because of me today. "In fact, I was never here either. I do not know anything."

She leans back in her chair and seems to consider whether I can be trusted. Swiveling back to her screens, she says, "Good."

Miles stands with an eye roll and takes me by the elbow. "Come on, Wade. Let's go get a drink. You look like you need it." He glares at Farrah. "I know I do." He waves an arm in the air, his attention focused across the room. "Bennett. Birmingham. Happy hour. Let's do this."

Leigh and I are the only two in the cafeteria. Dinner has long since been served, and it is so late that my eyelids droop. We sit across from each other at a long table, our backs to a cold, hard wall. Our drinks and a nearly empty bottle of whiskey sit between us. A line of dimmed lights over a clean, stainless food line is our only illumination. If not for the occasional lift and sip across from me, I would have thought Leigh had fallen asleep. I wonder if, like me, she is avoiding her dreams.

"I volunteered to be cloned." Leigh says this softly, yet in the quiet room, the sound could have been a grenade. The subject matter itself is atomic.

I sit up and stare for a protracted moment, unable to find the right words. What exactly do you say to someone about to throw her life away? "Why would you do that?"

She takes a slow sip of her whiskey. "The lie I would tell you is that I'm doing it for the good of women everywhere. Because someone has to and this is a surefire way of finding the cloning facility."

"And the truth?"

She fingers the rim of her glass. "The truth is I want what you have. I want a family."

A rising sense of panic claws up my chest. She cannot really mean to do this. I spin to face her and my boots slap against the floor. "You have no idea what you are giving up for a family you can get another way. The girls we rescue in the WTCs need homes. You could adopt."

"And a husband? Can I adopt him?" She laughs, but there is no humor in it. "Men, even our men, still only want a woman who can give them a child that is legitimately theirs."

"I do not believe that. Look at Noah. He is building a life with Sonya, yes?"

She narrows her eyes at me. "You can't be that blind. With you around, that relationship is on a fast track to Failsville."

A knot forms in my stomach. "You are changing the subject."

One of her perfectly sculpted eyebrows lifts. "I didn't bring up Tucker. You did."

Oh God. I did. I have to find a way to cleanse myself of him. "He is the only example I have."

Leigh turns to face me and cups her glass between her palms. She nibbles her lower lip for a moment, then says, "I was going to ask your opinion earlier, thinking I had more time, but then the timetable moved up. I had to make a decision, so I made it. I think it's the right one."

"It is *not* the right one. You do not want this."

"Give me one good reason why being a clone is such a hardship for you."

"Well, for one—"

"Your clock has been reset," she goes on as if I had said nothing. "You don't have to worry about losing your chance to have a family for at least another twenty to thirty years, and by then you'll be done."

"I also deal with a double standard nobody seems to think exists. What is the first thing you think about when you look at me? Do you see Emma Wade, the woman you hated once upon a time, or do you see a clone, the experiment with Emma Wade's face?"

She cannot look at me now because she knows I speak the truth.

"You are not the only one," I say. "Everyone looks at me as if I am some kind of freak. The only peace I get is when I am out in the world, where nobody knows me as anything other than a human woman. You do not want this; believe me."

"You think I don't know about double standards? At least after the cloning I can offer someone the family I can't now. Being able to do that, I can suffer the rest. I *will* suffer the rest." She stands and looks down at me. "I'm not looking for your permission. Just your acceptance. Tell me that when this is all over, I have a friend in my corner."

My heart breaks for her. How can she think otherwise? "Without question."

A smile cracks her serious expression and she breathes out a heavy breath. "Okay, good. You had me worried there for a sec."

I stand and we meet at the end of the table. "One thing is for certain," I tell her as we link elbows and begin to walk out. "You will know who your true friends are when it is all over."

"Who were yours?"

"From the beginning, it was always Foster. He never treated me any different. Declan, too, I suppose, but I do not count him. That is a different situation entirely. Not even Noah . . ." I pause and bite back all the negative phrases that come to mind. None of them is fair. "That was different, too."

"Nobody else?"

I shake my head. "What Dr. Travista did to me is unbelievable. How can anyone blindly accept me as the Emma they knew? Especially since I do not have all my memories. Maybe that will make all the difference for you."

She pauses outside the cafeteria. "If not, who needs them anyway? I can start from scratch, right? You'll be there."

"And Foster. I cannot imagine Miles will treat you any different either."

"No, I guess not." She gives me a small smile. "Thanks, Clone."

"Anytime, Human."

CHAPTER 21

Dr. Travista takes a long moment to study the still shot taken two winters ago. *"Emma was not a patient at that point,"* he says, and slides his glasses back on. *"But she was grateful to me for her remission, and volunteered to sit with Ruby Godfrey. She even tried to teach her to paint."* He chuckles. *"Ruby didn't take to the brush as well as Emma, but they enjoyed trying."*

"Would you consider them to be close friends?" the interviewer asks offscreen.

The doctor nods. A slow smile forms on his face. *"Of course they were. Emma cared for Ruby a great deal. She must be devastated by this news. Wherever she is."*

Noah asks me to take Adrienne at breakfast so he can meet the soon-to-arrive colonel. Sonya must be tied up somewhere because she never came down to eat with them. He looks wary to ask the favor, but I take the opportunity without hesitation. This is the first time in a week he has spoken to me. The first time he has looked me in the eye. He even brushes my hand in the pass-off of our daughter.

I want the moment to last, but he has erected a wall I cannot get past. He has made a clear effort to remain devoted to Sonya, and I promised myself I would let him go. It just may take more time than I would like.

Instead of going directly to day care, we walk around the hub for a while. She points at things and I tell her what they are called. She tries repeating most words, though combining certain sounds appears difficult. I begin to make out her particular sound pattern, though. What was only noise before becomes simple words.

We see Noah with Reid and the colonel at one point. Colonel Updike is average in height and quite a bit older according to the lines creasing his forehead and around his eyes. Despite his age, he is very attractive. He is bald and cleanly shaven, and sharp angles make up his bone structure. Muscles outline his arms and define his shoulders under his dark-brown T-shirt.

They are far enough away that we go unnoticed by Reid and the colonel, but Noah seems to sense us and turns. My heart gallops. I was supposed to take Adrienne to day care and I have clearly not done so. But he waves and turns back around, making it okay.

The rest of the morning passes quickly. She naps in my room for an hour; then we have lunch together in the cafeteria. It has been an exhausting yet perfect day. One I should feel guilty about wasting but do not. I need to work on figuring out what to do about Declan, but this time with Adrienne is precious.

Begrudgingly, I return Adrienne to day care. Once inside the room, she wriggles from my arms, takes my finger, and drags me to a low-lying round table. Multicolored shapes and crayons bounce along the touch-screen surface.

"Adrienne, I need to go bye-bye," I say.

"No." The one word is practiced; she says it with the skill of an adult, unlike everything else.

Adrienne pulls me down to sit and slaps the table. A menu of sorts appears. Coloring pages, virtual storybooks, stacking games . . .

I look around, and when none of the caregivers seem to notice or care that I am here, I tap COLORING PAGES, then GIRLS, then PRINCESSES. A large sheet of paper appears on the screen and Adrienne pulls the image toward her. The scene is from a princess story, complete with a pumpkin and a prince calling to the fleeing princess from a grand staircase. He looks desperate for her to return. Under the "paper" is a perfect row of crayons.

Adrienne crawls into my lap and leans over the colors. She hums a high-pitched *hmmm,* as if she cannot decide, then hits the pink. She begins swiping her palm around the screen, and pink strokes follow her movement. When done, she hits the green and repeats the process. She goes through all the colors in a very short period of time, then starts over.

I hug Adrienne's small, warm frame and dip my nose to the crown of her head, filling my lungs with the sweet berry scent of her hair. She scribbles away on the table, unaware of how much I already love her.

I am setting her up with a clean coloring sheet when a strange male voice fills the space. "Well, that looks fun. Mind if we join?"

The man walks up to our table with Noah and Reid on his heels.

Adrienne beams and reaches for Noah, who scoops her up without hesitation. "Emma, this is Colonel Updike."

I stand and reach out to shake his hand. "It is nice to meet you, Colonel."

He frowns and exchanges a look with Noah and Reid. He then gives me a small smile that makes his already thin lips disappear. "You don't remember me?" He has a low, comforting timbre to his voice, which helps me relax.

"My memory is very limited."

He scratches the cleft in his chin. "That's too bad. Well, anyway, if you aren't busy, I thought we could go somewhere and talk. Privately."

Privately? Why on earth would he need to talk to me privately?

I look at Noah, who gives no hint as to what this is about. After a long moment he nods once, urging me to agree to the meeting.

"Okay," I say. "Where would you like to talk?"

"Outside. I'd like you to come somewhere with me."

Outside? My heart flings itself against my ribs once, good and hard.

"Disguise yourself," he says, and heads for the exit. "Meet me in the command center in five minutes."

Noah hangs back as the colonel and Reid disappear. Adrienne rests on his hip, her little arms snaked around his neck.

"What is going on?" I ask him.

"He'll keep you safe," he whispers, casting a furtive glance around at the nearby caregivers, who ignore us.

"That is not what I asked."

He shakes his head, then smiles at Adrienne. "Daddy has to go back to work, chicken. Be a good girl for Alicia and Renae."

"Noah—"

"It's not my place," he cuts in, and sets Adrienne down. He pats her diapered butt and says, "Go play."

She runs off and into the arms of one of the girls. Noah watches for a moment, then leads me out of the room.

"Should I be worried?"

"No. Listen . . ." He trails off and faces me, his eyes cast down. "Just take care of yourself out there, okay? I have to go."

He turns away and leaves me with my heart stone still in my chest. *Take care of myself?* What does that mean? Why could he not look at me?

I have no time to consider this if I am to make it back to the command center, fully disguised, in time to meet the colonel. The best I can do with the little time remaining is to wrap a dark blue scarf over my head. The material is large enough that I am able to twist the length of my hair into a low-hanging knot, concealing every dark strand. I wish I had my old sunglasses but make do with a pair I find in "Emma's" box that are rectangular and tinted blue. I want to wear my leather jacket, but it will be too warm outside, so I stick with my black tank top and jeans.

Colonel Updike waits for me near the teleporters wearing a brown leather shoulder holster for a single HK pistol. The sight of his weapon gives me pause. He wants to take me outside and does not bother to conceal his gun?

With the way Noah was acting, a horrible thought surfaces. The colonel could be luring me to my very own assassination. The resistance would be better off without me around. With Declan searching the world for me, I can only bring them trouble.

I stop in front of him and he leans close to whisper, "You're wearing your suspicious face."

"Should I be worried about the gun you carry?"

"Only if you plan to attack me, in which case, definitely."

He looks amused, and I feel ridiculous for suspecting the worst. "I am sorry, but Major Reid has made it clear he suspects me of working for Declan, and he is not the only one. You understand my hesitation."

"Believe it or not, Ms. Wade, I like to draw my own conclusions and don't listen to idle gossip."

He turns and steps into a teleporter. "Have you been to San Francisco Island in your recent travels?"

I step inside the tube. "No."

"Good. You used to like visiting new places. Is that still the case?"

The last time I fawned over a city was my first visit into Richmond, but that was because, at the time, I had no memory of seeing a city outside of pictures in a book. The West America states are different from the East. I have yet to find a city I can appreciate. "Loose" is a word I would use to describe the West. There is no control in the freedom they allow themselves there.

"Not really," I tell him.

He punches in a port number and says, "Well, you always loved San Fran. Let's see if that's still the case."

The scent of spearmint encompasses the teleporter, and the hub blends into sunlit, foot-traffic-heavy streets. Except the "street" is an eight-lane high-street expressway with a wide pedestrian walkway. A shoulder-high guardrail separates us from an impressive drop into a fog-laden city.

Silver and blue structures escape the low cloud cover with pointed tops. Identical high streets like this one curve throughout the sky, weaving around the tops of skyscrapers and in and out of the dense fog.

We step outside, and a strong, cool wind threatens my balance. Goose bumps rise on my arms. While the sunlight glares, the wind off the Pacific cuts off any heat. I should have worn my jacket.

Colonel Updike leads me to the railing on our side of the street. The fog below ends in an impenetrable roll over the Pacific Ocean, which shines a murky blue. I have learned that the ocean water near land is too polluted to swim in, though the governments are working diligently to clean it up. They seem to have made tremendous progress here in comparison to some of the other cities I have been to.

From here I make out part of the forty-mile suspension bridge that takes travelers to the mainland and into Los Angeles. The structure is solid silver with beautiful curves for guardrails snaking along the sides. I find it hard to believe that, once upon a time, none of this existed. I have heard stories of the quakes shifting the land in opposite directions, and of magma bursting up to create islands, but they seem like mere fairy tales in light of this view.

"Look over there." Colonel Updike points in the opposite direction of the bridge. He has to yell so I can hear over the rush of wind. "That's where we're going."

Floating in the ocean are islands with lush greenery making up the base, and honeycomb windows linked together and leafing out like enormous flower petals. Suspension bridges link all of them together.

"Lily communities," he says.

I see how the shape lends to the name "lily" but am clueless how the community part comes in to play. "What are they exactly?"

"Self-sustaining islands, roughly twenty miles in diameter apiece, with everything to meet the community's needs. They recycle their own waste, produce their own food, and are completely solar powered. Each pad farms fresh seawater fish, which they manage using a filtering system to keep out the impurities in the ocean water."

Interesting. "And why are we going there?"

"I have an apartment there." He lays a hand on the small of my back. "Come on. Let's rent a vehicle."

We walk for nearly a half mile in silence while I take in the incredible views of the island. I wish I could see the city below the fog, but maybe it is for the best. My experience with the other cities must hold true here, too, which would ruin the effect.

While the area seems to be a place of peace, the one thing telling me otherwise is the weapon-laden pedestrians. Colonel Updike is not the only one carrying a gun. Not that anyone appears to need one. Not a single fight, verbal or otherwise, has broken out. Maybe the guns are a deterrent to anyone who would cause trouble.

A parking lot curves off the main road, and Colonel Updike leads me into the area. "Car or motorcycle?"

If I have ever been on a motorcycle, I have no memory of it, but I think I will like it. "Motorcycle."

With a nod, he chooses a sleek, black bike. He stops at a stand where a computerized male voice speaks to him. "Cash or credit?"

Colonel Updike taps the credit button on the rectangular touch screen.

"Place thumb on biometric scanner," the voice instructs, and after the colonel does so, the voice says, "Thank you, Nathanial Updike. Enjoy your stay on San Francisco Island."

I wait for him to climb on before straddling the black leather seat behind him. He uses his thumb on another scanner to start the motor, which sends a mild vibration throughout my body.

Seconds later, we weave in and out of traffic on the high streets, taking turns with ease. We never dip below the low cloud cover and are far beyond it by the time the expressway slopes toward the surface.

We take a suspension bridge across the water to one of a dozen lily communities. A sign near the island itself reads LILY STATION 6 and WELCOME HOME.

After parking, we enter through a set of glass doors and travel down a long hallway that ends in an open, round space. The dome, which would make up the center of the lily, is also constructed of honeycomb-shaped glass. The "petals" of the station rise around us on all sides for what seems like miles. Glass elevators travel between the stories.

The air smells heavily of seawater. Green plant life bursts from large pots and entwines columns. The floor, too, is glass, showcasing the ocean below our feet. Seaweed floats against the surface with an array of sea life swimming in and around each green vine.

Colonel Updike's apartment is on the twelfth floor. It is an expansive room with glass facing the Pacific, white walls, and sand-colored tiles. The room's furniture is sparse, and what there is looks square and uncomfortable.

I hang my sunglasses from the front of my tank and sniff the sweet-scented air. "Do I smell a cigar?" Peter always smoked a cigar at the end of every day on his front porch.

"Probably," he says, and chuckles. "Connelly!"

From the outside deck, a head peeks around a lounge chair. His thick, tight, white curls flutter in a heavy breeze, and his black skin has a sheen of sweat from the sun. A white-toothed grin lengthens once he sets his dark eyes on us.

I start for the glass doors, a smile on my face. "Peter?"

CHAPTER 22

Peter sets his cigar in an ashtray beside the lounge chair and opens his arms to me. "Little dove," he says in a vibrating baritone.

I melt into his strong embrace and inhale the strong, sweet scent clinging to his button-down shirt. Underneath is the distinct scent of his horses, which brings with it a sense of serenity. It feels as if years have passed since my stay with him in Montana, rather than weeks.

I look up at him. "What are you doing here?"

He nods behind me to where Colonel Updike watches us from the railing. "Ask him."

The sky behind the colonel is a clear blue with a small scattering of white clouds. He wears a faint smile and looks relaxed, while I am fraught with confusion. From the moment I met this man, I have been both on edge and at ease.

I leave the enclosure of Peter's hug and face Colonel Updike. "Colonel?"

He lifts a white eyebrow. "You used to call me Nate, you know. And since this is an informal meeting of old friends, I think it's more than appropriate, don't you?"

That remains to be seen. "Okay, fine, but—"

"Peter and I will explain everything, but in the meantime, why don't you have a seat. I'll get us all a drink." He points to Peter. "You better have another one of those cigars for me when I get back."

When Colonel Updike disappears into the apartment, I face Peter. "What is going on around here?"

"Always so impatient to get answers. They aren't going anywhere." He motions for me to sit in a chair that angles off the white railing.

I draw in a calming breath and try to gather my racing thoughts. I cannot imagine why or how I have ended up in this situation, but at least I know now that I am in no danger.

Once seated, I say, "Things are different now. I have little time for patience these days. Declan is looking for my parents, which means I have to find them first."

Miles and I have spent every spare moment he has searching but have come up empty. He is a good friend and tries to hide how discouraged he is becoming, but I am not blind. I am just glad that Declan has had about as much luck as I have in finding them. They are still safe somewhere.

"Yes, I know," he says. "I've seen the news."

I begin unraveling the scarf from my head. It feels good to let the wind blow through my hair. "But that is only part of it. Things are time sensitive, and even being here now . . . Do not get me wrong. It is great to see you, but this thing with Declan could lead to something about me becoming public if I cannot stop him first."

"Is this about you being the Original Clone?"

A flush races through my body. I had not told him for fear of judgment. "How did you know?"

"I told him." Colonel Updike appears with a bottle of liquor in one hand and three glasses pinched in the fingers of his other.

Peter takes one of the glasses and rests it on his jean-clad knee. "I'm surprised you didn't tell me yourself."

"We barely know each other."

He tilts his head and one side of his lips curves up just enough to hint at a deep dimple. "Some things are beyond reason. I don't offer a home to everyone who pops in unannounced. No one, in fact."

Colonel Updike hands me a glass with two fingers full of an amber liquid. "He's a damn good judge of character, which is why you aren't locked in a jail cell right now."

I set my untouched drink on the glass table beside me. "Noah—"

"—couldn't save you if I wanted you locked up for safekeeping." The colonel sits and begins cutting the end off a cigar. "I know you remember a small part of your life before, but you lived with Declan Burke for months as his wife. Until I heard from Peter, I was on my way to handle your return myself."

Both men watch me with raised brows that burrow deep lines in their foreheads.

I shift uneasily and rub damp palms down my pant legs. "You said before you do not listen to gossip."

"I don't. Facts are not gossip or speculation. You would have been jailed until my questions were satisfied."

"So you are satisfied I am not a spy?"

"I am." He tucks the cigar into one side of his mouth and his teeth clamp down on the end.

"Then what am I doing here, Colonel?"

His brown eyes narrow as he draws in a deep drag. Ashes form on the burning end.

Peter reaches out and clasps my knee. "We want to offer you a choice."

I look at Colonel Updike, my heart tripping in my chest. "I did not realize I needed choices. Do I?"

Peter leans away and sips his drink. "I offered you a place to call home, and the proposition stands." He waves a hand dismissively in the air. "I don't care about this clone stuff. You're an innocent girl who deserves some peace."

"That is kind of you to say, thank you, but I could never put you in that position. If Declan were to find me—"

"You would let me worry about that if the time came. I'm old, not helpless."

"Even so, I cannot leave my daughter again."

Colonel Updike clears his throat and lays his arms along the sides of his chair. "Your other option, then, is to reenlist with the resistance."

I find it hard to breathe suddenly. Reenlist? Become that woman who murdered her way into a WTC only to end up shot and dying? "That is not a choice. That is insanity."

"It's been made clear to me you're still capable of—"

"But I am not that woman anymore. I have not struggled to maintain my freedom just to enlist in your army."

The men exchange a look; then Colonel Updike says, "Emma, I can't let you live in the hub unless you're enlisted or married to someone who is. It's just the way things are."

"I am married," I say automatically, and a sense of relief washes over me. Nothing has to change. "To Noah."

He sits deeper in his chair and rubs a hand across his chin. "Tucker and I have already been through this. Your marriage dissolved the second your death certificate was signed. Is it a technicality? Yes. But I can't make any exceptions."

Not married? It is one thing to know I cannot have him anymore, but quite another to know our marriage is legally over. At least before I still had that part of him. For a little while longer, at least.

Tears prick my eyes. "You would make me leave my daughter if I said no?"

The colonel sits forward and rests his elbows on his knees "You would have visitation rights, of course. As often as you want. But, Emma . . . I don't want you to leave. We need you."

I cannot believe I am hearing this. Why is everyone set on stripping me of my freedoms?

Colonel Updike swallows the remains of his drink. "Take the day to decide, but tonight you'll go with Peter or myself, and it will be final. I'm sorry, Emma. Truly."

"We only want to keep you safe," Peter adds.

They cannot do this to me. I will not let them.

Adrenaline rages through me until I am shaking. I stand with fists clenched at my sides. My heart thunders all the way to my temples. "You forgot to mention the option where I am free to go," I say, and storm into the apartment.

I have no destination in mind, only that I will not have these two men dictate my future for me. Thank God I had the foresight to wear Declan's wedding ring around my neck and can sell it in the first pawnshop I find on San Francisco Island.

By the time I open the front door, my chest feels tight and my vision blurs with a building of tears. Will this mean giving up rights to my family? Noah will understand, right? This is not desertion, but preservation. He will let me visit Adrienne. She is my daughter.

But five steps outside the lily community, I am fully aware of the mistake I am about to make. My stung pride clouds my judgment. I cannot last on the outside without help, and no excuse I tell myself makes leaving Adrienne okay.

I stroll to the bridge walkway and sit on a white bench. Seagulls peck the cement walk around me. A cool, strong, brine-laden wind catches my loose hair up from behind and shoves it forward, where the thick strands cloud my field of vision. I should not be outside without my scarf, but I cannot bring myself to return for it. Not yet. Not until I decide what to do. Enlist or let the world go to hell around me while I watch, stripping me of a normal life. A life with only visitation of my daughter. Groaning, I prop my elbows on my knees and bury my face in my hands.

"Is it really that bad?"

I peek out, glare at Peter, and cover my face again. "How can you ask that?"

The bench creaks to my right with additional weight. "Tell me what you're thinking. Maybe I can help walk you through this decision."

I sit back and hug my knees to my chest. "I think I already know the answer."

"You aren't coming with me, are you?"

"I made the mistake of leaving my daughter once. What kind of parent does that?"

"You can't beat yourself up over the past. Parents make impossible decisions every day, doing what they feel is best at the time. You're no different."

"Adrienne was hours old and I was selfish. Even if I could not stay for Noah, I should have stayed for *her*." I focus on the roll of fog on the other side of the bridge, a blanket over San Francisco Island. Electric cars whisper past us, occasionally obstructing my view. "I suppose I am paying for my mistakes now. Sonya is Adrienne's mother. Noah's girlfriend."

We sit in silence for a long moment before he says, "You could come with me and bring Adrienne along. I wouldn't be opposed to the idea. Even Noah can't deny she'd be safer away from the hub."

For a second, the suggestion feels like a viable alternative. I cannot have my husband back but do not have to live without my daughter.

Then reality sinks in. I might be her mother, but that does not give me any right to her. And Noah loves her too much to take her out of his sight.

I shake my head. "I appreciate the offer, but that is an impossibility."

"Can't blame an old man for trying."

I smile at him, then rest my head on his shoulder. "I guess reenlisting will not be so bad. And it does not have to be forever."

"Think of all the lives you'll save in the process."

I nod but cannot speak. My throat feels too tight. For a year the only life I was responsible for was my own. My first instinct has been self-preservation, but that was before I saw Adrienne and Noah again. Before I became a part of this community whose mission is to make the world a better place for every life, not just the government-chosen masses.

We sit for so long, the sun has dipped behind the other side of the lily station. Without its direct heat, the air is much cooler. Cold, actually.

"We should go in," I say, and stand. "I am sure Colonel Updike is anxious to hear what I have decided."

Peter stands and grips my shoulders. "It's the right decision. You know that, don't you?"

"One I will not regret until the very second Major Reid decides to give me an order; then you may find me on your doorstep."

He chuckles and leads me back to the glass structure. We shuffle through the entrance with a group of small children being herded down the long hallway by several men. They are all bouncing, laughing, and talking way too loud. The adults with them look as if their patience has long worn thin.

Inside the open area at the end of the hall, the group pauses so the men can do a head count. Peter and I have to shift through the kids, and they do not move as easily as a group of adults would have. I get stuck part of the way through and turn to see how Peter is getting along behind me. He catches my eye for a moment, which is all he needs to miscalculate his next step. The poor boy beside him gets tripped up with Peter and falls down.

He bends to help the boy up and I feel a punch in the upper part of my left arm. The force rockets my shoulder back and I twist, nearly falling. It came out of nowhere. *From* nowhere.

Peter looks up instantly, eyes and mouth open wide. Whatever he says is lost amid the abrupt screams of the young children.

And then I feel it. The searing pain in opposition to the cold slithering down my core. The glacial swathe tugs, and the floor seems to leap up to meet me. But then I blink. And breathe. Shake off the momentary bout of dizziness. And everything appears to be back to normal.

Almost everything. Charred skin lies around an open wound from elbow to shoulder.

Someone shot me.

Someone shot me?!

My following breaths come fast and hard. My head swims as I meet Peter's eyes. He is yelling something at me, but I hear nothing but my own heartbeat. Even the pandemonium surrounding us has been muted.

Someone *shot* me.

The screaming breaks through the silence in increments and I shake my head to clear it. This is not the time to fade out. Whoever did this is still here. I look past Peter, down the hallway, and find my assailant poised with a plasma rifle.

Aiming at Peter.

CHAPTER 23

P<sub>eter!"

I start for him just as an arm snags me around the waist from behind. The voice in my ear is familiar. Colonel Updike. "Let's go!"

Peter darts behind a column and out of the gunman's range. But if he steps to either side . . . He meets my eyes and mouths, *Go*, even as I struggle to get out of Colonel Updike's hold. I have to help him.

Colonel Updike yanks me from where I stand, my feet kicking nothing but air, as gunfire rains down from more than the one direction. Windows shatter and spray the room with glass. White clay pots sprouting plant life burst apart, filling the space with the scent of earth. Colonel Updike tosses a second HK to Peter, then takes aim on a balcony where a man in civilian clothes fires on us.

Colonel Updike points to our right. "Run for that hallway. I'll cover you."

"But Peter—"

"Just go!"

I start to go as instructed, shielding my head from the flying debris, but trip over the body of one of the men who was herding children. I crawl behind one of the few plant pots still in one piece, then look over at Peter. Like the colonel, he returns fire with precision and determination. His expression is quite unlike that of the man from Montana.

A dark cloud of movement behind him captures my attention. The sight of resistance fighters approaching the glass doors, faces hidden under solid black masks, releases all the tension from my body. One man steps up behind my shooter and puts a shot into the back of his head without a moment's hesitation.

They move in and take the focus of the gunfire, which helps me get to the cover of the hallway. Children run past me, their piercing screams rending the air. Adults lead them into a room at the far end.

Colonel Updike darts around the corner and immediately aims back out into the atrium.

Peter runs in a moment later and I let out a cry in relief. He gives me a quick scan. "You all right, dove?"

"Yes." Except for the fact that my arm feels tied down in a blazing pyre. The tendrils of heat reach as far as my fingertips, up around my shoulder, and into my chest, making it hard to breathe.

With a nod, he sets up behind the colonel to provide cover. I lean against the wall behind them, trying to regulate my heartbeat and contain the tears building behind my eyes. How can we possibly get out of this without anyone getting hurt or killed?

A resistance fighter bounds into our hallway and pauses at the corner opposite the colonel, looking out and firing at random. A full black mask covers his head.

He crosses the hall and stops in front of me, his attention on my arm. He keeps a light touch on my elbow as he examines the wound. Because the plasma fire cauterizes, the wound does not bleed.

The man lifts his gaze to meet mine and I know who he is before he speaks. Only Noah's eyes glow this shade of amber. Despite the fact that adrenaline and cold fear sweep through me, I want to cry and kiss him in relief. He came for me.

"You need a doctor," he says.

"Do you think so?" I start to chuckle but end up wincing instead.

Noah looks at Colonel Updike. "Burke called in some favors. Had all the surrounding teleporters shut down. I only got half my team through before they killed the power."

No teleporter. No direct link to the hub. "What do we do?"

"Declan Burke sent these men?" Peter asks. Sweat beads his forehead. "That doesn't make any sense."

"Why not?" Noah asks.

"They shot Emma first."

Peter is right. Declan would order me returned unharmed, but I know something he has not yet realized. "He was aiming for you. You bent to help the kid just as he pulled the trigger."

"She could be right," Noah says. "The orders were to leave her untouched and shoot to kill anyone with her."

Colonel Updike yells over his shoulder. "Get Emma out of here. Once Burke finds out you came, he'll send reinforcements."

Noah looks at me. I wish I could see more than just his eyes, but he has not removed his face mask. "Think you can hang on for a while?"

Considering the pain I am in, I would love to curl up somewhere and close my eyes. "Do I have a choice?" It seems I am all out of those today.

He lays a hand on the side of my head, leaving it there for longer than necessary before taking my right hand. He slaps a warm-handled HK in my palm. "Stay behind me."

"We've got your back," Colonel Updike says. "See you at home."

My heart lurches with the realization that this is it. Safety break is over. And I have no idea if my friends are here, or if I will see them again. My already light head spins. *Please let them survive this.*

Noah crouches and charges out of the hallway, gun raised. It takes me a moment to gather the courage to follow. This is a far different situation than the simulation. That was a room full of harmless cats compared to this hungry lions' den.

Noah and I duck behind columns and large cracked plant pots. We are trapped. Declan took no chances with this capture attempt. His men fire from several levels of glass balconies. Resistance fighters either take cover or lie prone on the expansive glass floor, where the ocean sways in a calm juxtaposition to the room above.

Then I hear it. The unmistakable pitched slice of a hairline break zigzagging across the thick glass bottom. In the chaos of the room, no one else has noticed. A crack starts and stops, angling in several directions into the room. The imbalance of temperatures must be creating thermal stress. The ocean too cold. The plasma fire too hot. Not every shot from above has met with a target, and I know personally just how hot they are.

I elbow Noah and nod at the new danger. He curses under his breath and taps the com in his ear. "The floor is breaking. Everyone out."

The second he finishes speaking, the crack darts into the center of the room. On closer inspection, this flaw in the glass is not the only one. More spiderweb into the middle and meet. The entire room watches in abject horror.

Noah takes my hand and we sprint into the open. Plasma fire rains down on the unstable floor. We are nearing the hallway, with its nonglass floor, when a massive splash fills the room. The floor collapses and I drop into the ice-cold sea.

The salt water burns my open wound. Noah, already having made it to the stable floor, never releases my hand, and falls. He lands on his chest with his arm sunk into the ocean. His grip around my wrist is so tight I think he might break the bones.

I tuck the gun—how I managed to hold on to it is a miracle—into the back of my jeans and kick. My boots are heavy, making the process hard, and I am grateful Noah has not let me go. I could very well sink under their weight.

In my frenzied paddle to the surface, my ankle gets tangled in the steadfast grip of seaweed. Not two seconds later, Noah yanks my injured arm, and I yelp reflexively in shock and pain. I lose what little air is left in my lungs. Bubbles sneak through my clenched teeth and pop on the undulating surface. Black spots fill my vision and my lungs burn.

I am going to drown, which is ridiculous considering Noah is *right there.* I cannot even call for help.

Noah twists aside as the blue shots of plasma fire seek him out. He releases my hand in the process, and I immediately begin sinking into the obsidian depths. I cannot see the bottom, and every kick makes my situation with the seaweed worse.

A splash draws my attention and Noah appears above me, his arms rowing in wide arcs to reach me. He wraps his arms around my waist and hauls me toward the surface, but the seaweed will not give.

I have also been out of breath too long. Darkness threatens to close in around me. Noah yanks his face mask up and his mouth closes over mine. Air rushes into my lungs, hot and humid. He then kicks to the surface, takes a new lungful of air, returns, and repeats the process. By then, it is more than enough. I nod to let him know, then reach down to free my ankle.

Noah returns with his lungs refilled and mask down tight. He points in the direction of San Francisco and we swim. I am nowhere near as fast as I need to be given the weight of my boots, and he has to help me.

My lungs burn for air before we reach the outer rim of the lily station. Noah pushes me through the surface first and I gasp too soon, taking water into my lungs. I cough and choke, finding it difficult to stay afloat.

Noah brackets an arm around my waist. "Almost there," he says into my ear. "Hold on."

If we were on dry land, and if I was not coughing out seawater, I would do more than hold on. I would hug him until he could not breathe. He saved my life. But we are not out of the woods yet. My gratitude will have to wait.

We swim to the suspension bridge and take a ladder up. My body quakes in response to the chilled wind coupled with my cold, water-soaked clothes. The hard, involuntary jerks make it difficult to move.

Deadly shots fire on us the second our heads come into view. Noah and I face the assault line and return fire. Behind Declan's team stand the remains of the resistance, who back us up. Abandoned vehicles crowd the wide bridge, creating a kind of barricade. They were strategically parked at angles to block traffic going in, but also to keep anyone from going out, which leads me to believe the resistance team drove them in.

Noah heads for one motorcycle in particular and presses his thumb to the biometric scanner while straddling the seat. The motor hums to life and I start to straddle the seat behind him.

"No, wait," he says. "You'll need to shoot behind us." He inches back on the seat and takes me by the waist. "Face me and wrap your legs around."

There is no time to question the arrangement, though I wish there were. A flush heats my cheeks before I get my leg across the top. Noah takes only a moment to help me adjust into a position where I am in no danger of falling before spinning the bike around. The front wheel remains stationary, while the back spins at a high speed in the turn, kicking up white smoke. The bike lurches forward and we speed across the bridge.

Two cars and three motorcycles trail behind us. "We have company," I yell over the whipping wind. I am surprised I can speak at all. Icy shivers rack my entire body.

Noah nods once. "They're all yours."

Great.

"I'll get us to the low streets," he yells. "That should help."

The low streets? "You mean to take us into the fog?" I cannot imagine how this will help. How will he see to drive? He must be having a hard enough time with his waterlogged mask and its constant drip of seawater. "Are you crazy?" There is no mistaking the high pitch in my tone.

He laughs. "Maybe."

We cannot get to the low streets from the suspension bridge, so we climb the expressway, tilting from side to side, weaving around cars and semi-trucks. At the peak of the rise, the first shots zip by. I aim my gun at the black car behind us, using Noah's firm shoulder to steady my shivering arm. Two motorcycles flank the vehicle for a moment before zooming outward through traffic to come around us from either side.

The wind whips loose pieces of my hair around my head, stinging my eyes. Forcing myself to ignore the annoyance, I aim for the car's driver, who hides behind the glare of the sun reflecting off his windshield. I shoot. The bright blue plasma fire sings through the air and pierces the windshield, making a perfect circle. Cracks web out around it. The car remains on course.

I adjust my aim and fire again. This time the car veers off and hits the blue vehicle beside it. The two cars cross the road as if magnetically attached and drive onto the pedestrian walkway before crashing into the railing. The barrier takes the brunt without breaking, saving the cars from ending up in the Pacific miles below.

Noah angles us around a car. Once past, we meet with one of the motorcycles. The rider aims a gun at Noah's head. My heart flies into my throat. I shoot at him but miss. The rider has to course correct, though, giving Noah time to race forward and away.

Seconds later, we are caged in by two semi-trucks. Noah removes a gun from his side and aims forward.

"Watch behind us," he yells.

I hear the rev of a second motorcycle behind me and twist around to look. The bike drives right for us, riding the lane-separating white lines.

"Are we clear behind?" Noah asks.

"Yes."

He fires at the front tire of the oncoming motorcycle. The bike flips end over end, and a clear, egg-shaped shield shoots out from the sides. The shield protects the rider, but seconds later, he and the bike crunch under the wheels of one of the semis.

White smoke lifts off the braking truck tires. The motorcycle remains, and two trucks careen dangerously toward us.

"Shit. Hold on!" Noah yells.

CHAPTER 24

Noah brakes hard, and we clear the back ends of the trucks by mere inches. He tilts us to the right, racing for a nearby exit. Cars swerve to avoid us, and horns blare.

"You are going to kill us," I tell him through chattering teeth.

"Not today, I'm not. Just hold on."

I wrap my good arm around his neck and lean with the angle of the bike as he maneuvers through a long line of cars heading to the low streets of San Francisco Island. The fog wraps around us and he downshifts. The bike's fog lights blink on, but with one glance forward I know they do little good.

"This is too dangerous," I say.

Noah reaches back and opens a small compartment. He hands me a pair of yellow sunglasses. "Put those on and keep watch."

I do as he asks, and my visibility increases to at least a city block. Storefronts glare with neon lights to pierce the fog, and nearly all the pedestrians wear the same glasses I do. Bright, light-reflecting clothes seem to be the common fashion choice.

"What about you?" I ask. He must need the glasses more.

"If I take the mask off, Burke will see my face on camera. It's not safe even in this fog."

And the glasses will never stay on over his mask. "Then I will turn around and guide—"

"Emma, a little trust, please? Just watch—"

At that moment, he lets loose a string of curses and veers sharply off the road onto the sidewalk. Car horns bleat in our wake. We nearly topple over, and it is a good thing I have him around the neck or I would have fallen off. People jump out of our way as he takes us back up to speed and off the sidewalk.

"Not a word," he says.

"I trust you," I tell him, failing to keep a smile off my face. "Until you kill me, of course; then all bets are off."

His eyes crinkle in the corners and I wish his smile was not hidden under the mask.

Plasma fire through the fog sobers us. Noah takes an abrupt turn up a steep hill that forces my weight into him. I use his shoulder to hold my arm steady while I aim and fire the moment two motorcycles appear. Another sharp turn and we race up a set of stairs heavy with innocent bystanders, who jump over railings to avoid us. I close my eyes and pray he does not hit anyone, while holding on to him with a death grip.

The bike soars off the top step and over a sidewalk. Noah swerves into traffic and tilts around vehicles that take the low streets at a much safer pace. We turn into alleys and take a couple of more streets before ending up on a road that becomes bumpy, jostling my aim. Giant cracks in the street break up the road, explaining the sudden lack of cars. We drive through a residential neighborhood with townhomes lining the steep street on either side of us. No car could possibly make it over the road, broken up the way it is.

After seventeen misses, one of my shots hits one pursuer and he topples over. One more to go.

"Hold on tight," Noah yells, then looks at me. "You might want to close your eyes."

Close my eyes?! "What? Why?"

Our speed increases and I hug Noah to me with my good arm. The ground disappears beneath us as the bike becomes airborne. My breath catches. Below us, the remains of the road lie in broken patches in another abandoned street.

My stomach drops as we land on the other side of the crumpled overpass. The motorcycle tilts precariously from side to side, and the tires catch loose gravel and skid. A warning bleep signals from the bike's emergency system. Noah cannot recover balance or traction and we start to go down. I tighten my hold, and one of Noah's arms braces around my waist.

Moments before the bike touches down, the clear crash shield flies free of the left side and catches us in its egg shape. I land on my injured arm and pain overwhelms me into breathlessness. Gravel and cracked earth skate under us while we lie in a tangled heap inside the protective shell.

We spin and slide to a stop. I lie still, blinking tears from my eyes. I did not think the agony could get any worse, but it has.

Noah rolls up to an elbow over me. "You okay?"

I shake my head, unable to speak. If I do, I will cry.

The rev of a motorcycle in flight rends the still air, and I know our last pursuer is on his way. Noah scrambles up and helps me to my feet. Everything spins and I fight the urge to be sick. He swings me up into his arms and runs across the road to the ripped-up sidewalk. He sets me down safely beside an abrupt drop-off to an area too fog heavy to know where it ends. Could be another street. Could be a deep ravine. Could be the depths of hell. There is no way of knowing.

Noah turns with his gun raised as the motorcycle lands. The rider sticks the landing perfectly but does not see our abandoned bike through the thick fog. The two pieces of machinery collide. The bike flips. The rider soars free before the shell has a chance to catch him and lands with a *thud* in the cracked street. He lies very still.

"Stay here," Noah says. "I'll be back."

My legs cannot hold me up and I sink to the ground the second he walks away. My body must realize we are as safe as we are going to be for a while, because exhaustion begins to take over. I am only slightly aware of what Noah is doing. He kneels beside the body and feels for a pulse. He must not find one, because he stands and tucks his gun away a moment later.

He returns with his hand outstretched. "Come on. We need to find a safe place to hole up for the night."

Noah and I walk through the fog, clinging to each other and shivering. Neither of us has dried much since our time in the freezing ocean, and now there is no sun to warm us. The residential area looks abandoned, and with good reason. Most of the homes on the precipitous street have cracks bisecting their foundations, and the frames perch with one side rising higher than the other. Roofs have caved in. Porch awnings block doors. The entire row looks precarious enough to topple over like a deck of cards in one good gust of wind.

Noah stops in front of one and squints through the fog at it. "This looks okay."

The home sits on a corner and curves around from the street we stand on to the road perpendicular. The building rises three stories and most of the windows are broken. I do not know what color the house used to be, but the outside is now a moldy shade of green and brown. Plants either sprout from behind the siding or thrive outside it. The entire lawn is as overgrown as a jungle.

"It looks haunted," I say.

He chuckles. "With any luck, by a kindly old lady serving something hot to drink."

I think I would give both my legs for something hot at this point and moan with pleasure over the idea. "Hot tea."

"Hot coffee."

"Hot chocolate."

"Hot apple cider."

Now he is speaking my language. "Sounds perfect." I tug him forward while glancing up and down the street. All is quiet; the neighborhood is completely deserted.

We break in through the back door and into a musty-scented kitchen. Cabinets and counters are warped as if holding additional weight, though they are bare of everything but inches of dust. The tiled floors connect to a hall with a dark hardwood floor covered by a faded red runner.

Noah pulls off his waterlogged mask. He looks pale and his lips have a blue tinge. His hair sticks up until he runs his fingers through it. "We must be the first people in this house for years."

"Why do you think that?"

He points to the footsteps I have made in the thick coat of dust. Mine and his are the only ones.

"Guess that hot drink is out of the question," I say, and a cold shiver punctuates the statement.

He takes my hand. "Come on. Let's see if we can get you warmed up."

Inside the spacious living room, Noah turns slowly as if searching for something in particular. After what seems an eternity, his eyes widen and he points to one of the walls. "There."

Instead of asking, I watch him activate a panel in the wall. Inside the four-by-four-foot recess sits a stainless steel box with dark brown stones on top. Noah opens another panel and smiles. He pulls out a white plastic bottle with green lettering. I catch only one word on the outside before he sets it down beside him: OIL.

He glances over his shoulder. "A lot of these older homes have ethanol fireplaces tucked into the walls."

"Why hide them?"

"A way to keep the historic look of the house." He looks around again from his kneeling position. "This place looks pretty well cleaned out, but look around and see if you can find anything useful. I'll get the fire started."

If "cleaned out" means stark and empty, he would be right. I doubt I will find a single thing in here.

"Watch out for weak floors," he adds as I head for the staircase.

One look at the stairs and I decide to make the upper level my last resort. I cannot imagine the steps are safe. But it does not take long to search an empty dining room, small bathroom with cracked and broken fixtures, and what might have once been a small office to see I have no other choice.

I take the stairs at a slow pace, analyzing every step before testing my weight in minute increments. The second floor has a full bathroom in the same condition as the half bathroom downstairs, with the exception of a few personal items left under the sink: a roll of dental floss, a cylinder too rust covered for me to read the contents, and a broken black comb. In one of the two bedrooms, I find yellowed white drapes lying in a heap and attached to a black rod. The dusty material is not as good as blankets but will do. I cannot get them off the rod one-handed, so I drag the entire thing to the stairs and toss it over the side, where it clatters below.

Noah peeks over the railing, hands clamped on the wood banister. "Giving me a heart attack won't make this situation any better."

A smile twitches the corners of my lips. "Oh, I see. You are all good with death-defying motorcycle stunts . . . but drop some curtains and—"

"Hey. Don't knock the curtains' potential."

"Oh, right. I forgot. They are the greatest threat mankind has ever faced. Just shake them out, will you? And try not to hurt yourself until I get back."

I start to turn and he calls after me. "You aren't done yet?"

"I still need to check the attic."

The attic is a treasure trove by comparison to the rest of the house. Not that we need an upright piano covered in several inches of dust. Gray light breaks into pie-shaped beams through one large hexagonal window. Wood crossbars brace the roof and walls. A double mattress sags against a wall, and I find upon closer inspection that it has become a home for mice—I refuse to believe anything larger resides there. Boxes sit open in one of the corners. One holds nothing but wire hangers. Another has old, hardbound books. Beside it are crumbling sheets of music for the piano.

I kneel beside the box of books and begin pulling them out, reading names on their worn spines. Tolkien. Shakespeare. Brontë. Poe. Bradbury. Tolstoy. Austen, which is where I pause and finger the gold title across what I believe used to be a hard, red cover: *Emma*. A faded pink ribbon marks a place somewhere in the middle of the gold-edged paper.

The floor creaks behind me. One look over my shoulder reveals Noah, who is just reaching the top of the stairs. He has removed his black jacket and T-shirt. I cannot tear my eyes from the dips and curves of his muscles. Dark blond hair coats his pectoral muscles and trails down the center of defined abs. Surrounding the sculpted lines of his chest lies his life in a road map of raised scars. One might call these imperfections. I see only proof of life. A life I once shared.

I tear my gaze away to look at the novel in my lap. My mouth has gone dry, and I find it difficult to speak with any show of normalcy. "I found a box of books."

He kneels beside me and starts lifting a few by the corner to read the spine. The scent of ocean has replaced his usual musk. "Classics. You hate classics."

Yes. I remember Her voice in my head telling me not to request any classics from Dr. Travista, which is why I stayed away from them until Peter. "What about you?" I ask. "Do you hate classics?"

One side of his mouth lifts ever so slightly. "No. I don't know how many times I tried getting you to pick up just *one* book that wasn't some kind of out-of-this-world fantasy. And I mean *literally* out of this world. Spaceships. Other planets. Anything that didn't take place on Earth."

This does not surprise me. "A way to escape Her life, maybe?"

He meets my eyes, a line deepening between his brows. "Her?"

"What?"

"You said 'her.'"

I cannot believe I said that any more than he can. But what he speaks of does not sound like me. I do not want to read books that take place anywhere else. My life is not perfect, but I do not want to escape it so completely.

I lift the book in my hand. "I think I will read this one while we wait."

He takes the novel and gives me a hand up. "Come on. I have the fire going."

CHAPTER 25

Downstairs in front of the fire, Noah has used one of the drapes to clean away the dust from the floor. His shirt lies in a wet heap with his jacket.

Noah sets the Jane Austen book in front of the fire, then takes up the discarded curtain rod to brace across the staircase banister. He had the forethought to bring a handful of hangers from the attic and begins hanging his shirt and coat to dry. Once done, he walks with sure steps toward me, his tone casual as he says, "Let's get your shirt off."

I blink rapidly in surprise. He wants me to strip off my clothes? Here? Now?

Noah cocks his head. The fire beside us casts shadowed flames across his bare chest. "What's the matter?"

You are a grown woman and have done far more racy things than strut around in front of a man in your bra.

I swallow hard and shake my head. "Nothing."

He waits in silence, but I cannot bring myself to begin the process. Maybe he has seen more of me than I like to think about, but I have no memory of this. Intimate moments in which we held each other? Yes. But I never saw his face.

"Do you need help?"

I nod because I have only one usable arm and am in too much pain to attempt jostling myself free just because I feel shy. But the second he reaches out, I step back automatically and bite my lip. "Wait. Sorry." My voice is tight and shaky.

His lips quirk up. "Come on, Emma. It's not like I haven't seen—"

"Maybe so, but I have no memory of it."

The smile drops from his face as quickly as it appeared. "Oh." Then he looks curious. "Really? Nothing at all?"

I close my eyes to avoid seeing his expression, my face growing warm. "Stop looking so surprised."

"Sorry. I didn't realize—"

My groan cuts him short. None of this matters. "Just . . . help me." I glance up at him and take a shaky breath. "Please."

He steps forward and fingers the hem of my tank. I think he tries to avoid touching my skin, but the wet fabric clings and it is unavoidable. His touch sends electric jolts to my system and leaves a trail of goose bumps behind his knuckles. I focus on his chest and note how his breath stills. Looking higher, I find the quickened throb in his neck. His Adam's apple bobs heavily.

I do not know if it helps or worsens the situation to know he is as nervous as I, and I do not consider it for much longer. The time has come to work the wet cloth over the burn encompassing my arm, and the pain is too much. I grit my teeth and try to breathe, but it is difficult. By the time he has finished, tears leak from my eyes.

Noah cups my face and uses his thumbs to brush away the wetness. "Sorry. You okay?"

I nod, unable to unhinge my aching jaw. My self-consciousness has been dashed away by the agony.

Noah steps by me to pick up and shake out a drape, causing dust motes to skitter around in a frenzy. Standing behind me, he wraps the stiff material over my good shoulder and up under my bad one. I clasp it together in shivering fists.

His hands rest on my shoulders. He lets out a slow breath before saying, "Jeans next," then comes around to face me. "I won't look."

My heart pounds so hard and fast against my sternum I think it will bruise. "I do not see *you* shedding your pants."

I am stalling the inevitable, and according to the look he gives me, he knows it. Holding my gaze until the last second, he bends to unlace and kick off his boots, then removes his socks. Finally, he drops his pants.

If my jaw were not set to an aching clench, it might have hit the floor. Noah in nothing but a pair of black boxer briefs sets loose a geyser of lust within me. I think he is lecturing me about hypothermia and clothes drying faster, but the words barely register. All I know is that I am awestruck and nodding without realizing what I have just given consent to until it is too late.

Noah's hands slide through the opening of my drape and unfasten my jeans. Has he left any space between us? His breath sweeps warm across my cheek. His knuckles brushing my belly jolt me to awareness, and my breath hitches.

"How did your meeting with Nate go?" he whispers.

I lift my gaze to meet his much steadier version. Is he trying to distract me by mentioning Colonel Updike? I am unsure distractions will work. My zipper lowering seems to take hours, and nothing else exists outside this situation.

I clear my throat. "All right, I guess."

Noah's thumbs slide inside the rim of my jeans against my hips. "What did you decide to do?"

I cannot believe this is happening. "Boots," I clip out in a rush, clenching my fists to the drape before I let it fall and touch him. "My boots are still on."

He kneels, and I take a heavy breath. I stare at the fire that does not crackle and smells strangely like clean water. The flames erupt in a perfect line from the middle of glossy stones. I brace a hand on his cool shoulder as he removes the first boot. The shadows of flame flicker along the hardwood below him but do not fill the room. The house grows steadily darker, especially with no late-day sun shearing the fog outside.

I need to focus on something other than our positioning. What were we talking about? Colonel Updike? Noah asking what I decided . . . A sudden thought occurs to me and nearly bowls me over. "You knew why the colonel wanted to see me." This explains why he acted so strangely this afternoon.

"He filled me in." He looks up as he works my sodden sock off. "He mentioned how you had only today to decide. Did you?"

Tearing my gaze away from his, I nod. I still cannot comprehend what I have gotten myself into by choosing to enlist. And what will Noah think? Would he prefer I left so his life would be made simpler?

Task complete, he stands. A frown weighs down the corners of his mouth. "You're leaving, aren't you?"

Air catches in my throat. He sounds disappointed by the prospect, stirring dormant hope. "No."

Every muscle in his face relaxes. "Good. I'm glad."

"You are?"

"Of course I am."

"I just thought, after last week . . ."

His hands return to my hips, where his thumbs dip under my waistband. "I don't want to talk about last week."

He edges the material down. I shimmy my hips to help get the jeans over them. Amber eyes meet mine for a protracted moment before he sinks to his knees. *Is he deliberately taking his time?* He cups my calf and drags the damp material past one foot. His eyes rise to meet mine and desire builds in them, breathing life into my body.

I rip my gaze away and stare at the dark shadows flickering on a far wall. Each intake of breath stumbles around my erratic heartbeat. Noah's hand takes my other calf, and a shudder rocks up my body, both from the shock of his touch on my now sensitive skin and from my building need. My eyelids flutter shut. I understand what is happening and am powerless to stop it.

The wet jeans have long ago made the sound of being dropped into a heap, yet his hand has not left my calf. His touch caresses up behind my knee, and when his second hand doubles the sensations on my other leg, my head drops back. Heat stirs low in my belly and unfurls into my limbs.

You cannot let this continue.

The warning enters my thoughts too late. I am already lowering to my knees, relishing the feel of his palms along the outside of my thighs. Hips. Waist. The heat from the fire is uncomfortable this near to my burned arm, but I am too deeply ensconced in Noah's gaze to care. His hands leave my skin, and one rises to slide into my hair. His amber eyes dart back and forth, searching mine before lowering his gaze to my lips.

The pace of my heart increases and I wet my mouth. I bite my bottom lip the second the invitation is out there, because that is what it is. In that one swipe of my tongue, I have practically begged him to kiss me.

Noah's chest stills on an intake of breath, and his fingers begin to gather a handful of hair at the nape of my neck. I lean in slow, giving him time to back away. Instead, he catches my gaze and meets me halfway. Our lips lie still against the other's for the longest moment, as if in disbelief. Then, with a sigh, he pulls my head closer while pressing his mouth harder against mine.

Heat erupts and flushes my entire body. It is more than lust coursing through my veins. More than need. What I feel is the claim he has on me. How could there ever have been any doubt in my mind that I did not belong solely to him?

Noah's shadowed chin is abrasive against my lips and skin. His tongue slides seamlessly into my mouth and I taste a hint of seawater. My reactive groan is no more than a murmur, swallowed by the sensual probing of his tongue. I take his moan, too, reveling in the soft vibration against my skin.

His weight presses against me until I float backward. He cradles me all the way to the floor. A hand slides between the folds of the drapes, finding and gripping my waist. I release the fabric and arch against him, needing to feel his skin against mine. Needing to fit my shape to his.

Noah slows the kiss and pulls away to look into my eyes. For the first time since I arrived, his feelings are unguarded, and I know how much he still loves me. I know I have only to say the word and he will be mine again.

"I thought I was going to lose you today," he whispers.

I touch his swollen lips, shaking my head. How has he not realized the truth yet? He never lost me; not then, and not now. Not ever. I lift my head and take his mouth back.

A hand sweeps over my collarbone and down the center of my ribs. His fingers catch on an object that I had forgotten about. He pulls back with a jerk and looks down. I follow his gaze to where my wedding ring—my safety net—rests over the tip of his finger. A bucket of ice water would have had the same effect as these diamonds.

"Oh my God," I whisper, and close my eyes. I do not have the confidence to face him in light of this.

"You'll always be on the run, won't you?" he asks, and the ring hits my chest.

His weight disappears, and when I open my eyes, I find him sitting near my knees. He has one arm resting on an upturned knee, his focus glued to the wall opposite him. Each breath is deep and measured, expanding his rib cage.

I sit up and rub my swollen, hot lips. I want so badly to explain that I have no intention of leaving, but maybe he is not wrong. It is not as if I have ever taken the ring off. What-ifs play in the back of my mind every day, and I want to be prepared for anything.

"Noah—"

"Don't." He cannot look at me as he drags a hand through his hair. "My mistake."

Mistake? This single word spears my heart.

He gets to his feet and picks up our discarded pants. The next minute passes in silence as he hangs them beside our shirts. In the foyer, he is nothing more than a dark shadow, and I wish I could see his expression. Is he angry? Hurt?

My heart sinks when his shadowed shape lowers and sits against the doorframe leading into the dining room. Not only can he not look at me, but he wants to avoid me. How could I let this happen?

I pull my legs to my chest and bury every inch of skin I can under the safety of the drape save for my burned arm and head. I rest my chin on my knees and stare into the fire. It is not the same without the scent of burning, popping wood, and thanks to the tension surrounding me like a living thing, the fire does nothing to warm my cold skin.

I wish I knew what to say to Noah but cannot begin to think what it is he needs to hear. Or maybe it is me who needs to hear something. Anything. Even a single breath to tell me we will get through this.

When I cannot take it anymore, I stand and shuffle across the room with the drape trailing long behind me. I sit on the opposite side of the doorway from him. One of his legs stretches out in front while his other is tucked up with an elbow resting across the top. He watches me sit and I am grateful at least a little light reaches this far. He does not look angry. Reserved mostly, which is better than I hoped for.

"Talk to me," I whisper.

He stares forward, then drops his chin. "Why don't you talk to me? When this situation with Burke is over, and you're free to go, what will you do?"

"Are you asking if I plan to leave again?"

He rolls his head around to face me. "Yeah. I need to know."

I look away and tighten my grip on the musty smelling drape, shivering in the cool dark. "I almost left today. After Colonel Updike gave me my two options, my first instinct was to run."

"What changed your mind?"

"Adrienne." I pause and take a deep breath, unable to believe I am about to say this. "I have made so many mistakes, and leaving last year is the most unforgivable of them all."

"Emma—"

"I will not leave her again," I cut in, and look at him. "I love her, Noah. More than anything. I would like to be a mother to her, but if you would rather I kept my distance—"

"You're her mother. I would never stop you."

Relief floods me to the point where tears brim my eyelids. I had not realized how much I needed to hear this validation from him. I want to thank him but do not trust my voice to work. If I nod, the tears will spill over.

Noah stands and helps me up. Once I am upright in front of him, he tucks my hair behind my ears. "And I would never use the word 'unforgivable.'"

"No?"

He shakes his head. "I forgave you the moment you came back."

I bite my lip the second my chin trembles, but I am unable to stop tears from rolling down my cheeks this time. I rest my forehead against his chest and his arms surround me in a warm embrace. His heart beats strong and a little fast against my head. He kisses my crown, then leads me back to the fire.

Wordlessly, we sit, with him tucked close behind me. I nestle against him as he lifts the book from the attic off the floor. He leafs through the pages until he reaches Chapter 1.

"*Emma Woodhouse,*" he reads, "*handsome, clever, and rich . . .*"

CHAPTER 26

Y*ou must be devastated."*

Declan smiles tightly at the man interviewing him from off-camera. He casts his gaze to his lap. *"Yes. This was the closest we've been to rescuing my wife yet."*

"What are your thoughts regarding the loss of life during the rescue attempt?"

Declan frowns. *"This has been my deepest regret. That the resistance would shoot first and risk the lives of innocent people. My wife is the most important thing to me, but not at the expense of the children aboard that station. Their lives are too precious. But I guess the resistance sees things differently."*

The camera switches to the interviewer, his expression set with a sympathetic frown. *"Absolutely. Absolutely."* He gives Declan a thin smile. *"One last question, Mr. Burke. Rumor has it your wife was spending time in the lily community for a reason. Can you share with us what you've learned?"*

Declan nods once, then covers his mouth again. He casts his eyes down and away from the camera. After a long moment, he clears his throat and looks up. *"They were taking her to see a specialist."*

"Can you confirm that Mrs. Burke is out of remission?"

He nods. *"Yes. It's true. This specialist was attempting to treat her for her disease but died in the attack. There's no way of knowing how much longer Emma can survive without Arthur's help."*

Colonel Updike perches on the edge of Noah's desk and laces his fingers over one leg. I have just denied reinstatement as major and left him speechless. I can hardly believe it myself. He even planned to give Major Reid another assignment to thwart any complications. Not that I would not love to see Reid go away, but making me Noah's XO after everything that happened in San Francisco ... Well, I think we are both better off not working together for now.

I cannot tell Colonel Updike any of this, but I have plenty of other reasons, and they happen to be true. "I have no memory of my training, let alone commanding however many men that entails. Besides, we both know this is only so I can stay with my daughter. Pretend I am just starting out. Should not be too hard. I sort of am."

He sighs and folds his arms across his chest. "You're sure?"

"I am."

"Private Wade it is, then. You won't be in charge of any men, and I'll talk to Tucker and Reid about keeping you out of combat situations."

I stand and extend a hand. "Thank you, Colonel."

He gives me a tight yet genuine smile and stands. He cups my hand between both of his. "I wish things could be different."

"Me too," I say, but doubt the things I would change are the same as the ones he would. He wants fighter Emma back. I want to be free of all this and to live somewhere quiet with my family.

Colonel Updike looks pointedly at my arm. "How are you healing up?"

I glance down at the white bandage protecting the new skin growing underneath. I spent nearly two full days in the hospital wing with

Sonya while she removed the damaged part of my arm and replaced it with new, cloned skin, tissue, and muscle.

"I am much better, thank you. I am seeing Sonya for my last appointment in an hour."

With a nod, he leads me to the exit. "Since Tucker is in meetings all day, you'll have to see Reid for your schedule. Report after your appointment with Dr. Toro."

"Yes, sir." I turn outside the open door. "You are leaving today, yes?"

"In ten minutes."

I feel an unexpected pang of regret and do not know where it comes from. "Maybe when you return, you can tell me why we were on a first-name basis." Since he last mentioned this in his home, I have wondered why I would feel comfortable enough to call my superior officer by his first name. In addition, he seems to care enough about me to make sure I am safe and happy while maintaining structure within the ranks.

"I would love to tell you why," he says. His eyes shine and lift with his smile. "Next time."

I enter my room a few minutes later wondering how I should fill the next hour. It is not enough time to do anything useful. Not enough time for a good run, either. I have already showered. Eaten. Everything.

I would go early for my doctor's appointment, but no amount of time in the last couple of days has made going to the hospital any easier. In fact, I think the wing has made my nightmares worse.

In addition to the abyss, I dream I am back in the tank watching Noah and Sonya raise my daughter, shoving their happy life in my face while I pound my fists on the glass. I cannot get out, and he never lets me out, and it is just as frightening now as it was two years ago.

I eye the stack of books on my bedside table. Noah brought *Emma* back with us from San Francisco Island—as well as a few other books he thought I would enjoy—and I read a little each night. It is not the same without his soothing voice reciting the lines aloud, but I am enjoying the classic novel despite how my previous incarnation hated them.

I consider reading while I wait but spy "Emma's" box beside me. More proof that I never planned to stay. Noah has not confirmed as much, but after the things he said, I know he believes I will jump at the chance to leave. It is no wonder he has kept his distance from me since we returned. He wants to protect his heart, and nothing I say will change things. Maybe my actions will.

Other than to rifle through the clothes, I have not dug deeper into the personal belongings yet. I could at the very least utilize my currently empty dresser. Pulling things out to wear, washing them, and then returning them to the box seems a ridiculous thing to continue.

"Time to move in, Emma," I whisper, and kneel.

It takes no more than five minutes to put the garments away, leaving me with the miscellaneous items in the bottom. While I had not wanted to go through the box before, I cannot help but wonder what else there is. And from the outside looking in, I am already curious what kind of woman I was and why I kept the things I did.

Two pairs of flip-flops that have seen better days sit on their sides, propped up by what looks like a wooden jewelry box. Beside that is a large, clear bag with bathroom necessities: toothbrush, hairbrush and bands, and a razor, among a bunch of other things I cannot see without pulling them all the way out.

I reach inside to retrieve a black journal. My heart pounds, wondering what She might have written. How far it goes back and when it stops. I open to the first unlined page. Instead of words, I find a drawing. I recognize the details from a long-ago memory. A hotel room, early morning according to the penciled-in sun rays. Emma stands in front of Noah wearing a robe. He is frozen with a hand combing through his hair, grinning down at her. I even recognize the clothes he wears. I know this moment and do not need the words She has left out. This was the morning Noah showed up to tell Her he loved Her.

No, not Her.

Me.

This is how the diary is laid out. In pictures. The pages depict so many moments, good and bad, before and through the beach wedding, the honeymoon, and long after. Most with Noah, some without. She—*I*—took so much care to remember every last detail of the important moments in such a way as to never forget them. Each line as important as the next. A visual memory.

My memory.

And suddenly, my memory does not feel as lost as it once did, because here it is. I only need the important ones, right? It is as if somehow I knew I would need this one day.

A knock on the door startles me, and I look up as the *shiff* sound fills the room. Leigh peers in and down, leaning against the frame. "Just heard you're officially a grunt. Drinks later to celebrate?" Her arched eyebrows pinch together as she realizes what I am doing. She walks in and shuts the door. "What's all this?"

Kneeling beside me, Leigh gathers her thick hair and twists it over her shoulder. I hand her the diary, then dip into the box for the rest of the treasures it might hold. I cannot believe I waited so long to look. I lift the jewelry box free while Leigh digs out a black knife hilt that fits perfectly in her palm. She presses a button and a sharp blade springs free. We exchange a look, though she looks a million times more impressed than I am.

I lift the case's lid and find smooth sea glass of various colors among seashells. Folded in opaque white paper are pressed indigo petals. My heart twists. These are items from the honeymoon. I have imagined these petals and painted them, but to have them in my hand . . . It seems too unreal.

Leigh fingers through the small pile of glass and frees a silver chain, the one piece of jewelry inside. Dangling on the end is a pair of intertwined hearts—a luckenbooth. On the left side of each heart is a row of sparkling gems. One heart's jewels are sapphires, the other, emeralds. Birthstones. Virgo and Taurus. Emma and Noah.

"Pretty," Leigh says. "You should wear it."

I try swallowing past the lump growing in my throat. "No, that would not be right."

Leigh rolls her eyes and clasps the chain around my neck. "How can it not be right? It's yours and obviously meant something to you." She sits back on her heels and studies how it looks. "I want to hate it, but I love it. It's really beautiful."

I glance down at the hearts that are meant to bind women to a husband not of their choosing. The same symbol that led me back to Noah. The hearts lie over a small lump under my shirt.

I pull Declan's wedding ring free and yank the chain until it snaps. My heart beats faster, but I will not need the ring anymore and may as well stop pretending I will. Actions, not words.

I take Leigh's hand and drop the jewelry in her palm. "Here. Just in case you need an escape plan."

She quirks a smile. "What exactly am I trying to escape?"

I shrug a single shoulder, then turn back to the box. In my periphery, I watch as she pockets my wedding ring without another word. This one action confirms I was right to give it to her. And maybe she does not need to escape right now, but Leigh is not as settled as she likes to let us all believe. She deserves a chance at happiness, and maybe that ring will help her get there.

"What's in here?" Leigh asks, pulling out a small wooden chest. It is locked, but she breaks it open easily using the knife. She opens, then slams it shut and cries, "Oh dear sweet baby Jesus." She laughs so loud I am sure everyone in the hall can hear her.

"What is it?"

She shakes her head and twists the container out of my reach. "Nuh-uh. Trust me, 2.0; you do *not* want to see this. It will ruin your fragile sensibilities."

"What are you talking about?"

Her skin flushes a deep pink and a vein snakes up her forehead. Her grin deepens the longer she holds out on me, but finally, she passes me the box.

Now that I have it, curious or not, I am scared to open it. "You do it," I say, passing it back.

Giggling, she takes it and opens the top just high enough for me to peek in and see the devices and lubricants clearly meant for self-pleasure. I gasp and slam a palm down on the lid. Heat fills my cheeks and I bury my face in my hands.

"Told you," Leigh says, going into another fit of giggles and snorts.

I point at the offending container, choking back my own laugh. "I can*not* keep that. That is disgusting."

"If you think that's disgusting, you clearly haven't lived. That said, it's like borrowing from a friend, and *that* is most definitely a do-not-use-or-abuse situation." She clasps my knee and winks. "You, me, a box of vibrators, and the incinerator. We'll have a funeral for the poor bastards tonight before we hit the whiskey."

"Can we do it now?" I cannot fathom the idea of them sitting here until then. What if someone walks in and decides to look?

"You can wait a few more hours." She lays the box back inside the larger one and says, "Man, who knew 1.0 was such a dirty bitch? I sure as hell didn't. Oh," she nearly squeals. "A vid screen and data-slips. I wonder if there's porn. Miles will love that."

She produces a four-by-five-inch flat screen and a black rectangular pouch. Inside the pouch are clear films the same rectangular shape and as thin as paper. Leigh squints to read the single lines typed across the sides. "Looks like home videos." She starts to hand me one. "Your wedding."

In a single heartbeat, I see the arch draped in fabric. Indigo flower petals lying on sand. A wedding I feel but have no actual memory of. I shake my head, overwhelmed by the idea of watching what I lost live and in color. Noah and me vowing to love each other forever. Memories this alive will only exacerbate the fact that I *lost him.* That I did not take him back when I had the chance. That I did not fight for him.

I sit back on my heels and stare at the data-slip, tightening my arms around my middle. "Not yet."

She nods once, her expression falling, and slides it back in the pouch. "Do you want to watch any of them? Some look harmless enough."

Standing, I say, "I want to forget they are there."

The room spins and I waver on my feet. There is so much of Her around me suddenly, yet I am still the wrong-shaped peg trying to shove my way back into Her square hole. No longer a circle, but a triangle, maybe. A rectangle. Never quite right. Not on the inside, at least. Maybe this is why Noah kissed me. Because outwardly, I look the same. I wear Her hair and Her clothes and Her smile and love Her family . . .

My family.

I cannot breathe. My God, what have I done?

Leigh jumps up and takes me by the shoulders with tight fingers. Her eyes are wide, and a worried line creases her brow. "Hey. No need to panic. We'll fix whatever it is. What do you need?"

Tears slip over the rims of my eyes. *I need Noah to love me, not Her.*

CHAPTER 27

I am late for my appointment with Sonya but cannot find it in myself to care. Once through the doors, I take only a moment to scan the room I know every inch of by heart. After all, it is the place my host body spent Her last nine months.

The tank is gone from the corner, and Sonya has placed more beds with privacy curtains in its place. The wall of monitors still resides along an entire wall, but with no patients to monitor, it is blank.

Sonya stands at the row of cabinets to my right, rifling through drawers. Her black hair is straight and pulled into a low ponytail today. "You're late, which means you'll be late to report in. You can't—" She looks at me and comes to an abrupt stop.

I cup the back of my bare neck automatically. Leigh helped me cut my hair, which is why I ended up running late. We found the scissors in Emma's toiletry bag and clipped my hair back into the short, angled cut I maintained before. Had I not been on the run all this time, I might have kept it short. The style is me. Not Her.

In addition to the cut, I have put a little makeup on. I used to wear it all the time, and according to Leigh, Emma did *not*. Haircuts and makeup came second to her job. No, not second. Dead last.

"I like it," Sonya says, and gives me a reluctant smile. "The cut has always suited you."

"Thank you. Will this take long? As you started to mention, Major Reid will be upset because I have not reported in."

"I'll be quick." She motions for an empty bed. "Have a seat."

I push up onto the side of the bed and she stands in front of me with a pair of shears. She gives me another tiny smile as she begins cutting up one side of my bandage. I do not understand the kindness she is attempting to show. She never smiles at me and has worked with nothing more than clinical efficiency these past couple of days. I do not know what to think or how I should react.

"Why the sudden change?" she asks, and glances up at me.

I bite my lip. She cannot know, nor does she need to know, why I needed to be myself again. "Will I have a scar?"

Sonya's eyes drop from my face and she frowns. "If you do, it will be minimal."

"Good."

"You're worried about scarring? That's not like you."

She says this so easily. Automatically. As if she knows me. Little does she know that this is the wrong day to confuse me with my doppelgänger. I am still too raw after the box incident.

An ache fills my jaw and I unclench my teeth. "Like me or like Her?"

Sonya blinks rapidly and stops cutting midclip, but soon finishes without another word. She parts the bandage and lays it aside, then examines the large area of cloned skin. The shade is wrong. My skin is tan from all the sun I have gotten this year, and this tone is a much lighter shade. A faint pink line surrounds the new skin and tissue.

"This will all change," she says, and presses her fingers around the area. "I wouldn't suggest going out for a tan just yet, but the color will even out eventually. And if you're that worried about scarring, I'll take care of that whenever you're ready. The guys around here have this macho thing with keeping their battle wounds, but I'm not so out of practice with removing them."

With a sigh, she straightens. "Looks good. Light weights to re-shape the new muscle and come see me if you experience any dis-comfort."

I jump off the bed. "That is it? We are done?"

"As far as I can see, yes."

"Thank you."

I am three steps past her when she says, "Emma, wait."

Turning, I find her biting the corner of her lip and staring at the floor, arms akimbo. She toes the tiled floor with the tip of her shoe, then forces her head up and gives me a determined look. "I can't ask him, and I like to believe you'll give me a straight answer."

My stomach sinks.

"What happened in San Francisco?"

My chest tightens and I have to pace my breathing to keep from reacting too strongly. She wants to know about me and Noah. How can she expect me to tell her the truth after how she has treated me? I do not want this tension between us, but I did not put the wall there. She did.

"You know what happened," I tell her. It is the straightest answer she will get from me.

"You know I'm not asking about the assault." She takes a step for-ward and casts her gaze to the side, biting her lip again. "He's being especially attentive."

Too much. I hold up my hands, palms facing her. "In my experi-ence, that is not usually a problem." I turn around to leave.

"Did you say something to him? Did he to you?"

Stopping, I turn back around and school my expression into the same kindness she tried showing me moments ago. "You want the truth? He cares about you. More than I like to admit. Do not question his attentiveness. Embrace it for what it is."

Her dark eyes narrow. "Embrace what? His guilt?"

It takes everything I have not to react. I will not betray Noah. This is his relationship to destroy, not mine.

Taking a deep breath, I straighten my spine. "We talked about Adrienne. I want to be a mother to her and he agreed. If there is any guilt to be had, it is over that."

Unlike me, Sonya is unable to hide the flinch of surprise. Her eyes glaze with tears, but she blinks them away and clears her throat. "He didn't tell me that." She gives me a twitchy smile. "But I can see why he wouldn't. He knows how I feel about her."

"I was there when Adrienne was born; did you know that?" She shakes her head and pales. "Those are my memories of her birth. My eyes that saw her for the first time. I just want a chance to love my daughter. I want to right my mistakes, and Noah is willing to let me."

"And what about me?" she asks, her hands falling to her sides. "Where do I fit in with your new plans?"

I smile though I do not feel it, wondering when we switched roles. She must now feel like the outsider looking for a way in, and I know how lonely that can be. I will not be as cruel to her as she was to me, because I would never allow Adrienne to be hurt over this. "Adrienne is lucky to have two mothers who love her, yes?"

She has no opportunity to respond, because Dr. Malcolm rushes in, winded and holding a finger up to ask me to wait. "Thank goodness. You're still here." As per his usual, he is disheveled and smiling, though with a bit of difficulty due to being so out of breath. He bends and braces on his knees. "I thought I missed you. Wow." He rattles his head and swallows hard. "I really need. To start an exercise. Program."

"I was just on my way out," I tell him. "And this time I really cannot be late."

He fills his lungs. "May I walk with you?"

"Of course." I send Sonya a parting smile, then exit the hospital. "What is it I can do for you, Dr. Malcolm?"

"I was hoping we could talk about your friend Ruby."

I stop and face him. "Do you know how she died? What did you find out?"

He wipes sweat from his brow with the flat of a palm. His face is so red I wonder if I should be concerned. "Nothing. We still have no idea what killed her, but I have theories."

"Which are?"

"The most obvious is that her husband killed her, but I don't believe that. In fact, I don't believe anyone killed her. Not since seeing the interview with her neighbor."

The old man who watched her collapse . . . *but she was dead, you see. Just like that. Dead.* "He could have been lying."

You're perfect, Dr. Travista's voice adds.

"But for what purpose?" Dr. Malcolm says, unaware of the darkness filling the recesses of my mind. "Actually, I'm inclined to think she just collapsed and died, and here's why." He raises both hands, palms facing me. "You ready for this? It's a good one, and seems so obvious now that I—"

"Dr. Malcolm."

"Electromagnetism." He says this as if to a background of oohs and aahs.

"Electromagnetism?"

He bounces on the balls of his feet. "The EM force is one of four fundamental interactions in nature. With the exception of gravity, it's responsible for—"

"Dr. Malcolm. I do not have time for a science lesson. I want to know what killed my friend."

I start back down the hallway and he catches up a moment later, his shorter legs having to jog to keep up with me.

"Balance is essential in nature," he says, now using large hand gestures to emphasize his speech. "And the EM field isn't just limited to the physical, but also the metaphysical. Not a popular school of thought, but I like to believe that we have an incorporeal—"

"What does this have to do with Ruby?"

"Dr. Travista, I believe, may have upset an electromagnetic balance during the transfer. You were bound to your host as long as she was alive. Think of this as the universe's way of trying to maintain the balance. Set things right. But with the host gone . . . Now what? The mind-body is electronic, and extremely sensitive."

I have not missed the fact that we have stopped talking about Ruby. "I am perfectly healthy, Dr. Malcolm, as you can plainly see."

"I do see that, yes."

"And I really hope this is not your way of trying to talk me into those tests you so desperately want."

His steps falter but catch back up. "No. No, of course not." He chuckles, but the humor is forced. "That would be just silly to request such a thing. Especially given your opinion. But . . ."

I stop and look down at him. "But what, Dr. Malcolm?"

He lifts and holds a shrug, his head tilting to one side. "Maybe you understand my concern for Miss Bennett?"

Leigh. Who is scheduled to meet with Dr. Travista in only three weeks. Dr. Malcolm must have realized this would trigger a response. A need to protect my friend.

I sigh and rub my eyes. "What is it you need from me?"

I am suddenly surrounded in his tight arms while he bounces. "Oh, thank you, Miss Emma. I promise this won't hurt a bit."

"What will not hurt? What will you need from me? Blood?"

He backs away, shaking his head. "No, I don't think so. Just a brain scan."

That sounds simple enough. "That is all?"

"Oh, well, yes, but you see, the scan will require a few days where I'll have you performing a few tests, such as math and listening tasks.

Among other things. In the end, I will have a very detailed map of your brain. From personality and talents to—"

"A few *days*?" Tests within a test? Not only that, but I seriously doubt I will have the time. "We will have to come back to this when I know what my schedule is like." And in the meantime, maybe I can talk Leigh out of this madness, which will in turn free me from this responsibility.

Dr. Malcolm holds up his hands and nods erratically. "Of course. I will work around you. You have no idea what this means. The future benefits for Miss Bennett alone—"

"Okay, but I really must go now. Major Reid is waiting for me to report for duty."

He hugs me again, and this time the squeeze forces all the air from my lungs.

"*Oh. Kay,*" I wheeze.

He lets me go and beams. "We'll talk soon."

I spin and jog toward the command center, shooting back a wave in response. Major Reid is going to kill me for being late. I may even let him because I cannot believe I just agreed to those tests. But I would do anything if it meant helping Leigh survive what is coming. At least she will not experience what I have. The nightmares when my host was alive. The nightmares after.

I slow to a stop around the corner, recalling something Dr. Travista said last year. *"I believe Emma may still be connected to the host body. That's why she's proven difficult to erase. I discovered a connection between Ruby and her host initially, but it ended the moment I terminated the original."*

What was it Dr. Malcolm just said? *"You were bound to your host as long as she was alive . . . the universe's way of trying to maintain the balance. Set things right. But with the host gone . . ."*

With the host gone . . . *what*?

"Wade, you all right?"

I look up at the sound of Foster's voice. He leans around the corner of the command center but enters the hallway after seeing my face.

"You look pale," he says. "Are you sick?"

I force a smile and shake my head. "Is Major Reid mad that I am late?"

"Furious." He attempts a light tone, but concern etches his expression.

"Good. I like him better when he is angry."

He wraps an arm over my shoulder. "You know what they're going to put on your headstone? Masochist unto death."

He has no idea.

CHAPTER 28

P*rivate*," Reid says in a tone that has far too much delight in it for my taste. He dismisses a small group of men and walks toward me with a computer tablet clutched to his chest.

"Major."

"You're late."

"Colonel Updike said you would have a schedule for me?" There is no sense in offering any excuses. He will only use them as ammunition against me.

Reid sits on the edge of one of the desks and scans the chatter-heavy room before answering. "You're getting off easy, Wade."

I am careful to hide my surprise. He has called me nothing but Mrs. Burke since I arrived. "Easy how?"

He passes over the tablet. "This is yours. I forwarded your schedule to your personal in-box; memorize it. Don't miss any of your training sessions. You never know when they'll come in handy. Obviously, we're tasking you to help with Declan Burke."

I tighten my steadily warming grip around the tablet. I stand here listening but cannot believe this is happening. I am taking orders from Clint Reid. "Okay."

He hands me a small plastic container. Inside is a single, nude-colored earbud. "Your com-link. In your ear. Every second you're on duty. Got it?"

I nod.

"Lieutenant Colonel Tucker is planning a mission he'd like you to sit in on today," he continues, "but until then, you need a few things to get started." He nods behind me. "Birmingham is going to take you around to get everything—locker, uniforms, weapons." He straightens. "Back here in one hour, Private Wade. Try not to be late this time."

I swivel around and approach Foster. His arms are folded across his chest, his stance wide. A smile lengthens the longer he stares at me.

"What is so amusing?"

"You. Ranked under me. I find that beyond entertaining." He motions to see my tablet. "Let's look at your schedule, Private."

I roll my eyes and hand it over. Everyone is having far too much fun at my expense. "Do you know anything about this mission Noah is planning?"

"I'm as clueless as you, but I'll be at the meeting." He squints at the screen and rolls his fingertips over the top, reading what must be my schedule. "Looks like you're in the gym every morning for combat training."

My heart leaps into my throat. *Combat?* "Colonel Updike said—"

"I'm sure it's only because of what happened in San Fran. You're lucky the team got there when they did. You do pretty good in a fight, and you know how to shoot, but another situation like that on your own and you'll be dead or captured."

Or worse: Declan's mindless, compliant wife.

"Weapons training," he continues, sliding his finger over the screen. "Weight training per doctor's orders. All this on top of your scheduled hours monitoring feeds. You'll have no time to eat or sleep, Wade."

As if I *want* to sleep. I take the tablet back. "I can live with that."

Foster reaches out and tugs a strand of my cropped hair, a smirk lighting his expression. "That's the spirit. Come on. Let's get you suited up."

It takes nearly an hour to get me "suited up." I am left with little choice but to wear the standard-issue black pants, shirt, and jacket like everyone else. I am also assigned my own set of HK pistols, which hang heavy on my sides.

We run to our scheduled meeting to make it in time. We arrive at a desk in the command center, where Noah leans with crossed arms and legs facing everyone. His eyes widen slightly when he sees my new haircut, and I admit to butterflies, wondering whether or not he approves. It is as if this is the moment of truth; will he want me for me, or will he realize I am not the wife he remembers and let me go?

Reid sits perched on the desk beside him, a cinnamon-colored brow raised at me and Foster. Leigh, Miles, and Farrah sit in chairs in front of them. Farrah spares me the same look she always has in the past, the one that says I do not belong here. She and I will never be friends, and I am okay with that as long as she does not do anything to cause trouble.

Miles rolls an empty chair toward him and motions for me to sit. "Jesus, Wade. I forgot how hot you look with a gun on your hip."

Noah shifts in my peripheral and I am careful not to look over for his full reaction. I do not want to see that he cares one way or the other, nor do I want to show any indication that I need to know. Especially since he has made it clear he wants to work things out with Sonya, guilt-ridden though the effort may be.

Miles winks as I sit, throws an arm over my shoulder, and leans close to my ear. It is intimate enough that I expect him to whisper, but he makes sure everyone can hear. "Remind me later to tell you about this dream I had about you . . . me . . . a—"

Foster smacks the back of Miles's skull. He points a rigid finger at Miles, who chuckles in response. "Watch yourself."

Leigh adds another love tap on the back of his head. "Seriously. Can you not be that guy for five minutes?"

"Not even if you paid him in porn," I say. "Believe me. I have tried."

Everyone laughs, even Farrah, who has been trying to ignore us from Miles's other side. Well . . .

Almost everyone.

Noah clears his throat, and the sound is enough to strip all traces of humor from everyone's face. "Eyes up here." He holds up the invitation given to him by Declan a while ago in his office. "I have a way to find the cloning facility," he says, and taps the envelope against his palm. "Once we find it, I want to blow it off the map. We're only getting one shot to make it count."

Over the following two weeks, we plan down to the most insignificant detail the mission to take place at the Fire and Ice Masquerade Ball. Noah will take Leigh as his "hired escort," much to Farrah's obvious disappointment; at least it was to me. Based on my observations, she watches Noah on a more than professional level. But what woman in her right mind would not? Noah is beyond attractive; his confidence alone is enough to snag positive attention.

Miles and Farrah will attend as guests Landon and Opal Winchester, personal friends of a particular board member who happens to be out of the country for the next two months.

Leigh's only job is to provide backup to Miles and Farrah so Noah will not have to. The whole purpose behind Noah "renting" his date is to avoid any personal involvement with her. It will not look good for him if Leigh is caught, but at least there will be no obvious direct link to the resistance.

Because the ball will be held inside Burke Enterprises, utilizing an entire floor and the majority of the building's security, Miles has the rare opportunity to access Declan's servers. In them, we hope to find the location of the cloning facility. Maybe even prove they are cloning girls in the WTCs.

Reid, Foster, and I have no involvement the evening of, except to provide visual support from the hub and to help organize the details beforehand. I sit quietly during the planning stages because they need me only on the off chance they have a question about Declan— his habits and reactions.

The weeks pass quickly, and I am so caught up in my new schedule, searching for my parents, and spending time with Adrienne that I manage to squeeze out of following through with Dr. Malcolm's tests. I tell myself every day to get them over with. That I should do it for Leigh. But the more I think about what he said about the EM balance, the more I fear the results. What if there is something wrong with me?

You are perfect, Dr. Travista's voice reminds me.

I want to believe him, and I would if not for the abyss that calls to me every night. If not for the fact that these dreams started the night She died.

The day arrives, and everyone is tense. There is so much riding on getting this one thing right—much to Leigh's disappointment. If this works, she will not have to be cloned. I know she will do her job, and do it well, but I wonder if it has crossed her mind to make sure it does not.

I wait in the command center for everyone to arrive. Farrah enters first and looks absolutely stunning. Her red dress is held in place high at the neck by a choker necklace and drapes smock-like to the floor, leaving her shoulders bare.

Underneath she wears a waist cincher that holds tools she may need to get into Declan's office. The front of the dress parts up the center and gives her easy access to them if need be.

Around her thigh she has strapped a leather garter for her gun, a knife, and a tiny canister of aerochlor. The only straps showing are the silver ones that circle up her ankles and calves from her heels.

No one will know how thoroughly armed she is, and I know only because I saw the items laid out for her just this morning.

Noah comes in behind her wearing a tailored tuxedo. While the ball is red-and-white themed, he wears black pants with a white shirt, white jacket, and white bow tie. He catches me staring like a fool, and a grin twitches his lips. It is a good thing I am not walking, or I might have tripped over my jaw.

I do, however, stumble over my words in an attempt to recover. "Wow. You look . . . really great." "Great" is not the best word choice, but "undeniably sexy" seems inappropriate given our tense relationship.

Miles arrives and I am not at all surprised to find he dared a red jacket and bow tie over his white shirt and black pants. "I dare you to try and use the word 'great' on me," he says, popping the ends of his shirtsleeves. He bathes me in his naturally sexy grin and winks.

"Daring me just earned you a 'great' too," I say with a chuckle, grateful for the distraction. "Maybe even a *just okay.*"

He feigns stabbing himself in the heart. "That's just wrong, Wade. So, so wrong."

Reid taps Farrah on the shoulder. He hands her a white half mask with beaded strings hanging chin length from the bottom. White ribbons hang from the sides and will tie around her head. The white masks he gives to the men are half as well, but with little to no embellishment.

"We should go," Noah says. He glances around. "Leigh isn't here yet?"

Everyone looks around except Reid, who says, "She still has another ten minutes. I'll send someone to make sure she's almost ready." He snaps at an analyst nearby who was listening in. The guy runs out of the command center without pause.

"Okay," Noah says, "but she *has* to meet me outside no later than eight fifteen."

This part of the plan has been drilled and drilled some more. Noah is meeting someone beforehand and will pick up his "date" outside the building. Farrah and Miles are leaving now, teleporting to a spot across tow. where they will meet a car to drive them over. Noah, who is leaving from his office upstairs, is taking another route. No one is allowed to teleport directly into the building for safety and security reasons.

I give Farrah a hug and wish her luck. Miles hugs *me,* then tilts me back in a romantic gesture that I swear is calculated to be a test on Noah's patience. These last two weeks have been full of situations like this, but only in front of Noah.

For half a second I believe Miles will actually kiss me, causing my heart to stampede in my chest. Instead, he grins and taps his nose to mine before hauling me back up and making my head spin.

"All right," Noah says in a near growl. He glances between me and Miles, frowning. "Playtime's over. Let's go."

"Good luck," I tell Noah, and his attention stops on me.

"Thanks."

The three of them take off, and since I am not needed for another half hour, I decide to go say good night to Adrienne. I head for Sonya's room, where Adrienne will be staying the night, ignoring the butterflies in my stomach. Sonya is expecting me, but this does not make sitting in the same room with her any easier. Especially while I read Adrienne her bedtime story—the same one I have read every night for a week now in Noah's room. He has been stepping out to give us time together, or maybe he needs to avoid being alone with me. Regardless, this will be my first time with an audience.

The door to Sonya's room slides open after one knock. She is moving aside to let me enter when Foster comes racing down the hall, yelling my name. Sonya walks out with Adrienne sitting on her hip, eyebrows pinched.

Foster slides to a stop near us, his chest heaving on deep breaths. "Damn heels. Went down some stairs. The guy threw the football too long and hit her."

"Hit who?" Sonya and I ask at once. Adrienne rocks on Sonya's hip, trying to get free, but Sonya has a practiced death grip on her.

"Leigh," Foster says. "Think she broke a hip or a leg or something. Screaming like she's dying."

Sonya and I race down the hall behind Foster and end up in the hospital wing, where Leigh curses in such a sharp tone that Adrienne slaps her palms over her ears. A comical cringe screws up her little face. Reid has a bunch of doctors racing around, and Sonya passes Adrienne to me so she can examine her patient.

Reid points to me with a straight arm. "You. Strip out of that uniform."

I start in surprise. Did he just ask me to *strip*? "Excuse me?"

He ignores my question. "Birmingham, take the kid. Someone get this dress off her"—he points at Leigh, who lies squirming in a red dress, then to me—"and onto her. Now. We have less than five minutes to get her out of here."

I am speechless as everything happens around me too fast to keep up. Someone else has Adrienne, because Foster is yanking my jacket off from behind. Somehow I get out of my boots and clothes, giving little thought to the fact that I am surrounded by men. My mind races around the fact that Reid is sending me to the Fire and Ice Ball. *Me*. In the same room as *Declan*.

Dread pools cold in my stomach as reality sinks in. "You cannot seriously mean to send me to the ball. I could be recognized."

Reid scowls as if I am dense. "You'll have a mask." He turns to shout, "Someone get me a wig. Blond. And where are those masks? We need one with full facial coverage."

"This is insane," I mutter, and race to hold up my bra, which someone has just unclasped with no warning.

"If you have a better idea, I'd love to hear it," Reid says, taking the dress someone passes to him. "You're the only other woman capable and knowledgeable enough to run this mission. You don't go, we could fail, and that's a fact."

There is no arguing with him, because he is right. This is dangerous, but I will be perfectly hidden all night. Masked, I can stand directly in Declan's eye line and he will never know it is me. And if something happens, I can back up Miles and Farrah without hesitation.

I reach out a hand. "Give me the dress."

Getting the outfit on proves difficult, as it has a built-in bustier and squeezes my midsection like a vise—Leigh is taller, but also thinner. The dress zips over the top of the corset and has a cowl neckline that reveals way more breast than I am comfortable with. Cross-diagonal pleating in the top leads to a floor-length skirt with a high slit up one leg.

Foster kneels in front of me while someone hides my hair under a blond wig that hangs straight to my shoulders. He reaches through the part in the fabric and belts a leather garter to my thigh. Like Farrah's, it hides well under my billowy skirts.

He jostles around with the garter and glances up at me. "HK outside thigh. Knife inside thigh. Aerochlor canister back thigh."

I nod and swallow, my dry throat clicking. "Tell me this is going to be okay."

He stands and grips my arms. "I'll be waiting here with a stiff drink for when you get back. We're both going to need it."

My eyelids drift closed and I try to breathe. My heart beats too fast. "Oh my God."

"Shoes," another man says, and puts a pair of heels in front of me. They must be five inches high.

Dr. Malcolm arrives at my side with an aerosol can. "For your arm."

I glance down at the new skin outside my left arm, and the mixed tones top off my panic. "This will not work."

The doctor smiles reassuringly. "Trust me. No one will know the difference. It smells a little, though." He looks around the room. "Does anyone have perfume?" Other than Sonya and Leigh, we are surrounded by men, who smirk in response.

"Just spray her arm," Reid orders.

Dr. Malcolm sprays the pale skin on my left arm until the color matches. And he is right. It smells. More than a little.

Sonya appears and sprays me with something that smells strongly of vanilla and sugar. The mist makes me cough.

"There," she says. "That'll cover it up."

Reid appears with a full mask. It is white with a red-and-gold half mask painted around the eye area to match heart-shaped lips. White ribbons hang from the sides.

Reid takes me by the elbow and rushes me down the hall, giving me orders the entire way. I am already too late to use the same teleporter stop Leigh would have used to meet her car. I will have to teleport someplace nearby, though this part is sticky for him. I offer to teleport into the gallery down the street from Declan's building, and he seems more than happy with this suggestion.

I tie my mask on outside the teleporter while he chatters on; he is clearly stressed by this turn of events but has efficiently worked out every detail. Personally, I pray I do not faint the second this adrenaline dissipates.

"You have your com?" Foster asks as he helps me onto the teleporter platform.

I waver in my heels as the floor gives, then nod. "Yes."

"All right. See you when you get back."

After one good breath in, I punch in the sequence that will take me to the gallery where Noah once planned to kill me. Maybe once he sees me, he will attempt to repeat the action. He is going to hate this more than I already do.

"Good luck," Foster calls as everything disappears.

CHAPTER 29

The gallery looks just as I remember it from my first visit with Declan. The walls feature a wide array of styles—paintings and photographs—with canned lighting in the ceiling. Cushioned benches are arranged in front of every piece, inviting patrons to sit and admire.

I, for one, would love to sit. Not because I want to appreciate the work but because what I am about to do has hit me. Entering this building has set me right into a piece of my old life and opened my eyes. I could end up in Dr. Travista's lab tonight, and Clint Reid may as well have put me there. Old instincts kick in and I consider cities to teleport to in the west.

Leave while you still can.

Oh, how I want to, but then all of Noah's hard work would be for nothing. Farrah and Miles are already set up to do this thing, and what if they need me? *Really* need me? Noah cannot help them, and he will not allow them to start without proper backup. Which happens to be me, of all people. Worse, if this fails, Leigh will submit to cloning. If I can stop that from happening, I will.

I head for the exit and end up rushing through the door when the gallery owner, Harold Geist, spots me. He cannot know who I am behind my mask but must see a potential sale and nearly bombards me with a pitch.

On the sidewalk, I pause to look up—*and up*—into the lights of Richmond, which are so bright they hide the stars. The last time I saw this district of town, the Christmas holiday had the streets lit up in festive decorations and music played over a sound system. It is nothing like that now, but I am still surrounded by clean lines and the friendly voice of a man stating the price for a *Richmond Times* download. There are ninety-nine suited men crowding the sidewalks to every one woman, all of them staring at me.

Sweat prickles under my mask, from both nerves and summer heat. The retreating sun has taken little of the simmering temperature with it. I fist the folds of my dress in warm palms and lower my gaze as I walk to my destination.

Noah paces outside Burke Enterprises, which urges me to pick up my pace. I must be ten minutes late at best. The closer I get, the hotter and more constricting the air becomes. He is going to kill me.

He spots me and lets out an annoyed sigh. Once I am in hearing distance, he says, "Do you have any idea what time—?"

He stops abruptly, eyes wide under his mask. His lips lengthen into a taut line. I follow his gaze down to my chest, but my full mask limits the movement. He reaches forward and hot fingertips brush the space between my breasts. The light movement of a chain tickles my skin.

Then I know. I never removed my luckenbooth necklace. All this time I have kept it hidden under my shirts; I doubt he even knew I wore it. Clearly he recognizes it and does not believe for a second Leigh wears it.

Noah fists the necklace between us until his knuckles whiten. "What the hell is going on?" He speaks in a whisper, but his shaking tone holds so much fury it makes my throat tighten.

Swallowing my fear, I say, "It is fine. I promise."

He bends to put his lips by my ear. His breath is hot and humid. "Explain to me how this is *fine,* Emma. You can't be here."

"There was an accident and Reid made the only choice he could." I whisper too, watching the long line of masked attendees entering the building on a red carpet. "You need me or this is over."

He straightens. "Then it's over. Of all the people to send . . . I can't believe you followed along."

"I did not see another alternative."

He continues as if I had not spoken. "You're going into a room with the very man who would erase you completely; do you realize that?"

"I am masked and wearing a wig. As long as these items stay on, he will never know."

He shakes his head, his focus on the concrete under our feet. "It's too risky."

"I chose to do this. You know me, and you know I would never have gone along if I did not believe we could do this. Let me help, Noah. Please."

He looks at me, unblinking, for a long moment. A heart-pounding eternity later, he reaches out and starts to unclasp my necklace. "I'll hold on to this. No hired escort in her right mind would wear this symbol." He pockets the jewelry and offers me his elbow. "Come on."

The Fire and Ice Masquerade Ball is on the second floor. Security checks invitations at the top of the stairs, then allows the attendees to enter an extremely large room with dim lighting that gives the atmosphere a romantic feel. Marble pedestals topped with round glass bowls surround the room. Inside each vessel is a flame that appears to float and lick the open air. Tables with ice sculptures or full bouquets of red roses for centerpieces are arranged around the outside of the room. A string quartet plays on a raised dais in a corner, dressed to match the guests in red and white.

Noah lays a hand over the top of the fingers I have curled around his elbow. The second we enter, his entire body relaxes, reminding me to do the same. He smiles and formally greets other guests, whom I do not recognize. Because I am an "escort," he does not waste time making introductions.

He pauses once we are deep inside the room and glances around. "Let's dance," he says without looking at me. He searches for someone, but I do not know if he looks for Miles and Farrah, who are not due to arrive yet, or Declan. As the host, he should already be here, but the room is too full to tell.

Noah finally looks at me, and it as if I am the only woman in the room. I have not been on the end of this intense gaze since San Francisco, and it makes my head swim in a warm haze.

He lifts my arm and spins me onto the dance floor. He follows the graceful move and guides me into his arms with ease, setting a hand on the small of my back and holding the other in the air.

I have no memory of dancing with him but do not find it hard to follow his lead. Each step is smooth like silk, his hold firm. Somehow he manages to ensnare my eyes with his and never missteps. Despite the recent tension, and in one look, I am all his.

"You look stunning," he whispers.

Heat prickles my chest and rises up my neck. "You do not have to say that."

"Why not? It's the truth."

I take a shaky breath. "Thank you."

A soft tone beeps in my earpiece, followed by Miles's voice. *"The Winchesters are in place."*

Noah pushes me out and spins me again. Once I am back in his arms, he says, "Tucker and guest in place."

I glance over Noah's shoulder and spot Miles and Farrah taking champagne flutes from a passing waitress. They do not look our way, and to any stranger's eye they look like a beautiful couple very much in love.

"Five minutes," Noah says softly, "then we go find our host. You ready for that?"

No. "It will be fine." I do not know if this affirmation is more for my benefit or his.

"Correct me if I'm wrong," Miles says, *"but your date sounds very much like—"*

Leigh's laugh interrupts the com. *"Oh it's 2.0, all right. And I'm kicking your buddy Jacob's ass the second I'm able."*

Relief floods me with the sound of her voice. "How are you?"

"Not now," Noah says. "We go on as planned." He turns us and bumps a shoulder into another gentleman, to whom he apologizes in an absent way, but then his entire body stiffens.

"Dad." The greeting holds no surprise, but no familial love, either.

My mouth dries up. Noah has a father. Who is here. As a guest.

"Hello, son," the man says, and pulls his young date to a stop. "I thought that was you." From behind his mask, amber eyes look down the bridge of his long, pointed nose at me. "I'm surprised to see you with a date."

"Thought it was time for a change," Noah says, and tightens his arm around my back. His fingers dig gently into my side. "Don't worry. I didn't do anything stupid like purchase a wife."

His father chuckles. "That *would* ruin the forever-a-bachelor image you're so desperate to protect, wouldn't it?"

Noah smiles, but it does not reach his eyes.

The man, whose only resemblance to Noah that I can tell is in his eyes, reaches a hand out to me. "James Tucker." He nods down at his date. "This is my wife, MyAnna."

"Tenth wife," Noah clarifies for my benefit, but still does not introduce me.

"Constance," I say with a Southern inflection, and take James's extended hand. There is no softness to his bony touch, and I feel as if he might break my hand with his overly firm grip.

The men lead us off the dance floor, where they stop one of the many young women carrying trays of champagne. Each girl wears an identical sequined, white shift dress and high heels.

James takes two flutes, and Noah takes only one for himself, as part of his act to be dismissive of me. Not that I can drink, not with this full mask on.

James starts to hand me his. "My son is very rude, Constance."

Noah raises a hand to stop me from taking it. "No drinking for my date. Part of the contract."

MyAnna lifts her chin and turns her face away, but I am careful not to react.

James takes a slow sip of his champagne, then says, "Reputation has always been my son's number one priority." He looks at Noah while speaking to me. "One wrong word, my dear, and he'll never hire you again."

"Reputation means everything in this town." I should probably remain silent, but I also have a strong need to defend Noah. He does not deserve this condescension, most especially not from his own father.

"Not everything," James says, and smirks in a way that has Noah written all over it despite Noah's lips being fuller. Adrienne, too, actually. "Can't forget money. After all . . . reputation alone can't buy one happiness."

Noah lengthens, his unforgiving stare never leaving his father. Finally, he turns his attention to me, and it is not much softer. "I think it's time we mingled."

I nod at James and MyAnna. "Nice to meet you both." Noah steers me away and I whisper, "Did you know he would be here?"

"I thought he'd show, yes."

"I take it he does not know he has a granddaughter?" I do not know why, but this bothers me. We have so little family, and faced with Noah's, I hate the idea of Adrienne never knowing him.

Noah stops, throws back what is left of his champagne, then sets the empty flute on a nearby table. "My dad thinks I'm a bachelor who lets business control my every waking decision. That's all he needs to know."

"And your mother?"

His cheeks flush and I sense a tide of banked anger inside him. He looks over my head but seems to be somewhere else entirely. "He sold her when I was young. He sells them all when he's done with them. Impregnates them once, sometimes twice out of his sense of duty, then moves on."

I cannot breathe. "What? Where is your mother now?"

Please do not say dead.

"Germany. Her husband moves around a lot."

"Does she know the truth about you?"

He nods once and his eyes come to rest on mine. "She loved you."

I have nothing to say, so I simply take his hand and squeeze.

"We need to look for Burke," he says, squeezing my hand back.

"We should split up, yes? If I see him, I will com you."

"That wasn't part of the plan. You need to stay by me."

"We lost time speaking to your father. Miles needs to get to the server room and Farrah needs to get to Declan's office. Security is still tied up with incoming guests. We have to utilize this time efficiently."

Noah sighs, then nods. "Okay." He scans me for a moment, holding me so I cannot turn away. "Slouch or something. I feel like your posture is a dead giveaway."

"That is the most ridiculous thing I have ever heard," I tell him, biting back a laugh. "Stop worrying about me. I will be fine."

He lets my fingers slide out of his, and I turn my back. I can feel his attention on me until I disappear around the side of the dance floor. I walk slowly and take a glass of champagne when it comes by for nothing more than to have something to do with my hands. I pass Farrah and Miles, and they ignore me as easily as everyone else.

I scan the outlying tables and dance floor for Declan, but he is nowhere to be found. I do, however, see the Thomases clustered in a dark corner. Evan and Daxton seem to be having a heated yet quiet conversation, which tugs at my curiosity.

Charissa Thomas sips from a champagne flute and looks elsewhere. Her sleek, dark hair has been curled into a chignon with ivory hairpins. Her white maxi-length dress is fitted from top to bottom, emphasizing her slim curves, and belted at the waist.

On the dance floor, I spot Richard and Lydia Farris, he in a white tux and she in a shade of red that suits her auburn hair. A sweetheart neckline gives way to an A-line skirt that sweeps the floor. She looks radiant tonight, and nothing like the skeletal, pale, day-old clone I met last year.

I am about to move on, but that is when I smell him. The bold musk that ties my stomach in knots while melting my insides all at once.

I want him, my body says, remembering all the expert ways he used to touch me, guide me, love me. Except . . .

I hate him.

Turning, I find Declan smiling down at me, a red half mask over the sea in his eyes.

CHAPTER 30

Forgive me," Declan says, the creases around his smile deepening, "but didn't I just see you dancing with Noah Tucker?"

I nod, my throat momentarily constrained. The bustier under my dress seems much tighter than it was a moment ago. Somehow, I manage my pitched Southern accent. "You must be Declan Burke."

"Shit," I hear Noah mutter through my com.

"I am, and you are . . . ?"

"Constance Wiseman. Mr. Tucker's date."

Declan takes my hand and presses a kiss to my knuckles. My God, that mouth. I used to love those soft lips. The thought makes my stomach swim with revulsion. His full attention remains glued to my eyes, the only visible part of my face, which seems entirely too recognizable all of a sudden. Will Declan know me from my eyes alone? I am now grateful for the oversweet perfume Sonya sprayed on me. Noah worried Declan would know me from my *posture.* Maybe he was not acting as paranoid as I thought.

"I'm surprised he left your side," Declan says.

My heart *thunk*s as he rises to his full height. He is impressive and dashing in his white tux jacket and bow tie.

"Oh"—I flick a flimsy hand in the air—"he had a small matter to attend to, is all. I am perfectly fine here for the moment."

He lifts an elbow toward me. "You shouldn't have to be 'fine' for even a second. That dress begs to be danced in, so allow me. Tucker won't mind."

"Emma . . . ," Noah warns.

"Are we a go?" Miles asks.

I glance to my left and catch Miles's back to me on the far side. Farrah watches over the rim of a champagne glass.

I can do this.

I look up at Declan. The plan is to keep a constant eye on him and stall in case anything goes wrong. Time is of the essence, and Noah is nowhere in sight. Minutes ago, he was headed to the other side of the room, and the crowd grows too thick for him to get back to me in time.

I set my champagne flute on a table beside me and take his elbow. "Why not?"

Reid answers Miles's question. *"We are a go."*

Declan walks us to the middle of the floor and skips the graceful turn Noah would have started with. He pulls me right into his arms. I wait for his hand to sit low on my waist, but instead, he places it near my midback. He even keeps a respectful distance between us.

"Have you known Tucker long?" Declan asks.

Glancing up, I shake my head. "We just met. What about you? How do you know Mr. Tucker?" The last thing I want to do is talk, because if anything gives me away, it will be my voice. I can only hope the accent and string quartet are enough to camouflage my true identity.

"We've had a few business dealings together."

I pick at nonexistent lint on his lapel to avoid looking up.

"So," he says when I do not speak, "if you just met Tucker, then I take it you aren't one of his employees."

"No. A last-minute call whose schedule happened to be free tonight."

"I see you," Noah says through the com. *"Twenty seconds."*

"I see," Declan says. "You're a professional escort."

"I am. You look disappointed." And he does, which I do not understand. Why would he care about Noah's date so much?

"Not at all. I guess I hoped Tucker might have finally decided to settle down."

"With a potential wife." These days, I suppose all women are prospective partners if they can be talked into cloning.

He nods. "I was like him once, taking escorts to events because my focus was on my business. But once my wife was well enough . . ." He trails off and looks over my head, lost in some memory.

"You must miss her," I say before I can stop myself. I already know the answer, but it has always surprised me how deeply he seems to care. He acts as if I am *everything.* As if *we* are everything. A part of me wants him to have that back, except half of everything will never make a whole. My everything will always be someone else entirely.

Declan looks confused by my statement, so I clarify. "I keep up on current events, Mr. Burke. I know all about your wife. I can only imagine how scared you must be, given her poor health. And all the media can focus on these days is how she knew that clone who died. Shameful."

Declan gives me a tight smile. "The media can focus on whatever they want, Miss Wiseman. I'll still find my wife and make those bastards pay with every last drop of their blood."

A chill tingles down my spine. "I have no doubt in your ability to do just that, Mr. Burke. No doubt at all."

Noah's soft musk surrounds me from behind, and I want to sink into the heat of his fingers grazing along my lower back.

Declan stops dancing and smiles over my shoulder. "Tucker. There you are."

"If you wanted to borrow my date, you could have asked." Facing

Noah, I find him smiling as if he had not just heard every word Declan said. He wears this friendly mask well. "For a fee, of course." Casually, he pulls me out of Declan's space. His fingers are tight on my wrist, and his palm radiates heat.

"Oh, of course," Declan says with a laugh. "Let's get a drink so we can discuss this fee of yours."

"Alpha Team," Reid says, *"you are clear to go."*

I release a slow breath. This com means Reid has successfully switched live for prerecorded feed on the two floors where Farrah and Miles will be running separate tasks. Foster and Leigh will monitor the live feed from the hub to forewarn them of any threat.

Off the dance floor, Noah and Declan take champagne from one of the waitresses—I am ignored again—and the two of them proceed to talk business. I tune out the second one of them mentions a recent tax increase that has gone into effect.

Noah releases my arm to have both hands free so he can emphasize his distaste with large hand gestures. Acting this expressive seems out of character for him, but it works because he does it so naturally. Declan certainly seems familiar with this version of Noah.

While they commiserate over the loss of fortunes they have yet to make, I survey the room and security placement. They are easy to spot, as they wear black tuxes with red shirts. Every now and then, one lifts a hand to his ear to speak to the team. So far they are unaware of the actions going on upstairs.

"Jaybird in position," Miles says. He has reached the server room.

"Jaybird, hold position," Foster says.

"Girl Scout in position," Farrah says, letting everyone know she has reached Declan's office. *"Logging onto server . . . Access code is Delta Bravo seven six two Charlie."*

My heart drums hard and fast. We are so close. In minutes, we will have more data on Declan Burke than we will know what to do with.

Through the com I hear the *shiff* of a door opening followed by a confirmation of entry by Miles.

Noah's abrupt laugh startles me back into the room. He jabs a thumb over his shoulder at me and glances back with a light in his eyes. "Who, her? No. I told you. It's for a cousin of mine."

I am immediately drawn to their conversation.

"Well," Declan says, tilting his champagne flute forward, "I'll throw her in for you if you'd like. I'll even put her at the head of the line. How does tomorrow sound?"

Noah belts out a single, hard laugh. "I don't even know this girl."

I have to bite my tongue. Declan still acts as if he is doing women—all of mankind, for that matter—a favor.

Declan leads Noah aside, but I hear every word through Noah's com.

He lays a hand on Noah's shoulder and bends toward his ear. "Think about it, Tucker. I'll make sure Arthur wipes her memory and she'd never be the wiser. You need an heir to that empire you're building."

"Come on—"

"You're doing me a huge favor with this Emma situation."

Noah shifts his weight and tucks a hand into a pocket. His champagne lies poised against his lower lip, ready to tip back. "I haven't found anything yet."

"But you will. I have every confidence."

The two men stare at each other for a protracted moment before glancing my way. Dumbfounded, I cannot move. I would love to storm off in a rage or step forward and slap Declan in the face. Instead, I flutter my fingers in a wave as if I am as clueless as Declan believes.

"Let me test her out first," Noah says, and a salacious grin tilts across his face.

"Like she's a car?" Leigh asks.

"He can test all he wants," I whisper just loud enough for the com to pick up. "He could not handle me."

Noah chokes on a sip of champagne and I hear several chuckles through the com.

"Focus," Reid warns.

"Found the server," Miles says.

"See you downstairs," Farrah responds.

Miles and Farrah have been little more than background noise until now. Farrah has been searching Declan's files for the right server number while Declan plotted overturning another woman's life for breeding purposes. He disgusts me and deserves everything that is coming to him.

"Wait, wait, wait," Foster says. *"Girl Scout, you have company."*

I stiffen and listen as Foster explains how Armand and Daxton have just entered the outer offices. Armand is showing Daxton something on his computer, and they do not seem to be going anywhere anytime soon.

Farrah is trapped.

I look around for Daxton's parents and find Charissa dancing with Evan on the dance floor. She looks away as he talks in her ear. Neither looks happy.

"Uplinking data from server now," Miles says. *"We have maybe five minutes, and if I return dateless . . ."*

"We can't run the duplicate video feed for much longer, either," Farrah says. *"Someone's bound to notice."*

We need a distraction to pull Daxton and Armand from the outer office. Farrah needs only a minute. I exchange a look with Noah, who stands a good three steps away with Declan. Obviously, this is why he planned for backup. Only the look he gives me warns me not to take a single step outside this ballroom.

One of the waitresses passes me on my left, knocking me with an elbow. "Oh," she says, and smiles. "I apologize."

"No problem at all," I tell her.

She turns away while I measure her size because suddenly, I have an idea. One I think might actually work.

I approach Noah and lay a hand on his forearm. "How about I mingle so you two can talk?"

He sets a firm hand over mine. "That's not really necessary."

Squeezing his arm, I giggle. "I was trying to be polite, but you have forced my hand, Mr. Tucker. I need to use the little girl's room, so if you would please excuse me for a few minutes." I nod at Declan. "Thank you for the dance, Mr. Burke."

Declan responds, but I do not hear him. I am already following the waitress from a moment ago. She turns down a brightly lit corridor where the waitresses have been coming and going all night.

"Prototype in play," I say into the com, repulsed by the call name Reid assigned me. He overheard Noah and me refer to Declan that way one day, and stuck it to me as well. "Base camp, prepare to run live feed on floor 182. I have an idea."

CHAPTER 31

I smooth my hands down the front of the sequined shift dress and give the waitress a sympathetic smile. She cannot see it because I sprayed her with aerochlor and she will be out for at least thirty minutes. My dress, wig, and mask lie across the desk in the shadowed office.

"Ready?" I ask Foster.

"I hope you know what you're doing," he says in response.

While I dressed, Foster recorded enough feed to run while I get in and out of the second floor undetected by video surveillance. To Farrah's annoyance, we have been running live feed on floor 182 while she hides under Declan's desk. Once I teleport to the same floor, I will let Daxton and Armand "catch me" in the act of something treacherous. I cannot have Daxton witness my arrival without involving the resistance, and Declan cannot believe the resistance has access to the foolproof security system installed by Tucker Securities. Thus the live feed.

"Prototype," Reid says, *"you are clear to go."*

"On my way," I say and slip out of the office, taking a moment to glance both ways.

The office I chose sits on the corner of the perpendicular hallway leading back to the ballroom. Several feet in the opposite direction is a set of stairs leading down to a bay of teleporters. Declan once took me to his office from there.

I pause at the bottom of the stairs and make sure the way is clear before racing to the nearest teleporter. My bare feet pad quietly on the marble floor. I rest a hand over the HK holstered to my thigh and enter the glass-encased tube. My heart beats loud in my ears, and sweat tickles my brow line.

With a deep breath, I type in the number 182 and appear outside a long hallway with a carpeted floor.

"Security hasn't caught on yet," Foster says.

I run down the hall toward the glass doors, which slide apart the second they sense my approach. Inside, I look to the right and let my attention land on both Daxton and Armand in the flesh. It takes them a moment to realize I have arrived because they are deep in conversation on the other side of the desk.

They eventually pause long enough to do a double take. They stand upright from their lounging positions, startled. I hold still to let them take a moment and recognize me. I look directly into the sharp blue eyes of Daxton Thomas and watch the realization take hold.

"Emma Burke," he says, with a smile that looks far too gleeful for my taste.

"Up here plotting against me, boys? Or was the plot against Declan? I forget which. They both sort of run together."

They have barely started to come around the desk before I dart back down the hallway.

"You've been spotted by security," Reid says. *"Get back down to the first floor. We've got your tracks covered from there."*

The second the glass door closes me inside the teleporter, Daxton slams against the outside. He tries getting in but the machine is already set to go and will not open for safety reasons. He slams a fist against the outside and meets my gaze. I punch in my sequence of numbers and watch him melt away.

The running taps of feet echo through the first floor when I reappear. Heart in my throat, I step onto the cool marble and recognize the unmistakable hum of another teleporter in use. Across the aisle from me, a woman appears wearing a red dress that is a perfect complement to her auburn hair.

Lydia Farris.

She steps down, her eyes wide and entranced as they look at me. "Emma?" Her voice comes out a whisper.

"Damn it," Reid says. *"Take her out and teleport her body out of there. It's the only way."*

"What? No."

"Once the witness gives you up, they'll figure out we have control of the feed because you won't be on it. *You'll have to kill her."*

Kill her? I cannot have any witnesses, but the last thing I am is a cold-blooded murderer. She only wants to be a good wife and mother. Just like me. I can almost feel the shift of places as I put myself in her shoes, staring into the end of my gun. I would think of nothing but my husband and child, because that is how much has changed in the last year. It is no longer about me. It is all about them.

"That's an order," Reid yells.

Tears brim my eyes and I reach down for my gun.

Lydia squeaks when she realizes I have gone for a weapon. Her chin trembles and she holds both hands up to stop me. "Please. I have children. You know how much they mean to me. I just kissed them good night, Emma, please. Don't let them wake up without a mother."

Her pleading tears at my heart. I do not want to hurt this woman, children or no. Damn Clint Reid. There has to be another option. Maybe if I make her understand.

I take my hand off the gun. "I have a daughter, too. Declan took me from her. He would take me from her still."

Hands still held aloft, Lydia glances from side to side, but no one is coming. The security has headed upstairs to floor 182.

"Goddamn it. What are you doing? Get rid of her," Reid yells.

I pull the earpiece out, cutting off communication, and cross the space. "I cannot have any witnesses to my being down here, Mrs. Farris. Do you understand?" *Come on, Lydia. Help me save your life.*

Lydia looks at me, tears shining in her eyes. "I will not tell. For the sake of your daughter."

"Promise me," I whisper.

Lydia takes one of my hands. "I swear on my life." She places a hand over her heart and closes her eyes. "Let the void finally have my soul if I break this promise to you."

She says these words as if they are a benediction. They are so much more than that.

"The void?" I ask, my chest tightening. A void wants her soul. An abyss struggles for mine.

The running tap on marble sounds closer, drawing my attention.

"Go," Lydia says.

But I cannot go. Not with all these questions struggling to burst free. Except there is no time. I will have to find a way to talk to her when this is over.

"Thank you," I say, then dash up the stairs to the second-floor offices.

After one last check to be sure the waitress is still passed out, I tie my mask back on. I am back to seeing things with limited eyesight, and it takes a moment to find the door activation switch in the dark.

One step outside, I run right into a man wearing a white tux jacket. My heart leaps, sure he must be Declan, and I start to back into the room. The door clips my shoulder blade on its way shut and cuts off my escape route.

I look up and let out a relieved breath. Noah. "I thought you were—"

"Caught?" He shrugs theatrically. "How would you even know? You removed your com."

The tensing of muscles in his jaw reveals how angry he is. His half-mask is long gone, probably tucked in a pocket, and I feel a pang of jealousy. My face is hot beneath mine.

"I know, but I have it right here."

Noah closes a hand around my fist where I have palmed the ear-piece. "You were given a direct order to take out that woman."

I straighten, unwilling to let him or anyone else turn what I did into a bad thing. "I trust her," I say, and step away from the door.

There is a hard tug on the back of my mask and it falls, clattering against the wall. Turning, I discover one of the strings caught when the door shut.

I reach for the activation switch to retrieve my mask, but Noah puts a straight arm between me and the button. "You don't have the luxury of trusting anyone, and neither do I."

He pauses to listen to his com. With a roll of his eyes, he reaches up and removes the piece from his ear. He continues as he pockets the device. "You know the risks here better than anyone. Coming here tonight was a risk. Going upstairs after Farrah the way you did was a risk. But this . . . letting that woman live was the dumbest thing you've ever done, Emma, and you've done a lot of dumb things, believe me."

My blood boils beneath the surface of my skin. He has spent so much time asking me to trust him. Why can he not trust *me*? "Good thing I got that clean slate when Dr. Travista cloned me, then. I can start all of these dumb things over from scratch."

I start toward his arm, thinking he will move so I can free my mask, but he angles into the space to cut me off. I focus on one of his shirt buttons rather than look into his eyes. "Please move."

He knuckles my chin up so I have to look at him. "Why you, huh?" His anger seems to have dissipated, and a quiet desperation has taken its place. "Why did it have to be you who came tonight?"

"You know why."

"There are a hundred other women—"

"None who knew this mission inside and out. There was no time."

He closes his eyes for a moment and sighs. "It doesn't matter. We need to get you out—"

Deep voices cut him off and we both freeze. They are too close. Probably about to turn the corner. And one is all too familiar.

"I want every floor checked," Declan says, and it is as if he is right on top of us. "She came for a reason and I doubt she'll leave empty-handed. I want her found."

Noah glances around, then picks up my mask, of all things.

"There is no time for—" I start, but he presses me to the door and lifts the mask to hide our faces.

I have no idea of the purpose until his lips slant over mine and he flattens me into the door's frame. I part my lips on a gasp and take his hot tongue deep inside. Every dormant cell inside me perks to attention. He tastes of expensive champagne and smells even better. He reaches through the slit in my dress, cups my thigh, and sweeps it up over his hip. His hand slides over the gun holstered there and stops.

I melt in his kiss, though I am torn between running because I know the men have come around the corner and giving in to this moment with everything I have. I grip Noah's lapels in my fists, both to draw him close but to also contain the vibrations coursing through my hands.

Declan and the men with him have gone eerily silent. I fear the mask is not enough to hide my face, though I am basked in its shadow. Noah, on the other hand, is only half-hidden.

Declan clears his throat. "Excuse us, Tucker. We'll let you have some privacy."

Noah pulls away from me only far enough to say, "I'd appreciate that," in a husky tone. His gaze burns into mine with real, unwavering heat. His chest heaves with every breath, pressing against me.

The footsteps and voices fade, yet we do not move. The bustier in my dress limits every breath, and I cannot get enough air to my lungs. My lips ache with memory and wanting. My fingers refuse to release his lapels.

"They are gone," I whisper, and my voice gives me away. I do not want him to move. Ever.

He nods, his gaze dropping to my swollen lips. His hand slides off the gun, moves back under my thigh, and yanks me closer. This close to him, I feel his hard length pressing against me, and it catches my breath. My entire body aches for him.

Noah drops the mask and grips the back of my neck. His mouth crushes mine, and it is as if air is returning to long-dead lungs. I melt into him like snow in the rain, snaking my arms around his neck and gripping handfuls of hair.

Noah fumbles blindly for the activation switch until the door opens behind me. I practically fall into the room, taking him with me. Our kiss fumbles but resumes unbroken as the door shuts us into the dark. Almost dark, anyway. A pale glow from the city lights outside illuminates our way.

He lifts me onto the desk and maneuvers himself between my legs. He pulls out of the kiss and looks at me, his eyes in deep shadow. With trembling fingers, he traces my lower lip, chin, and finally down the length of my neck.

"What are we doing?" he whispers.

I cannot help but think of Sonya now. Back in the hub with Adrienne, waiting for Noah to return. He is hers now, and I have somehow become the other woman. A woman I would have no respect for in any other situation.

I drop my hands. "I am sorry. I should not have—"

He places a finger over my lips to stop me. "I mean, what are we doing apart?"

My heart swells, but I work to contain my joy. I cannot get my hopes up. Not yet. "There is no easy answer to that question."

"Emma." His eyes pinch shut and he takes a deep breath. When he opens his eyes again, anxiety shines there. "Tell me you're done running. I couldn't take it if you disappeared again."

I sink into him, my soul flooding with every ounce of love I have. Somehow, some way, I will soak up every shred of fear he holds. I cup his face and look into his eyes. "I stopped running the second I came back. I belong to you."

His smile starts to encompass the dark room, but a soft moan slams us back into reality. The unconscious waitress rolls from her side to her back but does not wake yet.

"My mask," I whisper, and jump from the desk.

Noah finds and places the mask in my hand but does not let me put it on yet. He cups the back of my neck and presses his forehead to mine, his warm breath caressing my skin. The mere scent of him makes me forget how bad our timing is.

"We're doing this?" he asks. "You and me?"

I scratch my fingernails along his sideburns and kiss him. "There is only one person standing between us."

He nods. "I'll talk to her when we get back."

I cannot believe this is finally happening. He is mine again. "Then yes, we are doing this."

He is leaning in to kiss me when the door opens.

"I don't recall reuniting with past loves as being part of the plan," Miles says. "Major Reid has ever so kindly requested that you put your coms back in."

Noah winks before turning and using his tough boss voice. "Take the waitress to a teleporter and send her to the hub."

He unearths his com and tucks it back in his ear, reminding me I should do the same. Luckily, it is quiet on the other end. Maybe everyone is in shock. I know they saw us on the hall feed. I just hope Sonya is tucked away in her room with Adrienne.

Farrah comes forward, a frown on her face. "Thanks for the save."

"No problem."

Her blond brows rise. "This doesn't make us friends."

"Would never dream of it."

Noah holds out a hand for me, half his focus on Farrah. "Let's go say our good-byes."

CHAPTER 32

The good-byes are exhausting. Noah knows so many people, and because he has to maintain the image that I mean nothing, it makes it hard not to question if the kiss and declaration happened. We never run into Declan because he is busy searching for me. Not a soul in the room has a clue anything is going on.

Even Lydia Farris acts as if I had not threatened her life a half hour ago. I hate being so near and having no opportunity to speak with her about her "void." Do we dream the same thing? Does she feel the tug of an arctic abyss? Did Ruby? Do all the clones?

"Okay, I think that's it," Noah says with a final glance around. "They all think I'm off to fuck your brains out."

I gulp. "Excuse me?"

He laughs and bends to speak in my ear. "Playboy—*me*—rents date—*you*. What else are they supposed to think?" His hand skims down my side and cups my butt. I squeal and jump in surprise. "There. That should seal the image."

"Mr. Tucker, if you do not remove your hand . . . ," I say in a warning tone, but I cannot help but laugh. I am grateful to the mask for hiding my overheated face.

He circles an arm around my waist and pulls me tight, still whispering in my com-free ear as he says, "You were perfect tonight. Thank you."

We are so close I can feel the beat of his heart against mine. He leans back to capture my gaze. The heated swirl of amber steals my breath. The room full of moving bodies blurs at the edges of my vision, and the chatter of voices becomes a steady hum. If he does not release me soon, we will never make it to the hub tonight, and I refuse to take this further until he is one hundred percent mine.

I clear my throat. "We should go."

James Tucker's voice breaks up the molten tension surrounding us. "I heard you're on your way out, son."

Noah stiffens and turns to face his father. "I am."

James glances between his wife and son, then says, "A private word first." He lifts a hand toward me and guides MyAnna to my side. To me, he says, "I trust you won't mind if I steal him for a moment, Constance?"

I look to Noah for some kind of signal. If he would prefer not to go, I will happily refuse James. Of course, James could just as easily tell me my opinion does not really matter anyway. It is frustrating to be this powerless. But Noah takes his father by the elbow and leads him out of earshot. Once they stop, Noah surreptitiously removes his com so no one can hear their private conversation.

"What are they talking about?" I ask.

MyAnna faces me and smiles. "Why don't you just stand there and look pretty. That's what you were paid to do, isn't it? Leave the *family* matters to the *family.*"

Through my com I hear Leigh say, *"Oh hell. A pod-wife."*

It takes everything I have not to claim my actual right to ask and receive an answer. Not only that, but I am a complete stranger to her. Is this how she treats all women she meets? For her sake, I hope not. She is in the same precarious boat we are all in.

"Wife number five?" I say. "What is the shelf life for a James Tucker wife, anyway?"

Her mouth opens on a silent gasp. In my com, Miles snorts on a laugh and Farrah threatens his life if he breaks their cover.

I turn and step away from MyAnna. What I said was underhanded and cruel, but I have a feeling there is a long line of women who would tell me she deserved it.

Near the corner of the dance floor, I stop and take calming breaths. I have removed myself from the area where the Tuckers speak privately, but I am easily in Noah's eye line. I catch his gaze to be sure, and he nods once to let me know I am okay here.

But maybe not. Declan walks through the room as if on a mission. Straight for me. Or so I believe until he stops five steps away to speak with Daxton Thomas. I palm the soft folds of my dress with clammy hands and take a deep breath.

Remain calm. Look natural.

My heart slows as whatever Declan and Daxton talk about turns heated. Declan's hands fist, and Daxton jabs a finger in his chest. Heads swivel toward them and conversations stop.

"What's going on?" Miles asks.

"I cannot hear. The music is too loud." Can I get any closer without raising attention?

One quick sweep of the area reveals Charissa Thomas watching from the edge of the dance floor. She leans precariously and swallows half a glass of champagne. She exchanges her empty glass for a full one that passes a moment later.

She is my way in. I head over and touch her arm. "Monica, is that you?" I say in a pitched, cheery tone.

Charissa leans back and turns as if on a tilt-a-wheel to face me. She is mask-free now, and her dark hair is starting to come loose around her face. Her hazel eyes lean toward a lovely shade of green, a perfect match to Adrienne's. "No, dear, not Monica." She smiles and extends a hand. "Charissa Thomas."

I giggle and accept her handshake. "How embarrassing. You look the spitting image of a good friend."

"You're Noah Tucker's date."

"Yes. Constance Wiseman."

She raises her champagne to her lips, showcasing the branded luckenbooth on her left hand. She tilts too far back to take a drink and I reach a hand behind her just in case.

"Is everything all right?" I ask.

She laughs, her apple cheeks turning a brighter shade of red. Her eyes glisten. "No."

She angles her glass at her son and my ex. I still cannot hear them because, while heated, their discussion is very low. Declan leans very close to Daxton now and jabs a rigid finger at the ground. Daxton in no way stands down.

"See that?" she says.

The entire room sees them. "Oh, I had not noticed them before. Are they fighting?"

She does not seem to notice my inquiry as anything other than genuine curiosity. "Breaks his promises, that one."

"Which one?"

"Declan *Burke*." She sways and I take her elbow. She wraps an arm behind my back and brings us together. Most of her weight is on me and I fear I will go down with her if I am not careful. "Broke his promise to take care of her."

"Take care of who?"

She turns her head and rests her lips against my ear, but she does not whisper. The sharp pitch makes my eardrum ring. "Olivia. My baby girl." She pulls back with raised brows and nods as if she has enlightened me about something tremendous. "Andrew Burke promised. Declan Burke promised. They all promised." She lists again, then links our arms so she can hold my hand. "He'll get her killed."

Daxton's raised voice draws my attention back. He throws his arms up and yells, "Why wait? Maybe I'll just tell them all right now." He sweeps an arm to encompass the room. "I'm sure they'd all love to know about what's *really* going on with that wife of—"

"Daxton!" Charissa rushes forward, forgetting to release me. Her hand crushes mine. "You can't."

Evan arrives in an almost too calm manner on the other side of Charissa and glares between Declan and Daxton. "What's going on?"

Declan points at Evan. "Did you know?"

Evan squares his shoulders and loosens the hold he has on his wife, his gaze skipping to Daxton. "Know what?"

"My wife was here," Declan says. "She asked your son if he was plotting against her. *Against me.* Come to find out, he's the one who's been leaking everything to the press."

Charissa squeezes my hand so hard my knuckles rub together, making me wince. "She is here?"

"*Was,* Mother. She *was* here." Then to me, Daxton says, "You know, this is a private—"

"Oh, don't you dare," Charissa says, clinging to my hand. While she had scarcely been able to stand on her own before, righteous anger now gives her a steel spine. "You plan to make everything public anyway. And you don't care who gets hurt in the process, do you?"

Daxton stares in stunned silence at his mother.

I try removing my hand from her grip. While I had wanted to be near enough to hear before, this is far too close for comfort. "Mrs. Thomas, my hand . . ."

Declan watches me struggle, but his eyes are distant. Finally, he looks at Daxton. "What else have you been planning? And don't try denying it, because your mother speaks as if you aren't done."

"You deserve what's coming to you," Charissa snaps at Declan. Spittle flies from her lips. To Daxton, she says, "But not at her expense."

Evan grabs her arm, taking her attention. "Darling, you're drunk." Banked rage rims his eyes, but he stands steady and prepared to lob whatever balls come.

She glares at her husband. "He won't stop until he knows the truth."

"*Ah,*" I whimper as she rubs my knuckles together once again. I cannot free my hand. Not without drawing too much attention, at least. She is much stronger than she looks. "Mrs. Thomas, please . . ."

Noah's voice fills my com. *"I'm coming. Hold on."*

Charissa goes on with a single-minded focus. "They're both putting her in too much danger. We have to stop this, Evan. We're the only ones who can protect her now."

Cold trepidation weighs in my stomach. Pieces of our earlier conversation start to slide into place alongside the current topic. But I refuse to believe it. I am missing something else, or looking too hard at the information provided.

Daxton shifts the weight on his heels and narrows his eyes. "Protect who? Emma Burke? Why would you want to do that?"

Declan glances between the three of them. "I think I'd like to know the answer to that, too."

Charissa finally lets me go so she can approach Declan. I stumble back but am caught around the waist by Noah. He asks if I am okay, but I ignore him, torn between running and staying to hear where this leads. Except I fear where this leads. I do not want to know this truth.

Mrs. Thomas shoves Declan in the chest. "You were supposed to protect her. That was the deal."

"What deal?" Declan looks behind her to Evan. "What deal?"

Noah walks us back several paces, but nowhere near out of range. I cannot take my eyes off the scene.

"In exchange for our cooperation," Evan starts slowly, "your father promised our daughter would be safe. We changed Olivia's name to protect her from the resistance. They'd find her and use her against us, otherwise."

"What does that have to do with me?" Declan asks.

"Oh God," I whisper. I already know. My worst nightmare unfolds before me.

"Part of keeping Olivia safe was to place her into a good marriage. With you."

Charissa shoves Declan again and begins sobbing. "And you killed her. Turned her into one of those . . . those . . . *things*."

Evan takes his wife around the middle and drags her back, but his eyes remain glued on Declan. "Emma is our daughter, you son of a bitch. And with my dying breath, I promise you'll pay for what you've done to her."

CHAPTER 33

I cannot breathe. These people—*these traitors*—cannot be my parents. But they are. I know because I look like my mother. I see it in the color of her eyes. The rounded tip of her nose. Her bone structure. We are the same height and have the same slim build.

She gave me away.

A sob thickens in my throat. Tension builds behind my eyes and throbs in my temples. But I cannot cry. Not here. Not yet.

"Holy fucking shit," Miles says.

"Keep it together, 2," Leigh says, but it is too late. Tears already break the surface and slide under my mask.

I cannot hear anything anyone says, though the floodgates are open. Questions and accusations are being flung like plasma fire between Daxton—*my brother*—and Evan—*my father.* Declan stands looking as numb as I feel. Charissa sobs into her hands, a heavy weight in Evan's arms.

"Noah," I whisper, though I barely hear the word myself.

His arms tighten around my waist and I realize my knees have given out. "Hold on," he says. "We're leaving."

But going where? There is no distance too great from this.

He weaves us through the crowd, down the stairs, and into the teleporter bay. "Give me your com," he tells me, his expression calm.

I wish his tranquility would leak into me, because I am a gale-force storm about to strike land.

I remove it with shaking fingers, staring into his eyes. Needing them to hold me together. "Did you hear that?" I ask, but it is a ridiculous question, because of course he did. What I really want to ask is if what I heard was real. It does not feel real.

"Get inside," he whispers, and helps me into the teleporter. "Base camp, we're going radio silent."

He pockets our coms and types an untraceable code on the illuminated keyboard, then a port number. We appear in the park he took me to on my first night, and it is just as empty now as it was then.

I strip off the mask and savor the warm night air on my wet face. The breeze is a tangible thing I can ground myself to. So is the tickle of grass against my exposed toes. And Noah's scent.

A sob shakes loose in my chest. "It is not real. What they said. It cannot be real."

Noah takes the mask from my fingers and hurls it into a copse of trees. "Come here," he says, and his arms surround me as I fall into them.

I stain his shirt with tears, clinging to the fabric, holding on to what is tangible. Trying to focus on what I *know*. I know I have Noah and Adrienne, and that I have finally found my home, though it is not where I expected it would be.

If I'd been asked just over a month ago, home was with my parents, Stephen and Lily. Until now, they were faceless names typed in a WTC record. The family I have been desperate to reunite with. But they do not exist. That is why I have been unable to find them. I lost so much time on this. Too much time. Wasted time. I am *always* wasting time.

Heat ignites and soars through my bloodstream. I push away from

Noah and scream behind clenched teeth. I rip the wig from my head and throw it. Turn my back on Noah and clutch the hair at my temples.

Hands wrap over my shoulders. "Say something, Emma. Talk to me."

I laugh hard from deep in my chest. *What a joke.* "Emma. Emma?" I spin around. "That isn't even my *name.*"

Noah stands coolly in front of me, supporting me with only a look. Ready for the barrage of anger he must guess is coming. But I am unsure if he can withstand it.

"I risked everything," I say. "I walked away from you and Adrienne and stayed away all those months because I was scared to return. Scared you would reject me. So I focused on finding them, because they would never reject their own daughter, right? Why would they? I gave you up for them." A barely restrained sob restricts my throat. My temples throb. "I lost you for them. And they did not even want me. They never did."

He takes me by the upper arms. "You can't believe that."

"Everyone wants to design my future for me. From the very beginning. My parents changed my name and sold me into marriage. Declan wants me to be his obedient wife and give him an heir to his madness. Doctors—even yours—want me to be a good test subject. You want me to be that girl you fell in love with who would collapse entire nations if it meant saving just one woman from slavery."

Noah flinches and drops his hands. I have hurt him but cannot stop the flow of emotion ravaging the air in the form of words containing only a fraction of the venom absorbing my heart.

"What about what I want?" My voice carries on the warm breeze, and luckily, we are very much alone. "I do not want to be Olivia Thomas, and I do not want to be Emma Burke, and I do not want to be calm and willing for the doctors, and I do not want to be Emma Wade, destroyer of evil men."

He takes my arms again so fast and so hard, I am jolted back into reality. Amber burns in his eyes. "You are none of those things."

"You are more right about that than you realize. If you are expecting me to be anything like the woman you married—"

"I knew who you were the moment we talked in the gallery last year. No matter how hard I tried denying it, no matter how hard I forced old images on you, you radiated with a strength I didn't recognize, and that scared the hell out of me."

"No. That is not true. You said I reminded you of Her."

"You want to know who I saw when I looked at you? The woman I knew She could be, but Her past wouldn't allow it. That's why I've been looking for you from the moment you walked away. You, Emma. I love *you*. Not Her. I love you because you are none of those things you think I want, and more."

He cups my face and presses his forehead against mine. "God . . . *Emma*. Be whoever you want, and believe me, I will love you anyway."

Tears stream at a steady pace over my cheeks. He knows exactly what I need to hear, but . . . "What if I do not know who I want to be?"

He pulls back just enough to look into my eyes. "But you do know."

"Not anymore."

He tucks my hair behind my ears. "You told me in San Francisco, remember? You want to be a mother to Adrienne. So even if everything else is up in the air, at least you know you want that."

Adrienne. Of course. With everything twisted around my mind, I had forgotten the one positive thing that has driven my decisions these past weeks. My daughter. Noah is right. I do know who I am.

Adrienne's mother.

I nod because I do not trust my voice to work. Neither of us speaks again after that. I already feel better having vented my frustration, and what has not healed is supported by his arms around me. By the time we prepare to return to the hub, I know one other undeniable thing about myself: I am the woman Noah loves.

Noah ports us into his office. I am grateful for the privacy of our arrival because my face feels hot and swollen from crying. That and I am not ready to face those who witnessed our indiscretion at the ball. All I want is to splash cold water on my face and curl up in bed. Not to sleep, necessarily, but to be alone with my thoughts.

We cross his dark office in silence, the room lit only by the glow of his computer's screen saver—a mosaic of pictures of Adrienne. Noah pauses with a hand over the door's activation switch, then lets out a long breath. His next intake halts as if he wants to say something, but he does not.

"What?" I press.

"I have to go see Sonya. Now. It shouldn't wait." He says this softly, as if he can lessen the impact.

I had already assumed this and thought I was prepared, but I am nervous for him. I am also worried she will make things too hard. Can she talk him into staying with her somehow? Turn him against me by reminding him of how I deserted my family? Play on his guilt? Guilt is funny like that sometimes. It can make us do things we do not want to do.

Noah faces me and gives me a lingering, soft kiss. When he comes away, his nose circles mine. "Should I come by after?"

The idea both thrills and terrifies me. "I would not turn you away."

He smiles. "Good to know." He stands back with a heavy sigh. "Time to face the music."

We are not two steps outside his office before confronting what we dreaded most. Sonya. She lays a stinging slap across my face, then his. Her bloodshot eyes are wide with fury, her hair a mess. She still wears her day clothes despite the late hour, and they are untucked and rumpled.

Sonya raises her hand to slap me again, but this time Noah snatches her by the wrist and twists her arm away. "That's enough." His tone holds no room for argument. "If you need to blame someone, blame me."

But she ignores him. It is as if she and I are the only two who exist. "I *asked* you for the truth," she says.

"I never lied to you."

She laughs with no humor. "No. You just skirted around the question. You're good at that." She yanks her hand free of Noah's hold and glares at him. "You should have ended this weeks ago. Saved me the humiliation. I've been walking around with people looking sorry for me. The poor idiot who can't hold on to the man she loves."

Noah glances furtively at me. "Let's not do this here."

She throws her arms up to encompass the dimly lit and empty hallway. "Why not? We're alone, which is a step up from how the two of you have been carrying on." Angry tears roll down her cheeks and she swipes them away. "You couldn't even have the decency to let me go before you started screwing on camera."

I gape at her. "We are not sleeping together."

"Who told you that?" Noah asks, hands hooked to his hips.

She wipes at her nose with the back of her hand, then sniffs. "It doesn't matter. I know it's true."

Noah throws his hands up in defeat. "Fine. Whatever. Where's Adrienne?"

"With the only person in this godforsaken place who saw fit to look out for me."

His eyebrows shoot upward, waiting for a better answer. I would like to know who has my daughter as well.

"Farrah," she says, and folds her arms, almost daring him to do something about it.

Pieces click together. I thought maybe Sonya saw everything for herself, but she would never leave Adrienne alone in her room just to go watch a mission unfold. That leaves one other option: Farrah told Sonya. She did it to hurt either Noah, whom I firmly believe she has feelings for, or me, the woman she cannot stand.

"You left my daughter with *Farrah*?" Noah says in disbelief, then heads off in the direction of the living quarters, leaving me alone with Sonya.

"For what it is worth," I start, gaze cast down the hall after him, "this is not how I wanted things to turn out. It was never my intention to—"

"Don't you dare. If you didn't intend for this to happen, you should have *left*. You told me you were leaving, so why the hell didn't you?"

"I could not leave my daughter again."

She throws her hands up over her ears and pinches her eyes shut. A low, gravelly moan sounds through her clenched teeth. Then she tosses her arms out to her sides. "You're so selfish, Emma. Everything is about you. The second you came back you made sure everyone saw how fragile you are, how needy. All anyone wants to do is shelter you from the things *you* perceive as danger. You wreck everything you touch. You left him a ruined man last year, and you'll do it again. You'll leave because that's what you do. Only this time Adrienne will be hurt too."

"No." I can scarcely get this one word through the tightness in my throat.

"Yes. I'm right, and I'll be here to pick up after you again. And again."

Does she have so little self-respect? Even if she were right, why would she do that to herself? But it does not matter. There will be no pieces to pick up, because I am not going anywhere.

I open my mouth to respond when my vision goes completely black. Frigid air winds around me and tugs downward. I tunnel into the nothing of my abyss as easily as I would slip into a tub full of ice-cold water. But this is not happening. I am awake.

Right?

In the span of an eyeblink, I find myself back in the corridor, shivering, knees weakened to the point that I am beginning to collapse. Shooting a hand out to the wall, I steady myself and draw in a deep breath.

"A fainting spell? Really, Emma? That's the response you want to go with?" Sonya shakes her head and starts to leave, then thinks better of it. She puts a finger in my face. "This isn't over."

I watch her follow after Noah, my heart pounding in my ears. A fainting spell? No. That was my nightmare seeping into my waking hours. That was my abyss showing signs of impatience. Something hungry and dark comes for me and shows no sign of stopping until it has me.

CHAPTER 34

I startle awake the second I realize I am beginning to drift off. The bathroom light spills through the cracked doorway. The glow from my tablet leaks from around the edges where I have it pressed against my chest.

I need to get up. Move around. Sleep is the last thing I want right now. Especially after what happened earlier.

Rolling from the bed, I make my way out to the hallway, where I am greeted by cool air. I glance toward Noah's room. If he is there, I have no way of knowing. He said he might stop by after, but there is a good chance he will need to be alone after the conversation with Sonya.

I slide to the ground, my back flush against the coarse wall, and look down at the tablet screen. Declan finally made it home around two and has not left his living room since. It is nearing three in the morning now, and from the looks of it, he is nowhere near ready to go to sleep. He sits in the corner of his couch, tuxedo shirt open to a white undershirt, staring into a cold fireplace. He has one arm draped over the back of the couch and the other over the side, fingers clutching a glass of bourbon off the end. Dark skin rings the underside of his eyes.

What does he think about the bomb dropped tonight? Does he feel as betrayed by his father as I do by mine? All those years ago, Declan agreed to marry me under the assumption he had a choice in the matter. In truth, his options were as nil as mine. Our lives were never fated.

Welcome to my world, Declan Burke. How does it feel to have your life plotted as if it is a piece on a bigger chessboard?

Declan's cell vibrates from the cushion beside him. He answers by saying, *"Did you find anything?"* Sitting forward, he rests his elbows on his knees and listens to the caller's response. *"You expect me to believe she just strolled into my office for no reason?"*

"What are you doing up?"

I startle and peer down the dark hall where Noah approaches. His tux jacket hangs from a hooked finger over one shoulder. His shirt has been unbuttoned and pulled free of his pants. He looks tired, and maybe a little stressed, but also happy to see me. He lowers to the empty spot beside me with a tired sigh and takes my tablet to see what I am watching.

"Well, that's basically what you're telling me," Declan says. *"She was there for a reason and I want to know what it was. I want every last detail from every video of every floor scoured for anything out of the ordinary. Nobody sleeps until I have answers; do you understand?"*

After cutting off the call, Declan swings his arm and hurls his glass at the fireplace. The glass shatters against the gray brick. Bourbon soaks blackened logs.

Noah's eyebrows pinch together. "Why are you watching this? If you're worried he'll find something, don't. I have guys making sure all our tracks are covered."

"I am not worried about that."

What I am worried about seems ridiculous now. I had the idea that if I watched Declan have a nightmare, I would find the proof I need to show the clones are connected somehow in my abyss.

"It is nothing."

Noah hands the screen back. Declan has started dialing the phone and paces the sunken living room, his face red. He starts yelling at someone a moment later, and I mute the sound.

Noah nods pointedly at the screen. "Nothing must have been something at some point if you're watching this."

I do not want to burden him with this, especially when I have no idea what is going on yet. But I do not want to keep him in the dark either. "Lydia Farris said something earlier that I cannot stop thinking about."

He takes my hand and skims his thumb across my knuckles. "What did she say?"

"She . . ." I pause, steeling myself for how absurd this will sound once voiced aloud. "She vowed to let the void take her soul if she were to give me away to Declan."

I expect him to laugh, or at least smile, but he looks completely serious. "What does that mean to you?"

I drop my head back, and my skull *thunk*s against the wall. "The phrase reminded me of my own nightmares. Of the abyss I feel tugging at me. I saw this connection that cannot possibly be there."

"What does this have to do with Burke?"

I take a second to put the screen to sleep and set it beside me. "I thought I could catch Declan having a nightmare." I smile at Noah, though the action is forced. "I think I am just desperate for a distraction and will create something out of nothing at this point." Except it *was* something to me the moment Lydia made her promise.

Noah does not return my smile and seems to study me with his intense gaze. "You sure that's all?"

I shrug. "How can we share dreams?"

For that matter, how can dreams threaten your waking mind? This has gone far beyond a simple dream. I just wish I knew how and why. How do I even begin to understand?

His hand tightens around mine and he looks straight ahead. "I don't know."

I need to change the subject. Speaking of the abyss has made me cold. I bump his shoulder with mine, trying to air lightheartedness, but my heart stampedes in my chest. "How did it go with Sonya?"

He frowns and several heartbeats pass in silence. "It wasn't pleasant, but it's over."

"I am sorry. I know that was not an easy decision to make."

"Easy, no. Obvious, yes."

"Is Adrienne still with her?"

He nods. "No sense in waking her. I'll pick her up in, oh . . ." He glances at his watch. "Three hours."

His hand drops heavy to his lap.

"I could get her," I offer, though in all honesty, I cannot imagine that going over well.

"Thanks, but no. Things are bad enough."

Nodding, I tuck my knees to my chest and twist to face him. He leans toward me and lays a soft kiss on my lips, then drops his forehead against mine and closes his eyes. We sit like this for a long time, letting the quiet and nearness soak in.

Noah yawns, breaking the serene moment.

I run a palm over his whisker-shadowed cheek. "Go get some sleep."

He nods, but the only other movement he makes is to pick up my tablet. He blinks hard as if to clear his vision and wakes the computer up to Declan's living room.

"What are you doing?" I ask, peering over to see Declan still pacing his living room, yelling into his phone.

After a shake of his head, he passes the screen back. "I don't know. Nothing."

He stands and helps me up. He hugs me and kisses my temple. In my ear, he whispers, "I have something of yours."

Leaning away, he produces my luckenbooth necklace. He opens the clasp and makes me turn so he can put it back on. Once done, he kisses my shoulder where the curve just meets my neck. Heat flares under my skin and stirs low in my stomach.

I lay a warm hand over the linked hearts and turn. "Will you tell me about the necklace?"

His brows knit together. "You don't remember?"

"I found it in a box after we returned from San Francisco. I assume it meant something important."

A grin tilts his mouth and he leans a shoulder into the wall. "Yeah. To *me*. I hoped it would have meant something to you, too, but you never wore it. Maybe only the one time because you felt obligated to, but..." He looks down and frowns. "You always hated that symbol. I'd foolishly hoped to turn what brought you darkness into something beautiful and only ours."

"That is why you branded your hand?"

Standing upright, Noah peels away the Plasti-skin covering the brand on his right hand. He takes my left in his right and links our fingers so our palms lie flat. He twists my hand so he can see the spot where I used to have a brand. Another twist shows his. They had been strategically placed, as if one set of hearts burned through to the other, binding us forever. Without mine, our link is now broken.

"I have considered having the brand returned," I tell him.

"To fend off any would-be husbands?" His tone holds jest, but his eyes do not.

I cannot look at him as I admit the reason. "My first painting was of our beach the day we were married. The arch. The flower petals. And a luckenbooth in the sand. I had no memories of you at that time, but on a subconscious level"—I meet his eyes—"I was trying to claw you to the surface."

He blinks in response, apparently speechless.

"This symbol has always been my link to you, and you did that. If I wear it, then I carry you with me always." I take a shaky breath. "What do you think? Do I have your blessing?"

Noah catches me around the waist and lifts me from the floor. His nose circles mine, and a grin lengthens across his face. "You have it. All of it. Me, my blessing, my soul, and my love, Emma. You always have. You always will."

"In today's news: a thwarted attack by the resistance at Burke Enterprises. And the self-proclaimed Moirai strike in Chicago"—a symbol floats in the holo-vid behind the news desk: three crescent moons connected back-to-back-to-back and held together inside a circle—*"killing mogul Titus Belleview."*

The newsman swivels to face a second camera angle. *"But first, reports from the White House show a dramatic decline in new volunteers for the cloning project. And the number of women withdrawing their names has tripled. When asked, Dr. Arthur Travista refused to comment, but sources can't deny the timing. The decline seems to have started following the announcement of Ruby Godfrey's death.*

"While some speculate Mrs. Godfrey's death has a direct correlation to knowing Emma Burke, others can't help but wonder if this has anything to do with the resistance at all. New groups seem to be rising up every day, most of them crying that these women are unnatural, and believe that God himself had a hand in her death."

Miles points to the long list of girls on his screen. The other side of his desk, where Farrah normally sits, is empty. I hear she has asked to be reassigned to another partner, but nothing official has happened yet.

Because I sit alone in the back, partnerless, I hope to take her empty spot. Miles and I work well together.

I lean closer to the screens, blinking tired eyes to focus, but the list is still just a bunch of strange names to me. "What am I looking at?"

"There's at least ten girls—sixteen, seventeen years old. All of them transferred into this WTC in the last six months. Their hospital records from their originating center have been archived."

"I do not understand."

He holds up his hand and begins ticking off fingers. "One, transfers are rare at this age. Two, why archive hospital records unless they're trying to hide something? Wouldn't they want the new doctors up-to-date on all information, including their fertility status?"

"Are they fertile?"

"Yes. And"—he ticks off a third finger—"according to these records, the girls entered the center with below-average weight. You'd probably expect them to supplement their meals, right?"

I shrug. "I suppose so." Who am I to know what they would or would not do? I have next to no memories of my time in a WTC. And it is not as if they have the best reputation for caring for the girls.

Miles shakes his head. "They were put on a special diet. Liquid to start, then graduated to bland solids; nothing processed or seasoned. Sound familiar?"

Yes. Intimately, in fact. I have little memory of liquids in my early post-cloning days but remember the tasteless meals Randall served me for months. "This still is not enough proof. Declan will have some excuse prepared if anyone asks."

"Obviously. The man can spin a steel post into a Christmas tree with a wave of his pinky finger."

He wags his eyebrows and grins. Not exactly the look of someone who believes he is out of options, and I think I know why.

"You need to see the archived records," I guess.

"Archived records I'd stake my entire life on that say those girls weren't fertile prior to transfer."

I am suddenly sitting a lot taller and my heart leaps. We might have real proof. "So hack into the archives. Is this not what you do?"

Miles shakes his head. "I might be able to access the records if I had the hard drive, which is back in Burke Enterprises' server room. Even if I could get back in to pull it, I'd never make it out. Their hard drives are attached to the security grid. Pulling one out would initiate a lockdown."

I fall back in my chair, my back slapping the hard surface. "So we are back to square one."

He grins. "Maybe not."

"But you said—"

"That's in Burke Enterprises. I said nothing about a WTC."

I straighten, hearing where he is heading. "We go to the originating WTC and pull the hard drive."

"Under the guise of a raid," he adds. "That way the focus won't be on stopping me, but the rest of the group. I still have to clear the idea with Tucker and Reid, but if we pull an old-fashioned raid, I think I can get to those records. At least four of these girls came from a center in Alexandria, Virginia."

I stand and prepare to leave. "Okay. How about I go talk to Noah while you keep looking for the cloning facility? I cannot believe you have not found it yet."

He swivels to face me with a sly smirk. "A little motivation would go a long way. Pictures will suffice. I'll even take them myself. You won't have to do a thing but lie there."

I turn and wave. "Take your mental pictures as I walk away, you fiend."

CHAPTER 35

Noah calls for me to enter after I knock. I hover in the doorway for a second and watch him shift a serious look from Sonya, who sits in a chair across from his desk, to me. His eyes widen in surprise.

Sonya looks back, sighs, then stands. "Perfect. Would you like to tell her or should I?"

Dread pools in my stomach.

"Go ahead if it'll make you feel better," he tells her, and leans back in his chair. The springs *skritch*.

"Should I close the door for this?" I ask.

"No," she says. "Everyone will find out soon enough anyway. I'm leaving."

I glance between them. *Leaving?* "For how long?"

She laughs from a deep well in her chest. "As if I'd return and put myself through any more humiliation. And you two aren't going anywhere, so . . . I'm leaving. Leaving the resistance. Leaving the east. I never liked it here, anyway."

Was she not just lecturing me about doing this very thing? How she would be here to pick up the pieces? What happened to that? "So everything you said to me last night . . . ?" I shrug. "Was about what exactly?"

"About me reacting in the moment. That's all. I'd apologize, but . . . Well, you understand." She shoots me a quick, thin smile.

That is not good enough. She preached to me about breaking their hearts, but what does she think will happen to my daughter? "What about Adrienne? You are the only mother she has ever known. Why would you—?"

"Emma," Noah says. "It's done."

Sonya's chin drops and she stands with arms akimbo. "It's for the best. Better now while she's still too young to know better. In a few weeks, she'll have already forgotten me."

"You cannot really believe that. She loves you." As much as I hate to admit this, it is true. I have seen and hated every second of the bond they share. Adrienne will be devastated.

She turns back to Noah. "Anyway. I'll get with Phillip and transfer all my files. He'll be up-to-date by the end of next week at the latest."

Noah looks down at his lap and nods. "Fine."

"You know, there's a bright side to all this." She casts us both a glowing smile. "I know you're getting anxious about Leigh going to see Travista. We all are after hearing Phillip's theory. Maybe now you can nudge your girlfriend into helping with *your*"—she emphasizes the word and looks right at me—"clone project."

Noah stands so fast his chair rockets back and crashes against the wall. "Get the hell out of my office."

I cannot take my eyes off Noah's face as she starts out, and he cannot take his eyes off her. His neck and face flush with anger.

Sonya pauses beside me, our shoulders grazing. She lowers her voice to say, "Or you could just leave and avoid the process altogether. But you've probably already considered that."

I look her dead in the eye. "Not once."

I watch her leave, fighting to control the tide of anger that ends in a throb at my temples. Noah passes me and closes the door. The second we are shut in, he turns and gives me a small smile. "Don't listen to a word she says."

I scrape my hair back and release a slow breath. "I know what this project means to you, and I know I promised Dr. Malcolm I would go, but—"

"No need to explain." He encloses me in a hug and kisses the crown of my head. "I get it. You'll go if and when you're ready. No pressure, okay?"

"But there is pressure. What about Leigh? If for some reason she has to go through with the cloning—"

"She backed out this morning."

I jerk my head back. "Are you serious?"

"She was a little full of righteous anger over how Burke tried to have you cloned and wiped last night."

I seriously love that woman.

While I am glowing with happiness over Leigh's decision, Noah nuzzles closer and bends near to my ear. I hear the smile in his tone. "What do you say we pack a bag and the three of us go away for the night? I keep an apartment in the city for appearances—dinner with my dad or associates, etcetera. . . . It's private, and no one has to know we were there."

Can we leave now? The idea of going away with him and Adrienne sounds amazing and just what we need, but there is so much going on lately. Can we just disappear like that? I still have to tell him about Miles's plan. "What about work?"

He looks skeptical. "How much work can there be? It'll take at least a day to analyze the data from the drive."

"Miles has already found something interesting. That is why I am here."

We sit facing each other in front of his desk, and he pulls my feet into his lap as if he has done this a thousand times. He strokes my shins while I talk, which is very distracting. When I finish my short story, he remains silent for a long moment.

"What do you think?" I ask. Going through the details again, I find I am anxious to get started on this plan and even hope to go along with Miles. He will need backup, and how dangerous can it be if we avoid the main cluster of fighting? Not to mention getting the chance to have a personal hand in Declan's downfall. After he tried plotting the cloning of Noah's "date" last night, I would love a shot at him.

"That's a lot of lives at stake just for a hard drive," Noah says.

I pull my feet free and lean forward. "You want to nail Declan. This is a hell of a shot. In fact, I think this is *the* shot."

He leans into an elbow and rubs his beard-shadowed chin. He watches me through narrowed lids.

"Not even Declan can get away with this," I add. "Those girls are protected—though loosely, I admit—by a government-funded oversight committee. They are not to be touched."

"Someone's been reading up on their politics."

I ignore the comment. "If you make this public, imagine the outcry. The committee will be forced to act against Declan."

With a sigh, Noah leans forward and braces his elbows on his knees. Not much space separates us. "I'll discuss this with Reid."

"Admit it. It is a good plan."

"It is."

"So why do you look so hesitant?"

He drops his chin. "Because you want to go."

I bite my lip and look away. "You must want to chain me to a solid surface."

"Can you blame me?"

I shake my head in response.

He reaches out and skims fingertips across my cheekbone. "It's okay. Can't say I'm surprised."

"You will let me go?"

"Yes, but only because I won't let you out of my sight. I'll be going too."

My heart leaps into my throat. I am sick thinking of him in this kind of danger. "You do not have to protect me."

He takes my hands and rolls his thumbs over my knuckles. "Let's shelve this conversation for a much later date, okay? I don't want to fight."

"Okay. What *do* you want to talk about?" I would love to get back to the night away he mentioned.

He lifts his eyebrows. "Ready to talk about your parents yet?"

I stand and retreat automatically. "Not really." Never would be too soon.

"I did some digging."

I lift a digital frame that flashes through images of Adrienne from birth to now. I missed so much.

"They were right about needing to change your name. Our people watched the Thomases for years after they double-crossed the four hub cells, and probably would have taken you to hurt them. They lived under heavy guard for years. Daxton too."

My throat tightens, and I grip the frame until my knuckles whiten. "Noah, I really do not want to hear this."

"Parents make a lot of choices, good and bad, when it comes to protecting their children. They were looking out for you."

"They could have kept the life they had with the resistance. They could have kept their family together and happy."

Noah's hands wrap around my shoulders, startling me. "That was a different time. Had it been me, I wouldn't have had Adrienne anywhere near the hub."

"It is no excuse."

"They wanted to keep you close to home but also offer you a good life."

I shut my eyes and hug the picture frame. There are so many options in front of me to keep my own daughter safe, and choosing to hide her in a WTC and arrange her marriage is not one of them. I would sooner leave her with Sonya to raise.

"They love you," he says, and kisses the top of my head. "In a perfect world, they just would have loved you differently."

I turn and melt into him, pressing my cheek against his beating heart. I hear what he says, but the facts do not make it any easier to deal with. Everything I went through to find them, thinking at one time they might be in danger. So much wasted time and heartache. Maybe one day I will see through the rips in my heart and feel at peace with how things turned out.

Today is not that day.

"I would love to get away for a night," I say, and look up.

Noah tucks my hair back and studies my expression. He finally smiles and says, "I'll make the arrangements."

I have no outfits I would consider for a date, but I find a top made of a thin, taupe-colored material that hangs off one shoulder. My options for bottoms are my black uniform pants and boots, or jeans and old flip-flops. I settle for the latter and vow to shop for nice pants and heels the second this is over.

Noah and Adrienne come looking for me early in the afternoon. She reaches for me automatically and Noah takes my worn backpack. My heart flutters in my chest, and he has as much difficulty holding my gaze as I do his.

We take the private teleporter in his office and appear in a bright white room. The clinical nature reminds me of a lab but for the couches, chairs, and floor cushions—all white with black accents. If not for the thin, black strips of molding, I would not know where the white tiled floor meets the white walls meets the white ceiling.

Twelve narrow floor-to-ceiling windows line the two outer walls of his corner apartment. The sun works hard to penetrate the opaque white shades. White columns mark the corners of the spacious living room. To one side, a square three-quarter wall surrounds what must be a kitchen. A simple oak table for four sits just outside. Opposite the kitchen is a hallway with two doors. Along the inside wall over the teleporter and guest entrance is a white ladderlike staircase that leads to a loft the size of the living room.

Noah sets Adrienne down beside overnight bags he must have dropped off earlier. "I had some food delivered if you're hungry." When I shake my head—I am too nervous to eat—he shifts his attention to Adrienne. "Want to watch cartoons, chicken?"

Adrienne starts rummaging through a pink-and-white bag monogrammed AMT: Adrienne Marie Tucker.

He helps her retrieve a set of watercolor paints and book, then takes my hand. He kisses my knuckles. "Come here." He angles his head at Adrienne to follow. "Come on, you. We have a special corner."

She skips beside us and I ask, "Why do you not live here all the time? This apartment is beautiful."

"I hate it. It suits my image, but it isn't a home. Besides, all this white with Adrienne on the loose?"

"Oh, right. Catastrophe."

"Epic," he says, and laughs.

Around the wall to the kitchen is what looks like an office nook with a black-and-white painting on the wall. The art looks as if a child threw black color on a white canvas. A nice oak desk has been pushed up against the far wall to make room for a kid-size folding table. Nearer the outside is a drop cloth and paint supplies. An easel and blank canvas are already set up.

"What do you think, Momma?" he says to me. "Feel like painting something?"

Tears well in my eyes. This is the sweetest thing he could have ever done for me. "I could paint a million things."

He kisses my cheek. "So do it. We have all day and all night."

CHAPTER 36

The afternoon carries on as if the three of us have followed this routine for years. Not that I do much. Noah takes care of both of us. He paints with and reads to Adrienne. He naps on the couch while she sits enraptured through an entire full-length princess cartoon. Twice.

And all the while I paint a beach. The same setting I have painted a thousand times, except I change the angle. The new view is from the water, showing a long stretch of sand ending at green-capped cliffs. In the distance, I add a blond father walking with a blond daughter on his shoulders.

After the sun sets, Noah takes Adrienne to the spare room off the hallway for bed. Not long after, the scent and sizzle of cooking steaks wafts from the kitchen. Light jazz plays from overhead speakers. I consider getting up to help with dinner, and my back aches from sitting on the stool for so long—I have not used these muscles in this fashion for well over a year—but I cannot bring myself to stop. There is no way I can finish the rendering tonight, but I would like to try.

Noah appears and sets up two more stools—one behind me and the other beside me. He sets a single plate on one with a medium-cooked steak cut into bite-size pieces. For the side, he has placed baby spinach, halved cherry tomatoes, and tiny mozzarella balls on toothpicks, then drizzled them in balsamic vinaigrette. Last, he sets down a glass of pinot noir.

My breath stalls as he takes the stool behind me and finds a clean paintbrush. His musk fills my senses and removes all traces of the sharp acrylic scent. Without a word, he begins working on my painting.

Every now and then, the two of us eat from the plate and drink from the wineglass. I am warm and heady in no time, from both the alcohol and his proximity. The occasional kiss he places on my bared shoulder tantalizes and awakens forgotten places.

While I work on the waves and sand, he adds a woman walking with the father and daughter. She has short dark hair. A tiny dark head of hair peeks out from her cradled arms. I love that he sees this future with me, no questions asked. One day I hope to give it to him.

"Boy or girl?" I ask.

"Boy."

I grin over my shoulder at him. "What is his name?"

He grins back, lines fanning away from his eyes, but keeps his attention on the painting. "Mmmm . . . Good question. What do you think?"

The name comes to me, and maybe it will sound crazy to him, but it feels right. "Wade." For the woman he once loved as much for the woman he loves now.

Noah catches my gaze. "Perfect."

I turn back to the painting with a shuddering breath, because that one word sums up everything about today. I know we cannot stay forever, but this one day, this one memory, will remain untouched. And the best part is that it is mine, not Hers.

Noah's brush dips into the color I have mixed for the sand, and instead of taking the tip to the canvas, he runs the bristles up the length of my forearm until the paint runs out.

A warm shiver travels up and weights my eyelids. A smile twitches on my lips. "What are you doing?"

His nose skims over the length of my neck. Moist, hot breath coats my skin. "I've tried painting you like this. In this position."

An arm bracelets my waist and draws me nearer the center of his lap. His hard length presses against me and I float into a pleasant, tingling weightlessness.

He dips the brush and, again, paints another trail up my arm. "I can't ever get it right."

"All you need—"

A warm lap of his tongue pulls my earlobe into his balmy mouth. Teeth graze tenderly as he pulls free.

"—is a little practice," I finish on a wisp of breath.

Noah takes more paint and has to raise my arm back up to lay claim with another stroke.

"I think you know exactly what you are doing," I tell him.

He smiles against my shoulder, then kisses the skin. "I may have an idea, yes."

I glance back. "But I do not." He does not appear to know what to say, so I stand and turn. "Take off your shirt," I tell him, then straddle my stool, facing him.

He bites his lower lip, studying me. His gaze travels down my neck and along my bare shoulder. To the swell of my breasts. Every second of silence burns me alive. When his eyes settle back on mine, he reaches behind and grips the collar of his green T-shirt, then strips it over his head. His scent wafts around and stirs my already heated center. With his arms free, he grips the backs of my knees and pulls me toward him, wrapping my legs around his waist.

I hold the paint palette aloft and soak up every dip, curve, and angle of him. He is incredible to behold. "I think I can work with this," I say, and dip my brush.

Chuckling, he leans back to let me trail the tawny brown down the center of his chest. Once the brush runs dry, I nose his chin up, giving myself access to his neck. His pulse throbs heavy and fast under my tongue.

Pulling away, I note the flush creeping up his neck and how shallow his breathing has become. It gives me a lot of satisfaction to know this transition is my doing.

His heated gaze falls to my mouth, turning me into one throbbing heartbeat. My lips pulse for his mouth, my breast for his touch, my insides for his length to slide achingly deep within. He makes me ravenous, but I need to make a memory of this. I need to draw this in my mind's eye. Every torturous line of him. A memory I will never forget.

I let the paintbrush drop onto the cloth and settle for using my fingertips instead. A compromise between my aching body and covetous mind. I trace smooth, colorful lines into grooves of shoulder muscle and along his biceps. I paint the channels of his rib cage and curves of pectoral muscle. I pay special attention to each scar and comb my fingers through the dusting of his chest hair. I rub his nipples hard under the pads of my thumbs, pausing to kiss his collarbone, neck, chin. I then graze my teeth over the soft edge of his earlobe, eliciting a shudder in response.

His fingers knead deep into my hips. I roll against him in response. He nearly growls into my neck. "Shirt off."

I pause for only a moment to consider the fact that I could not wear a bra with this top. Noah slips the palette off my thumb so I can remove my shirt. Air-conditioned air hits and tightens my nipples.

With a groan, his mouth takes the curve of my neck. His chin is deliciously abrasive against my sensitive skin. I grasp the sides of his head and fist his hair, heedless of the paint coating my fingers. His chest hair tickles against my breasts, only adding to the rapid firing of my nerve endings.

"I think you know exactly what you're doing," he whispers against my skin.

I tilt his head up so I can look in his eyes. "I may have an idea."

"My turn," he says with a husky tone.

His fingers paint the curve of my breasts, my collarbone, and around my shoulders. I feel his passion with every molten caress, and I mold into a new shape that is not square or round or triangular. My new design is his and will slide seamlessly into whatever hole he fashions.

He finishes his rendering and grips the back of my neck. We breathe hard and fast. I drink in the utter devotion swimming in his eyes and feed him with my complete rapture.

"You're beautiful," he tells me on a slip of breath.

"Not beautiful. Yours."

His mouth slants over mine, and the sweep of his tongue enkindles the building fire inside me. It is a small wonder my entire body does not disintegrate into a pile of ash; my temperature has risen to astronomical degrees. My blood is no less than a flash flood of lava racing to the point of utter devastation.

Noah pushes my hair back to cup my head and holds my mouth to his. I kiss him deeply. Passionately. Endlessly. I explore the ridges of his back, chest, and abdomen. Trace the waist of his pants, wanting inside, gently running my fingernails across his soft skin.

He pulls back, robbing me of his mouth. Various paint colors adorn his luminescent skin. "I need you," he says, his voice deep and husky.

"Need" is exactly the word to describe this situation. Need to feel loved. Wanted. Whole. There is also a need to turn back the clock and forget the last two years ever happened. Forget that I was ever lost to him, in body and in mind. A need to make love as if this could be the last time.

"So take me."

"Hold on to me."

He knocks my stool aside and carries me off with my legs locked around his waist. I watch the white ceiling go past as he devours the unpainted curve of my neck. He takes me up the stairs and into the dark loft, lit only by the glow of the downstairs.

Once I am on my feet, we work at our clothes, shuffling free of our pants and undergarments. He kisses me until I am edged to the bed and lying on the cool black comforter. He kneels over me and crawls, shoulders bunching, until I have been successfully maneuvered to the center.

I am more than ready for him, but instead of positioning over me, he laves slowly up my belly. Goose bumps rise in a trail behind his hot tongue. Then he kneels between my legs and looks me over; a flame in his eyes makes my skin flush. Moist heat swirls in my lower abdomen and my ache for him increases. I forget how to breathe. How to move. I want to lie here rolling in his tide for eternity.

He seeks my hand out, then presses our palms together, threading our fingers together. He rests our clasped hands over my head and hovers over me.

His hot breath clashes with mine. "There are no words for how much I love you," he whispers.

Words are too insignificant. Too human. Too tied to a single existence. I lift my head and stop just shy of laying my lips on his. "I know exactly what you mean."

He sinks inside me. I gasp and press my head deep into the mattress. His weight settles against my body, though nowhere near heavy enough. Heat surges, branches out, and I know completeness. Draped in his warmth, submersed in his sigh, my heart swells with new understanding. Why I loved him while never knowing his face. Why my soul clung to his memory after death and well into this new life.

Nothing and no one in this world, the heavens, or the universe stood a chance of keeping us apart.

He eases in and out, his clear eyes watching me intently. I lift my head and take his mouth, relishing the burn of his whisker-coarse skin, but I need more. I roll him over, never releasing our linked fingers. He sits up and nudges my chin skyward with his nose, then traces his tongue along my neck. The moist heat of his breath coats my skin, sending shivers racing along my flesh.

Our lovemaking swiftly turns into a passionate frenzy, as I cannot kiss him hard enough or take him deep enough. Fast enough. He lets me set the pace without complaint or pause.

His only refusal comes when any slip of air passes between our palms—this hold he will not relinquish. This hold I once found too firm has finally managed to hold on to me. I am no longer fleeting. I am anchored. No longer glass blown to its thinnest point, and yet I am still beautiful because he loves me. Still shining because he sees me. Still solid because he accepts me. I am, and always have been, his.

Always his.

We shower the paint off, make love again, then take a long bath in an enormous soaker tub. Just like in my memories, we plan our future with as many babies as my body can handle. This time there is no worry of a cutoff date. No doubts. No fears. I have years and years to carry children.

Noah takes warm, even breaths behind me, his chest humming with the sound of his whispered words in my ear. Our fingers play, linked over my belly. Water pings from the faucet at our feet. And everything is perfect.

Except perfection never lasts.

The abyss comes for me. The glacial nothing sweeps across the hot water and sucks me through its wormhole until I float, helpless and alone. My incorporeal form jerks against the fragile tether banded around me. The unknown obsidian yanks, and I hear the strain and creaks as my bindings weaken. This is it. The abyss will finally take me.

Wake up, Emma. Wake up!

But I cannot wake up. This is no dream.

This is death.

CHAPTER 37

Noah's frantic voice manages to break into the looming dark and pulls me free. I wake, fluttering wet lashes and squinting at a white ceiling. My entire body racks with cold shivers that have nothing to do with lying free of the hot water. Nothing to do with the cool tile under me.

Noah lifts me into his arms so fast my vision whirls. I gasp for breath. Fight the walls threatening to close in around me. I hold fast to him, grounding myself to something real and solid.

I am not the only one shivering.

Noah walks out of the day care, where he just dropped Adrienne off. He is already suited up for a long day of work at Tucker Securities. An hour ago I watched him pace the floor, trying to talk himself out of going in, but he could not. He has meetings with potential new clients today, one being a government official. Tucker Securities first.

He takes my hand outside the room and continues our argument as if there had been no pause. "I could pull rank. Make you go."

The threat is only half-serious, so I let it go. "You would not do that."

"I would. You weren't *breathing.*"

"I still think that is a bit of an overreaction. I just fell asleep." I know better, of course, but his worry is not helping.

"I was about to do CPR, for Christ's sake."

"Lower your voice," I hiss. People are starting to stare. Or they already were. Everyone knows by now about his breakup and why. Even by holding hands we are fueling the gossip.

Stopping, I groan and drag my hands through my hair. "We cannot have this conversation in public."

"Phillip Malcolm is nothing like Travista. He would never hurt you."

The desperation in his eyes tugs at every string untethered by my resolve. "I will think about it."

"Today. Please go today."

Please. This word is akin to using "trust" on me. He knows I cannot refuse him. "I said I will think about it. I do have to work today."

He rests his hands on his hips, making his suit jacket flare back. The material is as black as my mood. "You officially have the morning off. Report back to work after lunch."

Damn it. He has a workaround for everything. "You are the worst boyfriend ever."

This brings a smile to his face, and I can tell he wants to kiss me, but that would cross the boundaries we laid out last night. Holding hands in public is our limit. He glances furtively around before leaning in and lowering his voice to say, "You're so damn cute when you pout."

I push him away and wish I could halt the grin leaking its way to my lips. The attention we are gathering from both ends of the corridor siphons heat from my center and infuses it into my cheeks. "Will you go to work, please?"

He walks backward, hands up in defense. "You're going?"

"I guess you will find out later."

Foster appears around the far corner and raises a hand, signaling for us to wait. Unlike everyone else, he shows no special interest in finding us together. "There you are."

Noah stops and I walk forward to catch up. The look on Foster's face does not sit well with me.

Foster slows to a stop beside Noah and rubs a day's worth of whisker growth on his chin. "Something happened last night. I was going to call you about it, but Reid said you were unreachable for the night and not to bother you."

Noah's hand slides into mine automatically as I sidle up beside him. "With what?"

Foster frowns at me. "I'm sorry, Wade, but you're out. Who your parents are. How you're really the Original Clone. The media cited Daxton Thomas as the source. Guess he was pissed as hell about the revelations that came out at the ball."

So the world now knows how damaged I am. No matter how this ends, I will never walk down a street without someone staring at me as if I am a freak.

Noah's hand tightens. "What about the rest? Do they know she's resistance? Or was?"

He sounds calm. I cling to that, hoping for an infusion of the same, because inside I am all over the place. So many emotions clamber to be first it is a wonder they have not trampled me into unconsciousness. It matters. It does not matter. I do not know which to hold tight to anymore. I have my family and it does not matter, but they cannot be my entire world—I need to have an identity outside them— therefore it does matter.

"No," Foster says. "Shockingly, he left the resistance part out. Guess Burke wasn't his goal with this revelation."

"He wanted to get back at his parents," I say. "*Our* parents. But he also wanted to protect their name. Revealing my being resistance would make them look bad, and him by extension."

He is such a selfish bastard.

Noah nods at Foster in a way that dismisses him. "Thanks for the update."

"No problem. Burke is scheduled to have a press conference at one."

"All right," Noah says. Once we are alone, he turns to face me. "You okay?"

I give him a single tight nod. I have to be, because I have bigger things to worry about. "You should go to work. I have to find Dr. Malcolm. My commanding officer is sort of a tyrant, and if I do not—"

Noah kisses me into silence. He pulls back a moment later and rests his forehead against mine. "Thank you."

Well, that was unexpected. Nice, and leaving me near breathless, but unexpected. "There are clear rules against this," I whisper, glancing around to count the number of voyeurs. There are more than a few. "Are you trying to get me in trouble? I could be court-martialed or something."

He chuckles. "I'm the one in trouble, and the punishment will always be 'or something.' I can promise you that."

"Scoundrel."

He beams me a smile that could level entire cities. "Reprobate."

A couple walks by, staring openly at us. Their chatter regarding our current state begins the second they pass.

Grinning like a love-struck fool, I hide my too-warm face in his chest and whisper, "God, I hate you."

He cups the back of my head and presses a kiss to my crown. His chest bounces with a silent laugh. "You're doing me no favors here, either."

"Dr. Malcolm?"

I catch him exiting the cafeteria after his breakfast. Something that looks suspiciously like ketchup stains the front of his wrinkled shirt.

He spins so quickly I am surprised he does not fall over from dizziness. "Miss Emma. How are you today?"

How do you feel today, Emma?

I shake my head to rattle away Dr. Travista's voice. "Is there someplace we can talk privately?" I shove shaking hands into my back pockets. "I will not take up too much of your time."

His smile is large and bright. "I would devote as much time as need be. Anything for you, Miss Emma." He swings an arm in a wide arc. "Shall we go to my office?"

His office is on a whole other sublevel from the hospital and living quarters, and we have to pass the shooting ranges to get there. The muffled sound of simulated war fills the stone corridor. We are nearly past the area when a door to one of the rooms opens between us and a thick crowd of men spills out, laughing and slapping each other's backs. The cool air fills with the scent of sweat. Dr. Malcolm whistles and bounces toward his office, upbeat as always, unaffected by the sudden gathering of loud men.

His office is twice the size of Noah's. I pause just inside and take in an examination table that sits opposite his desk, silver stirrups folded neatly inside square front cavities. I did not expect that, and it makes me reconsider what I am doing. But Noah promised Dr. Malcolm would be different. I just hope he is right.

Dr. Malcolm walks along a row of bookcases and taps the tops of vibrant-colored animal figurines, their paws curled over the front of the shelves. Their too-large heads bobble on spring necks. Medical books double-layer the shelves, but so many trinkets sit in front of the books, they leave little room to remove any of the gold-embossed volumes.

"Come on in," he says. "Have a seat."

Still hesitant, I glance around at the rest of the room. Pictures drawn by small children cover every available wall space.

"Do you like the art?" Dr. Malcolm asks as he sits behind his desk. "I know they're no Emma Wade original, but the kids and I think they're magnificent."

"The children color pictures for you?" I had not meant to sound so astonished, but I am.

He smiles with a twinkle of pride in his eyes. "I get a new one after every checkup. A work of art for an extra lollipop. It's a fair trade. Besides, the tots get a kick out of seeing their work displayed."

This is a side of Dr. Malcolm I never expected. There is a standard in which we love our children while maintaining some level of maturity. Then there is the degree where I find Dr. Malcolm: intelligent beyond reason yet still a child at heart. He must feel nothing but joy at all times.

This knowledge is all it takes to put me at ease. I know now I can trust this funny little man with my life, and he will treat it with all the care and tenderness of a devoted father.

Dr. Malcolm leans back in his chair and tops his shining bald head with his palms. "What can I d—" He tilts back too far, scrambles, and rocks forward with eyes wide and mouth set in an oval. He lays flat palms on the desktop and grins. "That was close."

I sit opposite him and begin fiddling with a zippered pocket that runs diagonal across my thigh. "I would like to speak to you about something, but I want to make sure it stays between us."

"Strictly between us? No other doctors or—"

"Nobody."

He stands and skirts around his desk. Before I realize it, he kneels before me and takes one of my hands. He kisses my knuckles and smiles warmly up at me. "Miss Emma, will you—"

"What are you doing?"

"—be my patient?"

"Excuse me?"

He stands and reaches across his desk for a computer tablet. "If you officially become my patient, then I can't talk to anyone." He sits in a chair beside me and starts typing on the screen. "My files are password protected against the other doctors." He glances up with a sheepish grin and bobbles his head from side to side. Not unlike one of his dolls. "Unless I die, of course; then obviously they'll transfer."

That covers Sonya finding out before she leaves. "Noah does not have access either?"

This makes him pause and look up. "This must be serious."

More than I have been willing to admit, but if it is as bad as I imagine, I want to be the one to tell him. He cannot find out through my records. "Maybe. I do not know yet."

He hands me the tablet. "Press your thumb to the scan box for a digital signature; then everything that passes between us will be confidential."

I do as he asks, relieved I do not have to talk him into complete silence. Then again . . . "You will not use the excuse that I am a clone with no rights and share anyway, will you?"

"Of course not." He scoffs. "You can trust me."

That will have to do. It is not as if I have another option available. "You mentioned there may have been an upset of the electromagnetic balance during my transfer."

"Yes. Considering the sensitivity of the mind-body, one has to wonder how it will try to balance itself out. Basically, where will your soul go when its home has vanished?"

"I call it an abyss. Lydia Farris calls it a void."

Dr. Malcolm grips the arms of his chair and sits back, blinking. "So it's true." He sits forward again, eyes wide. "What's it like?" Just as quickly, he pinches his eyes shut and waves his hands between us.

"I . . . uh . . . you can . . . never mind. Just tell me later. Sorry. Please continue." Then more to himself says, "Very unprofessional," as if scolding himself.

"I do not know if your theory is right or not. That is why I am here. I thought they were just nightmares, but I have recently had episodes while awake. It feels like dying." I look down at my clasped hands lying in my lap. "I promised Noah I would not leave. But what if there is no choice?"

"There's always a choice."

I meet his kind eyes. "I want you to run your tests. Just promise me one thing."

"Anything."

"If something is wrong, and if Noah asks, please let me be the one to tell him."

"When would you like to start?"

After last night, I do not feel there is much time. Ruby collapsed and died of seemingly nothing. If the abyss can pull me from my waking state . . . I want to keep my promise to Noah, and I also want to see my little girl grow up. "As soon as you have time to fit me into your schedule."

Dr. Malcolm tosses his tablet onto the desk and grins. "Does immediately work for you?"

CHAPTER 38

"It was not my intention to lie to the American people," Declan says to an off-camera interviewer. He links his long fingers across the knee of his gray suit pants. *"I've only ever wanted to protect my wife's privacy."*

The camera switches to a brunet man in a navy-blue suit. He smiles, but it does not reach his eyes. *"From more than half your board?"*

"The board would have been all over me about taking Emma public. Was it a gamble? Yes, but she's all I care about. She was dying and the process was untested. Time ran out and Arthur did the only thing he could. When she pulled through, I immediately set to work looking for a subject to satisfy the board."

"And the visit to the now deceased doctor in San Francisco? You claimed this was all about her illness, but obviously . . ." The man trails off and lifts his palms. *"You lied, Mr. Burke."*

Declan rests an elbow on the chair's arm and rubs his chin. A muscle pops in his jaw. *"Yes. I lied. The truth is, the resistance is studying my wife. They want the cloning process for themselves."*

"But there are hundreds of documented clones. They could pick up any one of them off the street. Why your wife?"

"Because she is *my wife. Until she's home and safe, they will always use her against me."*

The interviewer nods, seemingly appeased for the moment. *"Let's talk about Mr. and Mrs. Thomas."*

Declan's face hardens. *"That subject is not up for discussion."*

"Mr. Thomas, your CFO, is suing for custody of his daughter. Your wife. According to our outside sources, he has not only the right but the sympathy of the courts."

Declan stands and buttons his suit jacket. *"This interview is over."*

Miles faces a wall in Noah's office, where he points at a satellite video over Colorado. Barely visible through the mountain foliage is an L-shaped building.

"It was smart, really," Miles says. "Hiding it on our turf. So to speak."

Noah stands in front and at an angle to me. He is stripped down to his white shirt and pants, his sleeves rolled up over his forearms. To his right, Reid has propped a leg on a chair and rests his elbows across his knee. Both men stare at the enlarged computer screen in silence.

Miles glances at me over his shoulder. "It's not even in Burke's name, which is why we couldn't find it in any of his assets."

Noah tucks his hands into his pockets. "Whose name is it under? Travista's?"

"Mine," I say. "I never gave it any thought, but Declan once had me sign a bunch of paperwork. Financial in nature. He said he wanted to protect me if anything happened to him. He was making sure I was set up and would not have to remarry or work."

I had trusted Declan at the time and never read a single line. Had I not been so naïve, I could have saved us all the trouble of finding the facility's location.

Reid drops his foot to the floor. "What you're saying is, technically, nobody owns the building."

Noah's head snaps in Reid's direction and his hands come free of his pockets set in fists. He does not say a word, though. What can he say? Reid is absolutely right.

"Thank you for that kind reminder, Major," I say. "But that is not the real problem here." Everyone sets their full attention on me. "If the government catches wind of this asset, knowing I am a clone, they will seize the property and everything inside."

"But it's on the wrong side," Reid says. "They can't."

"I am not talking about the east's government. It is the west that concerns me. Everyone is guilty of wanting to get their hands on this information. Even if they refuse to use the facility, they could sell Dr. Travista's data. No one is above making a profit."

Reid nods and catches everyone's eye at least once before saying, "So we need to blow a hole in the ground."

Noah stares at the computer screen but seems to be looking past it. "We'll hit the facility after the Alexandria raid."

"I thought the goal was the cloning facility?" Reid says. "Do we even *need* to do the raid now?"

I step past Noah. "The goal is to ruin Declan Burke. Destroying the facility is not enough. When the government finds out he has been breaking the law by cloning these girls . . ."

Noah takes my hand. "We go after both."

Reid lifts his computer tablet from the desk. "I'll get started on the details."

"Trumble, go with him," Noah says, clinging tight to my hand. "Thanks for the hard work. You really pulled through."

Miles nods and winks at me on his way out.

We watch the two leave and do not move until the door slides shut behind them. Noah releases me to shut the wall monitor off.

"I cannot believe it is almost over," I say.

Noah sits in his chair with a heavy sigh and a *skritch* of springs. He really needs a new chair. "We'll hit them in a couple weeks. Then no more Declan Burke."

My stomach flips. No more Declan Burke. No more hiding. Not that there will be any sort of normalcy, but I can walk into a casino without worry of capture. I can remove my mask at a masquerade ball and drink champagne. Maybe I can even do it at Noah's side.

That is where the fantasy ends, because my brother and parents know who I really am. Noah can never be seen in public with me. And if my parents are truly fighting for custody of me, then I am in for a whole other battle.

"What did Phillip say?" Noah asks.

I sit across from him and pull my knees to my chest. "It is too early to know anything just yet, but he got what he required to start running some initial tests. I need tomorrow off to sit through the more in-depth examination."

"I signed off on his request an hour ago." He leans forward. "He also asked for some really expensive nanorobotics."

Dr. Malcolm did not mention anything about using nanites, and the idea does not sit well with me. "I know nothing about that. Should I be worried?"

He gives me a firm shake of his head. "Not at all. He knows what he's doing."

"I hope so." I reach up and finger the patch taped over my heart. It is linked to a monitor and will shock my heart if it stops beating, alerting Dr. Malcolm immediately.

Noah drops his gaze to his desk and begins fiddling with a tablet stylus. "What did he say about the blackout?"

"He suggested it might be due to exhaustion, but honestly, I do not think he has a clue yet."

"Okay, well, until he figures this out . . ." He pauses to glance up

and back. His Adam's apple bobs heavily. "I have to consider removing you from active duty."

The blow rockets me out of the chair. "What?"

"I said I was considering it. And this isn't just about your safety,
but that of everyone around you. What if that wasn't an isolated incident?"

I am glad I decided to keep the full extent of my problem to myself,
but I guess it does not matter. No doubt he wanted a way to keep me
from going on the raid, and he found it. "You—"

A knock sounds on the door. Noah is quick to allow whoever it is
entrance. Anything to avoid my argument.

A young girl with strawberry-blond waves enters wringing her
hands. I recognize her as one of the caregivers in the day-care center.

Noah stands and darts around the desk. "Amber? Is Adrienne all
right?"

"Dr. Toro asked me to come get you. Adrienne's running a pretty
high fever."

My heart lodges in my throat and I am out the door before Noah.
Only a moment passes before he catches up to me, and we hurry to
the hospital wing together. I push through the swinging door with
Noah's hand on the small of my back. My gaze lands first in the corner where She floated in a tank of water, and a tightness wraps
around my chest.

Noah walks around me. "How is she?"

I follow the sound of my daughter crying—a pitiful, miserable
moan—and find Sonya rocking and crooning to her. Noah stops beside them and lays a hand on Adrienne's forehead. Her cheeks are
bright red.

"Fever is 102.1," Sonya says, doing a bouncy rock. "I gave her some
medicine. Should come down soon."

Noah has not moved to take Adrienne, and I stand frozen watching the three of them together. I know better, but the scene knocks me into last week, when the three of *them* were the family and I was the outsider.

Adrienne begins dry heaving and Sonya immediately shifts her out of the cradled position. No sooner is she upright than she is throwing up all down the front of Sonya's pressed white blouse. Sonya and Noah are practically statues until Adrienne begins wailing.

I run to a cabinet where Sonya keeps towels—after so many months in the tank, I have an intimate knowledge of where just about everything is. When I have passed a couple over, I open another cabinet and find a pair of clean black scrubs for Sonya to change into.

I hand Noah the scrubs and reach for Adrienne. My little girl takes one look at me and turns into Sonya, clinging and screaming. This seems to wake the two of them out of their shocked stupor while simultaneously sending me reeling.

Sonya rocks Adrienne and stares right at me as she says, "It's okay, baby girl. I've got you."

There is no doubt about that, is there? She has my family exactly where she wants them. Meanwhile, I stand here bleeding out from invisible wounds inflicted by my own flesh and blood.

Noah passes me the scrubs with a frown and takes our screaming child out of Sonya's arms. Adrienne kicks and throws her head back, but he does not let that stop him. Sonya's hands follow the girl over as if wanting to steal her back.

I place the fresh garments in her outstretched hands instead. Her glare leaps over to me, and if her animosity was not clear before, it is now.

Noah cradles Adrienne against him, heedless of the mess coating the front of Adrienne's clothes. "Come on, Emma."

At this, Sonya's attention shifts back to him, her nostrils flaring. "But—"

Noah cuts her off with a look. "I know how to monitor a fever and handle the stomach flu. She's fine." He takes my hand. "Let's go."

"The nation sits in stunned silence this evening," the newsman says, his expression somber. *"Lydia Farris, Arthur Travista's third successful clone, was found dead in her Richmond home this afternoon. No word yet as to her cause of death."*

CHAPTER 39

The following days pass almost too quickly, and with no further mention of removing me from duty. Miles and I spend our mornings devising a way to get to the server room deep inside the Alexandria WTC. I then spend the afternoon with Dr. Malcolm hooked up to monitors while he asks me questions the same way Dr. Travista used to, mapping my brain. If he has any idea what is going on, he keeps it to himself, much to my and Noah's frustration. Neither of us has broached the subject, but Lydia's death hovers like a black cloud. Another unexplained clone death blamed on the resistance.

As for the blackouts, they have occurred on a near daily basis, and I have been lucky so far to hide them from Noah. Only one happened in front of Leigh, and she thought I was having a fainting spell, then asked if I was pregnant. The others happened while I was alone in my room, and none have required the activation of my heart monitor.

Just shy of a week out from the raid, I spend some much-needed time in the gym sparring.

Foster swings at my head and I block with my forearm. "That all you've got, Wade?"

I grit my teeth and avoid another punch, then come back swinging. "I thought this was supposed to be realistic. My opponents do not usually talk."

He snatches my shirtfront and gets in my face. Those shining gray-blue eyes dart back and forth between mine. Sweat drips from his nose. "You want realistic? Then stop worrying about hurting me. Fight. Back."

He is wrong about one thing: My focus has been less about hurting him and more about our witnesses. They watch me everywhere I go, judging my every move. It is time to start forgetting about them.

I push him away and let the crowd surrounding us blur around the edges. My following attack puts him on the defensive more often than not. I do not know who is more surprised: me or him.

The sparring ends when I jump and kick out with both feet, hitting Foster square in the rib cage. I fall hard, my skin slapping the mats, knocking the air from my lungs. I dart a look in his direction and find him sprawled on his back, chest heaving. Claps erupt from the group surrounding us.

The round is over.

Leigh helps me to my feet. Her face is red from her own recent round. "Nice, 2."

Foster reaches out to shake my hand. Our palms are sweaty and slide. "Savor the moment. Next time you won't be so lucky."

I laugh. "Keep telling yourself that."

He turns with a smile and claps twice. "Good work, everyone. Same time tomorrow."

"Let's go before he changes his mind," Leigh says, and leads me into the locker room.

The three other women in our group are already in the showers. Steam escapes the tiled corners leading into the far room. At our lockers, Leigh strips from her top and shorts without hesitation. I have seen the long, thin scars covering her abdomen and back for a while now, but the idea behind them still makes me uneasy. The first time she caught me looking, she said, "Not everyone escapes the WTC with invisible scars," and left it at that. I refuse to ask for details, because I can imagine just fine on my own.

Leigh grabs two towels and hands me one. "Mind if I ask you something?"

"Of course not."

"Are you doing okay? Physically, I mean."

I am honestly surprised it has taken her this long to ask. It has not exactly been a secret where I spend my afternoons. Be that as it may, I have not devised a response in preparation.

"You don't have to talk about it," she says when I take too long to respond.

We enter the shower area and the pale yellow tile is slick with humidity. "I am not avoiding the question," I tell her, and glance at the others, who laugh and chat as if we do not exist. "I just do not have an answer."

Leigh flips the nozzle to a stall that stands out of earshot of the others. "But you are seeing Dr. Malcolm for a reason?"

I turn on a shower beside her. Cold water splashes up to warn me against getting under too soon. "Yes," I say, and scratch my head automatically. I cannot feel the nanites now residing there, but the idea gives me chills just the same. It has been two days since their insertion, and Dr. Malcolm is hopeful the tech will yield results he has not yet discovered on his own.

She steps out of her remaining clothes, partially guarded by a half wall between us, and steps under the spray. "Are you going to make me play twenty questions?"

"I agreed to let him run some tests for his clone study."

"Won't that be a moot point in a few days?"

"Not if something goes wrong with the existing clones."

She nods, appeased, and I soak my head under the hot water, rubbing the grime of sweat from my face.

"Sonya's leaving today?" I hear Leigh ask from under the rush of water.

I lean out and stare up at the silver showerhead. Heavy drops of water well up and fall from the bottom. The tension in my shoulders increases. "Yes."

"She took the breakup awfully well."

"I would not say that. We have had a few moments." The last being five days ago in the hospital wing with Adrienne. I can still picture her face as Noah and I walked away. How heartbroken and alone she looked.

"Yeah, but she hasn't beaten the crap out of you, or made it hard on Tucker. The people around here respect her. If they thought she wanted his life to be hell, they'd find ways to make it so."

"I hate this entire situation. I wish things could be different."

Leigh takes the shampoo bottle off the tiled wall between us. "Why? You're getting your family back together and won't have her around giving you the evil eye."

"I know. I just keep thinking about Adrienne. She will miss Sonya. But once she leaves, I will not have to look over my shoulder every time Noah holds my hand." I smile at the prospect. It will be a relief to not have to worry about sparing her feelings.

"Should we be expecting wedding bells in the near future?"

"He has not asked." The idea makes butterflies wing through my stomach. We talk of a future, but neither of us has mentioned renewing our marriage.

"Ask *him*. What are you waiting for?"

The idea brings me up short. I *should* ask him. He will say yes. I know he will. But there is only one thing left in my plan to prove to Noah I am not going anywhere.

"I have to do something first," I say. "Can you help me?"

Miles lifts my left hand off our shared desk. His nose squishes up as if he smells something horrid. "What the fucking hell did you do to yourself?"

The brand *did* smell at first but does not now. A spray of antiseptic and burn recovery healed the damaged skin, and my hand is as good as new. Except for the luckenbooth staring back at us. I cannot wait to see Noah's face when I show him.

I steal my hand back. "This is none of your business."

He grunts and returns his attention to his four screens. Behind a forced cough he says, "Lucky bastard."

"Excuse me?"

He grins but does not look at me. "Mind your station, Wade."

I roll away and flip on my four monitors. Miles and I are examining every inch of the Alexandria WTC for weak points and have to report later today. Except my heart is not in it. I feel a little glowy and happy and have a burning need to see Noah. But he is upstairs in his big office with windows overlooking a perfectly sunny day.

I grin. *Lucky bastard, indeed.*

I open a chat window on one screen and find Noah on the available list. I click his name and a white box appears.

"THINKING OF YOU," I type.

"DETAILS."

"IT WILL HAVE TO WAIT."

"TEASE."

I look at the hearts permanently marking my hand and smile. "I HAVE A SURPRISE FOR YOU."

Miles peeks around and tries to read my chat screen. "Sexting again, Wade? Really? I expect better from you."

I push him away and laugh. "Stop it."

He grins. "I thought we agreed you'd invite me next time."

I roll my eyes and read Noah's response. My screen blinks as if ready to go out, but then returns to normal. "CAN'T WAIT. LUNCH?"

"HOLOGRAM ROOM?" I want to show him the brand on our beach. "I'LL BE THERE. NW."

I smile and can almost hear him say the phrase we have said since our night at the apartment: "No words." We could say "I love you," but in the end, they are only three little words. For us, there are none.

"NW," I type, then close the window.

When lunchtime approaches, I practically fly from my station. "See you later," I tell Miles.

"Slow down, Wade. Should I be worried about a fiery inferno erupting in a second?"

I laugh and shoot him a wave over my shoulder. I thought most of the morning about it ånd have decided to ask Noah to marry me today. Now. I do not want to wait. A hologram room is not very romantic, but is a step up—quite a few, actually—from his proposal years ago in a command center during a fight in front of hundreds of witnesses. And anyway, the location does not matter.

I am so lost in thought, planning my little speech, that when I turn a corner too sharply, I run directly into Sonya. I am beginning to apologize when she grabs my shoulders in a tight grip.

Her eyes are wide and frantic. "I was just coming for you."

I blink. *Me?* "Why?"

She tugs me in the direction from which she just came. She is practically running. "It's Noah. He's hurt. Come on."

Any questions I have lock in my throat and I stop trying to hinder her progress. I race behind her, my heart *thunk*ing against my sternum. I cannot live without him and pray to whoever is listening that he is okay.

Moments later she darts into Noah's empty hub office. I had assumed she was leading me to the hospital wing. Not once did I think she would bring me to this room when he was working upstairs today.

I pause in the doorway. "What are we doing here?"

She opens the panel to his teleporter, climbs inside, then motions for me to hurry up. "What the hell are you waiting for? Let's go!"

Trepidation sinks like lead in my stomach. If we need a teleporter to reach him, we had been closer to the ones in the command center when I ran into her.

"He could die while you're standing there," she says, which is all it takes to yank me forward.

I climb in and inhale her too-sweet vanilla scent. She punches in an untraceable code—*Why does she need that?*—and the scent of spearmint envelops the tube. Noah's concrete office dissolves, and wood floors, each slat a varying shade of brown, take its place. We face a glass wall. A sunken living room. A small kitchen. A bedroom open to an unmade bed.

And Declan Burke.

CHAPTER 40

Sonya steals the HK from my hip and sticks it into my side. "Get out," she whispers, her eyes on Declan.

What is happening? Sonya—*Sonya*—brought me here? But why? "What the hell are you doing?"

"What I have to. Give me your com."

I finger the device from my ear and drop it into her palm. "You will not get away with this."

Outside the booth, Declan watches in silence. As if he cannot believe I am finally here. He is clean shaven and wears a navy-blue T-shirt, my favorite color on him. His hair has grown out enough that he has combed it back in his old style. He is very nearly the husband I once loved.

Declan opens the teleporter. The ghostly scent of burned wood wafts inside the glass booth. He reaches for my hand and I recoil.

"Go," Sonya says.

I have no time. I slam an elbow in Sonya's face, forcing her to stumble back. The gun never goes off, confirming what I suspected: She would never have the nerve to shoot me.

Just as I go for the keypad, Declan reaches inside, fists my shirt, and drags me out. He twists me around and brings my left arm up behind me at a painful angle. I cry out. Even pushing up on my tip-toes does not relieve the pain in my shoulder.

"Let me go," I grit out, twisting despite the agony jolting through my arm.

Declan kisses the crown of my head. "Not a chance, love."

Sonya steps out of the teleporter, wiping blood from her busted lower lip. She avoids my eyes. Stares up at Declan. "Do you have what I want?"

Declan's hold tightens as he walks us to the kitchen island and lifts a small, opaque envelope from the countertop. "Sure you don't want the money instead?"

"If that data-slip has everything I asked for, then yes, I'm sure."

I cannot believe she is doing this to me. Of everyone, not her. "What was so important, Sonya? What could you want so badly that you would just hand me over?"

She takes the extended envelope, then slides her gaze over to me. At least she has the decency to frown. "I'm sorry, Emma. I really am."

Backing away, she opens the envelope and removes the clear strip that resembles the home videos Leigh found in "Emma's" box. Tucking the HK under her arm, she removes a palm tablet from her pocket and inserts the data-slip inside. She plays with the screen for a half minute before a self-satisfied smile breaks her bland expression.

Her eyes shine at me as she tucks the tablet away. "Some things are worth far more than your life. And in time, I'm going to make him believe that."

Him. Noah. Comprehension wrenches up my spine and twists. Bile burns the back of my throat. "This has nothing to do with that data-slip at all, does it?"

"I'm getting a two-for-one deal," she says, and steps inside the teleporter. Her fingers hover over the keypad. "You can take comfort in knowing that I'll take care of them."

Moments later she is gone.

My wrists and ankles are bound by mag-cuffs. My arms and legs ache from the battle I lost trying to get free after Sonya disappeared. But my head clears of the adrenaline rush and my thoughts begin to line up straight. I only need to wait. Someone in the hub will see me and alert Noah. He will come for me.

So I wait and wait and *wait* for rescue that never comes. Can no one back home see what is happening? Then the answer hits me like a steel fist in the stomach. Sonya did something to the feed, which can be done from any location in the hub. She had to in order to get away with this. Which means I am on my own.

Declan sits on the opposite side of the couch from me, a glass of bourbon in his hand. He holds the glass out. "Would you like a drink?"

I would, but I need my thoughts sharp if I am going to escape. "What did you trade for me?" I have to know what Sonya found worth the risk.

"Everything Arthur has on cloning. I take it that woman is with the resistance?"

I look directly at him for the first time. He has no idea who he was dealing with? "Does it matter anymore? You have me. She has the data-slip."

He sips his drink, then seems to give it a second thought and downs the entire thing. Ice *clinks* in the glass. He stands and enters the kitchen for a refill. "That woman? Sonya? Called me four days ago to make the trade."

Four days ago. The day after the incident in the hospital with Adrienne. Had I walked away that night, left Noah and Adrienne in her care, would I be here now?

He turns and leans against the island, drink poised at his lips. "She wouldn't answer any of my questions. Just asked that I be fair and give her what she wanted."

His second drink disappears and he sets the empty glass down. He returns to the living room and sits in the center of the couch, only inches from me. The sharp scent of alcohol penetrates the air.

Declan tucks my hair behind my ears and whispers, "You cut your hair back. I'm glad."

I angle my head away from his touch. Tears burn the backs of my eyes.

"Do you hate me that much?" he asks, pulling back.

How can he ask that? I am just getting my life back together, and the pieces are only scraps of what remained. That is his doing.

But fighting with him will not help me. It never has. There has to be another way to do this, and I can think of only one way that has worked in the past. He was always fairly easy to manipulate. Maybe he still is.

"I do not hate you," I say. "I am just scared."

"Of me? I would never hurt you."

"No. Starting over. I am scared of starting over." I look him in the eye, and a tremulous sea stares back. "I wish I could make you trust me."

Declan takes a moment to tuck my hair on both sides. Fingertips graze over my cheek. His eyes dance over the contours of my face, soaking me in for the first time in more than a year. His gaze stops on my lips. "I want to."

But he never could, and that was our biggest problem. Now the issue between us is one he cannot fix without wiping my mind completely, and who knows? Maybe not even then. Noah will never stand by for this a second time. Not after everything that has happened.

Declan's eyes lower to my black uniform and he lets out a slow breath. "I hate seeing you in these clothes. You're one of them. It isn't right."

A voice from one of Her memories surfaces out of nowhere. *Keep as close to the truth as you can. They can spot a flat-out lie a mile away.*

Toni always gave me good advice. "I had no choice. They would not let me stay otherwise."

"You always had a choice. Why couldn't it have been me?" His voice breaks on the end, and I know he has had too much to drink. The alcohol has loosened his strength of will. Or maybe this is the effect I have on him. He has never been ashamed of his feelings for me.

"I have a daughter, Declan." He takes a sharp breath. "I told you my host was pregnant. She died during childbirth."

Tears slip unbidden from my eyes. My chest and throat ache. This, at least, is real. "She looks like me. You have no idea what that is like. To see yourself in another human being. Maybe I did not create her, but she is mine, Declan. I only want to raise my daughter."

He stares into the cold fireplace, expression impassive except for the minute ticks in his jaw. Standing, he crosses the space and leans into the mantel, head bowed. The sun lowers behind the trees outside, and the shadow of their sway dances along the side of his body.

I stand, but that is all I can do. The mag-cuffs attached to my ankles may as well have me encased in cement. Their magnetic link is too strong to shift. "The last thing I want is to hurt you with this. But you have to know the truth. You were right all along. Trying to stop loving you has been impossible, but my little girl . . ." My throat tightens and halts any further sound.

Declan turns, letting his hands fall heavy at his sides.

"There is no choice. It will always be her."

His approach is careful. Wordless. But his goal is clear. It goes beyond being near me. He wants under my skin, drinking from me, taking what is his. I never should have told him I loved him. Of all the lies to come out of my mouth, I should have stayed clear of that one.

But it is done, and he cups my chin in those long, strong fingers so he can tilt my head back. And I want to fight this, but I will never escape if I cannot gain his trust. I close my eyes and push the remains of tears out. "It is not fair," I whisper. "I want you both."

His lips press against mine and force them to part. Taking his bourbon-soaked tongue into my mouth stirs both guilt in my belly and sickness in my heart. Everything about this is a betrayal to Noah.

Declan deepens the kiss, his whisker-coarse skin burning against mine. His hands roam down my back and under my bound arms, forcing our bodies together.

He hardens against me, and this response shocks me into reality. He will want to have sex. What am I doing? Would I go so far as to sleep with him to gain my freedom? Would I do that to Noah and possibly wreck everything we have built? The answer to that is a resounding no. Sex is not an option. I will never willingly give myself to Declan ever again.

I pull out of the kiss and look away, but he takes me by the chin and forces me to look into his lust-filled eyes. He smooths my hair back.

"Thank you," he whispers, then gives me the tiniest of kisses.

I feel sick. "For what?"

"For reminding me just how low you'll sink to meet your own ends."

He pushes me down on the couch and strolls back up to the kitchen, where he pours himself another drink. I stare after him, shock zip-lining along my spine. He played my game, knowing the rules, and swept my feet right out from under me. And I was blind to the entire thing.

Declan turns with a newly filled glass and sips while staring down at me. His gaze rakes over me, shameless, peeling away the layers and saying *You. Are. Mine.* Confidence oozes from him in the way he squares his round shoulders and opens his posture to me. In the purposefully slow way he draws a sip from his glass, never taking those eyes off me.

I stand, hop twice until I am facing him, and raise my chin. "You have no idea how far I will go."

A grin slides across his face. "I love a challenge."

A buzzing vibration breaks the still air and he pulls his phone from his back pocket. He does not look at the screen before answering. "Is he gone?" he asks. After a single nod, he ends the call and tucks the phone away. "Time to go, love."

CHAPTER 41

The teleporter bay we appear in is unfamiliar, but I am not surprised to find a flock of men and a stretcher waiting for me. Dr. Travista stands at the foot and pushes his glasses up the bridge of his nose.

The second my body reanimates, I continue my limited struggle. Declan lifts me off my feet and carries me out. I attempt to roll from his arms. Bound or not, helpless or not, I will get out of this. I have no other choice. I have a family to consider now. I cannot lose these memories of our time together.

He drops me on the stretcher and several sets of hands push down on me as I twist and writhe. Someone demagnetizes my ankle cuffs. I kick and fingers dig bruising deep into my thighs and calves.

Declan belts an arm across my heaving chest and forces all his weight down until I cannot breathe. "Strap her ankles, goddamn it!"

Dr. Travista unearths a syringe from his pocket. He thumps the tube. "I'd hoped not to need this. I need her conscious for the mapping."

"Just do it," Declan says. "We've waited this long. A few more hours won't hurt."

No. "Let me go!"

A teleporter hums and everyone freezes, including me. To the far left, a man's static-like shape solidifies. Evan Thomas looks directly at us the moment he is aware of his surroundings.

He throws open the tube's door, jaw clenched tight, face reddening. "You waited for me to leave, didn't you? Thought you'd get away with it."

Declan squares his shoulders. "Every court in the nation can give you custody of her, but in the end, she's still mine. I'll revalidate our marriage—my lawyers are already working on it—and then what? What leg will you have to stand on then?"

Evan snaps his beige suit jacket down and taps his ear. "Call Charissa," he orders, then to Declan says, "We just so happen to be meeting with our lawyer right now. Your timing couldn't be more perfect."

He looks down at me for the first time. Whatever he is thinking, it is hidden behind a perfect mask of anger.

My heart, already racing, threatens to fly free of my chest. I do not know if him being here helps or hurts me, but it has at least given me a chance.

Evan looks absently at the floor. "Bring the lawyer and a police escort to the cloning facility. Olivia is here." He taps his ear again and scans Declan. "I want her off that stretcher right now."

I exchange a look with Declan, daring him to let me up. He *knows* why he should not comply, but what can he do? The police are coming. The lawyers. Apparently, at this point, he has no right to hold on to me. Good for me, at least.

Dr. Travista stops one of the orderlies from unstrapping my ankles. "Mr. Thomas, with all due respect, Emma won't go quietly. She's dangerous."

Evan does not so much as blink at Dr. Travista. "I want my daughter off this table now. The two of you are quite a pair." His gaze flicks between Declan and Dr. Travista. "How about a lawsuit holding you both accountable for your actions here today? I can have you served before you sit down to dinner."

Declan, holding Evan's intense gaze, lifts a small device and taps a button, and my cuffs demagnetize. "You'll want to rethink this."

"I won't have you, or anyone else, telling me what to think," Evan says. "I didn't work this hard to have it any other way."

My ankles come free of the straps. I roll off the side opposite Declan and beside Evan. He smells faintly of pine. I start to back into a teleporter, keeping my eye on everyone in the room. The orderlies are fast and appear ready to pounce if ordered.

"I am going back to my family," I tell them. "My *real* family. My daughter." I flash the back of my hand at Declan, showing him my luckenbooth. "And *my husband.*"

Declan's teeth flash behind taut lips. "You won't want to do that, love."

"Oh no?"

Two teleporters hum, signaling new arrivals. In one, my mother stands with another white-haired man in a pinstriped suit. In another, police officers in orange-trimmed navy. They probably do not even realize they are *way* out of their jurisdiction.

While I debate which of the two teleporters to fight my way to, Declan leans on the stretcher and shares a wordless conversation with Dr. Travista. Declan then nods his assent and the doctor looks between me, Evan, and finally Charissa, who walks up behind me in a pressed lavender pantsuit.

I back away from the woman who gave me away, though there is a visceral tug in her gaze. Her smile wobbles and tears glaze her eyes.

"Emma is dying," Dr. Travista says.

I tear my gaze off Charissa to glare at the doctor. "Is there no end to your lies?"

His hands spread in a placating gesture. "My dear Emma. Why would I lie about this?"

Declan meets my eyes. "All the clones are dying. You know I'm telling the truth. Whether you've admitted it to yourself or not, you know what I'm saying is right."

Charissa steps forward, practically vibrating. "You're lying."

Evan slips a hand around her wrist. He and Dr. Travista begin a dialogue about whether or not Declan speaks the truth. One I do not hear because Declan refuses to release me from his thrall. The sea in his eyes coaxes me to see the truth.

"Tell them." His lips shape the words, but no sound comes out. Then in a tone just above a whisper, he says, "Tell them about the cold, dark depths of hell. They're getting closer, aren't they?"

Evan and Charissa stop talking and look at me, but I cannot give them the confirmation they seek. I close my eyes. "No. It is not true." Despite my vocal refusal, I believe him. His mention of the place I call an abyss only confirms my suspicions. He knows from personal experience. And there is no denying the truth any longer.

I. Am dying.

A grieving darkness surrounds me, cradling me in swaying arms. Death, which I once thought a nightmare, has been my reality all along. A life with Noah and Adrienne . . . They were the dream.

Sonya was right. I will break their hearts again.

"Stay and let Arthur help you," Declan says.

I choke out a dry sob. "No."

He begins to round the stretcher, his motions as careful as those of a hunter approaching a skittish deer. His entire focus settles on me, and he works his way around as if the many bodies in the room do not exist. As if there is only us. As if we are everything. "It's been hard, hasn't it? Everyone knowing what you are. A mirror image of the person you were. An interloper. Alien."

"Stop it," I grind out.

"He doesn't *really* get it, does he? Stay and you'll never know that feeling again."

Noah loves me. *Me.* Not Her. Everything else, all the uninformed opinions and scrutinizing looks, will pass with time. I just need to be patient and wait it out.

"You do not know what you are talking about," I say, taking a step back.

"I've loved and accepted you since the second you opened your eyes. Can he say the same?"

This is where he gets me. By the time Noah accepted the truth, I was already gone. His hesitation, and mine, nearly cost us.

When I cannot respond, Declan presses forward, his eyes brightening. One of the officers stops him short of reaching me. "You're my world, Emma. My very life."

But that will never be enough, will it? He has not yet realized there is so much more. "I am his entire universe, and he is every life I have ever lived."

Declan flinches back as if my words are a physical blow.

Dr. Travista clears his throat, and the room snaps back into focus. "I've already found the source of the problem and have begun the process of curing every woman who has come through this facility. The process takes all of fifteen minutes," he tells me.

Lie still, Emma. This will take a while. It is imperative you don't move.

I shake my head.

You may find some discomfort, but I need you to try very hard to be brave, the ghost voice says, defiant.

I curl my fingers into fists, glaring at Dr. Travista. He wants me to be brave? I *will* be brave. "You will never lay another hand on me again."

Charissa reaches for me but stops short after seeing the warning glance across my face. "Let's talk things over first."

"As if you care."

Those eyes so much like mine, like Adrienne's, look stung. "Olivia. You're my daughter. I only want to help you."

I lean close. "My *name* is Emma, and you lost your rights to help me the second you put me in *their* hands."

I push her in the chest and out of the way. She falls into Evan's arms, and they are caught by two orderlies before going down. Someone yanks me back by the collar of my jacket. I slip out of the sleeves and race forward. Yells fill the space—"*Stop her!*"—and in the cluster of the small room, no one can.

I reach the teleporter, the port number that will take me home on repeat in my head. One foot on the giving floor and something stabs me in the neck. Cold swells under my skin.

I kick behind me, and my boot heel nails my attacker in the chest. I glance back. Dr. Travista falls into a group of orderlies and his empty syringe clatters to the floor at his feet.

The room is already beginning to swim by the time I pull myself all the way into the clear tube. The door closes me in and the teleporter enters safe mode. Try as they might, no one is getting in.

Four numbers into the code that will hide my port signature, Declan pounds on the outside glass. "Emma. You go back now, you'll die. Don't be a fool!"

I squint at the numbers, which are starting to overlap one another. I rattle my head to clear my vision. "I . . . am going . . . home." I have no idea if the words actually make any sound.

The last number goes in and I hit ENTER. I drop to my knees and lean against the glass front. Declan bends and yells my name, but I cannot hear him. My eyelids anchor down as the spearmint fills the tube.

I am barely conscious when the teleporter doors part and I fall through the opening, landing hard on a concrete floor.

"Oh my God, Emma," Noah says.

Relief floods me. Thank God. I typed his office port number in right.

He cradles me in his arms and pushes my hair away from my face. "What happened? Where have you been?"

Sleep swaths me in its heat, but I have to tell him. He has to know what she has done. "Sonya. Declan."

I wake in the hospital, blankets heavy and warm up to my shoulders. The privacy curtains surround me on all sides. Noah sits in a chair, elbows braced to his knees, fists laced and pressed to his mouth. Tired eyes stare toward my wrist, and muscles work in his jaw.

"Hi," I say.

He flinches upright, then pushes out of the chair. I try sitting up, but he holds me down. "Don't get up. Let me find Phillip."

I force his hands aside and rise before he can stop me. With a frown, he sits beside me, making the mattress dip low. He threads fingers into my hair, rests his forehead against mine, and snares me in his gaze. I am so grateful to be back in its encompassing hold that tears sting behind my eyes.

"I was scared to death," he whispers. "What the hell happened?"

The day comes rushing back. Sonya's lie. Declan. My parents. And finally, the revelation that I am in fact dying. How do I tell Noah that I have to leave again, only this time for good? There is no coming back from this.

I clear the thickness from my throat. "Sonya took me to Declan."

"I guessed that's what you were trying to tell me. The moment I told her you showed up in my office, the look on her face said it all. She's not talking, and believe me, I worked her over good."

"Where is she?"

"I had her locked up."

I am so relieved to hear this. After everything, if she had gotten away, too . . . "It was not for money. Declan gave her a data-slip with all of Dr. Travista's records on cloning." Noah straightens and leans away, but I continue. "She did it for you. For Adrienne. I think she hoped to regain your affections using the new information."

"I don't even care about continuing that project anymore. It won't matter once we destroy the facility. What the hell was she thinking?"

How can he question her motives? What would someone *not do* for the person she loves? I cannot say I would never go to extraordinary lengths for him.

"She loves you."

It is the same response he gave me about Declan once, and those three words held all the validation he required. I had been doubtful at the time, but what Sonya has done changes my point of view.

Noah scrubs his face and stands. Paces between the bed and chair, hands on hips. "Unbelievable." He stops and looks down at my clasped hands. "I'll kill him for hurting you."

I blink back at him in surprise. He is completely serious. "I am unhurt. I promise."

He meets my eyes, then blindly lifts one of my hands. "Want to try again?"

Burn marks and bruises bracelet my wrist—*wrists*—from where I struggled against the bindings at the hospital. I bite my lower lip.

He lifts my left hand. "And what about this?"

He glares at my new luckenbooth, but I am confused. Why is he so angry? He gave me his blessing after the ball.

"He branded you," he says, his voice tight.

I let out a breath, a weight lifting from my chest. "No. I did that this morning."

The curtains part before he has a chance to respond, and Dr. Malcolm flits to my bedside, smiling and rumpled as usual. "I thought I heard your voice. Glad to see you're finally awake, Miss Emma." He focuses on Noah. "Everything came back negative except for what I already suspected. Someone gave her a pretty strong sedative."

I rub my neck where Dr. Travista stabbed me with a needle.

Dr. Malcolm pats my hand. Bounces on his toes. "Other than that, she's perfectly fine."

You're perfect.

Except I am not. Not anymore. Maybe not ever.

Noah lets out a long breath. "That's a relief."

"So I can go to my room?" I ask, and shift my legs over the side of the bed.

"Wait," Noah begins.

"I don't see why not," Dr. Malcolm says over him.

I smile at Noah, who looks ready to give the doctor a million excuses why I need to stay. "Where is Adrienne?" I ask to distract him.

"Sleeping. Leigh is with her."

At least she is with someone I trust. "We should relieve her."

He nods but nibbles the inside of his lower lip. Rubs his chin. "I want to talk to Sonya one more time."

"Go on, then," I tell him. "I will be fine."

Noah looks to Dr. Malcolm for confirmation.

"I'll walk her back," the doctor says.

Noah hesitates a moment longer, then presses his lips to my luckenbooth. Another kiss on the cheek ends with a whispered, "That's what you wanted to show me at lunch?"

"Surprise."

His answering smile melts my insides. "I love it."

We kiss, and after another promise from Dr. Malcolm that I will not return to my room alone, he strolls from the hospital wing.

Once the doors sway shut, I meet Dr. Malcolm's bright eyes. "Dr. Travista says I am dying. Please tell me you can fix this."

CHAPTER 42

It is near midnight by the time I give Leigh the short version of events and see her out of Noah's room clutching a thin book of Edgar Allan Poe poems to her chest. Noah has not returned, and Adrienne sleeps soundly.

The last thing I want to do is sleep. I am alone with my thoughts for the first time, and the day crawls along my skin like a rash. There has been no time to absorb the details. Seeing my parents for the first time since knowing who they are to me. Kissing Declan. Being *so close* to becoming a patient of Dr. Travista's again.

The final punch of the day, the most devastating of them all . . . I am dying. Dr. Malcolm confirmed this was his belief as well but promised he was close to an answer. That I would not have to leave my family.

You go back now, you'll die, Declan said.

Or desert Noah and Adrienne; live only to forget they exist. How can these possibly be my options?

I slip into the shower. Going through these motions since my long talk with Dr. Malcolm feels pointless, but I do it on automatic. Cleaning the sterile scent of hospital from my hair. Washing the taint of Declan's touch from my body. I even take the time to shave. Maybe working this perfection on the outside will make me feel whole on the inside. But it does not work. No amount of flawlessness will halt death.

When I run out of things to do, I sit with legs folded up against my chest, the hot spray on my back. I cannot get out yet. Every move I make toward normalcy, every word uttered, is a lie.

Stay and let Arthur help you.

The process takes all of fifteen minutes.

My one lifesaving option. Taunting. Glaring. I hate that the longer time goes by, the more viable this opportunity becomes. I could save Noah and Adrienne the idea of my death by simply asking Dr. Travista for his help. With a plan, maybe I can escape afterward and return home. Or he will wipe my memory first and none of what happens after will matter.

I press the heels of my hands into my eyes, trying and failing to halt the hot tears from spilling. My throat aches as it works to contain the pain trying to unleash as sound. I told Noah I would not leave. I promised. I hate that I promised.

The shower curtain scrapes aside, drawing my attention up. My heart leaps at the sight of Noah, who kneels, his eyebrows pinched together. He must have been home for a while, because he wears nothing but pajama bottoms.

"What's wrong?" he asks.

I try to respond but cannot find the right words and only barely manage to contain the tremble in my chin.

The color drains from his face as he watches me struggle. "He hurt you, didn't he?"

"No."

One hand reaches out to cup the back of my neck, and the other grips the edge of the tub with white knuckles. Stray drops of water dot his arms.

"I am so sorry." My voice breaks and I cannot look at him. I rest my forehead against my knees. A sob claws painfully out from a deep well in my chest.

He rubs my head with a shaking hand. "Whatever it is, you can tell me."

I meet his bloodshot eyes, knowing he already suspects. I just have to be brave enough to tell him. "I am dying."

His eyes widen. He releases my head in favor of cupping his mouth. Water glistens on the pale skin of his hand. What seems an eternity later, he blinks and says, "What?" His tone is thick and broken.

I cannot take another second of this, nor can I say it again. I stand for no other reason than to take away the ability to look at him. The grief on his face is too much. But he stands with me. He steps swiftly into the shower, wraps his arms around my waist, and lifts me until my feet hang limp in the air. He holds me tight, quivering against me. I wish the arms preventing me from breathing were strong enough to keep me from floating away. Maybe if I cling to him just as hard.

"No words," he whispers in a hoarse tone.

"I know," I say. No words for the grief or the love.

We sit propped against the bathroom wall, wrapped in every towel we could find. His soaked blue pajama bottoms lie in a heap outside the tub.

With my legs draped over Noah's, I rest my head on his shoulder. The fingers of his right hand lace through those of my left, and his thumb rubs absently over my luckenbooth. Over the next few minutes, he alternates between kissing my forehead and kissing my hand.

Neither of us has said a word in a half hour, but the crying has finally stopped. My eyes feel hot and dry. My throat raw. He has not asked me how or why, and I have not offered the information. Several times he has taken a breath that would precede words, but he never spoke. I know he is torn between wanting and needing the details. He needs them but does not want them. I would feel the same if our roles were reversed. The facts do not matter when the result is the same.

"Dr. Travista told me," I tell him. "Declan confirmed it. I believe this is why he has been so desperate to find me. Dr. Malcolm thinks I will pass soon unless the cause is found."

Noah turns and rests his chin against the crown of my head. "How soon?" The words barely penetrate the suffocating space.

"He has based this on the time span between the death of host body and clone. Ruby's and Lydia's deaths did not happen at an exact number of days after host death, but . . . Anyway, his guess is that I have a week left. Maybe two."

"There's no time," he whispers, his fingers tightening around mine.

I nod against his shoulder. "You should know . . ." I almost cannot tell him about Dr. Travista's cure. The hope comes with its own loss.

"What?"

"Dr. Travista has already found a cure."

Noah sits back and angles my chin up. I hate the look in his eyes. The one that says he will tear down the world to find the answers we need. "Travista has a cure?"

"Yes."

"Let me guess. He's not offering it up for free. You'd have to go back."

"Yes."

His lips thin into a fine line. "Over my dead body."

"That is what I told him, but, Noah, if—"

"Don't." He stares at our linked hands. His fingers tighten and his chin trembles. "I'm not losing you to him again."

I grip the back of his head and draw him close, resting my forehead to his. "It could buy us time."

He taps my temple. "I'll lose you anyway."

I look down at the set of luckenbooths on our linked hands. He swipes a thumb over mine. The symbol that drew me from the dark. "I came back once."

"You would put all your hope behind . . ." He shakes his head. "There has to be another way."

"Listen to me." I meet eyes that glisten back at me. "My being here now, with what little memory I have, should have been impossible. I just think that if there is a way to fix this, it is there."

"There. With Declan."

He never uses Declan's given name, and I wish he had not started now. The name is a curse erecting a wall between us. The use speaks of betrayal. Of lost time. Pain. I refuse to give him that distance.

I grip his face in both hands. "This has nothing to do with him. I am scratching and clawing at any available chance to live. I do not want to leave you any more than you are willing to let me go."

His eyes clench shut. "It can't come to that, Emma. It just can't. I would risk everything"—he looks unblinking into my eyes— "*everything* to get you back. The company and the security of this entire operation. He won't have time to lay a single hand on you. Not again."

We nearly lost each other for the sake of the resistance. Putting it first. He believed this battle was worth every personal risk just a few weeks ago. The fact that he says otherwise now speaks volumes. And we are not only on the same page, but on the same damn word.

Us.

Not Them.

Noah sleeps fitfully while I watch from a chair. *The Complete Works of William Shakespeare* sits open in my lap. I tried reading *Much Ado*

About Nothing to take my mind off things, but not even the love-hate banter between Benedick and Beatrice can lure me out of the dark place I reside in.

My mind keeps going back to the raid. The facility bombing. In that building, with that doctor, lies my one escape from death. If we destroy it, I am most certainly dead. And so is every other clone who has not been back to see Dr. Travista. Hundreds of women could die.

Who will save them? Dr. Malcolm? *If* he figures out what is wrong with me. Us. But without full knowledge of how a clone *works,* how can anyone expect him to—?

This answer has me shooting up to my feet. The large book drops onto one of my toes. A lightning-hot pain zips up my foot and leg.

Noah bolts upright to find me bouncing on one foot, gripping my stinging toe. "What the hell?"

Adrienne stirs in her crib. Noah and I hold perfectly still until we hear the sound of her thumb sucking.

"I dropped a book on my toe," I whisper.

He climbs out and sits in my chair, pulling me into his lap. He takes my foot and tries rubbing the pain out for me. "What are you doing up?"

"Did Sonya give you the data-slip?"

My question is apropos of nothing, and the stunned, confused look he gives me is almost comical. "The . . . what? No. She didn't talk the entire time I was down there. I've had her room and office searched. No one found a data-slip."

I sigh and set my foot on the ground. "We need her to give that slip to Dr. Malcolm. It has all of Dr. Travista's notes. I cannot believe I did not think of this before." Though to be fair, I have been a jumbled mess since returning.

"Up," he says, pushing me to my feet. "Get dressed." He stops and looks at the crib. "Shit. We can't leave her alone."

"I will get Leigh."

He looks dubious. "It's nearly four A.M."

"She is awake. Trust me."

Leigh is up and all too happy to watch Adrienne again, but according to the look on her face, I have a girls' talk in my future. She knows something is wrong, especially if we need to make such an early visit to see Sonya.

The prisoner cells are on sublevel four. Our footsteps echo in the empty hallways and stairwells. It is so quiet at this hour I wonder if Noah can hear my heart beating.

Noah's hand encases mine with a viselike grip the entire way, and he walks as if the end of time bites at our heels until we reach the door outside the cell corridor. He peers through the rectangular glass. His breath fogs the surface.

"How should we do this?" he asks. "She's clearly not going to talk to me."

I nearly laugh. "She hates me, but I think I know what to say."

Muscles tick in his jaw. "This is so fucked-up."

Beyond. The woman who hates me holds the information that will save my life.

"Okay. We're waking her up, so she'll be caught off guard." He looks down at me. "I'll hang back. She won't even know I'm here."

I nod, though my heart kicks with an erratic beat. How can I face her after what she has done? How can I focus on getting her to talk when all I want to do is damage her beyond recognition? I was too close to losing everything to think clearly where she is concerned.

"She's in the third cell down on the right." He hits the door activation button and yanks me back to kiss me the second I start forward. "Good luck."

I take an extra second to inhale his scent and run my fingertips down the length of his sideburns. Then, turning, I face the corridor, which seems to elongate and narrow. Sonya's cell may as well be miles away rather than mere steps.

Noah and I step across the threshold. The door slides shut and the first motion-sensor light pops on over our heads. The glow is set to dim because of the hour, but I squint as if the bulb holds the radiance of the sun. Noah stays as I move forward, lights turning on as I go.

I stop outside the third cell. The final lamp clicks on, and Sonya startles out of sleep on a cot in the far left corner. Her head lies just past the line of dark shadow.

She sits all the way up and lifts an arm to shield her eyes from the glare. "What's going on? Who—?" Her eyes must have adjusted. Her arm drops like a weight. "They record this area."

"Noah knows I am here."

Her laugh is hard. "Does he, now? Send you on a little errand for information?"

"He is not the reason I am here."

"No, of course he isn't."

I step close to the bars and grip the cold metal. "Why did you do it?"

Sonya stands and saunters over. She wears a pale green outfit that resembles hospital scrubs. Her white socks scuff against the concrete floor with each step. She fists the bars, hands above mine, and meets my eyes. "You won't get me to implicate myself in this delusional fantasy of yours for the camera. What I will tell you is that"—she leans close to whisper—"not everything is about you."

"No, you are absolutely right. This time it is about you. I am only a casualty of your selfish motivation."

She averts her eyes. Her jaw locks seconds before she bows her head.

"This was never about retrieving the data-slip from Declan," I say. "As far as you know, the information will be practically useless the second we destroy the facility."

She looks up but says nothing.

"Declan and Dr. Travista will go to jail for cloning underage girls—*murdering* them. What good will that data be when the government is forced to reconsider the consequences of cloning? Especially after they hear the best part . . ." I let the sentence hang open-ended, drawing on her curiosity.

Sonya's hands fall and she steps back. Shutters slam home in her eyes. "I don't know what you're talking about. There is no data-slip. You're suffering from hallucinations."

"I wish that were the case. The truth is too horrific to be real."

This grabs her attention. "What truth?"

"Dr. Travista made a fatal mistake in the transference, only no one knows what that is but him. And now you, because *you* have every file and note he has ever taken. The only question now is, will you incriminate yourself to save hundreds of lives—including mine—or will you stand by and watch us all die?"

CHAPTER 43

Sonya laughs, but she searches for the truth behind the lie she believes I tell.

"You need to give the data-slip to Dr. Malcolm," I tell her. "Hundreds of lives depend on that information."

Playing on her sense of duty is the only thing that will get through to her. I know it. She is so stubborn that not even Noah could reach her. But from the moment I saw Sonya through Her eyes, I knew how seriously she took her profession. She will go to any length to save just *one* life. Adrienne is alive today because of her. Someone else would have just let the weeks-old fetus go.

"I don't believe you," she says, shaking her head.

Damn it. Why does she have to fight me every step? What will it take to get through to her? A sea of deaths? Frustration and anger burst through the calm facade I have tried maintaining.

I slam my palms against the bars. "I would not lie about this! Look at me, Sonya. Why would I be here if this were not a life-or-death situation? It took Ruby and Lydia dying for Dr. Travista to wake up and realize his precious creations were not *perfect*. You would doom all of us simply to save face? Would you?"

"No. Not them. Just you."

I push away from the bars. "You must take a lot of pleasure in knowing you were right about me. I will leave them and never come back. Just like you said I would."

"I take no pleasure in this. You've seen his grief with your own eyes. Would you want him to go through that again?"

"But that is exactly what you will do if you hold on to that data-slip. I would save him from that if I could, but unfortunately, this is all in your hands. It is all. About. You."

She glares at me for a long moment, then, with a sigh, she rubs her tired face. "Jesus. I can't believe this is happening."

"Believe it." My heart drums. I have her.

She looks around her cell, hands on her hips. "I want out of here."

"I cannot help you with that."

"You can and you will. I'm not telling you anything. You want that slip? Get me out of here. And you won't file formal charges against me. That's the deal."

My gaze floats to the keypad, which now glows like a beacon. I could type a few numbers and set her free. This could finally be over.

I look down the hall at Noah. His shoulders lift on a deep breath, then slowly lower. A pregnant moment later, he starts forward, I guess to input the number sequence, but I do not need it. I type the numbers that spell out "Europa." The locks *hiss* and *click*. The bars slide aside.

Sonya starts forward, shaking her head. "Are you that confident Noah will—?"

She steps past the bars and I slam a right hook into her jaw. She buckles over and clasps her face. Pain flares in my knuckles and I shake my hand out. "That's for taking me back to Declan Burke. And yes, I am sure Noah will let you go."

Noah reaches out and takes Sonya by the elbow. "Let's go."

She stares wide-eyed between the two of us. Her gaze stops on me. "He was there the whole time?"

"Unlike some of us, I try not to do anything behind Noah's back."

Noah nods at the door leading out. "You'll get us the data-slip. Then I want you gone before sunrise."

Her eyes glass over as she stares at him. "I'm sorry, Noah. I only wanted to protect you and Adrienne."

"That was never your job," he says. "Now, where is it?"

Sonya wakes Farrah for the data-slip. Noah is far more surprised than I am to discover they worked together. Only Farrah could have hacked her way into her old station, which was the blip of power I saw during my conversation about meeting Noah in the hologram room. She probably hid the live feed at Declan's, too.

Without blinking, Noah gives Farrah the same reprieve he has given Sonya. Gone before sunrise or he will put her in Sonya's old cell. We have more important things to worry about than prosecuting them for treasonous acts.

Noah and I split up after that. He escorts Sonya to her room so she can pack, and I go to wake Dr. Malcolm.

Then we wait. Hours. A day.

Days.

Nervous energy fills the hub. The raid is only hours away. Then destroying the facility. Noah second-guesses the bombing since Dr. Malcolm has had no luck with the data-slip. I think he questions, as I do, whether or not we should take the risk and force the cure from Dr. Travista somehow. The best we can plan for is to duplicate the raid. While teams escort innocent civilians out, Miles and I can search for the facility's server room and uplink every piece of data we can in the allotted time. The idea is last-minute and leaves Miles and me without a clear destination once inside. The building is so large, we may never find the room.

Two hours before we are set to leave, Noah, Adrienne, and I carve out an hour of alone time in the hologram room. Adrienne has no idea that Noah and I are going on this dangerous mission, and she refuses to let either of us hold her for long.

"I did not think it would be this hard to leave," I say, watching Adrienne chase seagulls around, flapping her arms.

Noah watches the tide slip forward and kiss the boot heels of his outstretched legs. "It never gets any easier, which is why I want to talk to you about something."

"What?"

He swivels and rises up to his knees, facing me. I mirror him and our fingers link automatically. Adrienne runs over and squeezes between us. She pushes against Noah's stomach and grunts from exertion.

I laugh. "Someone hates sharing you."

When I look up at him, he stares at me, his expression serious. He swallows hard. "I know things are . . . Screw it. Marry me."

Hot tears spring to my eyes. "Damn it." A wave of uncontrollable giggles hits me and worsens as the look of confusion deepens the lines in his face.

"What's so funny?"

"I was going to ask you. I have an entire speech and everything."

His beaming smile makes my head spin. "You do? Can I hear it?" He lifts Adrienne into his arms to stop her from pushing him. She wriggles to get back down and he sets her aside to chase a new seagull.

He looks at me expectantly and my cheeks warm. I take his hands back in mine and scoot close enough so that our bodies are nearly touching.

"Breathe," he whispers.

I draw in a needed breath and try to hold his gaze, but it is too hard. I cannot focus on the words while he looks at me with such devotion.

"I do not know exactly how things were before," I begin, my voice quivering. This will be harder than I imagined. "Why we loved each other or how. And I have a few memories that will forever be precious to me. But the truth is, they are Hers. Not mine."

Noah's smile falters and he averts his gaze.

"My first memories of you are frightening," I say, clinging tight to his hands. "You scared the hell out of me, if I am being honest."

"I wanted to kill you. Not the best first impression."

"No, but underneath it all, I was already madly in love with you. I felt it when we touched. In the way you looked at me. Despite everything to the contrary, you seeped into the vast dark of my mind and drew me out.

"My past or Hers, that is how deep an impression you have made on my soul. This is why I know that no matter how this ends, whether it be only days or years, we will always find each other again.

"I know who I am now, and she is naïve and scared *all the time.* She hates this uniform and using weapons of any kind. She does not want to save the world with her own two hands. She wants to leave all this. Live in peace on a beach"—I nod at the scene around us—"with her family. And she does not want to do that as Emma Wade."

Noah's eyebrows pinch together. "I don't understand."

"I would like to do that as Emma Tucker."

Adrienne shoves between us again, startling us out of the moment. Noah lifts her, and when he meets my eyes again, they shine with tears.

"Well?" My entire body vibrates with nerves because I have asked him not only to marry me but to consider giving all this up. The resistance and this constant battle against an entire world. I have asked him to leave everything behind for me.

"I resigned this morning," he says. My jaw drops open and he knuckles it back shut with a laugh. "That's part of what I wanted to tell you. I want the same thing, which is why I made an offer on the house in Mexico."

"You . . . *What?*" He is quickly becoming a watercolor through thickening tears.

"The man who owns it is old and I took a chance he'd want to unload it. Turns out he did." He chuckles. "It helped that I offered him a lot more than what it's worth."

"What?"

"The house is small but comes with a lot of land. We'll build onto it."

Am I dreaming this conversation? "What?"

"Is that the only word in your vocabulary?"

"No."

He lifts an eyebrow. "No?"

"Well, the most obvious word I know right now is yes. Will that one do?"

He kisses me, fingers wrapped around the back of my neck, until Adrienne starts trying to push us apart again. We laugh and kiss each side of her face until she wiggles and giggles in Noah's arm.

"Nate said we can stay until Phillip treats you," Noah says. He says this as if it is a done deal. I hope he is right.

The mention of Colonel Updike pulls at a growing curiosity. "What is my history with him?"

He gives me a tight smile. "How about I show you?"

He pulls me to my feet and retrieves the tablet off a table in the back. Moments later, the scene changes, but not drastically. Indigo petals lie on the sand. A small group of people stands on either side of an arch where Noah waits with a minister. He wears white pants and shirt, the material flapping in the wind. At the opposite end of the aisle is me. Her. She wears a white, maxi-length sundress. The wind pastes the skirt to thin legs. She reaches out with a smile to the man directly to her left.

"Nate gave you away," Noah says. "As far as you were concerned, he was the father you never had. The feeling was mutual. He loves you like a daughter. Always has."

Adrienne squirms to get down. Once freed, she starts running through the hologram of wedding attendees and giggling.

I wrap my arm around his back and watch our first wedding unfold. The relationship between Colonel Updike and me is clear from the moment the procession starts. One thing She got right that I never learned is that family is what you make it. It has nothing to do with blood and everything to do with the connections we nurture throughout our lives. My birth parents are strangers, but I have Noah and Adrienne. Foster. Leigh and Miles. Maybe even Colonel Updike—Nate.

CHAPTER 44

Noah stands on a desk at the far end of the command center. Every team is separated and grouped in different sections before him. I stand near the back with Miles, the two of us with our own mission, detached from theirs. Watching Noah like this, in his element, makes me wonder why he would ever consider giving this up. He is a natural leader and everyone looks up to him.

"Miss Emma?"

Miles and I look to my right, where Dr. Malcolm gives me a wobbly smile. His fingers play with the seams of his white lab coat, and his gaze bounces between me and Noah at the front of the room.

"Is something wrong?" I ask.

"Can we talk a minute? It's about the"—he clears his throat— "information you gave me."

Has he found the data he needs? "Of course."

Dr. Malcolm and I step into the empty corridor. I glance around and find we are very much alone before diving in to the conversation. "Did you find something?"

His mouth turns down in the corners. He cannot hold my gaze, which makes my stomach sink.

"There was nothing there, was there?"

He holds his hands up between us. "I have been through everything. I don't actually think the data-slip is *current*. If Arthur Travista did in fact find a cure, there's no mention of it in these particular notes.

"But I have been monitoring the data stream coming back from your nanites. I may have discovered the source."

These words knock the air out of me and I double over, bracing against my knees. For a moment, I believed all hope was lost. But it is not. Relieved tears burn my eyes.

"There's a lot of activity in your pineal gland whenever you . . . black out or dream, which makes sense in a way because the gland produces melatonin. That particular hormone modulates sleep patterns."

Dr. Malcolm's smile has returned, as has his bounce. "Did you know the pineal gland is also considered one's 'third eye'? And it's shaped like a little pine cone, hence the name." He winks. "Anyway, I don't exactly have a cure, but I'll dust off my old endocrinology books tonight. Maybe something will stir some ideas."

I reach out and hug the short man. "You will find it. I know you will. Thank you."

When I straighten, I find Dr. Malcolm a bright shade of red. "You're very welcome." He starts to turn away, double takes, then faces me again. "Good luck tonight. Not that you need it."

"Wade." I glance back at Miles, who leans into the hallway. "It's time. Let's go."

I follow him in to find a long line of men and a few women waiting to teleport out. We are all going to a remote destination where several trucks wait to drive us as close to the Alexandria WTC as possible. Those same trucks will take the rescued girls out.

Noah pushes through the crowd dressed head to toe in black. I cannot see a single strand of blond under the mask he has rolled up like a beanie, and black grease paints most of his face. I wear grease too, and I try not to think about how ridiculous I look.

"Were you just talking to Phillip?" he asks, and pulls me out of earshot of the rest of the group.

"He said the information Declan gave Sonya is old. The treatment for whatever is killing the clones is not on there."

Devastation, not unlike what I just felt, rolls off Noah like a physical entity.

I reach out and grab his hands. "But."

His eyes snap open. "But?"

"He believes he has found the source. With a little more time . . ."

He scoops me up and hugs me tight. "Thank God."

Once back on the floor, I glance around to discover we have once again gained a lot of attention. My cheeks warm. "You are doing terrible things to my reputation. Who knew you could be so dastardly."

"Says the thief of all my good sense."

I raise his zipper and smooth out his jacket. "Were you not supposed to go in the first group?"

He sighs and looks at the long line. "Yeah. I'm going. Just had to make sure things were okay first." His eyes light on me. "You ready?"

"I think so. Be careful, okay?"

He kisses me. "Try to come home in one piece this time, all right?"

"Promise."

I never see Foster or Leigh prior to the attack. They lead their own groups ahead of us. Miles and I watch everyone take position while we hang back in the safety of trees. Like me, he wears his mask rolled up, the black grease enough of a disguise. Others, like Noah, have no such luxury considering they work with the public.

My heart gallops like stampeding bulls in my chest. Sweat prickles my brow though I have yet to really exert myself. I fear for Noah and my friends, though I take comfort in occasionally hearing their voices through my ear com.

The whir of jets zooms overhead and I snap my gaze upward on automatic. Even if I could see through the thick foliage, they are long gone. Fire explodes inside the walls of the compound but nowhere near the actual building itself. The ground rumbles underfoot.

Blood pumps like fire through my veins. My hand aches around the grip of the HK. Reid's voice barely penetrates the blare of sirens and blast of fire as he orders everyone through the gates.

Miles holds a hand out in front of me, palm splayed as if to stop me. But I already know to wait. Not that I harbor any temptation to run headlong into the fray. A cold sweat breaks out over my skin, and the words "bad idea" play like a song in my head over and over and over. Then there is this part of me who thrills in this. Understands this.

The trouble is, I do not know which personality trait will get me killed the fastest—the coward or the daredevil.

We listen to the transition of squads entering for several minutes. I have memories of this part. Groups facing off members of the guard in teams. One taking the brunt of the attack to allow another past. And another. Until members are inside and retrieving the girls.

"Let's go," Miles says, then darts forward in a crouch.

My legs carry me as if pulled by his command, our feet a whisper on the grass. The closer we get, the more my head clears. It is as if I am back in the simulation with Foster, only this is entirely too real. One wrong move and I could die. On the flipside, this must be what living feels like, and I want to soak it into every cell.

Miles and I move through as swiftly as we can, taking down the enemy whenever necessary. I know I should feel guilt for every life I take, and maybe it will come later, but I am too focused on surviving.

We find the side entrance undefended as hoped—any extra security will have run for the brunt of the attack. Inside, the hallway is dark. One long window shows an empty cafeteria with a glow of red security lights blinking on and off.

We take the hallway at a crouch, keeping our heads clear of the glass on the off chance someone is inside with a gun. Near the end, we hear the echoes of grunts, curses, screams, and plasma fire coming from the great hall. Noah is there, according to the com chatter. So is Leigh. Foster has already led a team into one of the dorm wings.

Miles and I stop at the perpendicular hall, backs to the wall, then peer around. The way is clear, and we sprint left, leaving the cacophony of battle behind us.

We are only steps from reaching the next corner, when two men appear with rifles. I go for the one on the right, lifting my gun and preparing to fire. The man spins a back kick at my hands, and my HK clatters to the floor. To my left, Miles and his opponent grunt weaponless in a physical battle of their own.

I parry several attempts to hit my head with the butt of his rifle until he hesitates a second too long. In that moment, I knock his rifle aside with my forearm and swing my fist. He blocks my punch before I make contact. His arms, like iron fetters, force me around. My back to his front. Pinning me against him. My throat braced by the length of his rifle pressing hard into my windpipe. In one swift, well-calculated movement, he has trapped me. Cold metal cuts off my air. I grip the rifle and attempt to push it away, but the man is too strong.

He spins around and rushes toward a brown tiled archway. My heart collides against my ribs as realization strikes. He aims to slam me into the wall. Head first. I do not think as I run up the arch, then push with all the force my legs can afford. We topple backward and the rifle barrel loosens. I suck in a needed breath and, without another moment's hesitation, ram an elbow into the man's side, where he is not protected by gear. He grunts and I roll off him.

"Wade!"

Miles's voice alerts me to the HK he hurtles through the air. I catch the weapon and aim at the man's head. His brown eyes widen, and his chest lifts in quick, short breaths. His arms rise in surrender.

This is all I need to stop from pulling the trigger. I cannot shoot this man in cold blood. Not like this. But I cannot leave him to hurt someone else, either. I shoulder his rifle, then shoot both his legs just above the knees. His screams echo and collide with the growing torment from the great hall.

Miles's expression is pinched when I reach him. "Why didn't you kill him?"

I look at the dead man near his booted feet. "You deal with your conscience and I will deal with mine."

He quirks me a smile. "Those exist?"

"Ha. Can we go?"

He nods toward the hallway. "This way, my lady."

The corridor leads directly to a narrow staircase encased in large stone blocks that spiral up at a steep angle. Small, simple lamps hang overhead and dangle far apart from one another. We alternate between being bathed in brilliant light and disappearing in shadow so dark the stairs are invisible. It is by a stroke of luck I do not trip.

Halfway up, the pound of footsteps races toward us. *A lot* of footsteps.

Miles stops. "Wait." Muscles leaping in his jaw, he glances around, then leads me into the dark. "You're going to want to shoot to kill this time," he whispers. "If you don't mind."

I can hear the smile in his voice, though I cannot see him at all now. "The only thing you should worry about is losing to a girl."

He chuckles. "As if."

I aim into the light and wait, controlling each breath, longing to heave from exertion. My heartbeat drums in my ears. I palm an additional HK from my hip with a too-warm hand.

The soldiers finally appear around the tightly wound corner, shoulder to shoulder. My guess is they planned to surprise our group in the great hall by coming in from behind. The dark hides us, but we are still only two against . . . I cannot count how many.

"Now," Miles says.

The first few men are easy to take out. Bodies crowd the way down, making it impossible for anyone to come closer. If they try, we kill them. Several stay and shoot aimlessly into the dark. Others duck around the corner, where it is safe.

Miles and I back into the light and take cover in a deep inset of wall with a high shelf. Loose cobbles of rock make it hard for my boots to grip. I kneel facing the inset's curved stone, shooting around the corner whenever a new soldier appears.

Miles kneels behind me, one hand on my waist for balance, the other shooting up the stairs. We stay like this for what feels like an eternity. My legs scream, and my shoulder aches from holding the HK up for so long.

The soldiers either are all dead or have run. Either way, the firefight ends with the two of us unharmed.

Miles rests his forehead against my back and breathes deep. "That was close."

My heart feels bruised due to the rapid *thunk*ing against my rib cage. "Yeah."

"Hold tight while I make sure it's clear. Watch my back."

I lean out and aim a gun in both directions, listening for any sound that does not belong to us. Finally, Miles motions the all clear and we continue up the stairs until we reach a turret with an open area surrounded by crenellations. I glance over the side to see the back of the compound. Members of our team lead a stream of girls into the woods. The girls are older, telling me they are nearing the last of the groups. The younger girls are always rescued first.

"Almost there, Wade," Miles says behind me.

We find another hallway inside. Three uneventful turns later, we end up in a small room lined with computer equipment. Lights of various colors wink from black servers. Video screens high on the walls run a live feed.

Miles positions himself behind the desk and places a flat black disc on the surface of the main hard drive. A red light blinks from the center. He taps his com. "Jaybird and Prototype in position. Uploading data now."

After a quick file search, he says, "Server number is 937."

We run along the multiple rows, and several stacks of servers later, I locate the correct one. "Here."

Miles kneels and reaches behind, his expression strained as he works blindly to disconnect the back. Sweat streams down his temples. Something pops, and he grins. "Just like a woman's bra clasp."

I roll my eyes. "Focus."

He jerks the server free of the shelf. "Sort of takes the fun out of things, don't you think?"

From the back, Miles pulls a clear data-slip from a slot. I remove a protective shell from one of my zippered pockets and hand it over so he can tuck it inside for safekeeping.

I tap my com. "Target acquired."

"You heard her. Let's finish this up," Noah says. *"Detonation in ten minutes."*

I release a sigh of relief. He is okay. We are both okay, and this is almost over.

Miles taps my shoulder and winks. "Let's get the fuck out of here."

The main stairs are close and we take them to the second-level hallway overlooking the grand entryway. Bodies lie everywhere. Blood spatter darkens the brown-tiled walls. The enemy soldiers seem to be missing, and a few stragglers from our groups sprint for the exit. Reid is with them, waving them past. Foster and Leigh bring up the rear.

I should have been paying more attention to the hallway I pass, but I am anxious to reach the next set of stairs. Someone large barrels into me and we hit the stone railing. My shoulder and arm go numb on impact.

Miles is already partially down the stairs when the noise forces him to spin around. At least five men surround me and I lose sight of him. Someone strikes me in the jaw, sending a wave of pain through my face. Darkness threatens to sweep me under. Another man yanks my beanie off so hard he pulls my hair. The freed locks cloud my vision until a grip jerks my head back and parts the strands. The heated end of a gun presses to my temple.

CHAPTER 45

Plasma shots drive into my crowd of attackers. One of my HKs is long gone, but my left is holstered and I snatch it free. I shoot up and behind at the man who has me by the hair. Upon release, I fall forward, trying to ignore the pain screaming behind my eyes and the exhaustion coursing through my body. Miles comes into view and bodies fall dead around me.

Miles kneels and pushes my hair back. "You look a little worse for wear, Wade."

I try to smile. "Admit it. This is how you prefer your women."

He puts an arm around my waist and hauls me to my feet. "You know me too well."

"Seven minutes," Noah says in the com. I wonder if anyone else can hear the near imperceptible quiver in his tone.

I peer over the railing. Noah, like so many others, wears a mask pulled down tight to hide his face. He stands near the bottom of the stairs looking up at us and waves us down in a frantic gesture. Straggling remains of our team run past him.

The overhead lights in the building flicker and dim. Heavy footsteps pound the carpeted floor from the hallway behind us. I spin to face them but am unprepared for who stands there.

Declan.

Miles's arm tightens around my waist. The two of us raise our guns to the large crowd of men aiming at us.

Declan's gaze drops to where Miles slides his arm out from behind me to steady his gun. "You must be the husband I've heard so much about."

Miles jerks his chin up. Grins. Stupid, brave Miles. "Damn right. Gets under your skin a little bit, too, I'm guessing."

Declan motions to the men. "Get their guns."

There must be twenty of them rushing forward to surround us, rifles and HKs aimed at our heads. They snatch our weapons from our hands. Declan strolls forward and takes what used to be my gun. He turns it over in his palm. Back and forth. Studying.

When he looks up, it is with an intense, focused glare on Miles. My breath catches in my throat. I need no words to confirm the thoughts running through Declan's mind. The gun rises in a swift arc and the shot is off before I have a chance to say a word.

Miles drops heavily at my feet and I follow, stupidly intending to cushion the fall he will never feel. I hit the floor with his limp body, pain ripping up from my knees.

I cup his still face. "Miles!"

I shake him, waiting for that grin to tilt up. A joke to spill forth. A wink. Anything to tell me this is a fabrication on his part. But he only stares straight up, jaw slack. Blackened skin surrounds a hole in his forehead.

A scream freezes in my throat. My head feels too heavy. My chest too tight. Hot tears blur my vision, blessedly hiding the fatal wound.

"You killed him."

My fault. All my fault.

Declan believed Miles was my husband. What if this had been Noah? *Really* Noah? There had been zero hesitation. No thought. No time. And now one of my closest friends is dead over this case of mistaken identity.

This could have been Noah.

Plasma fire floods the second-floor landing from the stairwell. I look past Miles to the small group in black kneeling on the stairs and firing at Declan and his team of security.

"Emma," Noah's voice fills my head. *"We have five minutes to get to minimum safe distance. Get up. You have to leave him."*

But I cannot get up. Grief crushes me and I cannot feel my legs.

"Get the fuck up, Wade." Foster's demand holds no room for argument and is the fire I need to wake up. The building is going to blow. Miles cannot have died for nothing.

I lean close to Miles's body and surreptitiously drag my hands down his eerily still chest until I feel the hard bump. The data-slip container in his pocket. I fumble with the zipper and retrieve the item that ultimately brought us to this point.

A harsh grip yanks me to my feet. Declan forces me to face him, his fingers digging into my biceps. The blue-green of his eyes blazes. "Competition's over."

Plasma fire flies too close to Declan's head. His men rush forward to cover us.

Declan pulls me toward the hallway. Dragging my feet, I twist and tug to get free.

"Emma!" Noah's frantic call forces me to look toward the stairs. Though his face is covered, I recognize him rushing toward us.

Declan aims the gun, only this time I am prepared. I slam a knee in his gut. He doubles over but comes back swinging. A backhand to my cheek sends me flying to the floor. Declan aims again.

Panic sweeps through me like a brush fire. I jump to my feet and rush forward, putting myself in the bullet's path. "No!"

"Emma, what are you doing?" Noah asks. His voice is barely audible in my com.

"Get out of the way," Declan warns in a near growl.

"I will go with you," I tell him, tears thickening in my throat. "Just stop this. No more. Please."

He searches me for a trick but will not find one. I watched him kill Miles. I will not watch him kill Noah too. Finally, he reaches a hand out. The test I will not fail. I lay my hand in his. He leads me toward the hallway and I twist around to find Noah fighting another member of the security.

"Get out of here," I say. "There is no time." After everything, if the building blows up with him inside . . .

Noah looks up and starts for me. Declan's focus is on a room ahead, so I throw the container holding the data-slip, and Noah catches it easily.

Declan turns into an office and shuts the door. He punches a code on a keypad, and a click sounds the lock mechanism.

A fist pounds on the door outside. *"Emma . . . shit . . . hold on."*

I stare at the door, the breath still in my chest. "Go," I whisper.

"I'm coming," Noah says. *"I'm coming for you."*

"I know." I could not stop him if I wanted to.

Declan searches one of my ears, then the other, finding my com. He drops the device and stomps on it. He turns me toward a private teleporter. "Time to go."

We go straight to the cloning facility in Colorado. Declan remains silent as he leads me down a sterile white hallway. Windows face a parking lot lit by fluorescent lamps and beyond that, a dark, unknown landscape.

Opposite the windows are opaque doors under rectangular alcoves with curved corners. On the wall inside every recess, a touchscreen computer hangs above cubbyholes filled with various supplies. The ceilings and walls are a smooth white tile, but the floors are a grayish brown. The high sheen reflects the thin strip of lights above.

Red coats stroll behind us, arms tucked behind their backs. Yellow-scrubbed orderlies nod as they pass. Blue-coated botanists pass without so much as a glance up from their tablet computers. Then there is Dr. Travista in his white coat, stopped in the middle of the hallway, hands deep in his pockets.

He gives me a tight smile, and when we reach him, he says, "No fight today?"

"I killed her husband," Declan says beside me.

Bile burns my throat, and tears sting the backs of my eyes. Poor Miles. Why did he have to lie?

Dr. Travista scans me. "Probably in shock." To me, he says, "Why don't I show you to your room so you can get cleaned up and changed?"

I glance back in the direction of the teleporter room, wondering how long until Noah will come through those doors. Do I even want him to? If Declan finds out he killed the wrong man . . .

My stomach wrenches remembering how the light had just *vanished* from Miles's eyes. It happened so fast. An eyeblink. Gone. That cannot happen to Noah. I have to get out of here before he shows up.

Declan nudges me forward. "Let's go, love."

I throw a punch at his jaw that very well could have broken my knuckles for all the pain radiating up my arm. I am quick to follow up with an elbow to save from breaking my hand. The force I put behind the strike takes him to a knee.

As I prepare to kick, two red coats rush in and twist my arms up behind my back. An upsurge of panic sets my blood on fire. I have to get out of here. I have to. Noah cannot come after me.

"Hold her still," Dr. Travista says.

The needle appears in my periphery. Not enough time has passed for me to forget the effects of his sedative. If he sticks me again, this is over.

I stomp on one man's instep and blindly piston my head back, hoping to connect. I clip a jaw, I think, but nothing serious enough to get free.

The two red coats lift me off my feet and slam me chest first to the ground, driving the air from my lungs. The needle stings going into my neck, and cold spreads under my skin.

Dr. Travista leans straight-armed on the bed, gripping the steel sides, and watches me through glasses that sit near the edge of his bulbous nose. His smile is genuine yet small as he says, "Good morning, Emma. How do you feel?"

Morning? I squint into the sunlit hospital room. Large, square windows face a mountainous landscape. Very, *very* far in the distance, the tops of skyscrapers in Boulder, Colorado, glint in the sun.

Heavy blankets lie up to my chest. Someone has cleaned and dressed me in white scrubs. My stomach turns. Who would have done that? Declan? Dr. Travista? His favorite nurse, Randall? It does not matter. A violation has occurred.

I twist my bound wrists until they burn. An IV has been inserted, taped to the inside of my elbow, though nothing is connected. The smallest movement of my forehead tells me I have electrodes attached, and I see the slopes of more under my scrub top.

A hand comes to rest on my shoulder from the opposite side of the bed. Declan.

"Take your hand off me," I say.

He combs hair away from my face. "It'll be over today."

Dr. Travista pats my hand. "In an hour you'll be perfect." He looks up at Declan. "I think we can save some of her earlier memories. Save from starting completely over."

Declan shakes his head. "Too risky. We don't know when she started to remember."

"Stop talking about me like I am not here. You have to stop this. I have a daughter, Declan. She needs me."

He gives me a sad smile. "I'll find her just like I found you. We'll raise her together, love."

The words are a weight on my chest. "You will never lay a hand on her. Never." My threat must sound empty to him, because what he does not understand is that Noah will kill him first.

"That may be true, but in the end, will it matter? You won't know she exists, and our own children will fill any void that remains."

I jerk upward, wishing I could hurt him. "I did not want your children even when I loved you. Not that you could produce any. You were sterile."

He blinks. "How did you know?"

"Does it matter? You do not have that problem anymore, do you?"

Dr. Travista smiles beside me. "No, he doesn't. Thanks to you."

"What is that supposed to mean?"

"I'd been trying to talk Declan into the procedure for months, but he was reluctant. When you brought him to the brink of death—I'd just gotten to him in time to save his full memory—you forced his hand." He gives us both a placating smile. "You two will make beautiful children together."

"You both make me sick," I say. "You made me believe for months I was to blame for never becoming pregnant, when all along it was Declan."

"It's of no concern now." Dr. Travista moves to the end of my bed. "We should get started."

He looks at the wall behind me and I glance back, curious about what he looks at. The space behind me is one large monitor, showing my vitals.

"There's some interference in her brain activity," the doctor says. "Could cause some issues with the wipe."

"What sort of interference?" Declan asks.

"Electrical." He eyes me for a long moment. "Nanorobotics if I had to guess."

I look away, refusing to give him an answer one way or the other.

"Nothing concerning," he says, "and shouldn't affect the DMT."

Declan nods as if understanding exactly what Dr. Travista said. But I am confused.

"DMT?" I ask.

"Dimethyltryptamine," Dr. Travista says, pulling a prepared syringe from his pocket. "Medical grade. Fifteen minutes after injection, you'll be as good as new. No more bad dreams."

Declan shivers beside me. His hands tighten around the rail to my bed.

"Are you sure this is safe?" I ask.

Dr. Travista gives me a condescending chuckle. "It's quite safe when administered by a professional. Dimethyltryptamine is a simple compound found in nature. Mystics believe this hormone actually facilitates the entering and exiting of the soul. We all produce it naturally, but under stress, the pineal gland can produce too much or too little, creating an imbalance."

So Dr. Malcolm was right. Whatever is happening starts and ends in the pineal gland.

"I will give you an injection," Dr. Travista continues, "and when you come back down, everything will stabilize."

Declan releases a breath. "You'll feel it happen. It's like someone hit a reset switch."

"We shock a heart to get a normal rhythm," Dr. Travista says. "This is essentially no different."

He takes the cap off the syringe and I do the only thing I can. Squirm as far in the opposite direction as I can go. Declan reaches over me to steady my arm so Dr. Travista can insert the needle into my IV.

Security alarms go off as the word "no" sits poised on my tongue.

Declan's attention slings to the door. "What the hell?"

Dr. Travista pulls the syringe out and looks up at the thin strip of lights above. The white glow flashes red with a blue outline. "That's the bomb sensor." He rushes to the wall and presses a call button. "Evacuate the building."

Moments later, a computerized male voice sounds over the loud-speaker. "This is not a drill. For your safety and the safety of others, follow the evacuation procedure. Remain calm. This is not a drill."

The pounding of running boots fills the corridor outside, as does the occasional pitch of plasma fire and screams. Chaos approaches this room, where, under the wail of the alarm, time has frozen. No one moves to even breathe.

"Check every room!" The call reaches me and a swell fills my chest. Noah.

Declan points at the exit. "Lock the door."

Dr. Travista reaches for the keypad, but the door slides open, and several men dressed in black flood the room, guns raised. I try sitting up but the restraints cut me off.

The doctor raises the syringe, prepared to use it on the nearest target. One of the team members raises his gun and slams the butt on Dr. Travista's head. He falls, out cold.

Someone—a male—yells out the door. "In here!"

Noah rushes in a moment later, as maskless as the rest of his team. He raises his gun and aims directly at Declan. His jaw muscles tighten and release. Tighten and release. Red tints his skin.

My heart surges with both love and relief. He came for me, and he risked everything to do it.

Declan raises his hands, blinking rapidly, as if this will clear up the confusion he must feel. "Tucker?"

Noah takes one quick step closer to Declan. "I found your wife, Burke. And guess what? She just so happens to be mine, too."

CHAPTER 46

Leigh shoulders through the men, eyes red and swollen, tucking her gun in a holster. While she works on my wrist restraints, Foster kneels and checks Dr. Travista's pulse. Then, standing, he crushes the spectacles that must have fallen from the doctor's face.

I sit up and remove the electrodes from my temples while Leigh works on my last ankle strap.

Foster glances at me and asks, "You still there, Wade?"

They must have been concerned I had been wiped overnight. I cannot imagine what it must have taken to keep Noah from coming alone. "Yes," I tell him, and swing my legs over the side of the bed. The floor is ice-cold underfoot.

Declan watches me approach Noah, his gaze jumping between us. "At the ball. That was you."

I nod. "Right there in your arms."

"Surprise," Noah says. He has not taken a single eye off Declan. "We never did discuss the fee for borrowing her. The price is pretty hefty."

A salacious smile slides across Declan's face as he meets Noah's eyes. "She looked incredible that night. I imagined later what it would be like to take her in that dress. Guess I didn't have to waste so much energy trying to conjure up what she would feel like." His eyes cut to me and down to my lips, breasts. "I already know."

Noah has Declan to the wall, gun to his head, before I can blink. "Keep talking. I will kill you where you stand."

I recognize the look in Noah's eyes and am reminded of the gallery opening, when he put a gun to my head. He would have killed me if not for the past we shared. Declan has no such escape.

Having witnessed this cold hatred in action from Declan only last night, and losing Miles because of it, I cannot allow this to continue. Noah is nothing like Declan. He is considerate and protective and acts only when he has to. He is not a cold-blooded killer.

I lay a hand on Noah's shoulder. His muscles are tense, prepared to spring. I have to get through to him, and fast. "Noah, listen to me. We have everything we need. Let the government deal with him."

Foster lifts Dr. Travista from the floor and hands him to two of the men near the exit. "She's right, Tucker. Let's get them out of here and let the chips fall. They can't escape this time."

"No, screw that," Leigh says. "The fucker killed Miles. He deserves to die."

My heart sinks for her. Miles was my friend, but he had been Leigh's first. They had been practically inseparable. Family.

Foster wraps an arm around her shoulder and draws her into his chest. A moment later her shoulders shake.

Noah does not move a single muscle toward letting Declan go. Over his shoulder, he says, "Everyone out. Birmingham, you're in charge. I want this building clear when it blows."

They all obey his order without question. Foster follows last, catching my gaze. If I ask, he will stay. But I think the less interference we have, the better.

"Noah—"

"He'll never let you go," he says, cutting me off. He reaffirms his wide stance and pushes the gun hard against Declan's forehead. Declan's hands flatten on the space of wall behind him. "You'll never be safe."

"But I *am* safe. Think about what you are doing. This is not self-defense. Killing him like this would be murder."

His jaw muscles pop, and his chin drops slightly. Hesitation. Finally. "He's seen my face," he says, and a lot of the vehemence has left his tone.

"And we are leaving this place forever. It will not matter." I lay a hand over his heart. "Take me home. Please."

Noah's chest rises with a shaky breath. By the time he lets it back out, he nods and takes several steps away. "You're going to jail, Burke. For a very long time."

Declan swings and knocks the gun loose from Noah's hand. The weapon slides across the tile and stops with a *thunk* against the wall. The three of us dive for it.

Declan scoops it up first, spins, and latches a fist on the back of my head. He yanks me toward him and pain slices through my skull. I reach back to try and alleviate some of the pressure. Any movement on my part only makes the pain worse.

Noah pulls a second HK from his holster. He peers along the sight and no doubt has a perfect shot. Gritted teeth flash behind tight lips. "Let her go."

Declan presses the gun to my temple and we walk backward toward the exit. "You know, I'm beginning to wonder if she's worth the trouble."

A tiny muscle twitches under Noah's eye. "We both know you won't kill her."

They know it, and I know it. Declan loves me and would never consciously hurt me. If I can only get him to loosen his grip a little . . .

"Declan," I say, wincing as his fingers tighten. I do not have to reach too deep to instill a certain amount of pleading in my tone. "*Please. You are hurting me.*"

The moment I feel his tension ease, I take his wrist in both hands and force the gun up as fast as I can. Everything that follows happens in a matter of seconds, but it feels like a lifetime.

Declan releases my hair and I twist away, holding tight to his wrist. I maneuver his arm out straight and turn it at an awkward angle, gun aimed safely at the window. This position is risky because he is so much stronger than I am, but maybe if I move fast enough, I can dislodge the gun and get Declan back in a prone position.

I kick high at the back of his legs, and he falls to his knees with a grunt. He struggles to aim the gun at me. My heart kicks in a panic as I try to keep his arm out. Declan fires and the *ping* of glass breaking is a relief. Better the window than Noah or myself.

I swing a leg over his head, straddling his shoulder, and roll forward, taking him to his back. He moves with the momentum and pins me to the floor a moment later. I blink up at the gun barrel in my face and shove it aside seconds before it goes off by my head. Ear ringing, I twist his wrist with all my strength. He cries out and I wrench the gun free.

Then his weight is off me. Noah has Declan by the collar and throws him into the wall. He meets him there and slams a knee into his stomach. Declan doubles over with a grunt. Noah spins and lands an ax kick to the side of Declan's head.

Declan falls flat to his stomach and does not move for several long seconds. Blood spills from behind his ear, where Noah's boot broke the skin.

Bending, Noah presses the gun to the back of his head. "Get up." His chest heaves in tandem with mine.

Declan rises to his knees and looks up at me. Sweat dots his brow. "You can't run from me forever, Emma."

I tighten the grip on my gun. "I have heard that one before. This is over."

Declan pistons an elbow back into Noah's knee, then rises fast to strike him in the face. By the time I think to aim the gun, Noah has him around the throat, and the two of them are turning and trading head butts into the wall. I cannot keep up with them long enough to shoot, and I do not want to accidentally hit Noah.

I drop the useless gun and race forward. The first opportunity I get, I jump on Declan's back and hook an arm around his neck. I squeeze my arm to cut off his air. If I can just get him to pass out . . . With a choking wheeze, he releases Noah.

Declan lumbers back and slams me into a wall. Black dots float in my vision, but I manage to maintain my hold, loose though it is. Noah slams a right hook in Declan's jaw. With a yell, Declan reaches back, takes me by the shoulders, and throws me over his head.

I hit Noah and we both go down in a jumbled heap. By the time I roll off him, Declan is already lifting the gun I had discarded moments ago. He aims at Noah.

Flashes of Miles's death hit me like a truck. "No!"

The shot rings past me and Noah twists with the impact to his right chest. He hits the floor and I rotate back around to check on him.

"Noah," I cry, hovering over him, cupping his face. He cannot die on me. Not like this. Not now. Tears in my eyes make it impossible to see the extent of the damage. All I know is that his chest rises under my hands.

"Okay," he says in a tight, breathy tone. He shows me the gun, gripped in his hand and hidden between us.

"She's going to be mine again," Declan says behind me. He sounds winded from our fight.

Noah struggles to sit up and I help him, though every part of me wants him to remain perfectly still. To wait for help. He grips the gun, hiding it in my lap, and wordlessly meets Declan's gaze. Blood streams down his face from cuts to his forehead, cheek, and mouth.

I look back to watch Declan approach with the gun aimed at Noah's head. The sea in his eyes shines, and his smile says he knows he has won.

"And maybe when she's run out of her usefulness," Declan continues, taunting, "I'll find your daughter. And I'll take her too."

Fury explodes in my chest. He can threaten me all he wants, but Adrienne? I will kill him first. And now I intend to.

Noah's face contorts into such rage, I stop reaching for the gun in my lap. His muscles are locked so tight I am surprised he can manage to say his next words. "What's mine is yours; is that it?"

Declan snorts a laugh. "You could say that."

"Here's something of mine you forgot."

The gun comes around and up past me. The shot fires before Declan realizes the danger he is in. And Noah's aim is perfect. Declan slumps to the ground and falls to his stomach. At this angle, I can just make out the blackened skin on his forehead.

Noah's arm drops heavy between us. "Clone your way out of *that*, you bastard."

Dr. Malcolm stares at the syringe and back at me. A wavering grin tilts on his face. "I'm a little jealous."

Jealous? My heart pounds in my ears and I have already broken out in a cold sweat over the idea of this injection. What if Dr. Travista was wrong and this DMT stuff kills me instead? I have had to wait days for this so-called lifesaving drug, and my mind has conjured all the bad things that could go wrong. It is not like I have had the best luck lately.

Noah takes my hand, eyeing Dr. Malcolm with amusement. "I take it you've tested this out on yourself before?" He perches on the edge of the bed, his right arm bound to his middle. He has spent the last few days in various stages of surgery to replace a damaged lung, muscle, and skin. I am more than relieved he could get up and around today for this.

Dr. Malcolm blushes and bobbles his head from side to side. "I may have smoked some during a particular phase in my youth. The high is incredible. There's nothing like it."

I gape. "You can smoke it?"

He waves a hand. "It's nowhere near as potent as this is going to be."

Great. He had an incredible high from smoking it, and my version is more potent. "I will not be doing anything crazy, will I? Like stripping or something?"

Noah grins. "I wouldn't mind that, actually."

"Maybe you should leave," I tell him with a straight face. I am too nervous for his banter.

"You won't even leave the bed," Dr. Malcolm says as he starts to run the DMT into my IV. "Not your physical body, at least."

"What is *that* supposed to mean?"

He winks. "You'll see. I want to hear all about it when you get back."

"Get back?" My attention darts to Noah, who shrugs.

Then I feel it.

Death.

The crawl of the icy abyss through my veins. Arctic. The further the cold travels, the more my heart races. I am going to die like this. I know it. The abyss will take me, after all.

The room pulses with my heartbeat, and underneath the drumming is a gentle hum. The sound is low in the beginning but builds, then overtakes the beat of my heart and voices—*Are her eyes supposed to turn* black? *She's fine. Pupil dilation is normal.*

The hum reaches a point at which I believe I will shatter from the pitched frequency, but a gentle voice in the back of my mind says, *Relax and give in*. I know instinctively that if I vibrate the mild frequency of the room, I *will* shatter, but by allowing the hum to absorb me, to take me . . .

I give in.

And the room shatters like glass. The shards float away from a light so bright I think for a moment I have actually died. But on a whole other level, I am still looking into the hospital room. Dr. Malcolm monitors my vitals, and Noah holds my hand, watching in silence. Neither looks concerned, which means I am okay.

I am also experiencing something that can only be described as time. Birth. Death. Reincarnation. Time folds and shapes and makes no sense while making perfect sense. Pieces of my life come together, beginning to end, until the last layer takes its place and—

—I float in nothing.

I *am* nothing, yet I am everything. More than Emma. More than human. More than a clone. I am who I was meant to be. Eternal. Ethereal.

The white light turns yellow. Wherever I am, it reaches far beyond the abyss, and it is warm and peaceful. I know I will be okay here, but this is not the end of my journey. I have light-years to go, and I am anxious to get there.

The space ends with a door made of honeycomb-shaped glass. Rainbows of light rise from the glass like wisps of smoke, but not to ward me away. They beckon for me to come home. To break through; to let go the final layer of this mortal coil.

I rush through the glass and let the nothing behind me take the shards. The space beyond is familiar to my soul. I have been here a million times before. A waiting room of sorts for every life I have ever lived and will live again. I have friends and family there. They greet me with their light, and I know that, no matter what, everything will be okay because I am stripped of my humanity and handed the freedom to simply *be.*

My sensory awareness returns a piece at a time, a minute at a time, an hour at a time, a year, a century. . . . Eons of time have passed by the time I return to my body.

And it *is* my body.

My soul tethers itself inside.

I blink.

Dr. Malcolm squeezes my hand. "Welcome back, Miss Emma."

"How long was I gone?" I ask. It is difficult to have felt such a fracturing of time and space, then return and find everything how I left it.

"Fifteen minutes."

That is all?

"How do you feel?"

"Perfect," I say, and look at Noah. My head swims with a gentle hum that I hope wears off soon, but . . . "Absolutely perfect."

CHAPTER 47

Arthur Travista, the father of cloning, was charged today with twenty-three counts of murder. The victims, young girls from facilities owned by the late Declan Burke, were forced to partake in the cloning program.

"While their cloning was successful, Quinn v. Vincent protects all girls under the age of eighteen from experimentation of any kind.

"As for the cloning program itself, the government has put a freeze on the project, and not because Dr. Travista is out of the business. A spokesperson from the White House told EBS that they may have moved too quickly on this and, with proper planning, will reintroduce the possibility in the near future."

"... and in other news ...

"A surprising development today out of Burke Enterprises. Recently named CEO Evan Thomas sells the remaining WTCs to rival companies. He had this to say earlier today."

The image switches to prerecorded film outside Burke Enterprises. Evan Thomas stands with one hand resting on a podium, the other tucked in a pocket of his gray suit. His white hair flutters in the wind.

"We need to start looking toward the future," he tells the ocean of

reporters. *"Declan Burke had the right idea, but I believe he was misguided.*

"Closing the WTCs at this juncture isn't the right call—we still need to maintain some amount of control over our population in order to grow. But with the sale, Burke Enterprises now has the money to put to other uses. We are still funding the mass cure for existing clones, and I'm working closely with lawmakers to make sure these women get the recognition their hosts had prior to their change.

"We're also searching for a safe alternative to cloning. It's out there, and I intend to find it."

Noah adjusts Adrienne's weight. "You sure you want to do this?"

I peer through the one-way glass into his office, considering what I am doing. My heart beats hard and fast. "Want? No. But I need to."

Over the past few weeks, as we watched all the pieces fall into place the way we hoped, something felt unanswered. That is, until we had a short visit from Noah's mother, Bridgett Schwab.

Bridgett was quick to accept me and was beyond happy to see her son and me back together. While I enjoyed her doting attention, it only widened the chasm between me and my own mother. My father. Even my brother.

I need some sort of closure, one way or the other, before we leave for Mexico.

Noah wraps me in his free arm and kisses the crown of my head. "It'll be fine. Don't worry."

"You are taking a huge risk to make this happen."

"Tucker Securities is going to bed with Burke Enterprises. The deal is done. Evan won't want to wreck the good press he's getting from that. Besides. I have a good feeling about this. Trust me."

It has been a while since he has used the T-word on me, but it still holds the same power. I will trust him to my dying breath.

I nod and take Adrienne. She wraps her little arms around my neck and we watch Noah enter his office. When the glass closes behind him, Adrienne presses a flat palm against it and taps it a few times.

She points inside. "Dad-dy."

"Mm-hm, there is your handsome daddy," I say, and kiss her cheek.

Noah sits behind his desk, unbuttoning his suit jacket. A moment later, Leigh enters, dressed in a simple white blouse and gray pencil skirt. She agreed to play secretary for the next hour on the off chance we need backup.

"Mr. Tucker, your two o'clock is here," she says. She then ushers my parents in without waiting for the okay.

Charissa's left hand rests inside Evan's right elbow. They are a handsome couple, dressed in tailored suits for this requested meeting. Mouth dry, I busy myself with straightening out Adrienne's dress and taming her hair. Every wiggle she makes after that undoes all the work.

Noah stands and buttons his suit jacket. My stomach warms as the action defines his masculine form. "Mr. and Mrs. Thomas. Thank you for coming."

Evan shows Charissa into one of the chairs facing Noah's desk, then takes the second. Noah strolls around and perches on the desk between them.

"You said this was important," Evan says. His expression holds no nonsense, no show of emotion, but this is true of every occasion. He is one to study for the ultimate poker face.

"And of a personal nature," Noah says. "I understand you've been working to have Emma's rights restored."

"Olivia," Charissa corrects.

"Emma," Noah fires back. "I mean you no disrespect, Mrs. Thomas. Believe me."

"What is this about?" Evan asks, eyes narrowed.

"It's about Emma." Noah cuts a look at Charissa that dares her to argue, then continues. "If you were to find her, would you still continue to work toward restoring her individual rights? Or would you hold true to the current custody papers that deem her your property?"

Charissa leans forward, hands gripping the edge of her chair arms. "She's our daughter. We only want her to be happy. That's all we ever wanted."

Evan places a hand on her arm to stop her. "The custody was the only means we had of getting her away from Declan Burke. As you know, it was all a moot point in the end. He's dead, and she's hiding out with the resistance."

Noah glances toward the glass that from his side is nothing more than a wall showing his computer's screen saver. "Before I get to the point, I'd like to remind you that my company has now given yours financial backing. In the eyes of the media, we can do no wrong. Would you agree?"

Evan's chin inclines but does not lower to complete the nod. "I would."

"Until a few weeks ago, I led the resistance hub that destroyed the cloning facility and the Alexandria WTC."

Evan rockets to his feet, and Charissa gasps behind her palm.

"Emma is with me. And she's safe."

Charissa sits forward on the edge of her chair. "Where is she?"

Noah raises an eyebrow at her, then looks at Evan. "Give me your word that everything said here today stays in this office."

Evan snaps his suit jacket down. "You've left me with little choice, haven't you?"

"You're right. That's because I would lay down my life to protect my wife."

Evan sits slowly in his chair, and Charissa cries into her hands. Happy or sad, unknown. I do not know if Noah has anything left to say, but I take this as my cue to enter.

The glass parts in front of me and I walk through with Adrienne. I settle my gaze on Noah for strength, and straightening from his desk, he gives it to me in a single nod.

My parents stand with wide eyes, and after only a few moments, their attention drifts to Adrienne.

Noah comes forward to take her from me. "This is our daughter, Adrienne."

My mother glances between the three of us, eyebrows furrowed. "But she's too old."

"Noah and I were married almost six years ago. My host carried Adrienne to term and died shortly after from complications."

A small cry escapes Charissa's lips. Tears spill down her cheeks.

Evan takes her hand, then says to me, "Are you well?"

Noah laces his fingers through mine and smiles down at me. "She's perfect." He kisses my knuckles, erupting a swarm of butterflies in my belly.

"I have had the DMT injection," I clarify for Evan. This is what he really wanted to know. "Anyway, I wanted to—"

I stop, my throat closing around the words. Why am I feeling so emotional all of a sudden? They are complete strangers. But I cannot look at them anymore, because the longer I do, the more of myself I see in them.

Noah hugs me to him. "*We* wanted to thank you for the steps you've already taken. And to let you know that we're leaving Richmond. The States, actually. For good."

"What? Why?" Charissa asks. "We won't turn you in." She looks at

Evan for validation of her statement. He neither acknowledges nor denies. He simply stares at us, hiding his thoughts under an impassive expression.

"I only wanted to tell you that I appreciate what you are doing and that I forgive you." I swallow the lump in my throat. "If your intention was to make sure I ended up happy, then you can sleep well at night." I hug Noah closer. "Because I am beyond that."

A dimple forms in Evan's chin and he lowers his head a moment later.

Charissa rubs his arm, then steps past him. "Can I—" She stops to clear her tear-thickened throat. More tears flood and breach her eyelids. "Can I hug you?"

I cannot breathe, and before I realize what I have done, I am in her arms. She holds me tight, the way only a mother can. And I know deep down, despite the drunken, awful thing she said at the ball, she loves me.

My eyes are closed, so I do not realize Evan is there until he strokes the back of my head. I look up and he presses a lingering kiss to my forehead. Then, looking behind me, he says, "Take care of her."

"I will," Noah says.

I back away from my parents, swallowing an aching sob. My mother holds on until the last possible second, her hands hovering in the air. My father grips her shoulders and stares at the painting behind Noah's desk.

"You should take it," Noah says. "My replacement won't care for it, and I know the artist." He smiles warmly down at me. "She'll just have to paint me another."

"Thank you," Evan says.

Noah and I back toward the opening in the wall.

"Let us know how you're doing," my mother says.

I nod but can do no more than that. I do not trust my voice.

Noah sees me through the opening, then turns back to say, "You'll want to keep this from Daxton."

Evan nods. "Don't worry. Even if we knew where he was . . . I know exactly the type of man my son is, Mr. Tucker."

The wall closes and I watch my father fold my sobbing mother in his arms. A moment later, tears slip from his eyes, and his back shakes with a quiet cry.

Noah slips his hand in mine. "Let's go home."

Noah takes the duffel bag and box from my arms so I can say good-bye to Leigh and Foster. He takes them into his office, calling after Adrienne to follow him. She run-hobbles with a gleeful giggle.

Leigh hugs me first. "We'll see you in a couple weeks for the wedding. I can't wait. It'll be my first real vacation since . . . ever."

Foster steps over and holds me out by the shoulders, eyeing me down the bridge of his nose. "I don't want a repeat of your last disappearance."

I chuckle. "I will call you. I promise."

He lifts me in a tight hug and kisses my cheek. "Take care of yourself, Wade." He sets me down. "I can't even call you that anymore, can I?"

"For a couple more weeks," I say, then shrug. "But who knows? Something tells me the name will pop up again sooner than you think."

My friends look confused, and Leigh says, "I don't get it."

And she is not supposed to, so I go for a change of subject. "Noah tells me you got reassigned to Chicago?"

She folds her arms and averts her eyes. Kicks the concrete with the toe of her boot. "No, not exactly. Some special assignment for Colonel Updike. Looks like I'm going undercover for a while."

Foster elbows her. "At least you're getting out of here. I'd take an assignment like that in a hot second if it meant breathing air that hasn't been recycled a million times."

She shrugs. "Yeah, it'll be okay. I need to get out of here anyway. Since Miles . . ." She pauses and works to control her expression. "I just can't be here anymore."

I know what she means. Miles is everywhere and nowhere.

"When do you leave?" I ask.

"After the wedding." A grin peeks out from under her deep scowl. "Which calls for a really good drunk girls' night beforehand."

"Miss Emma!"

We turn as Dr. Malcolm comes running, hands strapped to his chest to keep his lab coat from flying out. He steps on a loose shoelace and stumbles, nearly falling only three steps away. Beside me, he bends over and braces himself, chest heaving for breath. He holds a finger up between us, asking me to wait. Why he always thinks I will walk away from him is beyond me.

"I thought. I missed you," he wheezes.

Noah walks up behind me, Adrienne in his arms playing with a small doll with long blond hair. "We almost ready?"

Dr. Malcolm straightens, sucks in a deep breath, and swallows hard. "I forgot to give you . . ." He rummages in his pockets, starts pulling things out, then places them in my hands. Large bottles rattle with pills. "Ginger to help with the nausea," he says, and my heart leaps instantly into my throat. "And your vitamins. Can't have you and the wee boy unhealthy."

Noah sighs and rubs a hand across his mouth. "Phillip."

Dr. Malcolm glances up, confused, then seems to realize how Leigh and Foster are gaping at Noah and me. "Oops," he squeaks.

"I guess the secret is out," I say.

Leigh yanks me into a swinging embrace. "It goes no further than here. Congratulations."

Foster slaps Noah on the shoulder. "Nice."

Noah beams at me, and I cannot help but beam back. The pregnancy was an accident, but a happy one. And only the first of many, I hope.

Reid appears around the corner, eyes glued to a computer tablet. He does a double take when he sees us standing outside the office. "You guys aren't gone yet?"

Noah takes my hand. "You can wait sixty more seconds to claim my office, Major."

"Lieutenant Colonel, Citizen Tucker."

Noah and I embrace everyone one last time, and it is a tearless good-bye considering we will see them again soon. Inside the teleporter, we step around the piles of duffel bags and very few boxes of belongings we could not part with. "Emma's" box among them.

"Ready?" he asks, bouncing Adrienne in his arm.

I take a deep breath. "Ready."

He kisses me on the lips, the nose, then the space between my brows. His amber eyes are aflame when he pulls back to look at me.

"No words," I say.

"Not a single one," he says in return.

He keys in the port number to a public teleporter in Arizona where a car waits to take us across the border into Mexico. We lift our hands to wave a final good-bye to our friends before we freeze and the room melts away for the final time.

EPILOGUE

I float in nothing. Blissfully numb. My tether binds herself to me for the final time.

I drag a hand through my hair, grounding myself before I drift further into this vision of perfection. Sand lifts on gusts of wind to sting my eyes, but I can't look away as she approaches. Smiling that crooked smile. Happier now than I've ever known her to be. As if our entire world was never turned inside out and upside down.

My hold on her is far from fragile. I'm never letting her go again, which is why I take her hands the second she reaches me. I sink into her eyes, hazel pools with flecks of green and gold, and tune out the entire world until she says, "I do," and steals my breath. Sends me reeling into the vast universe, where I have nothing to fear but her letting me go.

Wake up, Noah. You must be dreaming.

But this is no dream. She's so much more. My wife. My partner. The soul I will follow out of this life and into the next, because I'm as bound to her as she is to me.

What I float in is forever, and with her by my side, there's nothing left to fear.

ACKNOWLEDGMENTS

I would NOT be here if not for the incredible support of my husband, Tad, and our two boys. Thank you for sucking up all the "fend for yourself" nights.... I really needed that time off to continue this mad obsession.

Behind a ton of these brilliant ideas is the ever-amazing Charissa Weaks. This one was our big test, but we made it through! Don't you dare go anywhere. I couldn't do this without you pushing me to dig deeper. Be greater.

New to my crazy, Mary Cain. I thank you, and Miles thanks you. Or should I say the table thanks you ...? *coughs* *Ahem*. No, seriously, without you and Charissa, this story would have come out a complete disaster area.

Crystal, my incredible, supportive sister. Thank you for stepping outside your nonfiction box to read my pages and for going above and beyond to support this crazy career I chose.

Jodi Henry. For always checking in. For always guiding me through particular minefields. For squeeing at just the right times. And for proving that people out there still use the word *rad*. (You see that, CW? *Rad*. I was gonna get it in a book somehow, and look. I did.)

Jennifer Weltz. My incredible, sanity-saving agent. My Sonya expert. I'm so grateful to you for those early-draft phone calls and your patient guidance that led me to find the real story here. I only had one meltdown, and it will forever be #SonyasFault. I love that you see right through the BS and give it to me straight. (Then turn around and speak Yoda.) My favorite person, you are.

God. Denise Roy. I *cannot* tell you enough how much I adore you. Just put me in that long line of Fans for Life. I truly lucked out getting to work with you and your incredible team. Each and every person at Dutton, from editing to marketing to sales to whoever else I'm completely oblivious to, has made me look like a rock star. I am continually in awe of those who catch the most ridiculous and obscure issues within the many, many, MANY pages. Seriously. Thank you.

ABOUT THE AUTHOR

M.D. Waters lives with her family in Maryland. She is the author of *Archetype*.

A **150**-YEAR PUBLISHING TRADITION

In 1864, E. P. Dutton & Co. bought the famous Old Corner Bookstore and its publishing division from Ticknor and Fields and began their storied publishing career. Mr. Edward Payson Dutton and his partner, Mr. Lemuel Ide, had started the company in Boston, Massachusetts, as a bookseller in 1852. Dutton expanded to New York City, and in 1869 opened both a bookstore and publishing house at 713 Broadway. In 2014, Dutton celebrates 150 years of publishing excellence. We have redesigned our longtime logotype to reflect the simple design of those earliest published books. For more information on the history of Dutton and its books and authors, please visit www.penguin.com/dutton.